LARK ASCENDING

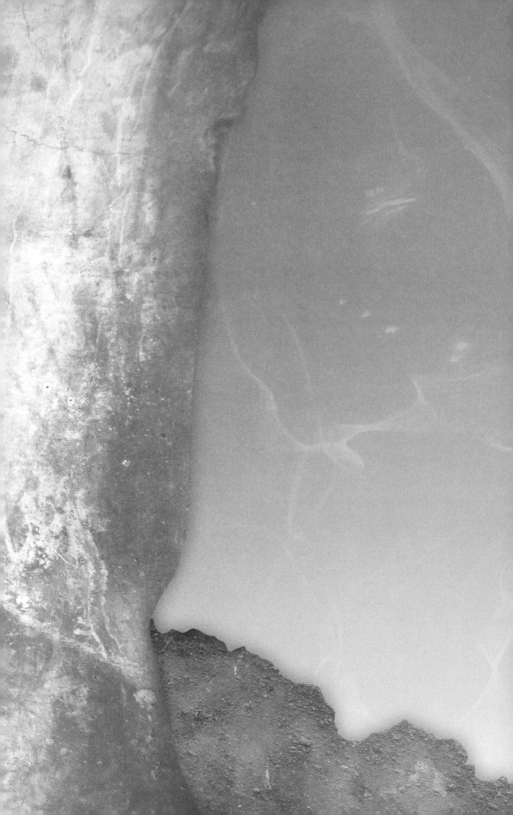

LARK ASCENDING

MEAGAN SPOONER

carolrhoda LAB

MINNEAPOLIS

Text copyright © 2014 by Meagan Spooner

Carolrhoda Lab™ is a trademark of Lerner Publishing Group, Inc.

Carolrhoda Lab™
An imprint of Carolrhoda Books
A division of Lerner Publishing Group, Inc.
241 First Avenue North
Minneapolis, MN 55401 USA

For updated reading levels and more information,
look up this title at www.lernerbooks.com.

Cover and interior photographs: © Illustrart/Dreamstime.com (rusty metal);
© Igorsky/Dreamstime.com (metal sheet); © Negativex_digital_photography/
Dreamstime.com (plasma); © iStockphoto.com/Crisma (sea); © Voyagerix/
Dreamstime.com (metal with rivets).

Main body text set in Janson Text LT Std 11/15.
Typeface provided by Linotype AG.

Library of Congress Cataloging-in-Publication Data

Spooner, Meagan.
        Lark ascending / by Meagan Spooner.
            p.   cm. — (Skylark trilogy)
        Summary: The final volume in the Skylark trilogy finds Lark fighting
    her way back into the City Behind the Wall, the place where it all began
    and where she will finally discover the cause of the cataclysm that caused
    the world to fall.
        ISBN 978–0–7613–8867–8 (trade hard cover : alk. paper)
        ISBN 978–1–4677–4629–8 (eBook)
        [1. Fantasy. 2. Survival—Fiction. 3. Magic—Fiction.] I. Title.
    PZ7.S7642Lar 2014
        [Fic]—dc23   2013046702

Manufactured in the United States of America
1 – BP – 7/15/14

For Josh·
There's no one I'd rather have
on my team, fighting for me
and for my stories.

And for Andrew:
Who will always be the voice of
my shoulder devil, telling me
to write the harder, darker,
more impossible things.

PROLOGUE

Their clockwork sun is rising. In these half-forgotten tunnels beneath the city, the sound is like the roar of a rainstorm, lashing my ears again and again. The swell of magic washes over me like a tide, flooding my senses; I taste copper, and I don't know if it's magic or blood from my bitten tongue. Breaking through their barrier drained me of every ounce of magic I had, making this surge overwhelming. It nearly drives me to my knees in the ankle-deep water. My sloshing footsteps are lost in the din as I stagger forward, bracing myself against the tunnel wall. The stone bricks are slimy to the touch, wet with decades of mildew and mold.

I pull myself upright again, a moan echoing away from me down the tunnel. There's no telling what security sensors they might have—for all I know, the city's forces are on their way already, wondering what foreign danger breached their defenses for the first time in a century. I can't be here when they arrive. I keep moving through willpower alone.

It was Dorian who taught me how to do it. He deciphered the theory of it, spent months locked up in his house, poring over equations and diagrams. Sometimes in the night I'd awaken, consumed with fear and doubt about what lay in store for me. I'd look out my window and see, across the darkened sea of the Iron Wood, a single light—like the solitary lantern in a lighthouse, calling to me, drawing me to him.

I always knew he could teach me how to get inside, but only I could break through the flawless metal dome enclosing the city. Only I am strong enough to magic iron.

I'm too drained to even conjure a light, so I rely on the dim illumination that filters through the occasional grate in the street overhead. As the cacophony of the sunrise fades, I begin to hear the noise of carriages and foot traffic here and there as the city's citizens shuffle off to begin their days.

With the fading of the sunrise's harsh magic comes the return of my senses. The city itself is an utter mystery to us— no outsider has been inside since before the cataclysm over a century ago. There are no maps, and I can't risk showing my face aboveground until I absolutely have to. We don't know how many people live here, or whether they'd recognize me as a stranger if they saw me. In the Iron Wood, we all know each other. We'd recognize a newcomer in a heartbeat.

So I have to follow the scent of magic. The moment I crossed through their barrier I could feel it, a shining beacon in the hazy unknown. Though there is magic in the air here, most of it resides at the far end of the city, in a complex of buildings. I could see them lit up like stars when I scouted from the rooftop in the predawn hours before I retreated beneath the streets.

If anything can tell me the secret of how this city survived the cataclysm that turned the rest of the countryside into ruins, it'll be there. Dorian thinks they had something to do with the end of the world. And we'll never be safe until we know they can't do it again.

Over the sounds of distant machinery and street traffic, something else catches my ear. A tiny buzzing, almost musical.

I pause, listening carefully. The sound is coming from down here—from the tunnels. And it's coming closer.

I pull back against the wall, tucking myself into an alcove. Whatever it is has magic, I can feel it now, bobbing nearer and nearer. They have sentries even down here. Carefully I pull the last shreds of magic I have close around myself, imagining a hard, iron shell. *Camouflage.* Holding my breath, I wait.

Eventually, a tiny machine flits into view. Its wingspan is no bigger than my pinky finger, and if it hadn't buzzed through a shaft of light from the streets above, causing its copper body to flash, I never would've spotted it. I hold even tighter to my shell, willing the sentry to move on past.

Though it pauses to scan its surroundings—I can feel the sweep of magic slide past me—its senses don't penetrate my camouflage. It hums off into the distance again, leaving me alone with my pounding heart.

I have so little magic that I feel naked, vulnerable. If that sentry had spotted me, I'm not sure I could have destroyed it before it took word of my intrusion back to its masters. Summoning my strength, I step out of my crumbling alcove and slip on through the maze of tunnels.

The knot of magic at the end of the city draws me onward, and eventually I feel it start to shift. It's no longer ahead of me, but all around me. Somewhere above my head are the answers I seek.

The world around me is nearly pitch-black now, no more grates leading to the streets. There are buildings above me, and no more easy escapes. Swallowing my fears, I send flickers of magic ahead of me, feeling the way they caress the stone and bounce back from the metal. I'm forced to form a picture of my surroundings the way a bat does, ghostly images coalescing in my mind.

There—a ladder. I grasp for it, fingers curling around

the clammy iron. No hiding underground anymore. I have to cling to the rungs for nearly a minute before I summon the courage to step out of the water and climb up to the hatch above.

The wheel-lock screeches as I open the hatch, but it gives way—there's nothing blocking it from the other side. The trapdoor is heavy, forcing me to lean my shoulder into it awkwardly as I try to shove it up and away while balancing on the ladder. Finally I manage it, and it falls back with a clang. Light floods my eyes.

I stagger out of the hole in the floor and let the hatch drop closed again, and then catch my breath. I'm in a vast room, larger than any I've ever seen. The ceiling is a huge dome with skylights to let in the artificial sunlight, crisscrossed with tracks for machinery. As I watch, an immense ring with a fiery sun on it ticks over, a simulated passage across their simulated sky. The floor is polished marble—when I look down, the hatch is nearly invisible, masquerading as a beautiful compass rose inlaid with gold at the center of the floor.

Corridors lead in every direction, labeled with signs. Most of them I cannot understand, despite being one of the few in the Iron Wood who can read. *Biothaumatic Laboratory*, reads one sign. *Museum and Archives*, reads another.

Archives. That one, I recognize. I take a step forward.

"Hello." A voice echoes out from behind me, freezing my blood and making me whirl.

A woman stands there. She's older than I am, but not by much. She has short black hair and a round face with keen, narrow eyes. She's a little plump, wearing a long red coat that reaches to her knees. Around her neck she wears a gold necklace adorned with an ornamental version of a drawing tool I've only ever seen in Dorian's office, used when he studies his maps and diagrams. *A compass*, my mind supplies.

She doesn't seem surprised to see me—she seems only interested, curious. Even pleased.

My thoughts tangle, trying desperately to seek out some excuse, some reason for being here. My pant legs are sodden from my trip through the tunnels—in the silence I can hear them dripping on the immaculate floor. The droplets strike out a rhythm against the floor like the ticking of a clock, measuring the time since she spoke, the time I've failed to reply. *Too late. Too late.*

The woman's head tilts to the side as she studies me the way Dorian would study one of his maps. "Welcome to the Institute," she says. "What's your name?"

I open my mouth, my dry throat working soundlessly. Finally, painfully, I whisper, "Eve."

She smiles, but the expression leaves me cold, makes me wish I'd stayed in the damp, musty tunnels underground. Her smile makes something at the base of my skull ache—her smile lifts the hairs on the back of my neck.

"Hello, Eve," she says. "My name is Gloriette. I think we're going to become the best of friends."

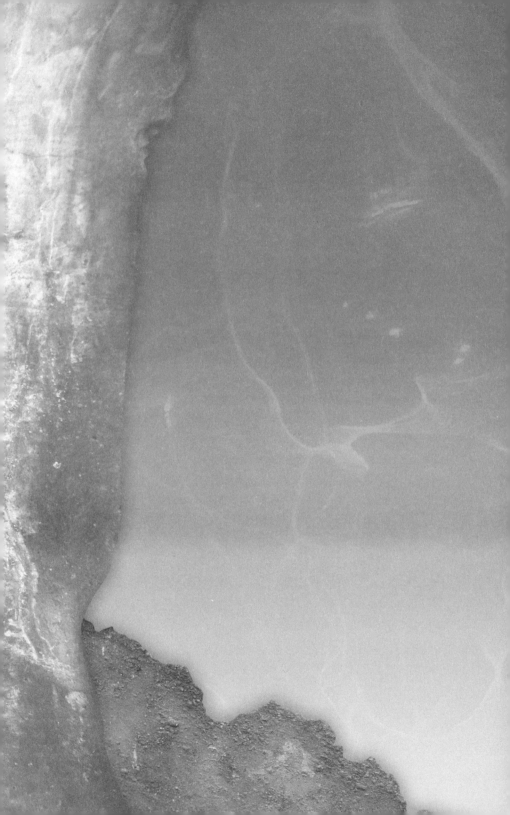

PART I

CHAPTER 1

My hands ached, my lower back screaming a protest. I longed to move, but even so much as a tiny shift to relieve my sore muscles might give away my position. I had the advantage up here, in this tree—but moving would shake the branches, and the tiniest shiver of leaves would be all Oren needed to find me.

In a way, I was grateful for my discomfort. The pain grounded me, drove away the fragments of my dream that kept coming back, no matter how often I tried to dismiss them. The dreams came more often now, the closer I came to my home, to the city where I was born. They felt like memories, but of events that never happened. At least, not exactly. I'd been in those tunnels under the city, but I'd been trying to break into the school, not the Institute. I'd been caught by Gloriette, but not in the rotunda. Her smile had made my skin crawl too, but she was so young in this memory, so much younger than I remembered.

Unless—unless it had happened that way. Unless my memory was wrong, warped somehow by everything that had happened to me. Perhaps I was the one becoming twisted.

But this—this branch, its rough bark digging into my palms, carving deep impressions in the skin there—this was real. I tightened my grip.

A small, tinny sound prompted me to lift my head, slow and cautious. The buzzing grew louder, more familiar, and in spite of my aching body, I smiled.

"Anything?" I whispered as Nix winged in and lighted on my shoulder.

"He's moved off in the wrong direction," the pixie said smugly. "He lost your trail back by the river when you walked in the streambed."

My heart surged with relief and no small amount of satisfaction. I'd outwitted *Oren*, the best tracker and hunter I'd ever met.

If Oren was headed for the wrong end of the copse we were in, that meant I could move. I straightened with a badly stifled moan for my cramped limbs. My jerky movements made the branch I was clinging to leap and shudder, and I was glad for Nix's scouting. I could sense the dark pit of shadow that was Oren when he was nearby, but once he got out of my immediate range, I had no way of tracking him.

Carefully I started climbing down the tree. I could double back to where he'd already searched for me—it'd take him hours to come back around again, and he didn't have that kind of time to waste. The second to last branch was about six feet off the ground, and I let myself down to dangle there.

Before I could drop to the leaf litter, a face melted out of the foliage—fierce blue eyes, and white teeth bared in a grin.

"Gotcha," said Oren.

I shrieked and let go of the branch, landing heavily and rolling when I hit the ground. Dazed, but heart pounding, I started to scramble to my feet. A hand closed around my ankle.

"Oh, no you don't!" Oren gasped, dragging me back. "I found you—don't try to get out of this one!"

"Nix!" I screamed as the pixie danced around just beyond the reach of my grasp. "You little traitor!"

"You're too trusting of your allies!" Nix called in a sing-song voice. It gave a little shiver of its wings—*laughing* at me.

"Do you yield?" Oren was laughing too, in that quiet, breathless way he had.

I made one last attempt to break free, but his grip was too tight. I went limp. "Fine," I muttered. "You win."

"Don't sulk," Oren said, kneeling over me. "You came close that time."

"I hope you know that I *could* get out of this," I told him. "But you could get seriously hurt in the process."

"Ah," said Oren gravely. "Well, thank you for deigning to be captured, in that case."

"Shut up."

His grip relaxed, though he gave no sign of moving to let me up. "I was watching you back there," he said idly. "I saw your face go blank—those dreams again?"

That he'd been there, watching me while I thought I was completely alone—his skill at camouflage, at using the forest as a tool, it never stopped amazing me. In the city Lethe, he'd been like a caged animal. Here he was free. Here he was home.

I nodded. "Or whatever they are. I can't get a moment's peace—it's all the time now, when I sleep, and even when I'm awake, bits and pieces come back to me constantly."

"Nerves," Oren suggested quietly. "Going back to your city, facing down the people who did this to you."

"Maybe." I gazed past him, up at the shards of blue sky scattered through the leafy treetops. Spring came as we traveled south from Lethe, leaving the last of the wintry frost behind. We'd needed only a few weeks to reach the outskirts of my home city, but here, in the south, the spring came quickly. The trees were alive with tender leaves and blossoms that shattered at a touch.

"Lark is ready," Nix said confidently. *"Lark can do it."*

"This is why we're training." Oren reached out but stopped a few inches short of touching my cheek. He was so careful to avoid that touch, knowing the currents it sent through me, the reminder that his shadow was always there, draining my magic. The reminder of what he was. "Even in the city without a tree in sight, this is how you beat them. How you stay hidden, stay quicker than they are."

His eyes were so earnest that I found my smile and nodded. How could I tell him that training my instincts and my reflexes wasn't going to make the difference in fighting the people who'd turned me into a monster? It was a different kind of strength I'd have to draw on there.

But the training helped in other ways—vented my nervous energy, gave me an outlet for my fears, distracted me from what was coming. Helped me trust my arm again, which I needed to get used to being healed, despite the way it ached still during the cold spring nights.

Oren leaned down, touching his lips to my hair. Even that touch, though he avoided brushing my skin, was enough to set my nerves shrieking. Something inside me responded to the monster in him, always. Though I longed to tilt my face back and let him kiss my lips, the rest of me shuddered away.

Then he lifted his head and pulled away, but not before I saw the darkened eyes, the brows drawn in, the not-so-hidden grief in his expression. My heart ached, and I concentrated instead on the magic, reaching out to find Nix as it flitted off through the forest.

Then I froze. Nix wasn't the only thing out there with magic.

"Oren," I whispered. He sensed the urgency in my voice, his body going instantly rigid. "There's someone out there.

"Shadow?"

"No—human. Not a Renewable, but there's something. I

can't tell—there's something strange about him. His magic is shielded somehow; I can't tell how far away he is. I think he's coming closer."

"We'll hide. Quick, back up the tree."

I wanted to groan a protest, but I knew it was the smartest course of action. We'd had few encounters with shadows on our way back due to our vigilance. They traveled in small packs, but when one pack found something worth chasing, their howls drew the others. Whatever was out there, if it found us and caused a ruckus, it could bring every shadow for miles sprinting straight for us.

Oren sprang to his feet and reached for my hand. But before I could take it, something leaped out of the undergrowth and swung at Oren's head. The impact knocked the breath out of me in sympathy—a huge branch had sent him sprawling with a grunt of pain.

"Oren!"

I kicked out, knocking whoever it was back into the brush. I sprinted for Oren's side, feeling for injuries with both hands. The shadow in him stirred at my touch, drawing greedily on the meager reserves of magic I held. Oren gave a soft, half-conscious groan when my fingers encountered wet, sticky blood in his hair. Something rustled behind me and I whirled, gathering my magic, ready if the thing in the brambles made a second attempt on him.

The bushes parted and a man ran out, still brandishing his branch. I readied a blast of magic, lifting my eyes to his face—

—and stopped.

I knew this man. His clothes were ragged and torn, revealing scratches on the skin underneath. The brown eyes were wild and desperate, and a dark, thick stubble had spread across his jaw and throat. But in the heat of the moment, I knew him.

"*Kris?*" I gasped.

CHAPTER 2

"Is it dead?" Kris rasped. He sounded as if he hadn't spoken for weeks. "Lark, get away from it—it could still hurt you—"

"Kris, what the—what are you *doing* here? This is Oren. This is—" My thoughts were so jumbled I could barely spit them out in the form of words. Abruptly I realized that Kris and Oren had never met, that the name would mean nothing to him.

"I thought it was a shadow," mumbled Kris, the branch dipping until it rested on the ground. "It had you pinned, I thought—he looks like a shadow."

Oren was stirring feebly, to my relief. I looked down at him, helping him sit up when he reached for my hand. He was as dirty as I was from weeks of travel, as fierce as ever, as though he hadn't spent all that time learning to control his ferocity in Lethe. If I didn't know him, and didn't know better, I might think he was a monster too.

And, of course, he was. But so was I.

"Kris." I couldn't stop saying his name. "What are you doing out here?" Kris opened his mouth, but I interrupted. "Never mind—not now. Help me get Oren up. There's a stream a ways back, where we broke camp—let's get back there. You can tell me what's going on after we make sure you didn't just kill him."

. . .

Though Kris tried to help me as I set camp back up again, he was absolutely useless. Eventually I made him sit still while I built up the fire—sitting on the *opposite* side from Oren, who was propped up against a dead log. Though Oren watched Kris in stony silence, holding a cold cloth, wet from the stream, against his head, Kris just huddled, shivering as though it was the dead of winter, watching me.

My mind raced with questions, making my fingers clumsy. But they still knew the trick of this, and I held my tongue until the fire could sustain itself. I put a metal bowl in next to the crackling wood, filling it with water to clean the gash on Oren's head once it was hot. I rinsed Oren's cloth in the stream, watching the blood dance through the water, then brought it back freshly sopping and cold. He took it, still silent, still watching Kris through narrowed eyes. I could feel his unasked questions behind that stare, but he was waiting.

Waiting for me.

I braced myself and turned to face Kris. He was so changed from the boy I remembered—gentle, handsome, charming. He looked older, but more than that, he looked frightened.

He was still staring at me, through me. When I looked at him he didn't even react—it wasn't until I nudged his leg with my foot that he started, blinking and refocusing on my face. I handed him the canteen and he grabbed at it, gulping down half the water inside before wiping his mouth with a rasp of his sleeve against the stubble on his face.

"Well?" I prompted him. I kept my voice gentle. This was the boy who'd betrayed me, who'd used me to lead the architects to the Iron Wood—but he'd also tried to save my life. And he looked as though he'd been through every trial I had, and worse.

He swallowed. "I don't know where to start. God, Lark, I've—" His hand moved, as if he'd started to reach out to me before his mind caught up with the impulse.

I glanced at Oren, who hadn't moved. "What are you doing out here? Why aren't you in the Institute with the other architects?"

"There is no more Institute." Kris hugged the canteen to his chest as though it were all that stood between him and some abyss yawning before him.

My breath caught. "What do you mean?"

"The city's split in two—the Institute no longer controls it. Half the population is with the architects, behind the barricades. The other half is in open rebellion. It's all fallen apart, Lark."

I stared at him, trying to imagine my precise, orderly city fallen to pieces. "I don't understand—what happened?"

"The attack on the Iron Wood took all our reserves. We expected to come back with all the power we'd ever need. We didn't expect—" He blinked at me, swallowing.

I knew what he meant. They hadn't expected *me*.

"When we got back we had nothing," Kris went on. "The Wall began to falter. People are panicking—word got out that the Institute was hiding a captive Renewable, accusations were flying everywhere. People found out about you, that you were a Renewable and ran away. At least, that's what they were told. I—" He closed his eyes. "I left the Institute to fight with the rebels. I told them what really happened, what the Institute did to you. They're on your side; they fight in your name. I couldn't stand what Gloriette was doing, the lengths she was willing to go."

I reached out to lay a hand on Kris's arm, squeezing it. "But how did you end up out here?" I asked, still trying to absorb all that had happened since I'd defeated the army of machines as they marched on the Iron Wood.

"I was going for help. I volunteered to go—I'd been out here before, I knew how to use the storage crystals to fight the void."

"But where—"

"The Iron Wood." Kris stared at the fire. His face was thin, exhausted. "I thought that—well, my enemy's enemy is my friend. The Renewables there have every reason to hate the Institute, and maybe they'd help the resistance if they knew what was happening. I took the last stores of magic we had and went out, but they're gone. The Iron Wood is empty. Not a single Renewable, no trace."

I glanced again at Oren, who met my gaze this time. We knew where the Renewables had gone—they'd gone to join my brother Basil, to seek refuge in Lethe from the architects of my city, in exchange for helping to sustain Lethe with their magic.

"But that doesn't matter." Kris lifted his gaze, speaking in a whisper. "I've found something better."

A sick dread twisted in my stomach. I knew where he was heading with this. "What do you mean?"

His arm shifted until he could wrap his fingers around my hand, cradling it between both of his. His touch was warm and solid, no trace of darkness in it. "I found you."

• • •

Later, when Kris had fallen into a deep, exhausted sleep, Oren finally moved from where he'd been sitting. Night was coming fast, and the dusk brought with it the scent of night-blooming flowers. The temperature was dropping, a sobering reminder that winter was not far gone, and a late frost could still rise up without warning.

Nix had returned earlier, confused to find us gone from where it had left us before in the clearing. The little machine had been thrilled to discover his creator there, sharing none of my confusion and suspicion. Nix was now dozing beside Kris's head, an oddly moving double portrait.

I lifted a finger to my lips, warning Oren not to disturb them.

"Do you trust this man?" Oren spoke quietly, crossing over to my side of the fire and staring down at Kris where he slept.

I looked up at him from where I sat, arms wrapped around my knees. "No," I said with a sigh. "But I do believe him about this."

Oren sat down next to me and wrapped his arm around my shoulders. Despite the fire crackling in front of us and the way our inner shadows stirred, I was grateful for his warmth. "He seems to care a great deal about you."

My throat tightened a little. "We have a complicated relationship," I replied, trying to keep my voice light, dry. "He's the one responsible for tricking me into fleeing my city, finding the Iron Wood. He's the reason for all of this."

Oren didn't reply immediately. I knew he wasn't thrilled at the idea of someone joining our little twosome, especially not someone I knew. But I couldn't leave Kris, not in the shape he was in. Finally, Oren shrugged, shoulder shifting against mine. "Then I suppose I owe this man a debt of gratitude for sending you to me."

I laughed, turning my head to stifle it against Oren's shirt. "Is your head okay?"

"I've had worse."

"That's not an answer."

Oren just shrugged again. I detected a note of irritation in the movement, and abruptly I realized that it wasn't all jealousy prompting Oren's surlier-than-usual attitude. Oren was embarrassed that Kris—desperate, half-starved, city-boy Kris—had gotten the jump on him and knocked him flat with only a dead tree branch for a weapon.

"What will you do now?" Oren asked when I didn't speak again.

I knew what he meant, and hesitated. Lifting my eyes, I gazed through the trees. We'd gotten our first glimpse of the Wall this morning when we scaled a crumbling ruin for a vantage point. If we'd kept going today, we would've reached the edge of it by nightfall. There was nothing to see now, but even so, I imagined I could sense it there, waiting for me.

"This doesn't change anything," I said finally. "I still intend to go back. Maybe even more, now. All those people. If the Wall fails for good, they'll be easy targets for the shadows. And those who don't die immediately will falter in the void and become shadows themselves eventually."

"And you can stop it?"

"Maybe not. But I can try. And you heard what Kris said—it's chaos. They need someone to lead them." As soon as the words were out, I grimaced. "Or maybe I shouldn't go after all."

Oren caught the expression and leaned away so he could see my face better. "You *are* a leader, Lark. I told you once I'd follow you anywhere, and I meant it. And it's not just because I need you to stay human."

"You're biased," I told him, flashing him a smile that was usually guaranteed to distract him.

"I mean it." His voice was low, serious. "You saved me. You saved the Iron Wood. You saved your brother, you saved the resistance fighters there, you saved all of Lethe. Why is it so hard to accept the truth of it?"

I pulled my gaze away, sick. "I couldn't save Tansy."

Oren wrapped his arms around me. "You can't always save everyone. But you try, and that's what makes you what you are."

"A monster?"

"A hero."

I laughed, but it was an uneasy sound. I was powerful, that much was undeniable. And Kris had said they fought in my name, after learning the truth about what had happened to me at the Institute. Maybe they didn't need me to be a hero. Maybe they just needed *me*, someone to rally behind.

"Look at the bright side," I said, heaving a sigh and leaning my head on Oren's shoulder. "Originally, it was just going to be you, me, and Nix against the entire city. Now we've at least got half the city with us against the Institute."

"I have enough trouble working with the bug," muttered Oren. "I don't think I'm ready for half a city's worth of questionable allies."

CHAPTER 3

The next day, we reached the edge of the Wall by the time the sun began to dip below the treeline. Though Kris could keep up, he wasn't the quietest of traveling companions, and more than once I had to stop Oren from unleashing a lecture like those he used to give me when we first started traveling together.

A night of uninterrupted sleep and food and water had done wonders for Kris. His gaze was still haunted, still changed, but his shivering had ceased, and when I handed him his share of our evening meal he smiled at me. In it I could see the ghost of the boy who'd smiled at me my first night in the Institute, the one who'd teased me about devouring all the watermelon and made me blush. Relief, tangible and warm, swept through me. The old Kris was still in there.

Our camp was in a part of the city that had, until recently, been inside the Wall. There were no trees growing up out of the roofs, no vines overtaking the crumbling mortar. Instead it was just silent, eerie, a sobering reminder of what would be should the Wall fail entirely.

As Oren set up camp in the ground floor of what used to be an apartment building, I went outside. Nix flitted along beside me, leaving Kris behind to get in Oren's way. I stifled the brief flare of unease at leaving the two alone together and slipped down an alleyway.

The Wall spread before me, a vast iron expanse that, even now, stole my breath away. On the inside, the Wall was crackling energy—pure magic. It took no special skill to leave the city, but returning was supposed to be impossible. Even with magic, the outside of the Wall was as impenetrable as iron. Only those too broken to fit within the perfectly oiled clockwork of the city ever left. Adjustment, it was called. As if a human life was nothing more than a bent cog: disposable.

Even now, part of me wanted to flee. Inside were the remains of the Institute and the people who'd created the monstrous shadow in my heart. Inside was Gloriette, whose voice in my memory made my skin crawl and my mind shrink with terror. Inside was a group of people depending on me to lead them, counting on me, as though I had any right to lead anyone.

I lifted both hands, pressing my palms to the vast surface. I expected a tingle of power, some sign that there was anything on the other side of this iron barrier, but I felt nothing except the cool, slick metal under my hands.

The curve of the metal distorted my reflection grotesquely, and I was struck by a vivid wave of déjà vu. It wasn't so very long ago that I had stood here, heart pounding, taking my first steps beyond the Wall after leaving the city. Less than a year had passed since then, and yet my own reflection was unrecognizable to me.

A tinny clang jolted me out of my thoughts, and I lifted my head to see Nix buzzing against the Wall. Its spindly legs scrabbled against the metal, trying to find purchase against the slope. Eventually it landed on my shoulder, mechanisms whirring frantically with the effort it had expended.

"What an unpleasant blight on the landscape."

"Aesthetics, Nix?" I asked, tilting my head back to see the Wall stretching up toward the sky and away. "Did Kris program that into you?"

"I am perfectly capable of determining the aesthetic value of an object on my own, based on a number of parameters including relative size and proportion, balance of color, approximate field of—"

"It doesn't have to be pretty," I murmured. "It just has to keep everyone safe."

"How will you get inside?"

"My brother gave me a key."

Nix slid forward onto my collarbone and hooked one of its needlelike legs into the chain around my neck. Like someone hauling a rope through a pulley, it drew the chain up until the little vial at the end of it emerged from under my jacket.

"It does not look much like a key."

I curled my fingers around the vial Basil had given me. "I know. Maybe it amplifies magic. Maybe it makes iron more susceptible to it—I don't know. Maybe it doesn't even work anymore. Basil was supposed to come straight back when the Institute sent him out. That was years ago."

"And if it doesn't work?"

"Then I'll force my way in," I said grimly. "I can magic iron. It's not pleasant, but I can do it."

I leaned forward, pressing my cheek against the cold iron. Experimentally, I let a little tendril of magic snake out, ignoring the way it tried to recoil from the iron. In his never-ending lessons during my time in Lethe, Wesley had taught me that brute force was almost never the solution when it came to doing something with magic. But I was never very good at finesse, and when it came to magicking iron, nothing but force was going to get me inside.

With my senses trained so carefully, I felt rather than heard

Kris approach from behind me. He said nothing, but my concentration was already shattered. Instead I let my magic seek him out, learning the shape of him by feel this time. There was something different about him, something I couldn't quite put my finger on. When I'd left my home city, I had so little control over my abilities that I never could have explored someone's soul this way. But compared to the citizens of Lethe, there was something about him that made me uneasy.

Before I could push any further, the taste of copper flooded my mouth, my every hair standing on end. A ripple ran through the metal surface where my cheek rested. It was barely more than a flicker, but it was all the warning I got before the world exploded.

Magic blasted through me in a wave, electrifying every nerve and muscle. For an instant, I could see buildings and streets stretching away in front of me, the world inside the Wall. I could hear screaming as if from a long way away as pain seared through my body. I was flung backward away from the Wall, striking the ground hard.

For a moment I wondered if Kris had somehow gotten his hands on a weapon. But the charge had come from the Wall itself—Kris was trying to help me.

He'd thrown himself down on his knees and was sliding a hand under my shoulders and picking me up, cradling me on his lap. His mouth was moving, asking me questions, but I couldn't hear him over the ringing in my ears. It felt as though every hair were standing on end, like fire had coursed through my body and left only singed nerve endings behind.

Through a thick, muffling haze, I heard shouting, running footsteps from our campsite. Kris was shoved aside so hard he fell over, and Oren's face appeared above mine.

I dragged myself half upright and pulled away from them both. "I'm okay," I croaked, my voice wavering. "Calm down."

Nix flew at me and huddled in the hollow of my throat.

"What the hell was that?" Oren spat the question at Kris, who was picking himself up off the ground and staring back at Oren with naked contempt.

"The Wall's unstable, I told you." Kris's eyes slid back to mine. "I had no idea the anomalies were affecting the outside too, or I would've warned you."

"Anomalies?"

Kris nodded. "Ripples that run through the Wall. They were our first warning that something was wrong with it, that the Renewable was finally failing. At first they only happened once every couple of weeks, but they've been coming more often now."

"That can't be good." I closed my eyes, fighting the adrenaline coursing through my body. "We've got to get inside, and fast. We'll camp here tonight, and in the morning—"

Oren held up a hand, his head lifted. I knew that tense, distant look on his face well, and fell silent, waiting, heart pounding.

Kris glanced between us, brow furrowed. "In the morning, what? What's going—"

"Hush!" I hissed. To his credit, he listened, going still.

I couldn't hear whatever it was that Oren had sensed, but his senses were sharper than mine. There was no in-between state with him; either he was the shadow or he was human, but even as a human he had better senses than anyone I'd ever met. They were all that stood between him and messy death, no matter what form he was in.

Finally, Oren's whisper knifed through the quiet. "Shadows. Five, maybe six. Too many to fight."

"Coming here?" I staggered to my feet, trying desperately to ignore the way my muscles were spasming in the aftermath of the blast.

Oren's eyes flicked toward my face. "They must've heard your scream."

"Can you get us inside now, tonight?" Kris's voice was low, nervous. I could almost feel his fear; my own wasn't much easier to deal with.

I shook my head, shivering. "I can barely stand."

"We've got to run." Oren made for the shelter and packed up our supplies as quickly and as silently as possible.

Kris, for once, made himself useful, damping the fire and drowning the embers with armfuls of dirt. I wondered if he'd encountered any shadow people on his way to and from the Iron Wood. His face was white, though; if he hadn't encountered them himself, then he had certainly heard stories.

Oren tossed me my pack and then slung his over his shoulders. Kris had his own supplies, though his bag was tellingly light. He hadn't counted on finding the Iron Wood empty, and he'd had nowhere to restock before trying to make it back to the city.

We kept to the circumference of the Wall, trusting that the density of the ruins there would keep the shadows at bay. They preferred the wilderness for hunting, largely giving the remains of the city a wide berth, the same way they did the Iron Wood. The afternoon sunlight dazzled my eyes, playing tricks on me, making me imagine I saw movement at every step. In broad daylight there was nowhere to hide except in the buildings, and I'd been trapped in a building with a family of shadows before. It wasn't an experience I wanted to repeat if I could possibly avoid it.

I could sense them now, around the edges of my range. Dark pits of nothingness yawning hungrily, only minutes behind us. I could feel eight distinct shadows—either Oren had estimated wrong, or others had joined in the chase.

Somewhere behind us, a desperate, lonely howl rose over

the sound of our harsh breathing and ragged footsteps.

"We'll have to find a place to hole up, barricade them out," Oren blurted. "Lark?"

I cast my power out in a net, trying to get a feel for the shape of the city before me. "There—a basement in the last building on the right in the next block. It's clear of debris."

Oren put on a fresh burst of speed, leaving me and Kris in his wake. If fear and adrenaline weren't keeping me focused, I could have stopped just to watch him run—long, even strides that ate up the ground at an astonishing rate. He reached the building and slammed into the door—it groaned but didn't give way. Kris and I kept running as Oren lowered his shoulder and tried again, and again, with no luck.

I could hear the shadows now, their snarling voices so distinct I felt I'd be able to see them if I turned. We skidded to a halt, and Kris grabbed at Oren's arm as he started to make another run at the door.

"Together," gasped Kris, winded. But Oren understood and nodded, wasting no time on bravado. In unison this time they charged the door, and under their combined weight, the whole thing finally gave way at the hinges and crashed inward.

Oren went sprawling but Kris kept his balance and then reached down to drag Oren to his feet. I broke into a jog again and found the door to the basement. This one was unlocked, and I breathed a soft moan of relief. We piled through it and then locked it behind us with a loud, solid clank of iron deadbolts.

We half staggered down the stairs in pitch-blackness, and I nearly fell when I reached the unexpected end of the steps. I didn't want to risk a light, so I felt my way forward. From the feel of the air, cold and damp, it was a concrete basement, good for little more than storage. My fingers encountered a brick pillar, and I let myself slide to the ground, still gasping for air. For all Oren's training as we traveled south, nothing could prepare me for running for my life from the shadows again.

A hand touched my knee, and I reached out. As his fingers curled around mine, I recognized the touch—Oren. Strong, callused fingers. Steady, despite the headlong flight we'd just taken. Though his touch caused an answering, unpleasant tingle of magic draining through my arm, I didn't pull away. Even that was better than nothing in this darkness. Footsteps approaching told me where Kris was, and he dropped to the ground beside us, his legs pressing against my feet. Then, finally, a tiny buzzing form lurched out of the darkness and buried itself beneath the curtain of my hair.

We were all here.

Over the harsh sounds of breathing and the occasional scrape of clothes on stone, I could hear heavy footfalls overhead. The shadows had found the building.

Oren's fingers tightened through mine. I was half afraid Kris would reach for me too, but he didn't, staying where he was, pressed up against my legs. I heard him swallow, though, the sound audible in the echoing blackness.

A howl lanced the silence from above—first one, then more and more joined it in a dreadful, chilling parody of a chorus. Then, a thud—and another, and another. They'd found the door.

I closed my eyes, gathering in my power. The blast from the Wall had shaken me, but it hadn't drained me—it was all there, just roiling and impossible to control. Still, I didn't need control right now. I just needed power. If the shadows got through that door, I was the only thing that would save Oren and Kris. If the shadows got through, I'd rip them apart.

More thumps and howls echoed down, making us flinch with every noise. A terrible screeching lashed my eardrums as one of them tried to claw its way in, fingernails raking down the metal door. I ground my teeth against the sound until they ached.

The seconds dragged on into minutes, and the minutes dragged into measureless hours. In the darkness, touch was all we had—I could feel every movement Kris made, pressed against my legs, and Oren's hand remained warm and strong wrapped around mine. Nix made what I could only hope it intended as soothing sounds, a low droning buzz of its mechanisms—but I suspected it was only trying to soothe itself. I focused on the absurdity of a machine feeling fear and tried not to think about the bolts upstairs giving way just a little more with each time the shadows threw themselves against it.

Then the pounding stopped so abruptly that my ears rang, and I thought the pounding of my heart would fill the entire room. Ears straining, I heard a few shuffling sounds, some heavy footsteps, a dragging sound. Somehow it was even worse than the pounding.

"What are they doing?" Kris's voice was not even a whisper, only a breath.

I half expected Oren to shush him, but instead Oren replied in a low voice. "Waiting."

"We should stay quiet," I whispered.

"They know we're here." Oren took a long, deep breath. "They'll have to leave come morning to find something else to hunt, but for now, they'll try to wait us out."

"Morning." I let out a breath I didn't know I was holding.

"We can last until then." I felt Oren's hand relaxing around mine.

Kris swallowed audibly again and moved, the fabric of his clothes scraping against the stone. "Let's not do that again," he suggested, voice finding a little more strength.

"I don't understand what they're even doing here." I

leaned back until my head rested on the stone pillar behind me. "It's a city—they should be out in the countryside. The shadows hate it in the ruins."

Oren grunted agreement. Kris said nothing, but I could feel him tense, his body going rigid at my side.

"Kris," I whispered, "what is it?"

"It's—I think I know why they're here," he said. His voice sounded weak, sick. "The Institute doesn't have the resources to keep prisoners, not with half the city against them."

A slow dread began to build somewhere inside me as part of me began to understand before the rest of me was willing to even consider what he was saying. "Then what   "

"She Adjusts them." Kris swallowed. "Only there's no ceremony, no farewell. It's not voluntary anymore. Whenever they catch a rebel, Gloriette forces them through the Wall."

I felt the darkness spinning around me, horror robbing me of breath.

"I think these shadows are—I think they're our people." Kris's voice cut through the darkness. "And I think some part of them is still trying to find a way home."

CHAPTER 4

The night came and went, though only Nix's internal clock alerted us that it was day again. I had dozed now and then, my consciousness dotted with strange dreams of things I'd never done and places I'd never been. I tried to shake them, but the feeling of familiarity lingered even as I stretched out my cramped limbs.

We let Oren unbar the door with his ear pressed against it, listening for any sounds that might indicate we were still being hunted. But his prediction proved correct—sometime in the night, the shadows had moved off in search of easier prey, too hungry to wait forever.

The light stabbed against my eyes as we shuffled out into the morning, leaving the dark basement behind. The fresh air was cold with lingering winter, but far sweeter than the fear-soaked atmosphere belowground. The Wall was just beyond the far edge of the street, bisecting a row of townhouses. Its dull gleam reflected little of the morning's dim light, giving it a monstrous sort of immovability as it squatted in front of us.

"How's your magic?" Oren asked, stretching his arms over his head as he came up beside me.

"Better," I replied, and though my mouth opened as if to continue, no words came out.

My tongue felt heavy and unresponsive. Though I'd left my more immediate fears of being chased down and attacked behind in the basement, the dawn had brought on an entirely new set. Kris had painted an unimaginable picture of my home. No matter what, I'd thought I was coming home to what I'd always known, even if it wasn't necessarily what I longed for anymore. It'd be familiar, if nothing else. Comforting.

But now there was no telling what I'd find on the other side of the Wall.

Oren was used to chaos. He'd grown up in it, thrived in it. He didn't understand why even now I still gravitated toward rules and order and certainty. I wished I could explain to him why the idea of my city, my steadfast, ever-fixed city, falling into ruin was so terrifying.

And why the thought of letting him see me scared, after everything we'd been through, was so hard.

I could feel Oren's eyes on me as he waited for me to gather my thoughts. He never pushed, always sure I'd speak when I was ready. The product of having lived so many years alone, I guessed. But as the seconds dragged on and the weight of everything I couldn't quite say aloud pressed in, Oren finally took a slow, thoughtful breath. "I'm going to do a quick circuit," he said. "Make sure nothing's waiting for us out there."

I swallowed hard, locating my voice. "Be careful," I whispered. When I turned he was already gone, swallowed by the ruins.

I retraced my steps back toward the building where we'd spent the night until I could grab my pack. Kris and Nix were playing some kind of game that my eyes struggled to follow. Kris was passing a ration chit back and forth between his hands, hiding it, using misdirection. Nix was far better at tracking the chit's movement than I was, but even the pixie was fooled now and then.

"You're getting sloppy," Kris accused the machine, laughing.

"The mechanism that allows me to see was of your design," Nix retorted with a furious buzz, swarming over to Kris's fist to pry it open and search for the chit inside.

"Who would've guessed you'd end up so stuffy," muttered Kris before looking up and catching me watching them. "All clear?"

"Oren's checking." I watched as Nix seized the ration chit and Kris's hand went flat, allowing the pixie to examine the chit, turning it over and over in its little legs, clicking in triumph. "What're you doing?"

"An old calibration exercise," Kris said, letting his hand fall as Nix buzzed off, bobbing and weaving under the extra weight of the coin as if drunk. "PX—er, Nix, I guess—was the first pixie model to have eyes. Or, rather, sensors able to pick up the visible light spectrum, instead of just magic."

I knew that the other pixies I'd seen were blind except for their magic sensors, but I hadn't realized Nix was the *only* pixie to be able to see. "And you invented that?" I asked curiously, watching as Nix dropped onto a log and crouched over the coin like a feral animal guarding a kill.

"I had help," Kris replied, but the pride in his voice betrayed him. He flashed me a smile, and for the strangest instant I was back in the Institute, blushing because he'd seen me single-handedly eat an entire watermelon. "But mostly, yeah."

I caught Nix's eye and gave a little jerk of my chin. For an instant I thought it might rebel, but after giving the ration chit a definitive kick with one of its legs, Nix abandoned it and darted over to my shoulder, sliding in against my neck under my hair. I couldn't have admitted it aloud, but the familiar metal weight of its body against my neck was a comfort. Watching it play—or calibrate—with Kris made my stomach twist with unexpected jealousy.

"How'd you learn to do that?" I asked Kris, settling my pack over my shoulders carefully so as not to dislodge Nix.

"Invent eyes?" Kris's own store of supplies was nearly gone, but we'd transferred some of our gear over so he could share the load.

"All of it." I could hear the complex symphony of Nix's mechanisms whirring away below my ear and knew it was listening to me. "Most of the time Nix seems more like magic than machine."

"*That's because I am quite extraordinary,*" Nix said drily, thrumming its wings against my neck.

"Hush," I muttered.

I could feel Kris's eyes on me, but when I glanced over he'd dropped his gaze to the broken path we were following. "I was born an architect," he said simply. "It's in my blood."

I thought of his soft hands, the clinical neatness of his clothes when I knew him in the Institute, the flawless attention to every detail. Even now, the way he was walking, each pace measured and falling in pattern on the shattered cobbles so that his heels touched every third stone—this was the mind that had come up with the entire plan to manipulate me into locating the Iron Wood.

I found myself staring, as though trying to see the mechanisms in Kris's head, piece them apart the way he could piece apart Nix. I was so distracted that I didn't even notice when he returned my stare and slowed his steps. It wasn't until he came to a halt that I found his eyes on mine.

"We're raised to believe our blood makes us superior." Kris's voice was quiet, thoughtful. "We're direct descendants of the architects who built the city, who created the Wall. We're raised to believe we're the reason the city didn't fall like the rest of the world during the Wars."

"And yet you left," I pointed out. "Why?"

"I guess I realized that blood isn't everything."

"What changed?" A breeze stirred, parading a few errant leaves and petals down the path between us.

Kris's mouth twitched, as though at some joke I didn't understand. "I met you."

I realized he was still gazing at me, and abruptly my throat constricted. Even half starved and beaten by exposure, Kris was every inch as handsome as he was the day he first teased me in the Institute.

"Kris—" I began, my throat dry. But he shook his head, cutting me off with a gesture.

"Don't misunderstand me," he said, with one of those disarming smiles, "I wouldn't try to edge my way in now."

I was about to speak when Kris stepped forward, closing the distance between us to just a pace and a half. "I think you're more important than that," he added.

I slipped my hands into my pockets, hoping warmth would calm my tingling fingers. "More important?" I echoed stupidly.

"Gloriette and the others were right—you're going to save us." Kris let his eyes move past me, watching some distant moment unfold in his mind's eye. "You really were the one we were waiting for—we just didn't know what to do with you when we had you."

"But I don't know what I'm doing," I protested.

"Knowing what you're doing is overrated." The corner of Kris's mouth lifted a little, though he was still not quite meeting my eyes. "Look where all my plans got me."

My thoughts crowded in again. I couldn't help but see

faces half-forgotten, imagining the people I used to know as they must be now—desperate, hungry for a savior. The fears I couldn't tell Oren came rattling out of me in a rush, eager to find harbor in Kris's faith. "I don't know if I'm ready."

Kris reached out, his warm fingers encircling my wrist and pulling one of my hands free from my pocket so he could hold it in between both of his. It felt strange to be touched by hands that weren't Oren's—to feel no current of magic between us, no constant reminder of what he was. I could feel only the warmth of Kris's hands, the tiny flutter of his pulse at the base of his thumb.

Kris kept his eyes on our hands as he spoke. "This is what I meant. You're more important than me, more important than Oren. This goes beyond any of that. You're going to lead us; I believe that with all my heart. They'll follow you like an army. And I—" His eloquence faltered, and he stuttered to a halt. There was no sound, as if even the breeze had stopped to wait for him to finish. "I want to follow you," he said finally. "I'll be your soldier. I just wanted you to know that."

Though this section of the ruins wasn't as overgrown as the outlying districts, spindly trees had grown up through the cracks in the paving stones, and vines had overtaken the street lamps. Spring had prompted blooms to open here and there, and they glowed a pale gold in the morning light, framed by the young green of newly budded leaves.

The muddy remains of Kris's red architect's coat seemed even shabbier in comparison with the glorious morning, but he stood there with such dignity, watching me, waiting for me to remember how to breathe. He still had my hand cradled in his, and abruptly I realized it was no romantic gesture, but one of supplication, of respect. Of hope. My eyes burned; the blood roared in my ears.

A noise from a few paces away, sharp like a cracking twig,

startled us apart. Kris dropped my hand and I flew back, whirling. Oren stood there, clearing his throat a second time. He didn't look at Kris—his eyes were on me.

"We're all clear." Quiet, terse. Revealing nothing. "We should go before any of them circle back around."

CHAPTER 5

The walk back to the perimeter of the Wall was a silent one. Even Nix was quiet, nestled underneath my hair, as though demonstrating its loyalty. Oren walked in front, picking our path through the empty streets and alleyways—I could see nothing but the set of his shoulders, tense but unrevealing. Though I didn't turn around, I knew Kris was close behind me. I could hear his steps, nowhere near as quiet as Oren's, or even mine now that I'd learned better how to move quietly in the world outside the Wall.

My ears were still ringing with his words, with his loyalty and faith. Half of me wanted to scream that he was wrong, that he needed to learn as I had that heroes never lived up, that the more he relied on me, the more I'd disappoint him. I'd spent years longing for my brother to return, to make everything better, only to discover when I found him that he wasn't the hero I remembered. He was just a boy—just as I was only a girl, one girl against the entire city. I wished I could pound the truth of it into Kris's trusting heart—and yet something held me back.

True, Basil wasn't who I'd built him up to be in my memories. True, my faith in him was misplaced. But it had gotten me there. It carried me across a wilderness I couldn't have imagined and through a city I'd never seen. Maybe Kris needed the promise more than he needed *me*. Maybe all of them did.

. . .

We reached the Wall again by midmorning. Oren found us a section clear of obstacles, the harder for any errant shadows to sneak up on us. Kris dropped his pack next to ours and stretched, spine popping. "Once we get inside, we might not get a chance to rest for a while," he warned us. "I've been gone for weeks now; there's no telling how things have changed in there."

I glanced at Oren, who was crouching over his pack and taking inventory of the supplies inside. He still carried that tension, though, and didn't look up even though I knew he could feel my eyes on him.

"Kris—" I said hesitantly. "I'm going to need some time. To get ready."

Kris's eyes flicked from my face to where Oren crouched. "Right. I'll go keep watch. Nix?" His eyes met mine again briefly as the pixie launched itself off my shoulder to go to his. Kris's mouth curved in a small, quick smile. There was a broken-down, rusted-over walker machine not far away—he turned and made his way toward it, inspecting its legs and eventually starting to scale the machine for a better vantage point.

Oren and I would be able to sense any oncoming shadows long before Kris would be able to see them, but I appreciated the gesture. If this was the last time we were guaranteed a moment to rest, it was also the last moment Oren and I would have alone.

I waited until Oren had finished his inventory and cinched his bag shut again with a savage jerk. He stayed in a crouch, elbows resting on his knees and hands dangling.

"Regretting coming with me on this suicide mission yet?" I asked lightly.

His eyes flicked up to meet mine, though I could barely see them through the messy hair falling down over his brow. "Give it time." His voice betrayed nothing, and his face gave away even less.

Still, a flicker of relief coursed through me. A joke meant we were okay. I moved toward him until I could run my fingers through his hair, brushing it away from his eyes. "I'm going to need you in there."

Unmasked, his pale blue eyes were more telling. His brow furrowed as he gazed up at me, silent for a long time. "You're going to need him too," he said finally. "We're lucky he found us."

He was telling the truth. We needed Kris's information—without him we'd be going in blind. But there was something else there, a deeper wound Oren was hiding. And no one hid wounds better than Oren. I reached out toward his face again, but he straightened before I could touch him and my hand fell away.

"I saw your face," he said softly, unprompted. "Back there, with him."

My heart stuttered a little, remembering how it had felt watching him with Olivia in Lethe, even when nothing was going on between them. "I'm not—"

"I know. That's not—" It wasn't like him to stutter or hesitate, but he stopped, his gaze searching mine. "I mean that I saw the way you held his hand. He felt normal, didn't he? He didn't feel like a shadow."

Oren knew that every time we touched I could feel the tingle of magic flowing from me to him. It was a constant reminder of what we were, that neither of us was quite human, that there was a part of him that was and always would be a monster.

"That doesn't matter," I said fiercely.

For once, Oren's face wasn't hard to read. There was a naked longing there in his expression, one that cut me so deeply I struggled to breathe. "Of course it matters." He lifted a hand as if to touch my cheek, but his fingertips just traced a lock of hair and then fell again, avoiding the skin-to-skin contact that would trigger the flow of magic.

It doesn't matter to me, I wanted to say. But that wasn't what he meant. It mattered to him.

I could still sense the shadow in him, even when he wasn't touching me—but it wasn't as visceral a feeling. I could ignore it, and so could he. At least, we could pretend to ignore it. I let out a slow breath, willing my heart to slow too. His wasn't the only presence I could sense, anyway. "I think there are some shadows out there, way in the distance. I should—I should get to work."

I let him go to get Kris and Nix back and turned to face the Wall. I pulled the chain around my neck over my head so I could inspect the vial in my palm. My brother had given it to me when I left Lethe, saying it was what the architects had given him when he crossed the Wall, fully expecting to return.

The stopper was made of lead, and I reached for the knife in my boot as the others returned. Kris came up to look over my shoulder, fascinated. "What is it?"

"You don't know?" I asked, pausing to look up at him. "It's something the architects gave my brother."

"Before my time," Kris replied. "Basil was long gone before I became involved in the Iron Wood project."

"It was supposed to help him get back inside the Wall once he'd located the Iron Wood," I said, sliding the tip of the knife underneath the edge of the lead.

"Maybe some kind of magic amplifier," Kris mused aloud. "Or a signal that'd alert the architects to come get him when he got back."

"A signal?" Oren echoed, straightening. The last thing we needed was to bring a dozen architects to meet us when we entered the city.

"Unlikely," said Nix, trying to land on the smooth metal surface of the Wall, legs scrabbling awkwardly for a moment before the pixie gave up and buzzed off again to hover. *"And even if it was a signal, the odds that anyone is still looking for it now are low. Your brother was pronounced dead years ago."*

"True." I wiggled the edge of the knife cautiously until the lead loosened, then slid free with a clink of metal on glass.

Nix surged forward and landed on my hand, crowding the edge of the vial. It had no sooner stuck its head over the edge of the glass than it jerked back, stumbling and buzzing in alarm. *"Some form of acid,"* it said.

"Let's hope it works like they thought it would six years ago." I stepped forward and, taking a deep breath, upended the vial along the Wall.

The liquid hissed where it hit the metal, clouds of noxious fumes rising up and away. I dropped the vial as I jerked back, coughing, eyes streaming. The glass shattered when it hit the cobblestones.

Oren leaned forward, waving away the fumes. The acid had left deep grooves in the metal exterior of the Wall, turning a small section of its smooth, reflective surface into a scarred, pitted mess. He shifted his weight and gave the section an experimental kick, but the metal didn't budge—didn't so much as creak under the blow.

"I don't understand," I croaked, lungs still protesting the acrid chemical smell lingering in the air.

"It is six years old," Kris pointed out. "Maybe it's just not as strong as it was then."

I took a few steps away from the acid-scarred section, getting some fresh air—and a fresh stretch of iron Wall. "Well, there was always a chance I was going to have to do this the old-fashioned way."

Oren caught my eye, his brow furrowed, but I waved away his concern.

Gingerly, remembering what had happened the last time I'd tried to explore the Wall by magic, I leaned forward and rested my palms against the cold iron. Closing my eyes, I let my senses flow over the Wall, searching for any weaknesses. There was nothing—even the section of the Wall I'd scarred with the acid held fast. The Wall itself was magic, but the architects had made it absolutely impervious from the outside.

Every time I tried to push through, my magic just slipped and slid away, unable to find purchase. Sweat gathered between my shoulder blades and dripped down the small of my back, the blood pounding in my ears as I strained—for nothing. I took a few deep breaths, trying to clear my mind and start again. I pushed and pushed until spots floated in my vision, and it was only the sharp, sudden tingle of a drain on my resources that jolted me back, gasping.

Both Oren and Kris were dragging me backward—it was Oren's touch that had jerked me out of my concentration. One of them was saying something, but my ears were ringing so much that I could only hear his voice as a strange buzzing, like a low-frequency version of Nix's wing vibrations.

I shook my head, still gasping for air. My hearing cleared a little, and I could make out Kris's voice. "—just follow the harvester machines, they have to come in from somewhere. Maybe we can sneak in that way, through the Institute's warehouses."

Oren was half supporting me with a hand under my elbow, his attention on Kris. "That could work," he said slowly. "It'll just take more time. There'll be shadows there, no doubt. They'll be attracted to the noise the machines make. It'll be risky."

I shook myself free, staggering away half a pace. The boys were so distracted by making their plans that they let me go, and I was grateful for the air. As I regained my breath, the Wall swam into view in front of my wavering vision again.

Without warning, my mouth flooded with the taste of copper again—another anomaly, as Kris had called it, was about to sweep through the Wall. Last time it had shocked me so hard it had knocked me flat, and then I'd been at full strength.

But wait—there'd been an instant, before the blast knocked me backward, when I'd seen through the Wall to the other side. The illusion of iron had vanished for a split second, compromising the Wall.

"It's a weakness," I whispered aloud.

Kris was still talking, but Oren heard me and turned. "What?"

"The anomalies." My mind raced. I had only a second or two before the ripple came through the Wall. If it blasted me this time, when I'd used so much of my magic already to try to break through the iron, there was no predicting what it could do to me.

And yet . . .

Movement in the distance caught my eye. A ripple was racing along the edge of the Wall toward us.

Somehow, Oren realized I was about to move half an instant before I did. But I was ready for him and managed to dodge when he lunged for me. I threw myself at the Wall just as the distortion reached us. Magic seared my body, but this time I was ready for it, and I channeled the power back at the Wall. Every nerve screamed, on fire—but it was over in an instant, and I was flying through the air. I hit pavement and rolled, gasping. Hands pulled me up and dragged me along, a tangle of voices and a metallic, frantic buzzing emerging from the blood roaring past my ears.

I opened my eyes to find Oren and Kris leaning over me and Nix buzzing this way and that, their concern almost tangible like a warmth against my face. But even their worry couldn't distract me from what I could see beyond their faces. Instead of the clear, warm blue of the spring morning sky overhead, I saw only a broad, endless expanse of rippling, violet light.

We were in. I was home.

CHAPTER 6

Growing up, the Wall was always there. It was as constant as the air we breathed. It was impossible to imagine anything beyond it, anything more vast. To us, the Wall was the edge of the world.

It wasn't until I fled my home that I lived for the first time without its gentle violet glow bathing the world. Its absence was so profound that it throbbed like a wound. Even after I'd grown accustomed enough to the vast, empty sky that it didn't give me nightmares, I still missed the feel of the Wall around me, constant and enduring.

I'd expected to feel that sense of safety again, once I returned. Here there were no shadow monsters lurking. There was magic in the air, so Oren would stay human even without my presence. Not an abundance of food, but enough. Always just enough. No starvation, no running for my life.

But instead, gazing up at the shimmering curtain of magic, I felt nothing. My heart was empty but for the constant background ache of hunger for power. The shadow in my soul stirred sluggishly, sensing the vast energy source all around me.

"We should get moving." Kris kept his voice low, touching my elbow to get my attention.

I let him lead the way. From all that Kris had told me, I'd half expected to find my home in ruins, on fire, streets running with the blood of the rebels and architects alike. But instead it was quiet. The streets were deserted, though this close to the Wall that wasn't unusual. For a strange, dizzying moment I felt as though I was retracing my steps from the day I'd fled, in some frozen limbo. I could hear nothing: no hum of pixie wings, no distant sirens.

The air was so still that the hairs lifted on my arms. I'd never noticed the city's stillness when I lived here—I'd never felt wind before, knew no better. But now, my skin crawled. We were outside, in the open, walking down a street—and yet the air was close and still as though we were in a small, tight room. It was like being in a doll's house—a doll's city. As though everything around us was fake, like a set in a play.

I glanced at Oren beside me, knowing the stillness for him would be an agony. His jaw was clenched, but when he caught me looking at him, he nodded back at me. He'd survive, for now. All his time spent underground in Lethe had at least prepared him for this.

The sun disc hung low in the sky, only just visible through the buildings on the horizon. My body told me it was morning, as it was outside the Wall, but here in the city it was sunset. Night was coming on quickly, and my instincts told me to seek shelter—even as my mind pointed out that there was nothing to shelter *from* in here. Only the architects.

"Where is everyone?" I asked finally. My voice emerged in a whisper—though the streets were deserted, it felt like my voice could carry forever in the stillness.

"Curfew," Kris whispered back. "This is the rebel-occupied sector, but it's not safe here after dark."

Maybe there was something to shelter from after all.

My pulse quickened a little, eyes searching the lengthening shadows.

"Not safe how?" asked Oren.

"Pixie squadrons." Kris came to a halt at the mouth of an alleyway, pressing close to the corner of the building and peering around, scanning the broader avenue ahead. "The architects send them through at night. During the day you can see them coming, but at night, the pixies have the advantage—no eyes, the dark doesn't affect them."

"Pixies like Nix?" Oren's low voice was skeptical. "I think we can probably handle them."

I remembered my last moments in the city, cornered against the Wall as a flock of pixies a thousand strong came thundering at me. "One at a time, sure," I said, shivering. "You've never seen them en masse. Children here tell each other horror stories about what pixies do to lawbreakers."

Oren shrugged, doubt clear on his features, but he didn't argue.

"*That is legend only.*" Nix, who had been quiet through all this, crept out from the shelter of my neck and onto the edge of my shoulder. "*Pixies are programmed not to harm human beings.*"

"You've got a needle designed for stabbing," I pointed out drily.

"*There are many things different about my programming,*" said the pixie archly.

"Pixies *used* to be programmed not to harm people," Kris said quietly, straightening and looking back over his shoulder at us. "Gloriette has changed many things since the failure of the Iron Wood project."

Nix fell silent, even its mechanisms quieting as it rubbed its front legs over its jewellike eyes. I imagined it as a nervous gesture, like someone wringing their hands.

"But you know some place we can go for the night?" I asked, keeping one eye on the sun disc as it dipped toward the bottom of the Wall.

But Kris was no longer looking at me—his face was tipped upward, eyes on one of the apartment buildings across the avenue. As I followed his gaze, a sharp movement caught my eye. A window shutter slammed, echoing in the silence.

Oren twitched and withdrew back into the shadows of the alleyway. "Spotted us," he said shortly. "Let's move."

But Kris stayed put. "I told you, this is the rebel-controlled sector. That much hasn't changed; there'd be Enforcers everywhere if the architects had taken this street. We want the rebels to find us."

I wasn't so sure—just because one side was definitely my enemy didn't make the other side my friend. But these were the people Kris wanted me to lead, and I couldn't lead if I stayed hidden in the shadows. I took a deep breath, and before Oren could protest, I stepped out into the street.

My shadow flew out in front of me, forty feet long in the low-angled light from the setting sun disc. "Is someone there?" I called. "My name is Lark Ainsley—I'm from beyond the Wall."

I winced—it wasn't quite what I'd intended to say. I wasn't from beyond the Wall, I was from here. This was my home. And yet, that wasn't strictly true anymore.

Kris and Oren followed me, their shadows joining mine as it stretched down the empty street. For a few moments there was no response to my hail except silence. But then the door of the apartment building opened and an unfamiliar face peeked out. "Lark Ainsley?" said a voice. "The girl who left?"

I nodded, my throat dry.

The door opened wider, revealing a middle-aged woman standing there, staring at me. I didn't recognize her, but she seemed to know me. "You are," she breathed, eyes going from me to the boys and back again. "I recognize you from the posters. You'd better come inside before you're seen."

She ushered us through the door and into the lobby of the building. It was dark inside, but the woman crossed over to a bench and retrieved an odd-looking, clunky box with a handle. She grasped the handle and wound vigorously, causing mechanisms inside the device to screech unpleasantly—but when she stopped cranking, a cracked lens on the side of the box emitted a pale gold glow.

I'd never seen anything quite like it. I could sense magic from it dimly, but only after she'd cranked the handle. Kris didn't seem surprised, though, and reached for another such device from the bench.

"Institute cut off all power and oil rations for lighting when we returned from the Wood," Kris explained, cranking the handle of his own box.

"We?" The woman turned, peering more closely at him, one eyebrow raised.

"Figure of speech," Kris said, handing the mechanical lantern to me. In the dim light, his muddy coat looked more brown than red.

Kris had told us he'd betrayed the Institute to join the rebels—apparently not everyone knew of the existence of a former architect, and Kris wanted to keep it that way.

"Well, you'll want to head down to the base. I don't recognize your friends, but I recognize you—and if you vouch for these two, that's good enough for me."

"Down?" I asked, shifting my grip on my lantern.

"Sewers," the woman replied. "The rebels hide under the city—only place where there's enough iron to hide them from the pixies."

She crossed the lobby floor and opened a door to a tiny,

empty back alley dominated by the large manhole cover in the ground. The woman retrieved an iron bar with a hook on the end and looped it into a hole in the cover, then deftly levered it upward with a clang.

I thanked the woman for her help and lowered myself down until I could drop to the brick tunnel below. Kris and Oren followed, and then the woman handed her lantern down to Kris so we'd have two. As the cover clanged down behind us, I felt Oren let out a long sigh beside me.

Underground, once again. This time, though, there was a difference. I'd spent my childhood in these tunnels, following Basil and learning them like I knew my own brother. Finally, a spark of excitement flickered in my heart where the emptiness had been.

Now I was home.

CHAPTER 7

The tunnel dead-ended at the manhole to the street, so there was only one direction to go. I didn't recognize this particular part of the city—we were a few miles from where I'd lived with my family, and I'd never had any reason to sneak into any place on this edge of the city. Still, everything about it was familiar. The feel of the walls close around me, the slick damp under my feet, the smell of wet stone and mildew. Suddenly it was like no time had passed at all since that day I snuck into the school to get a glimpse of the Harvest list.

I took over from Kris leading the way. He wasn't any more familiar with this entrance to the rebel hideout than I was, and I was more used to leading than following. Nix flitted ahead, in and out of the circle of lantern light, reporting back with warnings about loose stones and slippery patches. I wished I could see the world as clearly as it could in darkness—I could sense things using magic, but not enough to form a picture of the world complete enough to avoid falling on my face.

It was only about ten minutes of walking before we came upon a door guarded by a skinny boy leaning against the wall. He straightened when we rounded the curve in the tunnel, and we all stopped for a moment to stare at each other.

"We're friends," I called, hoping to put the kid at his ease. I couldn't see him clearly, but he couldn't have been much older than I was.

"Sure," the kid called back, raising something clearly weapon-like to point in our direction. "Prove it."

I heard Oren growl a low warning behind me, and I took a slow step forward. The last thing I needed was this kid provoking him into warrior mode. "My name is Lark," I said carefully. "I've come back to help in the fight against the Institute."

"Lark," the boy echoed before barking a short, bitter laugh. "Right. And I'm Administrator Gloriette."

"Look, if I come closer do you promise not to zap me, or whatever that thing does?"

The boy didn't lower the weapon, but dimly I made out a nod at the edge of my ring of lantern light. "Slowly," he agreed. "And your friends stay where they are."

I felt Nix drop off my shoulder and zip back toward Kris, little more than a flash in the gloom, and hoped the kid hadn't seen it. If pixies were deadly now, having one riding on my shoulder wouldn't help my case. Carefully, I moved forward, watching the edge of the lantern light climb up the boy's body until I could see his face.

I stopped, staring. He was familiar—big ears, long skinny legs, a shock of hair red enough to be visible even in the monochromatic gold light.

"Tamren?" I gasped.

His eyes went round as he stared back at me, mouth falling open. In the half a year since he'd carried me away from the Institute in his carriage, he'd changed. He was still gangly, but he'd begun to grow into it, and there was muscle on a frame that had once been stick-thin.

"It is you," he breathed, and dropped his weapon.

It went off with a clatter of springs and machinery, sending something flying at me. I threw myself to the ground as the projectile shot past my face, so close I felt the air stir by my cheek. It glanced off the tunnel wall and went screaming down the tunnel, clattering off the stones a number of times before all went quiet again.

"Oh god, I'm sorry—" Tamren dropped to his knees, reaching for me.

"I'm fine," I managed, raising my voice so that Oren and Kris, who were sprinting in our direction, could hear.

Nix came streaking toward me, mechanisms buzzing wildly with concern, and Tamren scrambled backward.

"Pixie!" he choked, fumbling for his weapon in a panic.

"Stop! Tamren—it's a friend. It's *my* friend."

He paused, wide eyes going from me to Nix as it collided with my shoulder, scrabbling up to check my cheek where the projectile had so nearly hit me. "A friend," he echoed. "Miss Lark—what the hell is going on?"

"Perhaps the explanations can wait until we're inside." Oren spoke up. I could hear the tension behind his speech and knew Tamren had not made the best first impression by nearly killing me. "Night is falling, and apparently not all the pixies out there are friends."

Tamren looked from me to the boys, then nodded as he clambered back to his feet and offered me a hand. I let him pull me up, then stood back as he turned to the door. Though it was crudely fit to the stone, it was thick and solid. The opening mechanism was complex, and I lifted my lantern a little higher in an effort to watch him as he pressed a series of levers in a deliberate order. I wasn't sure if I could recreate the pattern, but I tried to commit it to memory anyway.

The door swung open, and Tamren led us into the base.

Once inside, we began to pass other rebels. There were

more intersections now, different pathways, and rooms that used to house the ancient machinery that operated the sewers when they were in use, long before the Wall went up. My mind dredged up images of my time in Lethe, living in the spaces between the walls, being a part of that rebellion.

What could I hope to accomplish here? In Lethe we *won*, and yet it had changed nothing. The Renewables were still in danger. The ordinary people still lived in fear of the outside world. All of this was a cycle just repeating itself over and over. How many times would I have to fight this same battle?

Tamren peppered me with questions, and though I longed to reach whoever was in charge and tell my story just the one time, I tried to answer what I could. Yes, I was back for good. Yes, I was going to lead the rebels. Yes, I had ideas on how to fight the Institute. No, I didn't know about the revolution until I found Kris. Yes, Kris was my friend.

Tamren seemed to recognize Kris after hearing his name, which put some of my unease to rest. When the woman above hadn't recognized him, I'd begun to wonder if he'd been telling the truth about fighting on the side of the rebels. Now I was beginning to wonder just how extensive this revolution was, if there were so many members that they didn't all know each other.

Eventually we emerged from a tunnel into a large cistern full of bustling people. It seemed to be some kind of communal workshop—makeshift tables dotted the area, some covered with papers and books, others with machinery in various states of disrepair. I thought of the neat, tidy War Room in Lethe, the quiet deliberation of Wesley and the other leaders there—this couldn't have been more different. Every bit of this was cobbled together, and even the people looked grimy and worn down.

Tamren seemed proud, though. "This is the heart of the

resistance," he said. "There are other cells that operate in other sectors of the city, but this is the Hub." Now that he said it, the room reminded me a little of a wheel, the arched ceiling of the cistern branching out like spokes, each little section of the room devoted to a different task.

"Where is everyone?" Kris asked, looking around. The room seemed full of people to me—those closest to us were glancing at me, some staring longer than others. Recognizing me the way the woman above had.

"The brass?" Tamren's smile faded a little. "They're out on a mission. They were due back this morning, but there's been no word."

"All of them, at the same time? Who's in charge?"

"No one, I guess, right now," said Tamren. "It's a big job. Biggest yet. Really dangerous."

I glanced at Kris, feeling less certain by the moment. All the key resistance members, out on the same big, dangerous mission, leaving no one specific in charge? No wonder Kris thought they needed a real leader.

"I guess we wait until they come back," Kris said, not quite meeting my eye.

We'd drawn a bit of a crowd as more and more people recognized me. I could hear whispers rising and falling like the rush of insect song at dusk, could feel the heat of dozens of eyes on my face.

Tamren turned to face the crowd. "This is Lark Ainsley—the girl who left. She's come back to help us fight."

The whispers turned to murmurs and gasps, and I felt my cheeks threatening to burn under the weight of their wonder. This wasn't the first time I'd been at the center of a spectacle, but this time I was ready. More ready, anyway.

I drew breath, hunting for the right words with which to make my first impression on these poorly led people. Before I could speak, however, a cry rose up at the back of the crowd.

Though I couldn't hear the words called, those closer did, and the whole crowd surged away, erupting into cheers. "They're back!" I heard one man shout, and I realized that the "brass" Tamren mentioned must have returned.

"She's here—" Another voice, cut off by the jostling crowd.

"They found her!"

"Thank god, we're saved."

The crowd pressed in around us, the current carrying us forward as they rushed to greet their returning leaders. I lost sight of Kris in the surge, and Oren kept by me only by grabbing me around the waist and pressing close.

The crowd must've gotten confused, thought that the brass were the ones who brought me here. It was a coincidence only, but the overflowing relief and excitement of the crowd was too strong for me to shout over them, so I let them carry us along until I saw a gap in the crowd.

Oren and I battled our way forward until we could stumble free, into a ring cleared around a number of people who'd just emerged from one of the tunnel entrances. I fought for breath, hanging onto Oren's arm and blinking as I tried to focus.

There were maybe half a dozen people there, two of whom seemed to be injured but still standing, wearing bandages spotted with crimson. There were men and women, and one figure wrapped up in a robe and a blanket over the shoulders. At the head of the group stood a man who—I stopped, staring.

I recognized him, but only barely. His once-feeble mustache had spread into a thick beard concealing the lower half of his face. One eye was covered by a brown patch tied on around his head, and he looked about a decade older than I remembered. As a child I'd found him intimidating—now he was utterly terrifying.

His one good eye swung over and landed on me, then widened. "Lark?" he whispered hoarsely.

I swallowed, my throat so dry I nearly choked. "Caesar?"

My older brother and I stared at each other for a private eternity as my mind raced with questions. What was Caesar, the Institute's most loyal Enforcer and the man who betrayed his own sister for them, doing at the head of the resistance? Was he a spy? Did the others know he'd once been an Enforcer? Did they know the role he'd played in my flight from the city?

Before either of us could speak, one of the other members of the team stepped up and murmured in Caesar's ear. He muttered a curse and turned to look at the robed figure, then straightened, eyes passing over me so he could address the crowd.

"Members of the resistance," he bellowed, summoning an instant hush. "Many of you know that we embarked three days ago on a mission to infiltrate the Institute."

Though there were a few gasps, most of the crowd just murmured and nodded, leaning forward, hanging on Caesar's every word.

"What you don't know is why we risked so much to get inside—we couldn't risk any of them learning our true purpose. Well, friends, I have the great honor of telling you all that our mission was a success. We've found her—our savior. We can win this fight."

Where had this orator come from? I remembered Caesar as a lazy, petty man. But listening to him speak, I felt my own heart stirring. Even I believed him when he said they'd found her.

I blinked. Found her? Was Caesar talking about me? Baffled, I looked around until I spotted Kris, who had emerged on the opposite side of the crowd and was staring at me. I wanted to ask him what Caesar was talking about, and how he could claim I was the product of their mission, but he was too far away. Still, as I watched him, something about the set of Kris's mouth and the pallor of his face made me realize something was badly wrong—something he had not seen coming.

Caesar turned until he could reach for the robed figure, his movements startlingly gentle. I'd never seen Caesar treat anyone so carefully before, and my heart twinged with something I barely recognized as envy. He helped the figure move to the front of the group, then pulled the blanket away and tossed it to one of the other brass. The figure laid a hand on Caesar's arm and straightened.

"I can stand," said a low, musical voice—a female voice. "Thank you, Caesar."

Bowing her head, the woman lifted her hands and pushed back the hood of her robe.

It was the Renewable. In the golden, artificial light she glowed like the sun disc itself. Every inch of her was white—her hair, her lips, the irises of her eyes—gleaming as she had the day I saw her last, suspended in the Institute's cage of glass. She shone like the Star standing guard over Lethe. I gasped, falling back a pace; she wasn't just blinding to my eyes, but to my magic as well. Far more powerful than any Renewable I'd ever seen, she was so strong I didn't even need to switch to my second sight to sense it—her magic bled over into the physical realm, emanating from every pore.

"Hello," she said, lifting her chin as her white, empty eyes swept over the crowd and her mouth curved to a tired, gentle smile. "My name is Eve."

With a jolt, I realized I knew that name. Her strange eyes fell on me—and there was an instant spark of recognition. She knew me; but more shocking, I knew her. Knew her as more than the creature of light that helped me escape the Institute. I could *feel* her, as though a tiny yet tangible thread connected us. I could sense her thoughts churning just out of reach, like movement on the other side of a curtain.

The dreams I'd been having with increasing frequency the closer I got to my home—they were memories. Eve's. The Renewable's. I was reliving her arrival in the city again and again, for reasons I couldn't explain.

Her tired smile faded, but I felt warmth as she gazed at me, a very real tingling that spread over me, bathing me in light. Around us the crowd surged, voices rising and falling with questions, exclamations; but I heard none of it. I couldn't take my eyes off of her. I stood, shaken, staring.

"Welcome home, sister," she whispered to me from across the cavern.

CHAPTER 8

Caesar hollered at the crowd gathered around to make a path, and he ushered Eve along at his side. Glancing over his shoulder, his eye fell on me, and he summoned me to follow with a jerk of his chin. He moved with a limp, turning away to move toward a tunnel. I realized I was still holding Oren's arm, and from the confusion on his face I knew he hadn't sensed the same thing I had from Eve.

I was stretched thin, wrung out—something about Eve had made me weak at the knees. Perhaps it was the revelation that my dreams had come from a real person, that I was sharing someone's memories. I stumbled forward a step, my feet tingling with pins and needles.

"Help me," I muttered to Oren, who started, looking down at my face. Though he hadn't had the same reaction to Eve that I had, he could tell instantly that something wasn't right. His grip shifted until he was half supporting me, and then he led the way through the crowd, worming our way forward.

Kris met us along the way, and the three of us shoved through the crowd in Caesar's wake until we emerged into a tunnel leading away from the Hub. I was starting to feel a little more steady, but I was relieved when Caesar turned off toward what had clearly once housed machinery, but was now a small room furnished with battered sofas and chairs. He eased Eve down onto a cot as Oren found a chair for me. I was struck by the similarities in the gestures, and again by Caesar's uncharacteristic devotion. I found myself watching his face, as much fascinated by the changes there as I was trying to avoid looking at Eve again.

When Caesar turned back, I expected him to have a thousand questions for me. Instead his good eye fixed on Kris and widened in surprise. "You're not dead," he exclaimed, leaning forward.

Kris declined to choose a seat. He also didn't answer, glancing at me.

"Why would you think he was dead?" I asked finally, breaking the silence.

"He used to be our man on the inside," said Caesar, eye narrowing. "But one day he just never reported back. We assumed he'd been found out and Adjusted."

"I left to try to find help," Kris spoke up, his voice tight. "I thought the Renewables in the Iron Wood might be on our side, given what the Institute tried to do to them. The enemy of our enemy ought to be our friend."

"Should've filled us in," grunted Caesar. He was still as gruff as ever—more so, in fact. I knew I was staring, but couldn't help it. He was so familiar and so strange all at the same time. He leaned against the wall, reaching down with one arm to massage the muscle in his bad leg, grimacing.

"I saw my chance to steal a crystal and took it," replied Kris, reaching inside his coat to pull out a thick, chunky pendant on a long chain. It was dull and quiet now, its power all used up, but I recognized it as magic storage, to keep him human outside the Wall. "No time to report back."

"Well?" Caesar didn't seem all that relieved to see Kris, but his interest was clearly piqued. "What'd they say?"

"They were gone," Kris said. His eyes flickered to the side, and I knew he was fighting the urge to look at me.

"Just as well," said Caesar, forehead furrowing in a scowl. "Renewables caused the wars that started all this. Don't need them complicating things."

If Eve took offense at Caesar's dismissal of her people, she didn't show it. Her face remained calm, relaxed, lips curved in the slightest of smiles.

"It doesn't matter anyway," Kris continued. "Because I found something better."

Both of Caesar's eyebrows went up, eye patch creasing his skin. "Better than an army of Renewables?"

Don't do it, I thought, willing him to keep quiet. Kris ignored me—but Eve anticipated him, her gaze shifting to my face. I could feel her watching me, the sensation as clear as warm water flowing over my skin. For an insane moment, I wondered if she could read my mind.

"I found Lark," Kris said, making my heart plummet.

Caesar turned to look at me, and I stared at the worn carpet on the floor, bracing myself for a cruel bark of laughter. It didn't come.

"The architects seem to think you're some sort of weapon," Caesar said slowly. His one good eye was fixed on my face, betraying nothing but an intense, clinical interest.

I shifted uncomfortably under his stare. "Not a weapon," I said firmly. "But I'll help in whatever way I can. Kris seemed to think—well, he seemed to think you needed some kind of unifying figure. Someone to stand behind for the fight against the architects."

Caesar made a noncommittal sound in his throat, still gazing at me, distracted. For all the changes he'd undergone,

this much, at least, was the same. From the way he was looking at me, I knew wasn't his little sister to him—I was a tool,
and my worth was only as much as it could benefit him. I
still had no clue how he'd come to be on the side of the resistance—but this was still the same man who'd betrayed me to
get ahead.

But before either of us could say anything more, Oren
spoke up. He'd retreated to lean against the wall behind my
chair, but now he straightened and pushed away. "Lark's exhausted," he said shortly. "And this woman looks about to
drop, too. Is there a place we could all get some rest, and we
can figure all this out in the morning?"

I flashed him a grateful look—being in Eve's presence
made my whole body ache, skin prickling as though I'd been
lying in the sun for too long.

Caesar waved a hand. "Of course. Kris, there are some
empty rooms on Delta Corridor, if you want to show them
the way?"

Kris seemed to know what Caesar was talking about, because he nodded and headed for the door. Though I couldn't
feel Eve's eyes on me anymore as I got to my feet and turned
to follow Kris, I felt her reach out nonetheless. Something
brushed against my thoughts, the same fluttering pulse that
I'd felt the first time she'd reached out to me through the Machine, during my agonizing torture at the hands of the architects. I shivered, repressing the impulse to turn back.

I just wanted out of there—I wanted to be as far away from
her as I could get. I couldn't have explained why the warmth
of her touch unsettled me so. She'd only ever helped me, and
she couldn't help what had been done to her over the years of
torment and pain.

Maybe it was just all too easy to imagine myself in her
place.

. . .

Kris led us to a dark, rubble-filled corridor that smelled of mildew. "It's not great," he said apologetically. "But it'll be safe, and you'll get used to the smell. Sort of." He reached for a makeshift door and shoved it open. It sat unevenly on its hinges and took a bit of force to muscle open with a screech against the stone floor.

I lifted my lantern so that it cast its dim glow into the room. It made my little nook in Lethe seem like a palace. It held a small cot and a packing crate to double as nightstand and storage, and nothing else. Nix crawled out of where it'd been hiding in my collar and made a tiny but vehement noise of disgust.

My thoughts exactly, I thought, my heart sinking a little. Still, Kris was right. It was safe. It'd do.

Kris took a step back so he could glance from me to Oren. "Should I see if the one next door is empty?" He spoke with such tact and poise, and yet I felt my face starting to heat. Inwardly, I cursed the genes that had given me this fickle complexion.

"The one room will do," Oren replied mildly, unfazed.

Kris cleared his throat. "Right," he said briskly. "Well, rest up. I'll try to get someone to bring you guys something to eat—even if it's just dry rations."

"What about you?" I asked, letting my pack slide from my shoulder to thump onto the ground.

"Like Caesar said, I was a double agent. I spent most of my time in the Institute; I never had quarters here. We'll see where Caesar puts me. You might have a neighbor soon."

Kris flashed me a smile, then nodded at Oren, smile dimming a little. "Nix'll be able to find me if you need something." He paused, smile vanishing the rest of the way. "Don't worry, Lark. I didn't think they'd be able to get to the Renewable

64

without my help, but this doesn't change anything. You're the one they need."

I nodded, my mouth dry. Part of me wanted to protest that inheriting this ramshackle rebellion was not my dream, that if Eve would suit them all better, she could have them. But Kris was so certain, so unwavering, that the words died on my lips.

"Good night, Kris," I said instead.

He left us, and Oren dropped his pack behind mine and put his shoulder to the door, shoving it closed again.

Nix buzzed from my shoulder to complete a quick circuit of the shabby room. *"If it's all the same to you, I may find someplace else to power down for the night."* Its voice was thick with disdain.

"Be my guest," I said with a sigh. "Someone may as well find a nice place to sleep."

"You're the one who wanted to come back here," said Nix archly before zipping over to the door, which was so ill-fitted to its frame that the pixie was able to crawl through a gap and vanish.

I set the lantern down on the nightstand. Its meager light seemed even dimmer now, the darkness closing in around us. I shivered in the damp, musty air.

"This is miserable," I whispered, closing my eyes.

I felt Oren's arms slide around me, and I gratefully leaned in against him. For a moment I could almost ignore how careful we both were not to touch each other's skin, to only touch fabric. For a moment it almost felt normal.

"It's not so bad," he said, his voice rumbling through his chest and straight to my ears.

"Says the claustrophobe," I pointed out. "How are you not absolutely losing your mind down here?"

"I'm thinking very hard about that tiny cot we get to share." Oren pressed his cheek to mine for a tingling moment, then pulled back enough so that he could look at me. "What your brother said in there—that the Renewables caused the war. What war?"

I sighed, pulling away and dropping down onto the edge of the cot with a creak of warped metal. "You really don't know anything about history, do you?"

"Not a lot of time to study up when you're a monster," Oren pointed out.

My laugh was tired, but his joke—however black—made the bands of tension around my chest ease a little. "They're the reason why the world is the way it is. It was over a hundred years ago, when all the cities still stood, and there was plenty of magic to go around. The Renewables, who provided the magic, started to hoard it and compete with each other. Competition turned to fighting, fighting turned to war. Whole cities turned against each other, supporting different groups of Renewables, all promising different things."

Oren grunted. "Like wolves snapping over the remains of a kill."

"Except with forces powerful enough to destroy the world," I replied, my voice dry. "Magic against magic, and eventually they poisoned the world so much that it became like it is today."

"The Renewables in the Iron Wood didn't seem hungry for power," Oren said slowly. "Aside from the fact that they wanted to kill me, they seemed okay."

"I guess fighting for survival changes your priorities."

Oren shrugged. "Just seems odd that an entire race of people would all start acting like dictators."

"I'm sure there were nuances, but that's what we all learn early on. Every child knows the stories, so we don't repeat our mistakes."

Oren was quiet for a moment, brow furrowed as he

watched me. "And who taught you that?"

"The—" I stopped short, voice stuttering. "The Institute."

"And they're always so truthful."

I shifted uneasily and then lurched to my feet, pacing past him in the meager confines of the room. "I know. But it's the only answer I have, the only one any of us have. That's part of why I had to come back. That the Institute was hiding more than just Eve."

Oren crossed his arms. "Yes, that woman . . . What happened to you earlier? You were fine, and then she spoke and— I've never seen your face go so white so fast. Who is she?"

"She's—" I hesitated, trying to find the right words. How could I explain to Oren how it had felt, realizing I'd been sharing this woman's memories for the past month? "She's the Renewable the architects here captured years ago," I said finally turning back toward him. "The one who told them about the Iron Wood, and who helped me escape."

"You don't seem happy to see her."

"No, I am." I laid my hand against his chest, smoothing the fabric of his shirt. It was an excuse to keep my eyes on his chest and not meet his gaze. "I'm glad she's out of there, that the architects aren't hurting her anymore. It's just— something's different about her."

"Other than the fact that she shines?"

"You can see that?" I lifted my head, blinking.

"She glows in the dark. How could I miss that?"

"I thought maybe it was just magic, that I couldn't tell the difference because it was so strong."

Oren shook his head, bemused. "No, she definitely glows. And—I don't know why, but I felt different around her." His eyes went distant, brows drawing inward. I could see his face change, the characteristic ferocity smoothing, the set of his mouth relaxing. It wasn't until I reached up and touched his cheek that he jerked back to the present, eyes finding mine again.

"Different?" I echoed.

"More—solid." He frowned. "I'm not sure that's the right word. It felt . . ." He trailed off, realization spreading across his features so clearly it was like a light coming on. I was close enough that I could feel his heartbeat—and I felt it quicken. I waited for him to speak, but he didn't.

"Oren, what's going on?"

He cleared his throat, giving himself a visible shake. "Nothing. I don't know, it must be whatever affected you. How are you feeling? Think you could sleep?"

I tried to hide my hurt and surprise that he didn't confide in me. I wished I could push him, ask what had affected him so profoundly. But Oren never pushed me when I wasn't ready to talk, and I knew I couldn't force it. He'd tell me when he was ready.

Besides, I was still exhausted. "Sleep? For a week," I admitted.

We found bedding in the packing crate nightstand and made up the cot. It creaked as Oren lowered himself onto it, the whole thing sagging in the middle. Never had I missed my sofa bed in my parents' apartment more.

Where *were* my parents? I'd been trying not to think about them, especially after I'd learned from Kris that the city had fallen apart. Were they rebels too? Which side occupied the sector where they lived?

Oren interrupted my thoughts, reaching for my hand to tug me down onto the bed beside him. The mattress was flimsy and bowed so much in the middle that it rolled us to-gether as soon as I tried to lie down. Oren cursed, trying to detangle limbs and blankets and only making it worse.

In spite of everything, a laugh fought its way free from

the tangle of emotions in my chest. Oren stopped struggling, dropping his forehead down against my shoulder and breathing a quiet laugh in response. He wrapped an arm against my waist and pulled me close, tugging the blankets over us both with his free hand.

I nudged the pillow into place under our heads and reached over to turn off the lantern. In the dark, at least, we could no longer see the exposed pipes and crumbling, rotting stonework. I sighed. It was better than sleeping on the ground outside—barely.

Oren pressed his lips to the hollow below my ear. "You can do this," he murmured, voice quiet but no less fierce for it. "I'm with you. Every moment."

When Kris told me I could lead these people to victory, it made me want to run the other way, to find some place where no one expected anything from me and I could just be normal, just a girl. But Oren's voice was different. His whisper in my ear felt real. When he spoke, I could almost believe—I could almost see myself as I knew he saw me.

He stole my breath. My heart pounded, skin tingling with the warmth of his arms around me. I wanted so badly to turn around in the circle of his arms, let him kiss me, sink into his embrace. But to touch him was to feel the shadow in both of us; to let that darkness overtake longing and turn us into something we didn't want to be.

I had no voice with which to reply, but I reached for his hand, weaving my fingers through his and pulling it up so I could kiss his palm. I could only hold it for a moment, the touch magnifying the tingling drain his presence caused. Then I let it go, and he pulled away enough for the buzz of magic to fade, just a little.

You can do this.

In the morning, we would have to find out if he was right.

CHAPTER 9

Kris came for me the next morning and found me wide awake. I'd fallen into an uneasy sleep in the small hours of the morning, my body not accustomed to the time inside the Wall. Oren woke before I did, pacing the room for a while as I dozed. I watched him now and then through my lashes, wondering all over again that he'd agreed to come with me. He didn't belong in a place like this, full of dank underground air and damp. He needed sun and wind on his face.

So did I, for that matter. Despite the way every inch of me responded to the familiarity of being home, in the tunnels I once knew so well, my mind still rebelled. I'd been under the empty sky for less than a year, and already I craved it, missed it like I'd miss my own arm.

Eventually Oren vented his nervous energy by dropping into a strength-training routine that Olivia must have taught him in Lethe. It was impressive how much he could find to do in the confines of our tiny, cell-like room. Pull-ups on a sturdier section of overhead pipe, push-ups on the driest patch of floor, sitting chair-like on nothing, back against the wall, until his legs started to quiver with the effort.

If it were anyone but Oren, I'd accuse him of showing off

for my benefit. But he wasn't even paying attention to me, focusing on his exertions so much so that he didn't even look up when I abandoned my pretense at sleep and sat up.

"Maybe you should teach me to fight, so you've got someone to pummel," I suggested, running a hand through my hair.

Oren dropped down from the pipe he was dangling from, surprised—then he grinned at me, the fleeting expression as startling as ever. The rarity of Oren's smiles made them all the more devastating. "I think you'd have an unfair advantage."

"What, because you couldn't bring yourself to hit me?"

Oren arched his back in a stretch, lifting both eyebrows at me. "No, because you could knock me flat with a thought."

"Well, true." It wasn't the most romantic of reasons, though.

Oren's smile was still lurking around the corners of his mouth, making it hard for me to look away. He crossed toward me and tugged me to my feet. His body was warm, flushed from his workout, and he smelled like sweat and nervous energy, but I leaned close anyway. Even down here there was something about him, a smell or an aura, that reminded me of the wilderness. When I closed my eyes, he kissed me, and for a moment he tasted of rain before the surge of magic between us overrode my senses, sending me lurching backward again.

Then Kris knocked at the door. "You guys up?" he called.

"You've got to be kidding me," I mumbled, tearing my eyes from Oren's mouth to look at the door.

"I could kill him," Oren offered.

I stepped away from Oren reluctantly and opened the door. Kris stood there with Nix on his shoulder. I wondered if the pixie had spent the night curled up on his pillow, and had to suppress the strangest surge of jealousy. Nix stared back at me evenly, flicking its wings.

"What time is it?" I asked. "I'm all turned around."

"A little after dawn," Kris replied. "Caesar wants to see you."

Oren came up behind me. "Do we have time to eat first?"

Kris's eyes lifted to look at him over my shoulder. "You've got whatever time you need. He just wants Lark."

My heart sank. When Oren was with me, and Kris and Nix, and we were surrounded by the other rebels, it was easier to look at my brother's face and not want to explode with rage. But alone, I wasn't sure I could face him.

I felt Oren tense, the tingle of magic between us shifting subtly.

"It's fine," I said before Oren could protest. I sounded more certain than I felt.

Oren wasn't pleased, but he knew better than to argue. I glanced over my shoulder to find him standing in the doorway, watching Kris lead me away. The light Kris carried drew further and further from him until he faded into the shadows.

The rebels hadn't done much to make the sewers habitable. From what Kris had told me, the rebellion had been going on for some time, but there weren't many resources to go around. Aside from some battered furniture that had been moved down from the apartments above, and a few pieces of valuable scrap hammered into place to make doors, there was little to dispel the pervading sense of dark, damp misery. I'd imagined something more like what Basil had unwittingly started in Lethe when he discovered the spaces in the walls, and I found myself longing for their wired lighting system and liberated air circulators.

Kris brought me to a door no different from the one at the room I'd just left, but when he opened it the space beyond was vastly different. "Headquarters," he said quietly as I gazed around.

Everything was still makeshift. But the shelf made from part of a police walker was laden with books, and the packing crate tables were covered with papers and schematics. Here there were overhead lights, though they cast the same unsteady glow that the handheld lanterns did. I assumed they had to be wound by hand as well.

Caesar was standing over one of these packing crate tables, frowning at whatever he was reading. The same habitual trepidation I'd always felt around him leaped back into my throat so abruptly that when Kris stepped back to leave, I almost turned and begged him to stay. Instead, I surprised myself by finding a smile. "Thanks, Kris."

The door clanged shut, leaving me alone with my oldest brother. He didn't look up right away, and I felt a flicker of annoyance at having been summoned—then ignored. So I headed for the shelf to look through the books there. They must have been stolen from the Institute, for there was nowhere else in the city that held these precious objects. They covered a random jumble of topics, none of which seemed particularly helpful to a group of rebels hiding in a sewer. I had started to reach for one called *The Life Cycle and Social Patterns of the Asiatic Elephant* when my brother's voice halted my hand.

"I don't really know what to do with you," he said. I looked up to find him watching me, though he was still hunched over the table, hands pressed flat against its surface.

"I'm not sure it's your job to do anything with me. I'm here to help the resistance." I turned my back on the books. "Not you."

His mouth twisted in a grimace. "You're angry."

It wasn't phrased or spoken like a question, so I said nothing. I found myself remembering the tactics I'd used to alienate people before I fled the city—if I just stared long enough, most people were too unsettled to make fun of the fact that

I was too old not to have been harvested. So I stared at him, letting some of the fury I kept bottled up slip free.

But if my stare unsettled him, he didn't show it. He gazed back for a few seconds and then straightened, emerging from behind the desk-like stack of packing crates to drop down into a faded, ripped armchair. "Fair enough," he said shortly. "I just want to make sure you're not going to be a problem."

"Me?" I burst out. "What about—Caesar, what are you even doing here? Why aren't you with the other Enforcers, fighting for the Institute?"

He gave a quick, sour bark of a laugh. "I haven't been an Enforcer for a long time, little sister."

I wasn't ready for the chill that shot down my spine at those words. Through the weeks and months since it had happened, I'd kept replaying the instant of my brother's betrayal the day I fled my home for the wilderness. I'd pulled apart the only hint of an excuse he gave for it until it had lost all meaning for me.

We are who we are, little sister.

All at once I found myself wanting to run again. Even Kris couldn't expect me to work with Caesar. I found my voice with an effort. "I don't know what your game is. But I'm not going to wait to find a knife between my shoulder blades. I don't need you. I can fight the Institute on my own."

It had been my plan, after all, before Kris had found us and derailed me into thinking I needed to lead a rebellion instead. I turned to leave.

"I couldn't care less." Caesar's voice, sharp and weary, halted me. "I'm not the one who wants you to stay."

I didn't turn, finding it easier to speak when I wasn't looking at his face. "You didn't even send anyone to go rescue Kris when you thought he'd been exposed. Why should his opinion matter so much?"

"Kris?" Caesar snorted. "He's clever, but tactics aren't his strong point."

"So? Who then?"

"Eve."

I froze. Her name alone was enough to make my skin prickle. She was a reminder of everything I'd left behind in the Institute, the weeks of torture. Except that, for her, it had been years.

"How did you free her?" I asked quietly.

"I'm no stranger to the Institute's research facilities."

Something in Caesar's voice made me turn back around. His expression hadn't changed, but it was hard to see much of it between the patch covering one eye and the beard he'd let take over the lower half of his face. I wondered if that was why he'd done it. The droop of his mustache had always given him away before.

He gestured to the chairs opposite him. "Will you sit?" Though his voice was gruff, at least this time it was a question and not a command.

The other chairs in the room were all faded and dusty and smelled of damp and mildew, but I sank down onto one of them anyway. Its frame creaked under my slight weight.

I wanted to ask him what he meant, how a lowly Enforcer could be familiar with the top-secret facility in the depths of the Institute where I, and Eve, had been held captive and tortured. If he had information I didn't, then I needed to know it. Even if I couldn't work with him, I could still use what he knew.

But when I opened my mouth, something else came out. "Why did you turn me in, Caesar?" I choked. "How could your promotion have been so important to you, if you abandoned it to become a rebel?" The words made my eyes burn, and I fought to keep from blinking away tears. I needed to know—and I wanted to flee. Indecision kept me rooted to the moldy chair.

Caesar rubbed a hand across his mouth, rough skin scraping his coarse facial hair like sandpaper. "It wasn't the promotion." His voice was flat, clipped. "I told myself it was, and it was probably part of it."

"What, then?" My jaw ached with the effort of keeping it clenched, of not saying the words I wanted so badly to say. *I know you never liked me, but you were my brother and you were supposed to love me.*

Caesar inhaled audibly before letting his breath out slowly. "They really did tell us you were sick. That you'd snapped during your Harvest and they were trying to help you."

"And you believed that?" I felt my hands curl so tightly around the arms of the chair that my nails ground against the upholstery.

Caesar's one good eye lifted to meet mine for a moment. "All I knew was that you were running. And there's nowhere in this city that they couldn't find you."

"What about here?" I cried. "You're hiding now—you're hiding all these people from them and you have been for months. Why couldn't you have hid me?"

"The world has changed, little sister." His voice rose, a fraction louder than mine. "It wasn't like this then. Then, there was nowhere for you to go but *out.*"

"You *made* me leave, you could have—you *should* have—"

"I lost my little brother to the world beyond the Wall." Caesar's voice cracked like a whip, making my face burn as though he'd slapped me. "I wasn't going to lose my little sister too."

"What a hero." My blood pounded in my veins, making me dizzy. The shadow in me sensed my fury and wanted prey—but there was none to be found. Caesar, and everyone else in the city, had been harvested of their magic as a child. I could devour the tiny scraps that were left, all that was keeping his heart beating—but even I didn't want to murder him. Even now.

"I never said that. Only an idiot claims to be a hero. But leaving the city is a death sentence, Lark."

"And yet here I am."

"How could I have known you'd survive where Basil couldn't?"

I hesitated only for a second. Some sign, some deadly instinct, told me that the truth would hurt him far more than my silence would. "Basil is alive."

Caesar's eye widened, and he sagged back in his chair, clutching at its arms. "Basil's—alive? How?"

I watched the memories of pain and sorrow and confusion dance across my oldest brother's features and felt no remorse. "Maybe we're both of us tougher than you thought."

Caesar found his balance after a few long moments of struggle. "Where is he?" he asked softly.

I stared at him. "I'm not telling you that. God, Caesar— why would I tell you that? I have no reason to trust you. I'll never have good reason to trust you ever again. I'd trust Kris with my life a thousand times over before I'd trust you."

"Kris isn't family," Caesar pointed out, his face grim.

"What does family even mean, now?" I had to stop to catch my breath, fury and hurt robbing me of oxygen. "Where are Mom and Dad? Why aren't they here, fighting with us?"

Caesar's face flickered for an instant; then he shrugged. "Somewhere in the architect-controlled districts."

"You mean—" I struggled to understand. "You mean they're not rebels? They sided with the architects?"

"They didn't *side* with anyone, Lark. Most people don't want any part of this thing. They just want to live their lives.

To them, the architects are still their leaders. Our parents moved there shortly after the barricades went up."

"But now I'm back—if I went, and I explained things to them—"

"You can't." Caesar interrupted me swiftly, his voice icy cold. "You have to understand, most people in this city think you're a traitor. All they know is that you were a Renewable, able to save us all, and you ran away. Our parents think you're dead, and it's better that they go on thinking that. Better for them, and better for you."

He might as well have punched me in the stomach; my eyes watered so that I almost wished he had. "You should have explained to them—"

"I thought you were a traitor, too."

"You were supposed to protect me," I choked. "You were my *brother*."

He swallowed. "I still am."

"By blood, maybe," I whispered. "But I'll still never be able to trust you."

Caesar was silent for a time as the pounding of my heart slowed, the roaring in my ears subsiding to a dizzying thump. My ebbing fury left me dizzy, exhausted, sick with adrenaline and grief.

"Blood," he echoed finally, bowing his head and letting his hands dangle where they rested against his knees. "That's what they found so fascinating too."

"Who?" I asked dully.

"The architects." He pushed down against his knees and lurched to his feet, too restless to sit. "Kris told me what happened at the Iron Wood, what you did. The architects would kill to have that kind of power at their disposal. If they could recreate you, they would. But only two people have ever survived what they did to you: you, and—"

"Basil," I finished for him.

He nodded. "Siblings. Something about our blood, some accident of the way our parents' traits combined, made you and Basil unique. But they believed Basil was dead, and you were too powerful to be controlled anymore." He rapped his knuckles against the packing crate desk. "Fortunately for them, there was a third Ainsley child."

My eyes flew to him, but his back was turned, revealing even less than his bearded face would.

"Of course, I was harvested over a decade ago. They couldn't do to me what they did to you and Basil, they can't reverse engineer something that was already gone. But that didn't stop them from trying to figure out what was special about you and Basil by running their experiments on the only source of your blood that they had access to."

I had only dim memories of the things they'd done to me in the Institute. Flashes of strange rooms and strange people, tests run with knives and needles and conductive pads that flooded my system with magic so potent every nerve screamed for it to be over.

"How long did they keep you?" I whispered.

"Three months," he said shortly. From his voice, he could've been talking about the time of day. But I saw the truth of it in the tension in his frame, the shudder in his hand as he lifted it from the desktop. His fingers quivered like those of an old man, feeble and uncertain.

"How did you escape?"

"They got sloppy. They left the door unlocked one night, I guess thinking that I was in too much pain to flee. They were wrong."

It all sounded so familiar—the convenient escape route, left just when things seemed darkest. It had to have been Kris; everything about it screamed of his involvement.

Caesar continued. "I made it as far as the tunnels before the pixies caught up to me. At that time the rebellion had started, and they'd started altering the pixies' programming to harm humans."

My stomach twisted as my eyes raked over his features—the ruined eye concealed beneath the patch, the beard that, now I looked more closely, had sparser patches, as though the hair struggled to grow evenly through the scarred tissue underneath. "They did—that?"

Caesar slipped a finger under the band of his eye patch, rubbing at the skin underneath like someone chafing at a too-tight collar. "There were too many of them. They held me down, swarmed over me, tore into my skin. One of them ripped out my eye—I could see it happening."

I wanted to vomit. I imagined Nix's needlelike appendages, the ones that appeared when it needed to repair itself, reprogrammed to seek human targets. The damage those machines could do. The pain they could cause. And from something so tiny it could fit through a drain, slip through the crack under the door, hide in your bed until you were asleep.

"And your leg—" I began, voice shaking.

"Ah, that." Caesar let his hand fall to rest on his thigh. "That came before. That's what ended my career as an Enforcer. A present from my little sister."

My stomach dropped. I'd replayed that moment in my mind over and over, when I'd knocked him over the railing of our fire escape and then left him broken and bloody on the pavement. I had nothing I could say, but Caesar didn't seem to be waiting for me to speak. He straightened and turned until he could lean back against the wall behind the desk. "I wouldn't ask you to trust me," he said evenly. "In fact, I wouldn't expect you to care if I lived or died. That bridge between us is burned. But Eve wants you here, and I believe her. I believe *in* her. I don't need you, but she does. And that's enough for me."

Before I could answer, he shoved away from the wall and headed for the exit, the limp making his gait uneven. The door opened with enough force to swing wide and slam against the wall, ricocheting back. By the time I'd gathered my wits enough to go to the doorway, the hall was empty.

CHAPTER 10

I was reaching for the door to our musty room when an ear-splitting sound, brassy and piercing, ripped through the air. My hands clamped over my ears, thoughts scattering before the shrillness of the noise. My heart was still in the wilderness, and my brain refused to understand, trying to figure out what could make such a racket.

The door flew open to reveal Oren there, alert and urgent; his eyes darted this way and that. "What's going on?" he hissed, tense and ready. His voice was like a boulder, a life raft. I grabbed his arm as much to ground myself as to hold him back from doing anything rash.

"*I know what it is.*" Nix buzzed up and hovered over Oren's shoulder. It must have returned to the room after Kris dropped me off at headquarters to talk to Caesar. "*It's from a police walker. It's a siren.*"

For a long moment I froze, too stupid with fear and memories—*They're coming for me, they'll chase me through the Wall again, I'll be all alone*—to move. There was more than one siren—I could hear the slight difference in frequency so clearly that the pitches throbbed in waves against my eardrums. People had begun to flood the corridor, running and shuffling past, a stream of grubby, panicked people blurring in front of my eyes.

Then Oren reached into the stream and plucked one of the fleeing people out by his arm.

"What's going on?" Oren demanded of him. "Where is everyone going?"

"The Hub, like we drill," gasped the man, out of breath. "You should know this, why don't you—"

"This is some sort of practice?" I cut him off, impatient.

He shook his head, fear quaking through his shoulders. "Not this time. They don't turn them all on unless it's for real."

"Tell me what the alarm is for," Oren shouted over the noise, giving his captive a little shake.

"Pixies." The man gulped. "It means pixies have gotten inside." He tore himself free of Oren's grip and vanished into the current. Oren and I sheltered in the doorway, letting the others rush past. Nix buzzed in under my hair to rest in the hollow of my collarbone.

"Pixies like Nix?" Oren said, brow furrowed as his eyes flicked toward the machine where it nestled in against my neck. I knew that look—it was the *city people, how weak* look. Yesterday I would have secretly shared in his disdain. But now all I could see was my brother Caesar tugging at his patch as he described the way the Institute's machines had torn his eye from its socket.

I swallowed. "It's different now. Kris was right. They've reprogrammed them."

"And someone like you cannot fight them," added Nix, its multifaceted eyes fixed on Oren. It sounded almost smug. *"We're too quick to fight without magic."*

Oren's jaw clenched visibly. Telling Oren he couldn't fight something was like telling the rain it couldn't fall.

"Let's go," I cut in before Oren could snap at Nix. "We'll head to the Hub as well—maybe they've got a plan for this. Maybe I can help."

I should have said *we*. Maybe *we* can help. But the words were already out, and I could see the tension in Oren's stance. But he just nodded. "Let's go."

We retraced the path Kris had taken when he guided us to our room. The traffic in the corridors had died down, and by the time we reached the Hub, it was packed with people. There were more rebels than I'd realized, far more than I'd seen the day before. Caesar stood on a table at the far end of the room, trying to shout over the cries and demands of the people gathered around him, but making no headway. If my heart wasn't pounding so hard, I would've smiled to see him so disorganized. No wonder Kris believed these people needing someone else to unite them.

I gave Oren's hand a squeeze and then let go, readying myself to start pushing through the crowd toward Caesar. But just as I reached the edge of the chaos, a shudder ran through my body, halting me. My ears rang, and for an instant my second sight clicked over and all I could see was a jumble of heartbeats and the haze of background energy that hung in the air inside the Wall. Then light blinded me.

I staggered back, jerking away. Eve stepped up onto the table behind Caesar, and if I focused hard, I could keep my second sight at bay, watching them with streaming eyes. She'd gotten her glow under control, and though her white skin and hair still gleamed in the lantern light, she no longer shone with her own illumination. At least, not to the ordinary sight.

The noise of the crowd ebbed in waves and gasps, all eyes on her. She was pretty, in an eerie, inhuman way, with striking features and grace—but it was something else that made the crowd fall silent, staring. An air about her, something compelling that even made me want to stop, to drop all my plans to fight the pixies. I tore my eyes away as she began to speak.

"I know I've only just arrived here," she said, her voice clear, carrying across the room even though she didn't sound like she was raising her voice. "But I want to help. I believe I can keep us safe. But I need all of you to trust me. I need you to believe in me. Can you do that?"

I kept my eyes to the side, not wanting to watch her—her speech was compelling enough as it was, making me long to just let her guide me, too, the way she'd guided me when I escaped from the Institute. *Follow the birds*, she'd told me then. When I'd wanted to bring her with me, she'd also said, *It's too late for me.*

What had changed?

Blinking, I realized that my eyes were gazing at a familiar face. There were a handful of people clustered around someone at the edge of the Hub. *Tamren?* There was blood everywhere, and the people gathered around were trying to stop the bleeding.

"Tamren! What happened?" I ran to his side and dropped to my knees.

"Pixies," he gasped, one of his lips swollen and cracked. His face looked like someone had tried to play tic-tac-toe on it, crisscrossed with scratches. "They came in my entrance."

One of the scratches on his face was a lot deeper than the others—this was the source of all the blood. One of the medics was trying to stitch it up, and though their movements were deft enough, I knew Tamren would have a scar there the rest of his life.

"Are you okay?" I asked, wishing I could reach out to give his hand a squeeze. But Eve's presence made the shadow lurking inside me hungry, and I didn't trust myself. Tamren had been harvested of most of his magic when he was a child, but there was still the tiny kernel inside him keeping his heart beating. I steadied myself with an effort.

Tamren started to nod, eliciting an irritated sound from the man stitching up his face. "Yeah," he said instead. "I'll be okay. I don't know how they found us. I don't know what I did wrong."

The other two medics tending to Tamren had begun to shuffle away toward the crowd. When I looked up, I realized that they'd turned toward the table on which Eve was standing with Caesar—they were listening to her. She was still talking. I could feel her influence in the room like a heavy mist, making it hard to breathe, hard to think. No wonder even the medics, with a job to do, were drifting away.

When the person stitching Tamren's face lifted his head too, I put myself in between him and Eve. "Focus," I snapped at him.

I didn't have time to analyze the power Eve seemed to have over these people, no matter how much I envied her ability to command a room. If only I had that power myself, I could be exactly the leader Kris seemed to think I was. Instead I was crouching at the back of the room, trying desperately to keep one man's attention long enough for him to stitch up my friend.

"Do you know how many there were?" I asked Tamren, whose own gaze had started to wander—though I couldn't be sure whether that was due to Eve's influence or the blood loss.

"Only one at first—but then there were others. A dozen, two, I don't know. And there were more coming. I managed to get the door shut behind me, but they know it's there now, they'll be breaking through. Maybe they have already. Miss Lark—" He broke off with a gasp as the medic tied off the last stitch with a tug.

I let the medic wander off—the rest of his supplies were scattered on the floor, and I retrieved a pot of salve and some sticking bandages.

Tamren's wide eyes were fixed on my shoulder, and I realized that Nix was still there, peeking at him through my hair.

"It's okay," I said. "Remember? Nix is our friend. He's not going to hurt you."

"There were so many of them," Tamren whispered. He was younger than me, younger even than I was when I first left the city. And he hadn't had my experiences, had never been in a frantic, scrabbling fight for his life. I was amazed he was forming coherent sentences.

"I'm going to stop them," I told Tamren firmly. "I promise. It wasn't your fault." I couldn't help but think of the way he'd almost shot me with his crossbow; Tamren wasn't the most competent of people, but it'd do no good to let him think he was responsible for this. Not right now, anyway.

Even Tamren was starting to drift. The pain twisting his features softened a little, eyes wandering past my face to fix on the crowd beyond me. From his prone position on the floor, he wouldn't be able to see Eve on her makeshift dais—and yet he stared in her direction anyway as if he could, as if he could see through the masses of people, flesh and bone and the miasma of panic, and lock his eyes on her.

"Tamren," I said—nothing. "Tamren!" I shouted more sharply.

His eyes refocused, blinking. "Miss Lark," he said, voice thick and rusty.

"Did you hear what I said?" I gave his arm a squeeze, the one not covered in scratches from the pixie needles. "I said I'm going to stop them."

Tamren nodded. "I believe you, Miss Lark." But then his eyes slid away again. "She—she'll save us."

I lifted my head again, letting myself focus back on Eve. Even I could feel the power behind her voice, the confidence and grace and charisma. People were standing taller, breathing easier. The fear was ebbing.

"With your help," she was saying, her white eyes sweeping across the crowd, bathing everyone in the gentle warmth of her smile, "I can protect us. Stay at my side. Have faith."

I tried to concentrate, to sense whether she was actually *doing* anything, but I couldn't perceive much beyond the general flare of magic writhing within her. "She's going to stupefy them into standing here while the pixies come," I said, heart sinking.

Tamren didn't answer, but I wasn't speaking to him. I turned toward Oren—or toward where I had expected him to be, at my side. He was gone. Heart suddenly pounding, I scanned the crowd until I spotted him, standing with the others, listening to Eve speak.

"I will go with you," said a crystalline voice by my ear.

"Nix," I whispered. "What's going on?"

"I believe she offers them something they cannot resist," Nix answered. *"Not even that one."*

"What?"

But Nix only thrummed thoughtfully, wings fluttering and stirring my hair.

I checked Tamren's bandage again, but there was no sign the gash was bleeding through. So I stood and made my way back to Oren, reaching for his arm. He turned as soon as I touched him, and I tried to see from his gaze whether he was as muddled as the medics. But it was too hard to read him.

"Let's go," I said, keeping my voice calm with an effort. "The pixies came in through the same entrance we came through, the one Tamren was guarding. If we go now we might be able to stop them before they find their way to the Hub."

Oren nodded slowly. But when I started to turn away, my hand still in his, he resisted. "I'm going to stay here," he said. My hand went limp. "What?" I whispered.

Oren tilted his head toward Eve, who was now addressing individuals in the crowd, smiling and reassuring them. "If the pixies get past you, these people will need someone to help them."

"You mean Eve will need someone to help her," I said. I couldn't hide the bitterness in my voice, and as soon as I heard it my heart shriveled.

But Oren only shook his head, his mouth twitching into a smile, grim as his voice was. "Lark, it's me. I wouldn't stay behind if I didn't think it was right. But you heard Nix, there's nothing I can do against these pixies. You've got the magic; you can fight them. But if they break through, Eve will need as many level heads here as possible to evacuate the people. I can help there."

If they break through, I thought, *it'll be because I failed, and I'm dead.*

Oren had never once left me to fight alone. I tried not to think of it as abandonment, tried to see it as the compliment it was. That he believed I could win, that I didn't need him looking over my shoulder. But instead I could only see the way Tamren's eyes glazed over as he listened to Eve. Nix buzzed quietly on my shoulder, for my ears alone. Not even Oren, Nix had said, could resist whatever Eve offered.

I could lose everyone and be fine. I could lose Tamren, and Kris, and my brother; I could lose every person here, and I'd be just as strong. But I couldn't lose Oren.

He must have sensed my turmoil, because he turned to face me properly, pulling me in close so he could dip his head and brush his lips against mine. "You've faced so much worse than this," he said softly. "If you trust me, believe me when I tell you that you don't need me."

It was true there was little he could do to help me in this kind of fight. But I wanted him anyway. I always wanted him. His faith in me made mine stronger.

I wished I could believe his decision was only logic and had nothing to do with the woman in white on the dais, murmuring gently to the crowd. But I nodded and stepped back. His arms fell away.

"Good hunting, Lark."

CHAPTER 11

The darkness in the tunnels closed in around me as I retraced my steps back toward Tamren's exit. I could have brought a lantern, but I didn't know whether these upgraded pixies were like Nix. If they had eyes, like it did, then they'd be able to see the light.

And so I stumbled along, trying to do what Eve had done in the memory-dream that we'd shared. She'd somehow managed to see using magic, casting it out in an arc before her and reading the way it bounced back from the stones. Between my half-blind groping and Nix's help, I managed to pick up my pace with only a few scrapes on my knees and one barked shin.

My pounding heart sent the blood rushing past my ears, roaring like the waterfall at the summer lake. There I'd been running from the shadows. Now I was running *to* the pixies. I tried not to dwell on the fact that I was pretty sure I'd prefer shadows. At least they were something like a real opponent.

"*Wait*," Nix buzzed into my ear. "*Stop.*"

I skidded to a halt, shoes sliding in the muck lining the floor of the tunnel. I wanted to ask the pixie what it had heard, but my whisper would carry. I waited, tingling.

"Tamren's door is just ahead," Nix thrummed. *"They haven't broken through yet. But they're close."*

Now that Nix had alerted me, and my own footsteps were no longer masking it, I could hear the faint pinging and grinding sounds. They were trying to cut their way in. I hurried forward until I reached the door, stopping just short of it. I ran my palm down its surface. I closed my eyes, reaching out with my magic, trying to get something, anything, even a hint of the shapes swarming around the exit. Nothing came.

The sounds were growing louder, and I risked a whisper. "I can't get to them through the door," I gasped to Nix, feeling sweat beginning to form at my temples, along the nape of my neck. Despite the clammy chill of the tunnels, my skin burned.

"You'll have to open it to fight them."

I shook my head, leaning against the door. The metal vibrated against my skin, quaking under the efforts of the swarm beyond trying to get inside. "I can't tell how many of them there are. There could be three of them—there could be three hundred."

"They will get through that door," said Nix. *"Wouldn't it be better to be ready?"*

Fight them on my terms. It made sense—except there was no way to be certain I could handle what was on the other side of the door. I leaned in close, pressing my ear to the cold metal. If my magic couldn't sense what was out there, maybe one of my other senses could.

I could hear them out there, whirring and grinding and clicking, testing the seams of the door and slamming against the hinges. The wheel-lock was too heavy and too tightly sealed; they were trying to break their way in. At least one at the top of the hinges; one at the bottom; one at the lower edge of the door, where I could hear that incessant, shrieking

grinding sound. At least three. No, four. There was a whining whir that buzzed from top to bottom; five. My ears continued to adjust, and I picked out a sixth, a seventh, an eighth
distinct sound. My heart sank more and more with each new
sound.

Maybe if I waited, Eve would come. If I stood guard here
and held my ground long enough, perhaps she'd come to help
me. Nix thrummed impatiently. "I'm thinking," I snapped.

Then a new sound broke through my indecision. A quiet,
metallic pinging came from somewhere over my head. It was
too dark to see, but I'd thought there was only stone overhead,
nothing that could make a metallic sound.

The tone of the pixies beyond the door shifted. The
grinding stopped, and then the hammering at the hinges too.
One of them gave a whining buzz that reminded me of Nix
when it got overexcited. It came again, a little further along; it
was moving, whatever it was.

Abruptly a memory flashed into my mind. These had once
been sewer tunnels. When Basil taught me how to navigate
the tunnels near our apartment and the school, he'd taught
me to look up—the tunnels were all the same, but for the net-
work of pipes that ran overhead, connecting all the buildings
to each other and to the water main.

The pixies were in the pipes.

I leaped back, eyes trying frantically to focus without any
light. It was so dark I couldn't tell whether my eyes were open
or closed. But one thing had changed: the pipes were made of
copper. I could see now.

The instant I called on my second sight I could see them.
Overhead, through the copper, was a line of tiny machines,
glowing with magic, crawling along a narrow section of pipe
that led straight back toward the Hub.

"*Lark*—"

"I see them," I hissed.

The shadow lurking inside me swelled, alerted by the adrenaline coursing through my system. Finally, here was prey I'd let it have. I reached up, grasping at the magic of the pixie in front, and gave a savage twist. It was barely more than a drop to the vast desert that was my inner shadow, but the pixie overhead went dark.

The others paused for a moment, processing the unexpected, instantaneous death of one of their number. Then, as I gathered myself for a second strike, all hell broke loose.

As one, the pixies in the pipe rushed downward with so much force that the soft copper tore from its socket. And like water from a broken dam, the pixies were free. They surged outward in a wave, filling the air with flashes of light and sound. Razor-sharp wings buzzed my face; something tore at my hair; I opened my mouth to scream, and one of them grabbed at my lip.

I swatted it away, flailing out in darkness, senses and magic battling for dominance. In every way except my magic I was blind, but the pixies were moving so quickly that my magic couldn't track them. I tried to strike out at a glowing streak just above my head, but by the time my darkness found it, it was already gone.

A metallic scream somewhere in front of me told me that Nix was waging its own battle, fighting against its brethren. Something crashed to the floor and shattered, and I knew at least one of the pixies was down. I couldn't tell how many there were—dozens, at least. And we'd only killed two.

Something slid in under the collar of my shirt and then went racing down my spine, a thousand needlelike legs stabbing into my skin. I gasped and threw myself back against the wall with enough force to daze myself, hearing the crunch of delicate mechanisms between me and the stone. The pixies were everywhere, swarming in my hair, against my face, crawling up the legs of my pants. One landed on my hand, and even as I tried to shake it loose, I felt it prying at my fingernails, trying to rip them away.

"Nix!" I screamed, unsure if my only ally was even still alive—that crashing pixie earlier could have been my friend. "Help—"

But if Nix was out there, it was too busy to come to my aid. I gathered up all my magic in a knot, letting it build and build until my ears sang with the pounding of my heart—and then I let it explode in a wave, knocking the pixies away.

For a moment, I could see everything. As the magic I'd just released ricocheted back to me, it was like dropping a torch down a bottomless well— the light rippled through everything and then vanished again. But I had what I needed. The pixies moved too fast to catch with my magic, but I could still target something that wasn't moving.

I spun and sprinted back down the corridor toward the Hub. My blast of magic had only bought me a few precious seconds, but a few seconds was all I needed. The pixies were faster than I was; I could hear them gaining on me, screaming the mad, vindictive whine that I'd heard only once before, a sound that still haunted my nightmares. This time there was no Wall to escape through, no leap of faith I could take to leave them behind.

Then the ground crumbled underneath me and my foot rolled on a loose cobblestone. "Nix, get clear!" I had no idea where my ally was, but I had to trust it could get out of the way. I threw myself forward, hitting the cobblestones and rolling. As soon as I slid to a halt I lashed out with my magic; out, and *up*.

There came a loud groaning of earth and stone, but for a moment nothing else happened. I pulled with all my might, seeking out a weakness in the arched, cobbled ceilings of the tunnel. Then something splashed heavily into the muck and a handful of sand pattered against my face; and then the entire ceiling was caving in.

I curled into a ball, lifting my arms to cover my neck. I'd been aiming for the ceiling halfway down the corridor, but the whole tunnel was coming down, and rocks pelted my arms and shoulders, the force knocking me half unconscious when one ricocheted against the back of my head.

Then, as abruptly as it began, the cave-in was over. For a long moment I couldn't move, and my panic surged. I was trapped. I was buried alive, and no one would find me, they'd all stay wrapped up in Eve's magic and no one would ever know what happened to me—

But then the adrenaline faded a little, and I found I was merely frozen, fear and shock turning my limbs to iron. Slowly, I willed the feeling back into them and managed to push up onto my hands, sending pebbles and dirt cascading onto the rubble around me. Behind me, the entire tunnel was a solid pile of rock now. I reached out with my magic, trying to find any signs that there were pixies unharmed.

There, a flash of magic. I turned, focusing in on it, letting the shadow out.

"Lark, don't!"

I reeled back, trying to rein in the hunger. Then another streak seared across my brain, and I whirled. There was one pixie left, flying straight toward the Hub. I cast out, hoping I could substitute raw power for precision just once more—and plucked the pixie out of the air.

I bled it dry and then let it clatter to the floor, lifeless.

"Well done," came Nix's voice out of the darkness. It didn't sound as smug as usual—instead its voice quivered uncharacteristically.

I let out the breath I was holding and fell backward, letting the darkness wash over me.

. . .

I only discovered the extent of my injuries as I made my way back to the Hub. Blood was dripping down my face from somewhere, and my left arm was difficult to move, no doubt from the impact of one of the falling stones. My ankle was twisted—not badly, but enough so that every step was painful. I had to rest often, and just for a moment, I was glad Oren *wasn't* there to see me stopping every ten yards to lean against the wall.

When I reached the Hub, the crowds were still gathered around Eve. She lifted her head as I came to a halt, her eyes meeting mine. She must have read my victory on my features, because she smiled and straightened. The crowd straightened with her, reading her body language.

"Breathe easy, my friends." She nodded at me, then shifted her gaze back to sweep across the faces of those clustered around her. "We're safe again, for now."

A ripple went through the crowd, relief making them press in closer around Eve. Caesar stood just in front of the table on which Eve stood, blocking anyone from trying to climb up there with her. I had no doubt that but for his presence, Eve would've been swarmed.

"It isn't her victory," came Nix's voice by my ear. It was taut with tinny hostility.

"It doesn't matter whose victory it is," I murmured, tasting salt and copper on my lips; blood and sweat pooled together from the scratches on my face.

"You don't believe that."

I didn't answer. Nix knew me too well. For all I knew, it could read the bitterness in my voice, sense my elevated pulse.

A dark shape separated itself from the crowd and drifted closer—Oren. The bands constricting my chest eased a little. At least he wasn't under the same spell everyone else was. He came toward me, half reaching out. I shied away, though—I couldn't handle the transfer of power between us, not right now. I was still too wired from the fight, too sensitive.

He paused, hand still outstretched, then slowly let it fall again. "Are you hurt?" he asked after clearing his throat.

I shook my head. "A few scrapes. I'm fine."

Oren's chest rose and fell visibly, the only outward sign of his relief. He glanced over his shoulder at the crowds pressing in around Eve, adoring, grateful. "You should have seen her," he said softly.

"Seen who?" But I knew who he meant. His voice held a hushed tension I couldn't—wouldn't—identify.

"Eve." His gaze was distant, fixed on her face across the room. "She kept them calm, prevented a panic that would've almost certainly cost a dozen people their lives."

"Lark stopped an infiltration that would have certainly cost everyone here their lives."

I wanted to hush Nix, but Oren wasn't even listening. "I know you don't trust her," he said. "But I think you should meet her. Really meet her, not just see her. There's something about her. Something—" He shook his head, searching and failing to find the words he wanted.

Abruptly I realized what was in Oren's voice, the current lightening it from his usual dark murmur. Like a torrent of cold water, I knew. *Admiration.*

I swallowed hard, my throat so tight it felt swollen. "It's taken me a year to learn to trust my instincts," I whispered, though it wasn't necessary—no one was listening to us. "I've been betrayed by more people than I can count. I won't let it happen again, not when my own people are at stake."

Oren finally tore his eyes away from Eve so he could watch me, brow furrowed. "Lark, I know you think I'm like them—that we're all under some sort of spell. But she's different. You said yourself that you weren't sure you were a leader. You didn't know if you were the right person for this task. Here's your answer."

I stared at him. "You're saying I'm *not* the right person?"

"No, I'm saying that Eve is a leader. What more could you have asked for? You can concentrate on what matters, on the fight, and she can be the flag these people rally behind."

He was right. I knew he was right, and yet my stomach was still in knots, my eyes still burned. I wanted to reply, but movement caught my eye. Caesar had climbed up beside Eve onto the table and was scanning the crowd. When his gaze met mine, he gave a jerk of his head that was an unmistakable gesture.

Come with me.

Then he climbed down and ushered Eve away, standing between her and the now-cheerful crowd of people like a bodyguard.

Oren shoved his hands into his pockets, chin tucked and watching me through his eyelashes. It was such a familiar habit that I felt myself breathe again, a little of my nameless fear easing away.

"You're right," I said, hoping I sounded more sure of myself than I was. "Let's go."

CHAPTER 12

Caesar brought Eve to a room I hadn't seen yet. It was furnished like a bedroom, but was much larger than the cell Oren and I shared. I wondered briefly if it was Caesar's room, but as we entered, Eve was sinking down onto the edge of the bed. If it had once been Caesar's room, it was no longer.

I had to fight the urge to grab the door frame. Only Oren half a step behind me kept me moving. I could not explain what made me fight so hard against Eve. I refused to believe it was vanity alone, or pique at having my people choose her over me. Nix was all outrage on my behalf, and I could feel it vibrating against my neck like a tiny, furious ball of spite. I felt no anger—no more than usual, anyway. When I looked at Eve I felt something else entirely.

Fear.

I stepped through the door, my eyes on Eve. She looked up as soon as I entered, her white eyes meeting mine and her pale lips curving into a smile. "Welcome, sister."

Caesar twitched at that, looking at me and then glancing away again. The word came more easily to this strange woman's lips than to his own.

"Hello, Eve." They were the first words I'd spoken to her.

The first words out loud, anyway. I could feel her mind fluttering against the edges of my own, as though drawn by the connection we'd once shared through the Institute's Machine. I hardened my thoughts, imagining iron, and the spiderweb touch faded away.

If Eve noticed my shutting her out, she didn't show it. Her smile didn't flicker; her eyes didn't leave my face.

"How were they able to rescue you?" I asked, forcing my gaze away from hers, to rest upon my brother. "The chamber where they were keeping you was in the very heart of the Institute."

"The architects had moved me," replied Eve, not missing a beat.

"Kris told us," interrupted Caesar. "Before he vanished."

"Moved you?" For once, I wished I *could* read Eve's thoughts. But fear kept me from meddling with the curtain that separated her mind from mine. "What were they trying to do?"

But Eve just lifted one white shoulder, seeming untroubled by the actions of her captors. "It doesn't matter. I'm free now." Her brows drew in as she watched me, and when she spoke again her voice was soft and warm with regret. "I am sorry the people out there didn't witness you fighting on their behalf. I could feel your battle. You are truly amazing."

Uneasy, I shifted my weight from foot to foot. "Thank you. It's all what the Institute did to me, though. This power isn't mine."

Eve's smile returned, though it was a smaller, more secret thing. Something more private. "Just because something is given to you doesn't mean it isn't yours." She lifted a hand so that I could see her white flesh, and the glow I'd seen when I first saw her returned, more dimly. "I am what they made me too."

I cleared my throat. "Oren tells me that you kept the

people here from panicking. That's no small task itself." *And probably not something I could have done.*

Eve shook her head. "If you had been there they would have listened to you as well. We aren't so different, Lark."

Her freckles, though faded a little, were still visible. All at once I was reminded that she wasn't from this city. She'd grown up under the sky, in the Iron Wood, a warrior and a scout like Tansy. I tried to see Tansy's fierceness and strength in Eve, and all I could see was—nothing. Eve was like a blank slate.

No—more like a window. Transparent, transmitting light and warmth and nothing else.

Oren cleared his throat. "I saw the way you handled those people," he said. "I thought we were going to have a riot break out, and you kept them all calm."

Eve smiled at him, but the smile didn't reach her eyes. Her gaze fixed on him, lips slightly parted. She looked as fascinated as everyone else was with her. Jealousy tried to surge up in a rush of bile, but I swallowed and ignored the impulse.

"Eve," I said quietly, "This is Oren, my friend. He's from the outside too."

"I can see that," she replied, her clear eyes never leaving his face.

Oren's face had drained of some of its color, and as soon as I saw him I knew why. Eve knew. I didn't know how or why, but one look was enough to realize that she'd seen what he was. It would take only one word from her to betray his secret and expose him as a shadow to the entire resistance.

But Eve just smiled. "It's a pleasure to meet you, Oren."

Caesar watched this exchange with a frown. I wasn't the only one fighting off jealousy. "Eve, do you need anything? Food, water?"

"Just rest," she replied, turning a fond look on Caesar.

His scowl vanished. To my astonishment, his eyes lightened and, as I watched, his mouth moved into the unfamiliar form of a smile. A true smile, not the grimace he'd always shown me. "You can talk to Lark later, then. Come on." That last was directed at me, and spoken far more roughly.

"Thank you, Caesar." Eve reached out to lay her hand over his. My head throbbed, eyes straining as though I was staring at the sun. I turned my head away, confused. "But I would like to speak to your sister a moment longer. Will I see you for dinner?"

It was a dismissal, not a question. As though her touch had robbed him of his senses, Caesar nodded, mumbling incoherently. He backed toward the door, and just before he closed it behind him, I actually caught him smiling broadly enough that his teeth showed briefly through the dark tangle of his beard.

I continued to stare after he'd departed, as though the closed door would somehow explain the transformation I'd seen in my brother right before my eyes. A small laugh behind me made me turn back.

"He isn't the dark, foreboding figure you think him to be." Eve got to her feet. Even that small movement was graceful, so much so that I couldn't help but stare.

"How do you know what I think of him?" I asked finally.

"He is your brother, and yet your reunion was colder than the meeting of two strangers. Caesar doesn't speak of you. You barely look at him." Eve shook her head, the gesture so full of sadness that my own heart ached in sympathy.

I felt an urge to confide in her, so certain she would understand; so sure that she could help heal the rift between my brother and me. I resisted, gritting my teeth. This was Eve's magic, not my own desire. With an effort, I said, "You said that you wanted to speak to me?"

Eve's eyes slid from my face to Oren's, who stood beside me, silent since it became clear what Eve saw in him. "I actually wished to speak to your friend, Oren. But I thought that might seem strange to Caesar, and the last thing I want to do is force you to reveal this secret before you're ready."

I swallowed hard, but I was saved from trying when Oren stepped forward, his face tight. "How did you know?"

Eve sighed, her eyes scanning Oren's features. She didn't reply for several minutes, but Oren didn't seem to notice, so tight was his focus on her. Finally she took a step forward so she was only a pace or two away from him. "You poor, frightened child," she murmured. "You've been lost in the dark for so long, all alone. What horrors you must have seen, what despair. To have no escape, no respite."

Oren swallowed. His voice, when it came, sounded strained, as if it was an effort to speak. "I have Lark."

My heart lurched in sympathy, but it was Eve who replied. "Yes," she agreed, her voice warm. "And now you have me, too. I cannot pretend to be what Lark is to you, but I will be your friend."

That was going too far—Oren was not the kind of person to share his feelings and have heart-to-heart chats with anyone, even me. I watched Eve's face, waiting for Oren's snort of laughter. It didn't come.

He made a choking sound instead. Astonished, I turned to see tears in his eyes. I couldn't move; I watched, horrified, as one spilled down his cheek, clinging halfway down. He didn't even lift a hand to wipe it away.

"You know what I am," he said hoarsely. "Why are you being so kind? Why aren't you frightened?"

"Because I know this wasn't your choice. If you could, you'd leave the shadow behind forever."

Oren nodded, speechless. I felt almost like an intruder, as

though I was spying on a moment so intensely private that I could not fully understand what was taking place.

"And because I can change all of that," she went on, her white eyes burning with empathy, with certainty. "I can make you whole."

The languor that had kept me silent this whole time snapped abruptly, and I found myself blinking between them. "Wait," I said, croaking through a hoarse throat, fear rising like a smothering cloud, though I had no idea why I was afraid. "What are you saying?"

But Eve just smiled, her eyes never leaving Oren's face. When she replied, she acted as though Oren had spoken, as though I wasn't even there.

"I can cure you," she said.

. . .

Caesar was waiting outside the door for us when we stumbled out. He was either used to the effect Eve had on people or was so befuddled himself that he didn't notice the state we were in. Oren was pale, jaw clenched so tightly I was worried he was going to hurt himself.

Eve had refused to explain further, asking only that Oren meet her tonight, after most of the rebel forces were asleep. No, "refused" wasn't the right word. She'd simply declined, and we were both so captivated, so under her spell, that we'd accepted her at her word.

But now my mind raced with questions, and when I glanced at Oren, I knew his must be too. But he didn't return my gaze, kept his on the floor.

"What do you think?" Caesar asked gruffly. All traces of that uncharacteristic smile were gone, but he was speaking to me, looking at me. That was a start.

"She's—" I struggled for the right word and ended up just

gazing helplessly at my older brother. There weren't any words.

But Caesar just grunted, the closest he ever got to a laugh. "True." He gestured for us to move along the corridor. "We've had some new intelligence. I'll fill Eve in once she's had some rest, but you may as well hear it now."

I glanced at Oren. He was still silent, tight-lipped, and I knew that he wouldn't be able to think of anything except Eve's cure until it happened. I wished we could slip away and talk about it, but the only excuse I could think of to give to Caesar was that we needed to rest. And the last thing I wanted was to seem weak.

He led us to the office where I'd shouted at him before, but gave me no second glance to tell me he was thinking of it still. It was as though the confrontation had never happened. Caesar limped straight to the packing crate desk on the far side of the room and picked up a dirty piece of parchment, so thin from being erased and reused that it was becoming translucent.

"Until now, the main thing standing between us and the Institute has been their machines." Caesar handed the parchment, which was covered in drawings, to me. "They had the magic, so they had the advantage. When we found out they were moving Eve, we had to assume they were planning something, using her power; we took that advantage back."

"And now they don't have Eve."

Caesar nodded. "We don't know how much power they have left in reserve, but unless they find a way to gather magic from beyond the Wall, they're stuck with what they have."

I let my eyes roam the surface of the parchment. It was covered in drawings of machines and mechanisms. Basil would have scoffed at the clumsy efforts of the artist, but they were enough to convey the idea. Some I recognized, like the pixies and the harvester machines—others were wholly new to me. "So we wait them out," I replied. "No need for a fight at all. They'll run out of power, and then they'll have to make a deal with us."

Caesar shook his head. "For all we know they have months of power in reserve, and we don't have the supplies to last that long."

I lifted my head, scanning his face more closely. He'd lost weight since I'd last seen him. The beard had concealed his thinner cheeks at first glance. "How bad is it?" My own stomach growled, and I realized that I hadn't eaten since the morning before I crossed the Wall into the city.

"The Institute still hands out daily rations, but only to citizens, not rebels. Some of us are still able to collect rations, live among the civilians and share what they can spare with us. But for most, it's too dangerous to go aboveground. We aren't going to last for more than a few weeks."

Oren cleared his throat, and I glanced at him. His eyes were still shadowed, but he was finally focusing on something other than the distant possibility of banishing his demons forever. "Not to mention that a cornered beast is a dangerous one. The closer the Institute comes to running out of power, the more they're going to consider an all-out frontal attack before they lose that chance."

One look at Caesar's grim face, and I knew we wouldn't survive such an attack. "What's stopping them from just attacking now?" I asked.

"They'd win, there's no doubt of that." Caesar ran a frustrated hand through his shaggy hair. I guessed he'd been cutting it himself; he looked nearly as wild as some of the shadows I'd seen. "But they'd lose a lot of resources in the fight. Maybe too much to survive afterward. In killing us, they'd be destroying themselves."

My eyes were stuck on one machine in particular, something a little like the police walkers with room for a human passenger. But instead of its usual blunt nose, a mechanism was mounted there like a pair of giant shears, each blade as long as a man's height. Underneath someone had scrawled the word *demolisher*, and I assumed the machine's original purpose had been to tear down buildings to make way for new ones. But here, in the headquarters of the frightened rebels, it was impossible to believe the Institute wouldn't use it as a weapon.

I shuddered. "All right. So we need two things. Food and information. The Institute must be maintaining the automated fields beyond the Wall or they'd be starving too. Have you sent teams out to raid them?"

Caesar spread his arms in a helpless gesture. "How can I? Until you returned, I thought there was no way to breach the Wall. Not to mention, we have no idea what's out there, whether I'd be sending my people straight to their deaths."

I struggled not to look at Oren. No doubt Kris had filled Caesar in on what the architects knew of the world beyond the Wall. Still, it was one thing to be told about the shadows, the magic void, the harshness of the wilderness—and another to live it, to survive it. Caesar was smart enough to know his people weren't prepared for it.

I could do it—I could leave, gather food, return. But I was only one person. If I brought Oren with me he'd be a drain on my power, cut my survival time in half. And even then we'd be able to bring back only what two people could carry. It'd barely be a drop in the bucket compared with what these people needed.

"So we let the city harvest it for us," I decided. "We take it from them after they've already returned."

Caesar nodded, but his face was still grim. "We've been working on plans for a raid for over a month. We're still stuck on how to bypass the machines guarding the storehouses."

I wondered if Kris had told him how I'd single-handedly leveled the army the Institute sent to take the Iron Wood. Caesar was watching me evenly, waiting for me to give him the answer. But I wasn't sure I could do that again. It had been a reaction out of fear, grief, anger, desperation. I'm not sure I could summon those things again, not the same way. With control had come caution, and I wasn't sure I'd survive another outburst like the one in the Iron Wood.

"Then we need information," I said, not meeting Caesar's eyes. "We need to know how much magic they've got left, whether they have some way of gathering it from the outside, whether they're planning an attack."

"Kris was our man inside—" Caesar began.

I shook my head. "He burned that bridge when he left to find the Renewables. They won't exactly welcome him with open and unquestioning arms when he turns up after having vanished for three weeks."

"We could rough him up a bit. He could claim we captured him."

I scanned my brother's face. Now I knew he didn't realize that Kris had to have been the one responsible for his escape from the Institute. Not even Caesar was so ungrateful as to suggest sacrificing his savior.

"I have another idea," I said carefully. If Kris hadn't told Caesar what he'd done, he had his reasons. It wasn't my secret to tell.

I felt more than heard Oren shift uneasily beside me. He had good reason to worry. My plans were never particularly good ones; this one, in particular, made my pulse quicken with dread.

Caesar was watching me with raised brows. "Yes?"

I took a deep breath. "Let me go talk to them."

Caesar gave a bark of laughter even as Oren burst out, "Out of the question."

"Hear me out," I cut through irritably. "Without Eve, the Institute is facing a losing battle even without us to deal with. They've been running out of magic for years, long before now. Eve was never going to last forever."

I thought of Dorian's haggard face when he confessed the truth about our Renewable, that she'd been a spy sent from the Iron Wood. *It's a miracle she's lasted as long as she has*, he'd whispered.

"And you think that'll make them willing to talk?" Caesar's lip curled in disgust. I didn't know if his derision was aimed at me or at our enemy.

"Maybe."

"They'll just take you again," said Oren, holding back his fury with a clear effort. "Torture you the way they did before, try to use you like they were using Eve."

I nodded, my mouth dry. "That's possible too." Everything in me wanted to give in, to let Oren's worry and Caesar's doubt change my mind. "But even if they don't talk, even if they try to take me captive again, I'm not the same girl they had before. I'm stronger. I can escape them if I have to, and I'll be inside, past their machines, able to gather information about their reserves and their plans. And if there's a chance they'll listen, that alone would be worth it."

Oren made a frustrated sound in his throat, like a muffled roar, and turned to pace toward the door and back.

Caesar, however, was quiet. Thoughtful. Watching me with something very different, unfamiliar to me. "It isn't the worst plan I've ever heard," he said, voice low and grudging.

I leaned forward. "I think I can help. You don't need me here; Eve has proven that. But I can help out there. I can teach them how to use the magic beyond the Wall, where it clusters, how to survive the pockets. If they can sustain themselves, they won't need Eve. They won't need to harvest children. And they won't need to destroy you."

Caesar reached out and took the parchment back, and from the direction of his eyes I knew he was looking at the same machine I was, the demolisher.

Oren, unable to restrain himself any longer, burst out, "This is ridiculous, Lark. You're not going in there alone."

"I can't bring you," I said sharply. While Caesar's eyes were on the parchment, I shot Oren a fierce look. He knew why he couldn't come, if only he'd stop to think. If the Institute drained my magic, or separated us, he'd become a shadow. And if that happened inside their walls, then killing him would be the least of all the potential horrors they'd perpetrate on him.

His mouth pressed into a narrow line, his frustration blazing like a tiny sun. "You can't do this," he said.

"I thought I could do anything," I replied, unable to resist throwing his words back at him.

His frustration ebbed, leaving him looking merely tired. "I don't *want* you to do this."

"Neither do I," I said dryly.

"I'll think about it." Caesar spoke up, interrupting us. "In the meantime, you should head to the Hub and get your name on a food roster. Someone might have some scraps for you and your overprotective friend." His gaze, as he watched Oren, was far from friendly.

Oren glared back at him, and I reached out to grab his sleeve and tug him toward the door. "I meant it," I said quietly, over my shoulder. "I'm not the same person I was back then."

As the door swung closed behind me, I heard my brother mutter, "No kidding."

CHAPTER 13

"Are you insane?" Oren blurted as soon as we reached our hole of a room.

"For once I'm inclined to agree with this one," Nix said, emerging from its favorite hiding spot beneath my hair. *"Your plan has many flaws and uncertainties. The probability of success is small, and the probability of your survival is even smaller."*

To hear my life expectancy analyzed so clinically made me want to shiver. "It's not what I want either," I assured them. "But this stalemate is headed for an explosion, and if there's a chance I can head it off, don't I need to take it?"

"You don't need to do anything for these people," Oren cut in.

"It was the Institute who tortured me," I replied softly. "Most people in the city don't have any idea what was done to me. All they know is that I could have saved them, and I ran away."

Oren's face was stern, grave. "You owe them nothing. You have no reason to need forgiveness."

I sighed. "Maybe not. I don't think there's any redemption for me, anyway. But it's my home, and I abandoned it. And besides, what if the Institute holds the key to understanding what really happened out there?" Though my gesture was at the wall of our little cell, I meant the entire world beyond the Wall. "To stop it happening again, to fix what's happening now. This city, the Iron Wood, Lethe—none of it is going to last indefinitely unless the world outside starts to heal. I believe I can start to find out how to do that if I can just get to the Institute's records."

Oren just gazed at me, stubborn, unyielding.

I pressed a little harder. "If the world began to heal, and the magic began to even out, you wouldn't ever have to become a shadow again. You'd never be without magic."

Oren shoved away from the wall and crossed to the bed, throwing himself down on it hard enough to make the cot's frame creak. "If Eve is right, then I'll never have to be a shadow again anyway."

I couldn't help but watch him, my eyes lingering on the eloquent sag in his shoulders as he dropped his head, elbows on his knees and hands dangling between them. I knew what Eve's promise meant to him. Even more, I knew what it'd mean to me. The ability to touch him without recoiling, to know that he'd never have to be in that dark place again; I wanted it so badly I ached, my heart straining. And yet my every instinct was screaming that it was *wrong.*

"We know nothing about her," I said softly. "She could be capable of anything."

Oren tensed. "She's powerful," he argued.

"So? I'm powerful, Oren. But all it means is that I can stop a man's heart with a thought; it doesn't mean I can change the way things are."

"You think there is no cure?" He looked up at me, and for an instant his heart was in his eyes. How could I break it?

I hesitated. "I don't know," I whispered. "I want it to be true."

"Then I'm doing it."

It was my turn to pace, the narrow confines of the room making it impossible for me to vent my doubt and confusion. "What's the harm in waiting? Get to know her better, find out what she can do, before she starts trying to change you."

"She's not changing *me*; she's erasing the shadow."

"That *is* you!" The words were out before I could stop them. Even in the tiny room they seemed to hang in the air, invisible and permanent.

Oren's eyes closed over, his face shutting down. I hadn't seen him look at me like that since the days we first met, when everything I did was wrong and weak. Now his gaze stabbed through me, my heart cracking.

"You've always said that I am not the monster," he said quietly. "That we're separate."

I shook my head, wishing desperately I could erase the last thirty seconds. "I meant that the shadow gives you strength; it's why you're here now, with me. It's terrible and awful, but it's a part of you. And I don't want Eve or anyone else changing you or taking you apart, even if they think they can put you back together exactly the way you were." The words spilled out of me before I knew what I was saying, before I had time to understand my own heart. "I love you, shadow and all. I love all of you."

Oren's expression was stricken. For what felt like an eternity, he just gazed at me, breathing hard. My thoughts screamed at him to speak, to break this awful silence—to say something, anything. When he finally did speak, though, I wished he had simply let the quiet hang.

"If you're in love with the monster, then you're not in love with me," he said quietly. "And all of this has been some sick, twisted charade."

Before I could reply, he turned and left, the door banging shut behind him. I could hear his footsteps fading down the corridor, swift and angry. I wanted to go after him, but I was rooted to the ground where I stood, my eyes burning in the gloom.

A warm metal body tucked itself close against my neck. *"He is frightened,"* Nix said. *"He will return."*

"Oren doesn't get scared," I whispered.

"He is human," Nix replied. *"More or less."*

• • •

Though I had no interest in eating while my stomach was twisting so unhappily, I knew Caesar's advice was sound. Particularly if rations were so slim, I couldn't afford to skip any meals. I didn't know where Oren had gone, but I felt certain he would not have gone to the Hub, angry as he was. He was still, in his heart, a loner. I still had time to convince him to wait before letting Eve attempt anything. I knew Oren well enough to know that I had to let him calm down before I tried to broach the subject again.

So as soon as I could walk steadily, I made my way from the room. I was getting used to the tunnels and managed to find the Hub without any wrong turnings this time. I half expected to find the mass of rebels still gathered, faces upturned, waiting for Eve to come back. But when I arrived, it was as though nothing had changed. Craftsmen were still working on bits of machinery, repairing furniture, and poring over schematics. On the far side of the Hub was a line of people shuffling past a low table, behind which a woman sat handing out crude dishes. Underground or no, I recognized a ration line when I saw one. I headed toward them.

As I threaded my way through the scattered clusters of people, a sound caught my ear. A handful of children were being led by a middle-aged man in a chanting chorus that I recognized—the lilting pledge of devotion to their leaders.

When I was a child we pledged devotion to the architects and the Institute that kept us all safe from the horrors beyond the Wall. As a little girl it had made me feel protected, loved, important. Worth keeping safe. In my clumsy, childlike way I'd always felt a surge of loyalty, standing there in my classroom with my hands clasped in front of my heart. I watched the children as I passed, wondering if they felt anything while they chanted, these children of war who never got the chance to grow up feeling safe. Did the chant help?

For a brief second I felt a strange urge to join them, to speak the words that had once so affected me, in the hope of recapturing some of that certainty. But I kept walking. Because this wasn't the chant of my childhood—the words had changed. They weren't promising their devotion to the Institute anymore. Who were they pledging to now?

I resisted the urge to break my stride and listen and made my way over to the ration line. The woman divvying up the food looked about ready to snap, the circles under her eyes making her look twice her age. I'd been heading toward the back of the line, but I paused and redirected my steps toward her.

"Can I help?" I found myself asking.

The woman looked up, startled. She had striking eyes, a green so pure it reminded me of the leaves just beginning to bud on the trees outside. Her face was so plain that I found myself staring, taken by surprise by her gaze.

"Who are you?" she snapped.

I recognized that hostility. She was waging her own war, here at this table, dividing too few rations among too any people, all of whom would have some reason why they should get more than their share. Each one with a story to break your heart.

"My name's Lark," I said, trying not to respond to the

barb in her tone. "I'm—"

"Caesar's sister," the woman interrupted me, surprised. I held my tongue—I would not have defined myself that way—and nodded. Her brow furrowed in confusion. "Why would you want to waste your time here? You're from beyond the Wall."

Word traveled fast, even if Eve was the main headline. I glanced at the line, which had already begun to stretch longer since I'd been talking to this woman. "Because I need something to do," I confessed. Part of me wanted to explain that I wasn't from beyond the Wall, that this was my home. But the words stuck in my throat, and I knew it wasn't entirely true. Not anymore. "I know nothing about machines, I've given my tactical thoughts to Caesar already, and you look like you could use a hand."

The woman stared a moment longer, but when the old woman at the head of the line cleared her throat loudly, she jumped. "Okay. Yes, thanks. Sit here, use that ladle. Three-quarter scoop of porridge for each bowl, no matter what." She demonstrated, then passed the bowl out to the impatient lady, who eyed me suspiciously and then carried her bowl off to eat.

I began filling bowls, trying to focus on the ladle. At first I kept dropping clumps of porridge on the table, earning a sidelong look from the woman each time, but eventually I learned the trick of it. I set the bowls down beside my partner, who handed them on to the hungry rebel masses.

After a time, the woman spoke again, startling me out of the repetitive trance I'd fallen into. "Talk to me about something. Martin's coming, and he's always got a sob story about why he should get more. If we're talking maybe he'll just take his food and go."

On the spot, I just gaped at her for a few moments. Then, stammering, I managed, "So—what is this stuff? That you're feeding them?"

"Grain mash," said the woman, one eye on the approaching Martin, an old man with thinning gray hair. "Everything goes in. Mostly it's ground-up ration crackers and the occasional handful of oats. We've got plenty of water, so we just add as much as we can to try and fill it out a bit."

I swallowed, looking down at the off-white mush I was dishing out. There were darker lumps in it, but I was sure I didn't want to ask what they were.

The woman let out a short, quick laugh. "Don't make faces," she said. "It's not as bad as you think. Whenever we get nuts or the occasional bit of dried fruit, we toss that in too. You get sick of it, but it does the job."

I watched as she handed Martin's bowl to him. He looked at it, then at my partner. I knew before he opened his mouth that he was about to protest, and so I blurted, "I bet if you ever managed to waylay some sugar beets, you could make a syrup for it that'd be pretty good."

The woman was watching Martin calmly. "The Institute doesn't send out luxuries anymore, only the bare rations. We make do with what the people above can spare, which isn't much."

Martin grumbled and moved on, glaring down at his meager bowl of mush.

My partner chuckled and glanced at me. "There, you've already made my job ten times easier. My name's Myrah."

I smiled and ladled another bowl of mush. "Lark," I repeated.

We continued to serve out rations, sometimes chatting, sometimes sitting through long periods of comfortable silence, for the next two hours. It wasn't until a familiar voice broke me out of my reverie that I realized how much time had passed.

"He's got you working the food line now?"

I jerked my gaze up to find Kris standing there, smiling that crooked smile at me. He looked tired, but not nearly as bad as he did when we first found him outside.

"My idea," I said firmly. "Not Caesar's. It looked like Myrah needed some help."

Kris nodded a thank-you to Myrah as she handed him his bowl. "Can you take a break and come eat with me?"

I glanced at Myrah, who smiled and made a shooing motion. "Go, we've made a big dent in this line. Thank you." Her face didn't seem quite so plain when she smiled. She pushed a bowl—three-quarters full—into my hand and then turned back to her task.

Kris led me to an unoccupied section near the edge of the cavern and sat down on the floor, cross-legged. I joined him, stretching my legs out and balancing my bowl on my knees.

"Not exactly the glamorous life," Kris muttered.

"I've spent most of the last year sleeping on dirt and bathing in creeks," I pointed out. "This isn't so bad."

Kris's lips twitched, but he was in too solemn a mood to let me coax a true smile from him. "I'm sorry about how this has turned out." He poked at his mush with his spoon, gazing at it as though it might provide him with whatever he was looking for. "I wasn't expecting them to get Eve."

"You told them she was being moved. You had to know Caesar would try to use that information."

"I told them to warn them," Kris replied drily.

"Do *you* know what they were trying to do? Why unplug their power source at a time like this?"

Kris hesitated, and though his eyes were fixed on his bowl, I detected a hint of a struggle there. "Not entirely. There's a lot that you don't know about the Institute, Lark. We're not all bad."

"I never said you were."

"I know, but you think—never mind. The only reason to take Eve off the power grid would have been to let her Resource build up to higher levels. When she's connected, the power flows out. But when she's on her own, it just continues to regenerate. That's what they were doing."

"To what end? As a weapon?"

Kris shook his head but otherwise didn't answer, his expression troubled. He was hiding something from me; but at the same time, if he was truly keeping secrets, he was capable of concealing it better. I had to conclude that he simply wasn't ready to tell me what he knew. In his heart, he was still an architect. Every moment he lived here with us must feel like torture, a betrayal of his own people.

"Maybe it's for the best Eve's here now," I said lightly. "Of everyone involved, you were the only one who thought I could lead these people. Eve's a born leader. It just means I can do the work and let her handle the people here."

Kris tipped his head to one side, conceding that much. "I'd bet a week's rations that you're the reason we're not all pixie food right now."

"I wouldn't take that bet," I responded. "I may have dealt with the pixies—but Eve's the one who kept this place from erupting into mass hysteria."

Kris snorted. "I'd take panicked and alive over calm and dead any day."

A laugh fought its way free of my throat, and I found myself grinning at him. "You have a point there."

"What exactly did she do?" Kris asked curiously. "To calm everyone?"

"Just talked. She has some kind of influence over people, some way of making them all fixate on her and only her." I glanced at him. "Weren't you there?"

Kris looked down at his bowl. "I left as soon as I saw her

getting up on that table." He shoved a spoonful of mash into his mouth.

"You knew what was coming," I breathed. "You knew what she could do."

Kris pointed at his mouth, making a show of having to take the time to finish his mouthful before speaking. It bought him a few moments, but even so, he hesitated after swallowing. "Not exactly. But I headed one of the research teams assigned to her when I worked at the Institute."

I was struck anew by how much responsibility Kris had had there, despite his young age. He was older than me, but not by more than three or four years, and he was the head of an entire team of architects. Now, he was just a boy sitting cross-legged on a dirty floor, eating soggy ration crackers.

"What is she?" I asked finally. "She's no ordinary Renewable."

"She used to be." Kris still wasn't looking at me, focusing on his lunch. "Until we began our work."

He still referred to the Institute as "we." Maybe that was why Caesar didn't trust him, thinking that he still considered himself one of the architects. But I knew better. For Kris, it was a constant reminder of his guilt. Of a series of decisions that had led him further and further from himself.

He set his spoon down and lifted his head, finally looking at me again. "Lark, how much do you remember from your time there?"

I felt my throat constrict. It would be easier to pretend I'd forgotten. That my mind had simply erased all memory of what had been done to me. Most days I pretended anyway, pushing it far away, as though it had happened to someone else. But it wasn't true.

"I remember everything."

Kris swallowed, his gaze hollow. "The nuances are

difficult to explain, but in essence what we did was fill you with magic, more than your system could handle, over and over again until you had enough to last you through the wilderness to reach the Iron Wood. But I think—I think there may have been side effects."

My heart lurched. He knew. He knew about the shadow inside me, that I was a monster no different from Oren, only more deadly, more perfect in the way I hunted and fed. I forced my voice to calm. "What do you mean?"

"The way you absorbed the magic from all of us and from the machines while you were defending the Iron Wood." Kris was watching me carefully. "I think that by dosing you repeatedly, we made your body begin to crave magic, become receptive to it. I think we *made* you what you are, able to absorb magic from things. Have you done it since then?"

Images flashed before my eyes. Putting an end to Tomas's pain outside the Iron Wood. Draining Tansy as we fell from the window in the ruins. Nina's comatose face, unmoving, unchanging, after I had drained her to the point of death. "Yes," I whispered.

Kris nodded. "Well, I think that we made Eve what she is, too."

I blinked away the sting in my eyes, forcing myself to focus. "How?"

"The exact opposite of what we did to you. We took her magic again and again, forcing her to regenerate far more often and more quickly than any Renewable normally would. My theory is that her system compensated by producing magic at an alarming rate, and that now she can no longer control it. I think it seeks out voids and tries to fill them.

"Voids," I echoed blankly.

Kris nodded. "We've all been harvested. I think what she does is ooze magic into those around her, for a time. Perhaps that was what was so comforting to the people during the pixie attack."

I thought of the blank, mindless adoration with which the crowd had regarded her. "It wasn't just comfort. It was euphoria."

Kris grimaced, nodding again. "Sometimes it would hit the architects like that too," he told me. "Magic can have that effect, on people who are starved for it."

I stared at him, recalling all too easily the mind-numbing agony of being pumped full of magic in their Machine.

"In small doses," Kris added, seeing my face.

I wanted to ask him about Oren, and Eve's promise that she could cure him. But doing so would require that I reveal Oren's secret, and as much as I had come to believe Kris really was my ally, I wasn't sure I trusted him to be Oren's, too. So instead I said, "Is there any chance Eve's power, giving people magic, could ever be permanent? If there was, say, a void—would she be able to heal it?"

Kris watched me, his expression solemn and thoughtful. He didn't answer right away, and for a heart-stopping moment I thought he'd guessed why I was asking. But when he did speak, his words surprised me. "I wouldn't go near her if I were you, Lark. You and she are opposite forces, and as any architect knows, opposites attract—but often with disastrous consequences. I don't know what would happen if she tried to use her powers to heal yours."

My mind raced. True, Oren and I were different. But we carried the same darkness inside, the same void longing to be filled with magic. But Kris had only confirmed my fears about what Eve had offered Oren. Even if she could cure him, it'd be by destroying the shadow—and who knew how much of the Oren I'd come to love would go with it?

"Tell me something, Kris." There was something still

nagging at me about what he'd revealed. "If draining Eve just made her stronger and stronger, why send me in search of the Iron Wood? I'd assumed the Renewable was faltering, losing power."

Though I couldn't be certain in the general gloom inhabiting the Hub, I thought I saw something flicker through Kris's expression. Fear? Guilt? "Her power wasn't why we were so desperate to find another source for the Resource."

But before he could continue, a shadow fell over me and a gruff voice said, "Get up, we've got to talk." Caesar stood there, backlit and looming.

I finished my bowl of porridge in a hurry—Myrah was right, it wasn't as bad as it sounded—and got to my feet. "Kris too?" I asked, though I kept my voice firm enough that it wasn't really a question.

Caesar glanced down at Kris, then nodded. "We're talking about infiltrating the Institute, he might as well come." Then he stumped away, clearly expecting us to follow.

A chill trickled down my spine as we followed Caesar. He was considering my plan. Now all I had to do was hope it was a good enough plan to work.

When we reached Caesar's office there was already a small handful of people there. There were a man and a woman about Caesar's age, and very clearly related—same dirty blond hair and gray eyes, same mannerisms when they looked up at the sound of the door opening. There was another man, one I recognized from the group that had brought Eve back with Caesar. And then there was Eve.

I was surprised to see her there; until now she hadn't been present for any of Caesar's strategic meetings. I glanced from her to Caesar, hoping for some hint of what was going on, but his face was expressionless.

"I've filled them in on your idea to return to the Institute,"

Caesar told me. "This is Asher and Alice," and he gestured to the brother and sister, "and this is Tek." The man who'd helped retrieve Eve nodded at me.

"And?" I asked.

Caesar shook his head. "It won't work. They can't be reasoned with. We can't risk sending anyone in there."

"But I said that I'd go," I insisted. "You won't lose any of your people, and given what we stand to gain—"

Kris interrupted. "What plan is this?"

"I want to go back to the Institute and try to reason with them, make some kind of deal. I can show them where the pockets of magic are, buy them a little time if they go to harvest it."

Kris's eyes swung from me to Caesar. "And you think this is a bad idea?"

Caesar grunted. "A stupid idea. You know the Institute will chew her up and spit her out."

Kris nodded, and my heart sank. I'd been counting on him to back me. "True. I'm just surprised you care enough to prevent that."

Caesar didn't even flinch. "Lark's a resource. Weigh up the variables and we need her."

"I agree." Kris was carefully not looking at Eve, but I could feel her eyes on me.

"Excuse me," I interjected, furious at the way they were talking as though I wasn't even there. "But it's my choice. I'm not one of your subjects, Caesar."

"True," Caesar agreed. "You can do what you want. You can go throw yourself off a roof if you really want to, though speaking from personal experience, I don't recommend it." That jab was meant for me, but I refused to give him the satisfaction of flinching. "But if you want to help these people, then we need you as a soldier, not a spy or a diplomat."

But what if I don't want to be a soldier?

Asher, the blond brother in the back, spoke up. "That still leaves us without a plan to move forward," he pointed out.

"We do what we'd originally planned to do," Caesar declared. "We have Eve, and she's agreed to help us power the machines we've salvaged and repaired. That gives us weapons. Not many, but enough for a small, calculated strike."

"The food stores," I muttered.

Caesar nodded, his steely gaze swinging back to me. "If we take out the machines guarding it, we can salvage those too. Grow our little army. Guerilla tactics, striking smaller targets, until we have enough for an all-out assault."

Kris rolled his eyes. "You're never going to have enough for an all-out assault," he said dryly. "The Institute has weapons you've never even seen before. You can't fight them that way."

"We've got no other choice," snapped Tek from the background, scowling at Kris. He was a slender man, tall, with a shaved head, and clearly not a fan of the architect-turned-rebel.

"Is losing Lark as a resource your only reservation about her plan to infiltrate the Institute?" Kris asked, ignoring Tek and watching Caesar.

"Aside from the fact that it's suicide to boot, yes."

"Then I'll go," Kris said simply.

My heart stopped. "Kris, no. They must suspect by now that you're with us. They'll kill you."

Kris shrugged. "Maybe. But I worked there a long time, and I don't think so. You all like to think that the Institute is made up of a bunch of faceless, heartless architects, but the truth is that most of them are just trying to save this city. Some of them are going to want a way out that doesn't involve flattening the lot of you under their machines."

Some of them. Meaning not others. "You can't," I said

firmly. "This was my idea—for *me* to go, no one else."

"Think, Lark," Kris said gently. "Even if they didn't need you here, I'm still the logical one to go. They know me. I speak their language. I know exactly how close they are to their own destruction, and ours to boot."

He was right. But it was one thing to sacrifice myself, to be willing to place myself in the hands of my onetime torturers and captors, and another thing entirely to send someone else to the same fate.

Eve, who had been silent up until now, spoke. "If there is anyone who has the right to believe that the Institute is filled with monstrous, unforgiving people, it would be me," she pointed out. "Yet I believe there is common ground. If this boy thinks he can speak with them, perhaps it's worth exploring."

Caesar looked at me. I wanted to protest, to scream that this wasn't right, that I was the one who was supposed to go. I shook my head mutely, silently begging him to understand. But before I could come up with a legitimate reason to stop Kris, Caesar made his decision. "Done," he said, nodding at Kris. It was as much a nod of dismissal as approval. "Go draw up a plan and have it to me by morning. If there's no reason to delay, you'll go tomorrow."

Kris inclined his head. He turned for the door, eyes lingering on my face for a moment before he slipped through it.

"Lark," Caesar snapped, frowning at me. "Stay focused. We'll need you to help us figure out where to target our strike. You can see magic—the rest of us can't, except for Eve, who's too easily spotted to go above ground."

I shook my head. "No strike until Kris is back. If we attack them while he's negotiating a truce, they'll kill him for sure."

"Of course," said Caesar. "But we need that plan in place, should Kris fail. Even you must see that it'd be foolish to just hope that everything goes well. We have to be prepared."

Prepared for Kris to die. But I had no choice. I nodded.

Caesar gestured to the table, where the others were leaning over a map of the city. "Let's get to work."

CHAPTER 14

I noticed time passing only when my stomach began to growl. Eve had long since left, begging exhaustion, and so it was only Caesar and his advisors. Caesar sent Asher to fetch us our evening rations, which I noticed were far more meager than the midday rations were. The meal was a silent one, each of us absorbed in thoughts of what lay ahead.

The part I would play was small, but crucial. Because of my second sight, I'd be able to see where the city was spending most of its resources. Kris had confirmed that they used vast amounts of energy to send their harvester machines across the Wall to tend and bring back the food crops, so it stood to reason that the areas with the most power would be near the warehouses. Machine storehouses were the second priority, if I couldn't locate food. With Eve to power them, the more machines we could bring back and reprogram to fight for us, the better our chances of being able to withstand a frontal attack by the Institute.

I longed to protest at every turn in the conversation that none of it would be necessary. Kris's silver tongue and charming smile—not to mention the unassailable logic of his argument, that a war would bring only mutual destruction—would see us through. But I knew Caesar was right. Despite Kris's confidence, the architects had never been entirely predictable. There was no guarantee they'd listen to him.

When our meal was finished, Tek slipped out to return to the Hub to oversee the engineers. His real name was Tecate, but he'd earned his nickname due to his prowess at deciphering the Institute's technology, adapting their machines to suit our purposes. I wished Basil could have met him—they couldn't be more different in temperament, but Basil would have loved to have someone who could understand him when he started talking about components and data storage.

Alice and Asher left soon after Tek, leaving me alone with Caesar. For a long time he didn't speak, surveying the map with furrowed brow. He was so intent I began to wonder if he'd forgotten I was there, and I took the opportunity to watch him more closely. His beard covered most of the scars on his face, at least from a distance. Up close I could see the lines where the tissue was too scarred for hair to grow, and I thought again of the pixies that attacked me. If I'd been a few seconds later in destroying them, would I have had to find some way to cover my scars, too? There were lines around his eyes, even though he was still a young man. He'd been so quick and so certain when he'd agreed to Kris's proposal; he'd grown used to making life-or-death decisions, forced by circumstance to grow old fast.

"Having Eve with us changes things," he said, startling me. I wondered if he'd felt me staring at him.

"Because she can power the machines?"

"And because of what she symbolizes." Caesar began to fold up the map of the city, taking great care with it. The sheet was ancient, well worn at the folds, ready to fall apart. "She survived the Institute. Subjugated for years, and she's still here, still fighting. If she can survive, then so can we."

I fell silent, my eyes going to the empty chair where she had sat. Her mesmerizing presence had been dimmed while she was here, but I could still feel it while we worked, a soothing, soporific effect. When she left I'd felt as though a cool breeze had wiped away a fog.

"You symbolize that too," added Caesar. I looked up from the folded map to find him watching me.

"Because I ran away?"

"Because you came back." Caesar shrugged, dismissive. Even so, his next words shocked me. "I'm proud of you, little sister. And not just because you can help us win this war."

"It's not a war yet," I said, trying to ignore the way my heart pounded in my ears. "I have faith in Kris. We can stop this; it's not too late."

Caesar just grunted and swiveled in his seat so he could tuck the map in between two battered books on the shelf. The light was dimming, and he got to his feet to wind it with a loud grinding of its ancient mechanisms. Once the light flared a little brighter, he let his hand fall, but didn't turn back to me. Instead he propped one foot up against one of the chairs and dug his knuckles into the muscle of his bad leg, trying to massage away the stiffness there.

"Why do you find it so hard to believe they'll listen to Kris?" I asked.

Caesar's fingers flexed, as though he was trying not to form a fist. "Because hope is impractical. You haven't been here— you haven't seen it all fall apart. Every step we try to take, they come back with stricter rules, harsher punishments."

"But you have hope. You keep saying that you think we can win this war."

Caesar didn't answer right away. His head dropped a little, his shoulders suddenly stooped, as though all the books and blueprints and schematics in the room were weighing him down. He was silent so long that I took a step forward. My shoe scraping on stone caused him to straighten.

"Of course. I believe we can win."

I'd always known my brother was a liar, saying whatever was necessary to get his way. But this time, for once, I could see how painful the lie was. How much he wished it was the truth.

Caesar turned, leaning back against the table and jerking his head toward the door. "Go get some sleep."

"Sleep? But it's dinnertime."

Caesar's lips twitched. "It's hours past dinner; we ate late. Most everyone is asleep except for first watch. Hard to tell time down here."

My mind froze. *Everyone is asleep.* Nighttime. When Eve told Oren she would meet him—and cure him.

"I have to go!" I blurted and whirled for the door, hearing my brother's startled questions ring down the corridor after me.

· · ·

I sprinted through the gloom, eyes watering with the strain of picking out my surroundings. With most of the underground asleep, no one was winding the lights in the corridors, and only a few were still glowing.

Eve told Oren to meet her after everyone was asleep, at the reservoir. I'd never been there, but she'd described its location to Oren while I'd been there. *Past the Hub.* My legs burned. Now that I was moving, I *knew* I couldn't let Oren go through with this. *Four corridors down, turn right at the air pump.* He was doing it for me—I did this to him, drove him to seek a cure. How many times had I recoiled from his touch because of the jolt that passed between us? *Continue on past the scrap depository.*

I dodged debris in the dark, wishing for dream-Eve's ease at navigating in pitch-black with magic. I knew I had to slow down; I'd never reach Oren if I broke my leg. But no matter how firmly I told myself to slow, my legs kept pumping.

Turn left at the—I turned and skidded to a halt just before I ran headfirst into the stone. This wasn't right; there was no left turn where Eve had said there should be one. I slammed my palms against the wall, trying to feel if there was a doorway I'd missed, but my questing fingertips found only crumbling brick and mortar.

I stumbled backward, tripping over a broken cobblestone and slamming my elbow hard against the wall. Heart pounding, I stared wildly around the darkness. "Oren!" I cried finally, screaming as loud as I could. But there was no answer except my own voice, echoing back to me as a despairing wail.

Stop. Think. It was always Basil's voice, that calm voice of reason. Even after he stopped being my hero, even when I realized he was a man like any other, he was still the one in my head who chided me when I was being unreasonable.

I stopped stumbling around and closed my eyes. I willed my heart to slow, stop distracting me with its painful banging against my ribcage. *Listen.* I could hear water. I felt around until my fingertips closed around the frigid metal of a pipe. I had no way of knowing which way the water was running, but on one end of it would be the reservoir where Eve was meeting Oren. I took a deep breath, picked a direction, and followed it.

Running water wasn't the only thing hovering on the edge of my senses. I could feel magic. And it wasn't far away. I picked up my pace, following the pipe and the magic, until I rounded a corner and saw light blossom before me, faint enough that for a moment I thought my eyes were playing tricks on me. But when I drew nearer, the tunnel opened out into a huge round cavern. Some distance away was a rocky shoreline where water lapped gently against the stones before stretching back, back into the darkness.

And standing knee-deep in the black water were two figures: one light, one dark.

"Oren," I gasped, stumbling forward. I could barely make them out, but my voice bounced around the cavern, amplified across the water. He didn't lift his head, and neither did Eve.

The stones shifted and rolled under my feet as I moved forward. It was like trying to run through a field of marbles. My aching eyes caught movement; Eve reached out for Oren, who stepped forward. Then another step, and another, until he fell in against her. She wrapped her arms around him, cradling his head against her shoulder. I bit back a cry and redoubled my efforts to reach them. The shadow was still there inside him, screaming, tugging at me from across the space between us. It wasn't too late.

I reached the shore, but at the same instant I felt water splash at my ankles Eve threw up one of her hands toward me, palm out. I hit something solid; invisible, but unyielding. I screamed at her to let me go, but no sound came out. Slowly she lowered her hand so she could wrap both arms around Oren again. The barrier she'd erected remained, and I struggled in its bonds. I couldn't move forward or back, could only watch in horror as Oren sagged in her arms. She tightened her grip, half supporting him, and then rested her cheek against the top of his head.

A spasm ran through them, a horrible wrenching, jerking movement that seemed to hit them at the same time. I tried again to make a sound, but nothing happened. I lashed out with all the magic I could muster, but Eve's barrier didn't even flicker. Eve glowed brighter and brighter, even to the naked eye, and Oren's skin too began to shine. I switched over to my second sight and, had Eve's barrier not been holding me up, I would have thrown myself backward.

Blinding brilliance lit the entire cavern, reaching to the far wall, which must have been over a mile away. Both Eve and Oren glowed so white-hot I could barely look, and I couldn't tell where one ended and the other began. Pain blossomed behind my streaming eyes; I couldn't move enough now even to close them or look away. I could see only this burning singularity, the rest of the world melting away.

Then a wave of blackness exploded, and at the same time the barrier released me. I collapsed in a heap in ankle-deep water, my panting breaths blowing spray and gravel everywhere. The flash—or implosion—had knocked out my second sight, and I was so shaken that I couldn't get it back. I could only cast my gaze around the cavern again, trying desperately to remember where I'd been standing, where Oren and Eve had been, how to get myself there.

Then, slowly, a tiny hint of light returned. I tried to focus, eyes streaming, on Eve, her gentle glow illuminating a circle around her and the boy in her arms. Then she released him, and he slumped down onto his knees in the water, then sagged sideways, facedown.

I gave an inarticulate cry and half swam, half crawled out to him. Eve stepped back, saying nothing as I threw both arms around Oren and started dragging him back toward shore. As soon as I could sit and hold his head above water I stopped, cradling him close. Pushing the wet hair back from his face, I scanned it, trying to detect in my panic whether he was even still breathing.

The glow grew brighter, accompanied by the sound of a gentle sloshing as Eve approached. "I am sorry I had to shut you out," Eve said softly. There was something wrong about her, something in her voice that made my skin crawl.

I lifted my gaze, water and tears obscuring my vision,

making her seem like a watery apparition. "What did you do?" I sobbed, pulling Oren's motionless body tighter against me. "How could you—I need him. I need him. Put him back."

"I did what I said I'd do." She reached out, and in my near-hysteria I forgot Kris's warning that we shouldn't come close. As her shining fingertips strayed close to my face I felt the hairs on my skin lift and reach toward her, a charge like static, like fear, rippling through my skin. I knew I couldn't let her touch me, and yet I didn't have the strength to pull away. I moaned, and she let her hand fall again before her skin could contact mine.

Then Oren coughed, spitting out water and dragging in a huge breath, choking on the air. The rest of him came to life, his hands grabbing at my arms. I thought I'd shatter with relief, pulling his head in against my chest, making sure he didn't fall below the water again.

I lifted my eyes to find Eve's face close to mine. Her white eyes burned, the pupils mere pinpricks amid the fire. Her cracked lips parted. "I can cure you too."

In that instant I realized what was strange about her voice. Despite the water, the cavern all around us, the cocoon of stone and damp—her voice didn't echo.

I had no response. I stared at her, the fire in her gaze, the fire transforming her. She blazed there, a hand's width away, and then withdrew, slowly leaving us in darkness once more.

I realized I was gasping for air as though she'd truly been on fire, drawing all the oxygen from the room. I shifted my grip on Oren and half crawled, half staggered toward shore, dragging him up to where the pebbles were dry. I let him go, and he fell away onto his back. Though there was almost no light coming from the corridor, where the last hints of lantern light still lingered, my eyes adjusted until I could see him staring at the ceiling, eyes wide, unseeing.

"Oren?" I whispered. "Talk to me. Please—say something."

His lips moved once, and then he squeezed his eyes closed. "I'm okay," he rasped in a voice that frightened me.

"I tried to stop you," I said, the words pouring from me in a rush. "I need you, and nothing is worth risking you over—not even a cure."

Oren's hand moved in the darkness, groping until he found mine. His water-clammy fingers curled tight around mine. *I'm still here*, said the gesture.

"What did she do to you?" I whispered, bending over him and pushing back the wet hair clinging to his forehead.

His tightly closed eyes relaxed, then slowly opened, the unseeing gaze focusing with some effort on my face. He swallowed, staring for a long moment; then his eyes widened, face going even whiter.

"She cured me," he whispered.

The bottom dropped out of my stomach. Fumbling, gasping, I tried to find my second sight again; when I switched over my vision was dazzled, still half blinded by the magical implosion that marked the end of Eve's ritual. I searched, my gaze sweeping over him again and again, but I could see nothing.

He lifted himself up on his elbows, shaken, cautious. "It's true, isn't it?" he said, watching my face. "The shadow's gone."

I met his gaze after a long moment, and he read the truth there in my eyes. The boy in front of me was a monster no longer; he was just a boy, no different from Kris or Caesar or Tamren. I could sense no shadow but the one always lurking, always waiting, inside my own heart.

I wanted to touch him. The impulse to reach out and lay my hand on his cheek started somewhere deep in my belly, traveling up my spine and down my arm until I felt my fingers twitch. But I'd been resisting that urge for so long that I just stared, unable to move, unable to speak.

Oren levered himself up, his movements ginger at first. His face was transformed, the bitter darkness there replaced by wonder and hope. He lifted a hand toward my face, making me flinch in anticipation. He hesitated, fingers a hairsbreadth away from me; then his palm curved against my cheek, warm and solid. No tingle passed between us. No jolt of power transferred.

I exhaled a breath I hadn't realized I was holding and closed my eyes, sending tears spilling down my face. I couldn't bear to look at his face, and I concentrated instead on the feel of his skin against mine. For a moment I forgot my fears, forgot my distrust of Eve, forgot even the certainty that this would change Oren, that he wouldn't be the boy I fell in love with. There was only the sensation of his fingers tracing the curve of my cheekbone, curling into my hair, pulling me closer.

When I opened my eyes again I knew he could feel it too. The change, that his touch was no longer a parasitic reminder of what he was. Gone was the stony-faced boy I struggled to read—for an instant his heart was in his eyes.

He bent his head, lips meeting mine in a rush as though he could wait no longer. His kiss was so familiar and yet so new; I tasted wind and rain, and his skin was wet from the waves, and yet I couldn't taste that tang of power, the metallic, electric taste of blood and magic.

Every time we'd touched and parted, unable to bear the burn of magic between us—it all came roaring back, flooding my senses. All the things I hadn't let myself do, or say, or feel; all the times he'd reached out, only to touch my hair or my sleeve or not touch me at all. A thousand unlived moments, each one fading away touch by touch: his hand sliding up my side; his lips behind my ear; his body warming from the reservoir to the heat of my own.

"Lark," he gasped, breaking away from me long enough to speak. "I'm sorry. We should stop, figure out—"

"Oren." My voice shook as I interrupted him, his wet locks tangling through my fingers. "Do you never stop talking?"

Oren's blue eyes met mine for an instant, surprised, recognizing his own words from the first time we met; then he laughed, quick and bright, and kissed me hard.

This was all I'd wanted from the moment I'd learned Oren's secret. I just wanted to be us. I wanted him to be just a boy, helping a girl, lost in the wilderness.

An image flashed before my closed eyes: Oren's face after I'd told him I loved all of him, shadow too, and that I didn't want him to change. *What did I know?* I thought wildly before lifting my arms so he could pull my shirt off. *I love him. As he is. Just Oren.*

And though neither of us spoke, I could hear it echoing in the waves lapping the shore, back and back through the cavern. *I love him.*

CHAPTER 15

I woke groggy and confused, blinking in the gloom. It was morning, which I could tell only because there turned out to be vents high in the ceiling to the streets above, where I could see the faint, watery light of the sun disc filtering through. It was cold, and I gathered my blanket closer around me, trying to remember where I was.

The sound of water nearby brought it all back. The reservoir. Eve. *Oren.*

I sat up with a jolt, realizing that the space next to me was empty. No, not empty at all; Nix sat there in the hollow where Oren had lain, eyeing me with that flat blue stare.

"Good morning."

Abruptly, I realized that my clothes were still gone and grabbed for the blanket. Oren must have gone off in the night to fetch it—I was certainly glad to have it now. "Where's Oren?" I gasped, face turning crimson.

"How should I know?" Nix said tartly. Then, after a brief but heavy pause, it added, *"You never came home last night."*

"What are you, my mother?" I cast about for my clothes, clutching the blanket up around my chest.

"I was worried."

"Machines don't worry," I teased it, dragging my pants closer. "Turn around."

"Lark, I'm not programmed to take any notice of—"

"Turn around!"

Nix gave a remarkably human sigh—and it wondered why I felt uncomfortable changing around it?—and turned.

I pulled on my clothes in a hurry, ignoring the sand clinging to my skin. What had felt right and perfect last night now just felt uncomfortable. I was stiff and sore from lying on the gravel beach all night, and I knew it was going to take an hour to get all the sand out of my hair. And where was Oren?

I staggered to my feet, which Nix took as its cue to turn back around. It fluttered up to my shoulder, clicking distaste as it twitched aside my sandy hair. *"Your brother wants to see you,"* it said.

I hesitated. Wherever my brother was, it was likely Eve was there too. I wasn't quite sure I could face her after last night. Somehow I felt sure she'd take one look at me and know what had happened between Oren and me, and that it was her doing. As grateful as I was, and as relieved to have been wrong about her, I wasn't quite ready to admit that to her face yet.

Still, if my brother wanted to see me, it'd have something to do with our plans, and the city was more important than my relationship with the shadow boy. *Or not so shadowy now.*

I gave my head a shake, nearly unseating Nix and making the pixie buzz a protest, and then headed back toward the Hub.

Caesar was waiting in his office, along with Kris, whose face was grave. Eve wasn't there, but it turned out I should've been more worried about what my brother could see, one eye or no. He took one look at me and scowled as I slipped inside the office. "Where have you been?" he demanded.

141

"I—uh. Got turned around last night, ended up sleeping at the reservoir."

"You?" Caesar snorted. "Basil's little protégé, getting lost in the tunnels? Right." His eyes raked over me, disheveled and covered in sand. "Where's your shadow?"

I choked. "What?"

"The guy always following you around. Oren. He sleep out at the reservoir too?"

I started breathing again with an effort. He didn't know—it was just an expression. *And now there's nothing* to *know,* I reminded myself. "I don't know where he is," I answered truthfully. I couldn't bring myself to look at Kris and kept my eyes on my brother.

Caesar grunted, and I felt a flare of indignation. What right did he have to feel protective of me now, after everything that had transpired between us? But when he spoke next, he changed the subject. "Plans have changed," he said shortly, tossing a much-recycled bit of paper down on the table.

"What do you mean?"

"Our eyes and ears have reported an increase in factory activity," he said.

"And how does that affect us?"

"The factories are where they manufacture their machines," Caesar replied, watching my face. "Used to be mostly harvesters, pixies, the occasional police walker. Now we know they're making war machines."

My heart shriveled a little inside my chest. "You think they're planning an attack."

"Maybe." Caesar leaned back against the table. "But that's not the only reason. We've had three people go missing overnight."

I frowned. "Missing?"

Caesar nodded. "Could be nothing. Could mean that they

were captured by the Institute, and they'll be giving up information at any time. Could mean they were moles all along and are headed back to their architect masters as we speak."

I exhaled slowly. I wanted to criticize my brother's organization, his leadership, but I'm not sure I would've handled it any better. With rebels flooding in from all districts of the city, it'd be easy for an architect spy to slip in unnoticed. I watched my brother's face and didn't speak, hating myself for the thought that came next: How driven *was* he to go on the offensive? Enough to stage the disappearance of his own people to create an imminent threat?

Caesar gazed back at me, unflinching, before continuing. "Any change means that something is on the horizon. In light of this new information, it seems sending anyone in to talk would be a bad idea."

Now I glanced at Kris and understood why his expression was so stony. "I'd still like to try," he said. "Lark is right, we can't win an outright war."

"I'm not sending anyone in there," Caesar repeated, raising his voice a fraction. "And Lark, we need you here in case of an attack."

"But the machine warehouses, the food stores," I protested, taking a step forward. "I'm the only one who can detect the telltale magic where they're being hidden. If they're about to attack, this might be our last chance!"

"And if the Institute attacks us while you're out wandering the streets?"

"You're weighing a certainty of death by starvation and lack of preparation against the possibility of an attack."

"Last time I checked, I was still calling the shots here," Caesar said in a low voice. "You want to take over? Make these decisions?"

I felt Kris's eyes on me, holding me, though all I wanted

was to retreat from that very question. "No," I snapped. "But I'm not yours to command. I'm going to go look for those storehouses, and you can either kill me to stop me, or let me go."

Kris spoke up. "I'll go with her as far as the Institute," he declared. "We'll watch each other's backs and make quicker ground."

Caesar's lip curled, but before he could deliver any further ultimatums, a soft voice by the door interrupted him.

"Let them go, Caesar."

I turned to find Eve standing there. She smiled at me when I met her gaze. There was no reprisal there, none of the smugness I feared. Nothing except her gentle warmth, flickering hot around the edges.

"Eve," Caesar choked. "You don't understand, they want to—"

"I know." Eve moved into the room, and I danced aside, not wanting to risk touching her. "But your sister and her friend are right. There's always room for talk." She reached out and took Caesar's hand, twining her fingers through his and coming to a halt at his side.

Caesar exhaled slowly, shoulders sagging as though his strength went with the air in his lungs. He met Eve's gaze for a moment, something unspoken passing between them. For a strange moment I felt like an intruder, some foreign observer on a private moment. "Fine," Caesar said finally. "But you go now. Today. This morning."

I glanced at Kris, who nodded back at me. "Okay," I said, thinking of Oren. Where was he? But I had no time to find out. I had to get ready.

I jogged back toward my room, stopping by the communal bathing area to hose off the sand still stuck to my skin. The water was frigid, but I took comfort in the way the other bathers gasped and shivered as much as I did. I threw my clothes back on over my wet skin and then headed for my room, praying Oren would be there.

He wasn't. I sent Nix off to search for him and grabbed my pack. I took out the extra set of clothes—I wouldn't be gone long enough to need it. I made sure the knife Oren had given me all those months ago was firmly sheathed in my boot and ran through my inventory of supplies. It was such habit now, running through it all by memory. At least I wouldn't have to live out of a bag for much longer. One way or another, this would be over soon. And I'd be home—or I wouldn't need one anymore.

I wanted to wait for Nix, but the pixie knew my route and could catch up with me if it came by the room and found me gone. So instead I slung my pack over my shoulders and headed for the Hub. I met Kris there and loaded my pack with food for a couple of days. Kris had decided against bringing a bag, pointing out that he'd be in the Institute in a few hours anyway. And if they weren't going to feed him, hunger would be the least of his problems.

"We should get moving," I said, once I'd filled a canteen with water and tucked it in the top of my pack.

"You don't want to wait for Oren?" Kris asked, brow furrowing. "Does he know what's going on?"

My heart twisted a little, but I shook my head. "Nix is trying to find him—if Nix can't, then I certainly won't be able to. When Oren doesn't want to be found, no one can find him." *Please don't ask me why he wouldn't want to be found.* It was taking all my mental strength not to ask myself that same question.

"Lark—you okay?"

"Fine." I hesitated. Kris was the closest thing I had to a friend outside of Oren, but he wasn't exactly someone I wanted-ed to confide in, not about why I was so frazzled. "I had a strange night."

"You're sure you want to go now? We could—"

I shook my head again, sharper this time. "I don't trust Caesar not to change his mind," I said in a low voice, keeping my eyes on the people going to and fro about their business in the Hub.

Kris's mouth twitched into a half smile. "Despite your history, he's done an amazing job holding these people together so far."

I shrugged. "Maybe. But I know my brother, and tactics or no, he's spoiling for a fight. He's waiting for a reason to strike."

Kris reached out and gave my shoulder a squeeze. "Then let's not give him one."

We headed northeast, toward one of the cordoned-off areas of the city. The tunnel entrances were all blocked off inside the barricaded section, but we could get close enough before emerging that we'd be unlikely to run across any patrolling pixies or Enforcers.

We came up in an alley between two buildings in a part of the city I didn't know very well. The sun disc was already halfway to its zenith. Even a few days underground made the sun disc seem brighter, more intense; my memories of the sun outside were fading. No wonder we had so completely lost our understanding of what the world beyond the Wall was like.

"The Institute's to the east," Kris murmured, holding the grate so I could wriggle free. He then eased it back into place and straightened, blinking in the light. "Your brother's intel points north, on the edge of the Wall. You should head that way." He jerked his chin toward the left.

"I'll come with you."

"And get us both caught? It's better if only one of us goes in."

I shook my head. "Just as far as the gates. I'll keep an eye out for trouble, in case they aren't happy to see you again."

Kris grinned at me. "I'd point out that it'd be you against the entire arsenal of the Institute, but somehow I don't think that'd stop you."

I wished I could be so cavalier about my destructive tendencies, but managed a wan smile nonetheless.

"Just remember that we want them to take me in." Kris led the way from the mouth of the alley, running a hand through his brown hair. "Don't blow your cover for nothing, okay? The Institute doesn't know you're back. Let's keep it that way for as long as possible."

"Right."

We walked in silence, each of us listening for the sound of pixies on the wing or the booted footsteps of Enforcers. But we saw only a handful of people going about their days. The children would be in school and most of the adults off at their daily labors; only a few people on errands and the occasional rickshaw rattling by disturbed the quiet. Life in this quadrant was so normal it made my heart ache. I knew I didn't want to return to life as a pawn in the Institute's games, but at the same time . . . it had been so easy then. All I'd had to deal with was the mockery of a few bullies.

"Are you going to tell me what's wrong?" Kris asked quietly, startling me from my thoughts.

"What?"

"You've looked half ready to snap all morning. And somehow I doubt it's my impending capture."

Though his grin was easy, my heart sank a little nonetheless. I knew how he felt about me, and how he must wish it *was* worry for him causing my disquiet.

"Something happened last night," I said finally. "With Oren."

147

"Oh." Kris cleared his throat. "Maybe I shouldn't have asked."

"No—" I could feel my face heating, mostly because Kris's assumption wasn't exactly false. "Eve did something to him."

Kris's expression changed dramatically, awkwardness replaced by interest. "Did what, exactly?"

I shook my head. "It's hard to explain without giving away something that I can't—that isn't my secret to share."

"That Oren's one of those monsters?" Kris asked blandly.

I stopped dead, heart pounding. It took Kris a few moments to realize that I was no longer moving, and then he stopped and turned.

"Lark, I'm not an idiot. I've got the most experience of any of the architects when it comes to beyond the Wall, and I know what the shadows are. Oren's not a Renewable. You met him in the wilderness. You keep him close at all times. I know what he is."

I stared at him, my heart still in my throat. "And you haven't told anyone?"

"Why would I?" Kris lifted a shoulder. "You're able to keep him under control out there, clearly, or you wouldn't be traveling with him. And here, there's enough magic to keep him human even without you. He's no more dangerous than I am."

I swallowed. At any time Kris could have exposed Oren's secret, and my brother would not have been as understanding about what his condition meant. Oren would've been gone faster than I could have said *leave him alone*. "Thank you," I said awkwardly.

Kris just tilted his head a little. "You said Eve did something to him?"

"Cured him," I whispered. "There's no sign of the shadow anymore."

"Shadow," echoed Kris. "That's a poetic name for it." His brow was furrowed in concentration, and I recognized the architect in him stirring. I knew part of him wanted nothing more than to run back to the Hub, find Oren, and hook him up to as many machines as possible. "You're sure it's completely gone?"

I nodded. "I could always sense it, though of course I didn't know *what* I was sensing until after we'd been traveling together a while. It's gone, he feels just like you now. Or like anyone," I added.

"Fascinating." Kris seemed to realize then that we were standing in the middle of the street, and he reached out to nudge me in toward one of the buildings. We were approaching the garrisoned section of the city, and we ducked down an alleyway to stay out of the line of sight from the Institute's gates.

"What you call shadow—it's not really accurate." Kris spoke earnestly. "Well, unless magic is a sort of light. Basically, what made Oren a monster is not just the lack of magic, but *anti* magic. A void, a vacuum that nature longs to fill. No matter how much magic he's given, the void inside him consumes it and seeks more. It shouldn't be possible for Eve to have done anything to change that."

"And yet," I said dryly.

Kris sighed. "I wish I could study him." He glanced at me, a sheepish expression creeping over his face. "You can take the boy out of the Institute, but you can't take the Institute out of the boy."

"For once I'm with you," I admitted. "I don't understand it. And I haven't been able to talk to him today. I think he's so shaken he can't deal. He thought he would be like that forever, and suddenly everything's different."

"And it was Eve who did it."

I sighed. "As much as I hate to admit it, she helped him. And I can't see any reason for her to have done that except to *help* him. Help me. Maybe all of my confusion about her is just a reaction to the way she feels."

"Feels?"

"I can feel what the Institute did to her. We're linked somehow."

Kris opened his mouth to reply, but a faint sound at the edge of my hearing made me lean forward and press my hand against his mouth. He went still, watching me. The sound grew louder, and I tilted my head, trying to tell what direction it was coming from.

A buzzing, whirring, humming knot of shifting, mechanically-twisted magic heading this way. *Pixies.*

CHAPTER 16

I pulled my hand away from Kris's mouth and held a finger against my lips. He nodded, and I pulled him down into a crouch against the alley wall. I remembered what Eve had done in the memory we shared, and I reached for that reserve of stolen magic inside myself. I pulled it over Kris and myself, imagining the cold, smooth surface of iron surrounding us, encasing us in a cocoon. The pixies had no eyes, only receptors for magic, sensitive enough to see even non-Renewables. But if I could shield us with the image of iron, maybe they'd pass us by. I couldn't afford to waste my power in a fight, not this far away from my goal.

My fingers were still wrapped around Kris's hand, and though I could have let go, I didn't. He had no power to give me, but the warmth of his touch steadied me, reminded me why I was doing this. I smoothed together the edges of my shield, focusing as I remembered Eve doing in my dream. There were gaps here and there, edges where my concentration failed. I hoped it would be enough.

Kris heard it now too. I felt his eyes swing over toward me, felt his hand grow clammy in mine. If anyone knew what these new, deadly pixies were capable of, it was the man who'd helped design them. I put thoughts of Kris aside and focused on my shield.

The swarm buzzed up the alley, rounding the corner in a rush. For a heart-stopping moment I thought they'd seen through my shield and were zooming straight toward us. But then the leaders of the swarm screamed on by. There were several dozen at least, and the sound of nearly a hundred wings all buzzing in unison was deafening. The wind stirred at my hair as they passed, and I held my breath, eyes watering.

How did Eve do this? Holding onto the shield was like trying to hold water in my hands. The more I tried to adjust, to keep it together, the more it fell apart and slipped through my grasp. Each pixie that buzzed past my face shattered my calm a little more. I blocked it all out, digging my fingers into my own thigh in an attempt to let the sensation ground me.

It seemed to last an eternity—it was Kris's voice that finally shattered the shield. He was shouting my name, and when I opened my eyes I found him inches away, shaking me by the shoulders. His face was white, and for a moment I though one of the pixies had gotten through and was attacking. I stumbled back, bracing my shoulder blades against the wall, staring wildly around for the source of Kris's alarm.

"Stop—Lark, stop! It's over, they're gone!"

I gasped, sucking in the first full breath I'd taken since I'd heard the pixies. I let my body sag, hitting the ground with a thump as my knees gave way. "They didn't see us?"

"No." Kris was still pale, staring at me with some agitation. "Are you okay?"

"Fine," I said, blinking. "Why?"

"You've been crouching there like that for fifteen minutes. You couldn't hear me—I thought you were having some kind of fit."

I looked up, but I couldn't see enough of the Wall between the buildings to tell where the sun disc was on its track. I took another shaky breath. "I had to block everything out. I'm not used to that kind of magic."

"What did you do?"

I hesitated. How could I explain that Eve and I had been inside each other's minds? "I was copying something I saw a Renewable do once," I said slowly. "A sort of shield to hide us from their sensors."

Kris's eyes lit as his concern started to ebb. "You mean you can use magic to hide from them? We thought their sensors were—" His gaze drifted past me, thoughtful and distant.

"Hey. Kris." My tone brought his eyes back to my face. "You're on our side now, remember? Us being able to hide from the pixies is a good thing."

"I know," said Kris, lips twitching. "But it'd be fun to try to fix that."

I ran a hand through my hair, getting slowly to my feet. My body felt shaky from all the adrenaline coursing through my system, but I could stand. Despite the effort it had taken, the shield hadn't cost as much magic as I'd thought it would. Eve was efficient, that much was certain. At least, she had been when she was an ordinary Renewable, infiltrating the city.

We were close enough to the barricades now that we snuck inside one of the buildings on its border and crossed that way, prying up the boards covering the windows. The city was split into districts by the undercurrent of hostilities. Most of the city still functioned as normal, patrolled by the Enforcers, but sections of it were controlled—more or less—by the rebels. The section immediately around the Institute, however, was controlled entirely by the architects. Anyone caught inside the barricades without a direct order from an architect would be assumed a rebel and prosecuted as a traitor.

When I asked Kris what had happened to the people living in those sectors, those with more power and influence in the city, he just shrugged.

"They're still here," he replied, carefully levering the boards back into place over the window we'd snuck through. "But everyone's closely watched. We'll have to stay out of sight."

But as it turned out, there was no need for stealth. When we emerged from the building again, on the Institute side of the barricades, the streets were empty. No people, no children, not even a lonely carriage driver pedaling back from his last fare. Not even the ruins above Lethe had been this still; there, at least, people in the buildings would peer down at Tansy and me.

"What's happened here?" I whispered. Despite the lack of people, I felt compelled to lower my voice.

Kris was troubled and trying not to show it. A crease above the bridge of his nose betrayed him. "I don't know," he murmured back. "This—this isn't right."

I slowed my steps. "Should we turn around?" Our plans were risky enough as it was, without adding whatever was going on here.

Kris shook his head. "Whatever's happening here will keep happening if we don't put a stop to it."

"Then we keep going."

The silence of the streets as we made our way toward the main gate of the Institute was oppressive. The hairs stood up on the back of my neck as my ears strained for a sound, any sound. I was glad for Kris's company, even though we walked without speaking—just hearing another set of footsteps was a comfort. Still, all too soon we would part, and he'd enter the Institute and I'd go on alone to scout for the food stores.

I missed Nix's metallic little body pressed against my neck, the hum of its tiny clockwork mechanisms and its occasional sarcastic remarks. I missed Tansy, with a pang that made my heart ache. I missed Oren.

Kris slowed to a halt at the corner of a building. When I leaned forward to peer around it, I saw the massive front gate of the walled Institute compound looming just ahead. Somehow, in my memory, the gate was smaller. The whole complex was smaller. I remembered what was underneath it as massive, many times larger than what was visible above. But now, looking at it again, I remembered how dwarfed I'd felt walking through those doors, even before I knew what fate awaited me there.

I glanced at Kris, crouched beside me. "You don't have to go," I whispered. "I can still be the one to—"

Kris tilted his head, just enough so that I could see his crooked, charming smile, and I fell silent. Even now it made my heart lurch a little, remembering when we'd first met. I'd thought of him as the only one there who really saw me; who treated me like a person. Even though it was all an act, then, seeing that smile now made me realize how much I'd come to rely on him. On his humor, his faith. On his friendship.

"This is my home," Kris said softly. "I have to go back. I have to try to find middle ground with my people. I know you understand."

"Me? Why would I?"

"Because you came back too. To your home."

I chewed at my lip. "Just be careful. Don't promise them anything, just say that we want to talk. Find out if they're even willing, that's enough for a first step. Then get out of there."

Kris nodded, and if it annoyed him hearing me list the same instructions for the fortieth time, he didn't show it.

"And Kris—" I hesitated. I was probably the best bargaining chip the resistance had, knowing how badly the Institute wanted to replicate what had been done to me. But we had to have something in reserve, something with which to shock them in negotiations. "Don't tell them I'm in the city again."

Kris nodded again, and reached out to take my hand. "I'll be fine. They're my family. Even if they're being unreasonable right now, they're not going to hurt me." He gave my hand a squeeze.

His touch ought to feel like Oren's, now that Oren was cured. But there were subtle differences even without the startling lack of magic. His hand was softer, warmer. And more expectant. He touched me like he was waiting for something. Or hoping for something.

I gave his hand a tiny squeeze in return, then carefully slipped my fingers from his. "Stay safe," I said by way of farewell.

Kris straightened, pulling his shoulders back and lifting his head. Suddenly he was an architect again, even without the red coat and ornamental compass around his neck. Every inch of him screamed authority and power. He strode around the corner as though he owned it and made his way toward the gates.

I should have kept moving so that I'd have plenty of daylight if I couldn't find the stores right away. But I had to know if they were going to take Kris prisoner or let him walk in unmolested. So I remained still, watching.

A trio of Enforcers came running out of the gatehouse as Kris approached, weapons in their hands. That was new. The Enforcers had always carried batons before, but never any kind of projectile weapon. But these were unmistakable, the way they pointed them at Kris. They reminded me of the magical talons that the Eagles carried in Lethe, but there was no telling what these might do. But Kris stood his ground, lifting his hands to show that he was unarmed.

They were too far away for me to hear what they were

saying, and too far for me to have any hope of reading their lips. But I could see their body language as hostility gave way to confusion and uncertainty. Two of the Enforcers remained guarding Kris while the third went into the gatehouse again. After a time, the gate opened and a pair of architects in red coats appeared on the steps. They, too, exchanged words with Kris and then waited. After a long, heart-pounding moment, one more person appeared on the steps. And this one I recognized instantly.

She looked the same as she had the last time I'd seen her, when she was smiling her cold smile down at me and telling me there was no cure for what they'd done to me, and that I—along with the Iron Wood I was protecting—was doomed. Gloriette's black hair was cropped short around her face, with no effort to soften it. Despite her round, fleshy form, she was all hard lines and malice. My throat constricted as I watched her approach Kris.

I was struck by how much older she was than she'd been in Eve's memory. I hadn't ever thought about how old Eve was or how long she'd been in the Institute. I'd thought it was no more than a year before I met her there. But when she'd met Gloriette, Gloriette had been at least twenty years younger than she was now. My stomach roiled unhappily. I couldn't begin to imagine twenty years of agony and torture, physical and mental.

It's a miracle she isn't insane.

I thought of her empty, white eyes and suddenly wasn't so sure.

Gloriette finally lifted a hand, gesturing to the Enforcers to stand down, and I let out my breath in a long sigh of relief. The other two architects accompanied Kris, leading him up the steps and through the big copper doors adorning the front of the main building.

Gloriette remained behind, scanning the ghost town laid out before her. I was too far out from behind my corner, but I couldn't risk withdrawing now, or she might see the movement. I watched her, certain at any moment that her cold, narrow eyes would fix on mine, that she'd smile that slow, saccharine smile of triumph.

But she didn't. Fingers toying with the sharp point on her architect's compass, she turned to make her way back up the steps. The gates swung closed behind her, slamming with a bone-rattling, metallic clang, and then all was still again.

CHAPTER 17

I picked my way through the streets carefully. Though there was no one living here anymore, I occasionally stumbled across a patrol of pixies or Enforcers on their way to a more troubled—and more populated—part of the city. I was ready for them and could always duck inside a building or down an alley, but it meant I had to pay attention. I couldn't let my thoughts wander, either to Oren and his arms around me and his pale eyes on mine, or to Kris and what might be happening to him at this moment inside the Institute's marble halls.

I scanned the streets with second sight now and then, but so far I could sense nothing. Certainly not the concentration of magic that would tell of a closely guarded food warehouse, or even a stockpile of war machines, my secondary goal. I kept walking around the perimeter of the Institute, watching for a change in the currents of magic, anything to signify a greater-than-usual tangle of the Resource. I was nearly at the northern gate—I should have found something by now, according to Caesar's intelligence.

I stopped when the northern gate came into view. There was nowhere to hide beyond this point, and I'd be easily visible from the gatehouse. I must have missed something.

I'd just turned back to begin retracing my steps when something flashed at the edges of my senses. I found myself turning blindly toward the east, searching for the source even though there was nothing to be seen except the expanse of granite wall surrounding the Institute. It had felt familiar, almost like . . .

Then came a blast of magic that knocked me to the ground, blinding me. The earth trembled, and a moment later the sound rushed after it. A physical explosion as well as a magical one. In an instant, I knew what it was. Eve. I could feel her magic in it, the too-bright, too-harsh glare of her hyperactive power. She was unstable, Kris had said.

I took off back the way I'd come. When I rounded the corner I could see smoke rising in the distance, an ugly blue-black plume that hit the Wall overhead and pooled there, spreading like oil on water. It was nowhere near the rebel base. It was right up against the eastern perimeter of the Institute. So close, in fact, that it might even look like an attack.

My heart stopped. *Kris. They'll think we've attacked them. And now they'll have a hostage.*

I broke into a sprint, heading for the gates of the Institute as fast as I could. I had to get there before they took the price of this attack out on Kris. He was so sure they were his family, that no matter what they'd accept him back. But I didn't share his certainty. I knew Gloriette. I knew her heart, through my memories and Eve's.

The gates were swinging open as I arrived. I half expected to see an army of Enforcers marching out to go investigate the explosion. Instead there were only two, and they were dragging something between them. Gloriette walked not five paces behind them, but I had no attention for her right now—my focus was on the thing the Enforcers were carrying. A body.

At a command from Gloriette they dropped their burden,

which rolled down the broad marble steps with a sickening sound until it came to a halt at the bottom. It was Kris. He lay motionless, eyes gazing upward, unblinking. I could sense nothing from him, not even the little magic that kept a person's heart beating.

My mind froze. I forgot Gloriette, forgot the Enforcers standing all around. I ran for the steps with an inarticulate cry and threw myself down between them and Kris, ignoring everything but the boy lying motionless on the steps. Let them take me, if they dared.

I tilted Kris's head toward me, bending low. I felt no breath stirring against my ear, and my fumbling fingers could find no pulse. There was no sign of what had done this to him, except that there wasn't a scrap of magic in his body. They'd taken it all, harvested the tiny flicker remaining that kept him alive. Now he was lifeless, a machine with no spark.

I couldn't take my eyes from the boy in my arms. The *dead* boy. My eyes burned, vision blurring helplessly as rage and grief mixed together. My anger made me hyperaware of everything around me, and I felt one of the Enforcers shift, raising one of those weapons they'd been carrying. I snapped a shield into place a split second before he fired, not bothering to look up.

"Hold your fire," snapped Gloriette, her voice crawling into my ears and skittering to awaken long-suppressed memories. The voice of my nightmares.

I lifted my head to see Gloriette watching us. For a moment her eyes were wide with shock, then transformed by the briefest flicker of something bright and hot. *Triumph.* Then it was gone, and she only watched, her thin lips pressed together, her gaze almost amused. I felt my magic building with my rage. I could kill her now, where she stood, with a single thought. I could stop her heart the way they'd stopped Kris's.

My tongue was thick and heavy in my mouth, no words emerging. She didn't speak either, and for a split second we froze in that tableau. Then she raised an eyebrow in a sickening, mocking challenge.

You thought you could save him?

I tore my gaze away from Gloriette's and laid Kris back down against the stone. Throwing a silent thank-you to Wesley for showing me how to do this, I folded my hands together over Kris's heart and thumped once, twice, three times—again and again, with the rhythm of my own heartbeat.

Once my body had the cadence of it, I let my concentration go to the store of magic hoarded by the shadow within me. Coaxing a tendril free, I let it drift down through my arms, past my clasped fingers, and into the motionless body in front of me. Kris's face was wet with tears, my tears, and each time I bent to breathe for him, I had a hard time gathering the strength. I was growing lightheaded, dizzy. I should stop and take a proper breath myself. But I couldn't. Not while Kris lay there like—like a dead man.

No magic. No pulse. No breath.

It was supposed to be me.

All my fury and helplessness erupted as I slammed my clenched hand against Kris's body where I'd been trying to restart his heart. I felt the magic explode, too, a dark blast of chaotic energy. All at once Kris sucked in a ragged breath and then rolled over onto his side, coughing and gasping.

I fell backward heavily. "Kris," I gasped. Abruptly I could feel my own body again, my breathlessness, my lips swollen from breathing for him, my hands sore from trying to jump-start his heart. I crawled back to his side and slid my arm under his shoulders to help lift him into a position where it'd be easier for him to breathe.

He groaned something that sounded like my name,

focusing on my face with some difficulty. It was a long moment before he spoke. "What're you doing here?"

I wanted to laugh, feeling the hysteria bubbling somewhere just below the surface. Instead I lifted my gaze again. The steps were empty—Gloriette was gone.

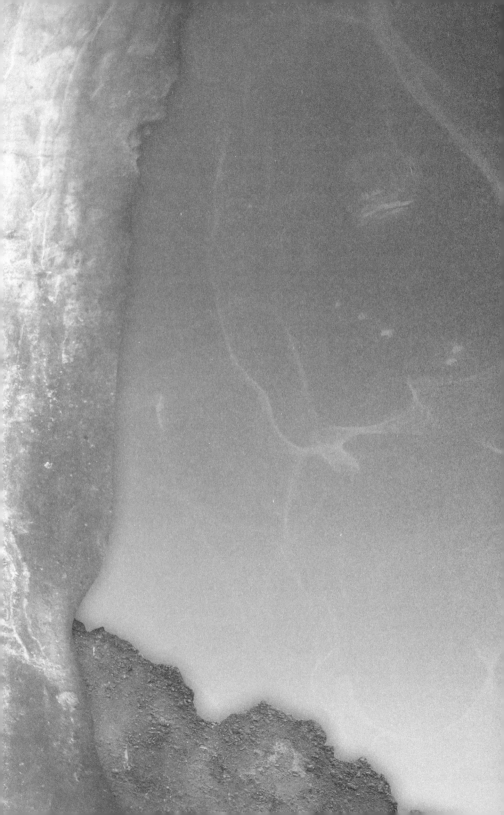

PART II

CHAPTER 18

I managed to get Kris a few streets away from the Institute gates before we had to stop. I needed the rest almost as much as he did. We fell in a heap, searching for breath and dragging ourselves back away from the door of the building we were sheltering in. Kris pulled his legs up and let his head drop between his knees. His face was white, so pale it seemed to reflect the purple Wall overhead and looked almost blue in the dusk.

"Thank you," he said, sounding as though he'd swallowed sand. "What happened?"

"I think it was Eve." I watched him closely, hunting for signs that he wasn't improving. Any sign that moments before, he'd been dead. "I don't know what she was doing near the Institute, but I felt it, I know it was her. It was like a bomb going off, and I think the Institute took it as an attack."

Kris was quiet, listening without much reaction. "That would explain their questions. I think they thought I was a decoy."

I swallowed, my heart still hammering with fear and regret. "I'm so sorry. I shouldn't have let you go in there."

"It wasn't your decision," Kris said softly, his eyes still

on the ground. There was no hint of a smile, no sign of the charm he always carried in a cloud around himself. "It was my call. They could have just as easily tried to kill you."

I hesitated uneasily. They could have captured me while I was trying to revive Kris. They *should* have captured me. Why didn't they?

"What did they do to you?" I whispered instead.

"What they've been doing to everyone else," Kris replied. His voice was detached, as though being fed through Nix's recording device rather than his own lips. "That's where everyone in the sections near the Institute went. They're all dead. The architects killed them."

The bottom fell out of my stomach. Through the roaring in my ears, I murmured, "No. Even they wouldn't—why? Why would they just kill everyone?"

"Because they're running out of magic, and we're the closest source of power."

"But everyone's already been harvested." But as soon as I said the words, I understood. Yes, we'd all been harvested by the Institute. But we were all left just enough of our innate magic to survive. Just enough to keep our hearts beating. Now the Institute was taking even that.

Kris reached down and traced a circle in the gravel underneath us. I thought for a moment that he was drawing me a diagram, about to launch into one of his barely comprehensible lectures on machinery and magic. Instead he just traced the same circle, over and over, his dusty finger etching a deeper groove each time.

"Are you okay?" My voice was almost as hoarse as his. "They took your last magic, wouldn't that make you—" My lips couldn't take that last step and form the word, but my imagination felt no such restraint. My mind's eye painted over Kris's form with brutal detail, draining his brown eyes to white, turning his veins black and his skin clammy gray. I could see teeth. I shook my head in a shiver that traveled all the way down my body.

"No," said Kris, interrupting my waking nightmare. "It takes exposure to the void to pass that final threshold into—into what you call the shadow men. But it doesn't matter."

I gaped. "How can you say that?"

Finally he lifted his head and met my eyes. His eyes raked over me, hollow and burning; grief-stricken, he could barely hold my gaze. "Don't you understand, Lark? We're *all* shadows waiting to happen."

"What?" My heartbeat pounded in my ears.

"People have a natural reserve of the Resource within them. It keeps them human, keeps them alive. If they were left to the void there'd be time. Days, weeks, even, before they became shadows."

"But we're not natural," I whispered, staring. "Everyone here has been harvested."

"Harvested to the point of nothingness. That cushion of time—we've destroyed that, with our machines in the Institute. The second the Wall fails—and it *will* fail—everyone in this city will become a shadow, hungry and mindless and gone forever. Me, Caesar, Gloriette, Tamren, your parents, every single living soul in this city. Everyone except you."

"And Eve."

Kris lifted a shaking hand to push his hair back from his face. "That had occurred to me too."

It was too easy to see the Wall gone, only the metal framework remaining. To see the buildings around us grow dark, to see the vines growing over the places where I'd played, the school where I learned my history. Too easy to see shadows around each corner, pouring out of the tunnels, lurking in the darkened halls of the Institute.

"So you understand now." Kris's voice was like lead, as heavy and cold and as unmovable. "Why the architects are doing what they're doing."

"Murdering dozens, maybe hundreds, of innocent people?"

"To save thousands."

My eyes burned, my skin crawling. "That doesn't make it right."

"It doesn't?" Kris's grief and his pain were like knives. I never wanted to see him like this. I wished I could turn back time and make him once again the cheerful, wry companion who watched me while I pretended not to notice. "What would you have them do instead? Let us all die?"

"Talk to us!" I burst out, my voice tearing like a sob. "There has to be—"

"It's too late." Kris tilted his head back, looking up at the thin, shimmering membrane that was all that stood between us and the darkness. "It's over. It's us or them, and we don't stand a chance."

I reached out to take his hand, to stop its shaking with my own. "You're calling the Institute 'them.' You never did that before."

"Some part of me always thought I could go back." Kris looked down at my hand around his as if confused to find it there. "But that's over now too." He took a deep breath. "I can't ever go home."

I swallowed hard. "Then you and I finally have something in common."

In time, I was able to get Kris on his feet again. He was heavier than he looked, solid despite his lanky frame, and he leaned hard enough on me to make me stagger. But I had to get him back to the Hub so that I could find Eve and Caesar and figure out what to do next. If I could just get Eve, or whatever was left of her, to the Institute, maybe I could show them that what happened was an accident. That we hadn't intended to declare war, and that we did want to talk.

Some of Kris's strength returned as we moved, but I knew that he was going to need days of rest and a few good meals before he was even close to normal. Not that I was certain he'd ever be normal again. His smile was another casualty in the long, long list of things the Institute had taken from me.

The corridors leading to the rebel hideout were empty, but I could hear a commotion echoing through the tunnels. Something was going on at the Hub. I caught Kris's gaze, and he read my intention before I could speak.

"Go," he said, unwinding his arm from around my neck. "I can make my way back from here."

I touched his cheek, all I could think to do to show him how sorry I was. I left him there, head bowed, hand pressed to the spot where mine had been, and took off toward the Hub.

I found the rebels all gathered, the crowd as dense and as perturbed as when the alarms had gone off to warn of the pixie attack. For a brief, panicked moment I thought we were under siege again, that the Institute had come back with a counterattack so swift we had no chance of winning. But then I realized that the agitation wasn't panic—it was celebration.

The sea of people was alive with cheers, dancing, people waving rags and brooms and bits of detritus in the air like flags. I could see Caesar across the crowd, up on the table-turned-dais, though it was Asher next to him roaring at the crowd, egging them on. There was no sign of Eve. Caesar looked about ready to drop, but he was smiling a grim sort of smile. He was *happy* about whatever had happened.

Fury seized me, and I fought my way through the crowd until I reached the dais. "What are you *doing*?" I screamed over the noise. Caesar heard and dropped his eyes, then started as he saw me. He shouted something in Asher's ear, then dropped down off the table. He grabbed my upper arm and started hauling me back toward the office, his limp dragging me off-balance.

He shoved me into the room and followed after, slamming the door behind him. "The hell are you thinking?" he hissed. "This is the first good news we've had, they need this for morale."

"Good news?" I shouted. "This has ruined our chances of talking to them and finding some sort of common ground."

"Who cares?" Caesar shouted back. "They won't soon forget that we're not powerless, and—"

My jaw fell open, shock and horror sweeping through my body. "You *meant* for this to happen? You did this on *purpose?*"

Caesar scowled at me. "You stroll in here and start telling us all what to do, trying to convince me to give it all up the moment we finally have a weapon, something to use against them—"

"Eve's not a weapon!" I cried. "She's a person. She's been used for years, decades even, and now you're just continuing to use her. Is she even alive after that explosion?"

"She wants this too," Caesar roared. "And she's fine. She needs to vent the magic as much as we need her as a weapon. Why do you care? A few more strikes like that and we can win this thing!"

"*Kris was in there,*" I retorted. "You sent him in there!"

Caesar's jaw hardened. "A necessary casualty," he said, voice lowering.

The fury building inside me snapped. "You have no idea that he's the one who saved your life, do you?" My voice cracked, whiplike, slashing at that core of arrogance and self-assurance that propelled my brother forward. "He did the same for me. He's the one who arranged for you to escape the

Institute. He's the reason you're not dead. And you sent him in there to die."

The sudden silence was deafening. Caesar gazed at me, impassive beneath his eye patch and his beard, impossible to read. But when he spoke, his voice betrayed him. "It doesn't matter," he rasped, voice breaking. "I'm sorry about your friend. But we had to do it. We had to strike before they got wind of our plans."

My stomach twisted, sick and empty. And there'd be no more food, not after I'd wasted the day searching for nothing more than a false hope planted there to get me out of the way. "Kris isn't dead," I said dully. "They tried to kill him, but I got to him before they could."

Caesar's visible eye widened, flashing with hot relief before he closed it, turning away. "Well done, little sister."

I stared at his back, thinking of the knife in my boot, of how easy it'd be to draw it. The white-hot anger swept through, building on my fury at Gloriette. The urge to strike, at anyone, at both sides, left me weak-kneed with exhaustion trying to fight it.

"Kris was right," I whispered. "It is over, all hope of salvaging this."

"There never was any hope," Caesar muttered.

"There was, before you destroyed it." I sank down on the edge of a packing crate, no longer possessing the willpower to stay standing. "Today the war started."

CHAPTER 19

Oren was waiting for me when I left Caesar's office. Nix hovered nearby but declined to give its usual trill of greeting. It looked tired, limping through the air until it could drop down heavily onto my shoulder and crawl over to slump against my neck. The pixie had been searching for Oren all day.

I wanted to summon some kind of anger or agitation at Oren for his abandonment of me, but one look at his face sent all my fury crumbling away, leaving me weak-kneed with exhaustion. He reached out, and I stumbled forward until I could lean against him and let him wrap his arms around me.

"Where've you been?" My voice was muffled against his shirt.

"I had to think," he murmured into my hair. "This changes my whole life. I couldn't just—I had to process."

I stared at him. "It changes my life too, you know."

Oren didn't respond immediately, and I could see something behind the pale blue eyes that I didn't recognize. Fear, confusion, doubt; something darker lurked there, something he wasn't sharing with me. I longed to ask, but after a moment he squeezed me, tight enough to make my blood sing. I could push him later to tell me what was going on. For now I could just close my eyes and revel in the fact that my cheek was touching his neck and it didn't burn with magic.

His touch invited me to stay that way forever, standing in the hallway outside my brother's office. The longer I stayed, the harder it was to move, like I was slowly turning to iron like the apple trees to the west. Then condensation dripped down from the ceiling, splattering against the crown of my head. I pulled back reluctantly.

"Kris was right about Eve." My mouth tasted like ashes, choking on the words. "I know she helped you, but she's dangerous. She let my brother use her as a weapon. And she's unstable."

Oren's expression didn't shift, but something behind his gaze hardened. "Then that's your brother's fault, not Eve's."

"Please don't fight me on this," I whispered. "If you trust me, you'll be on my side."

"There aren't two sides," he protested. "We're all on the same side in this war."

War. I swallowed. He was right, it was war now. And if it was us against the machines, we'd need the strongest weapon we had. We'd need to find a way to control Eve.

"No matter what," he went on, voice dropping to a whisper to match mine, "I'm on your side. Always. If you decided to destroy the world, I'd stand next to you while you did it. You know that, right?"

Mouth dry, palms sweating, I could only nod. "I'm going to go talk to her," I said. "Will you come?"

Oren just looked at me, shaking his head. His face was oddly pale, despite the thick gold glow of the magic lanterns. "I—no. I'll go train, I need to be alone for a while."

But you were alone all day, I wanted to scream at him. I wished I could keep him here until he told me what was wrong. But Oren was the last person on earth anyone could force to talk when he didn't want to. So I swallowed my frustration and nodded. "When you're ready, I'm here."

Oren vanished down the hallway, but not before shooting me a look that shattered my balance. He wasn't one to speak his feelings, but now and then he wore them plain for all to see. Or for me to see, at any rate. Heart pounding, I stood there for long moments before I gathered my composure enough to turn around and head the opposite direction—toward Eve.

. . .

She was waiting for me. She'd sensed I was coming, and when I knocked on her door I found it standing ajar.

The bond we'd formed while connected to the Machine came and went, but she was better at reading it than I was. I had only gathered scattered thoughts, half-formed images. A tower by the sea with a light high in its eaves. Small, mathematically perfect shells, something I didn't even have a name for outside her memory. She'd lived by the ocean. The images were calming, serene, and I took heart in that. Eve could be reasoned with, even if Caesar had convinced her that war was our only choice.

"Hello, sister," she greeted me. She was seated on the floor, despite the crates my brother had left to serve as seats. "Join me."

I fought the urge to remain standing and sank down onto the floor. I instantly felt the chill of the stone, even through the layered rugs there meant to keep out the cold and damp. "Are you okay?"

Eve smiled at me. "You are so thoughtful. I'm fine. I feel better than ever."

Kris was right, then. The power built up inside her to the point where releasing it was a relief. I scanned her features, noting that her skin glowed a little less, her eyes were a little more focused. "If I'd done something like that, I'd be in bed recovering for a week."

"I doubt that," replied Eve, her eyes on mine, a faint hint of amusement there. She so rarely even seemed human to me that I wanted to seize on that little flicker, draw it out.

"Well, maybe not," I agreed. The Iron Wood stood as a testament to that. "But I wouldn't feel great."

Eve tilted her head to one side, then the other, testing the muscles in her neck. "Your brother is happy."

I swallowed. She knew already what I wanted to talk to her about. "That's why I'm here. I know that Caesar rescued you, and you're grateful. I would be too. But—" I hesitated, the idea of telling this woman who was at least forty years my senior what to do leaving my mouth dry. It didn't help that she looked no older than me. "But don't leave one kind of slavery just to enter into another."

Eve's gaze never left my face, her eyes flickering over my features, my posture, my clothes; a scrutiny that made the hairs on my arms lift in embarrassment. I braced for the censure I knew was coming. "What do you know of slavery?" she said, finally. Her voice was gentle, though, and if there was any criticism in it, I could not detect it.

"Nothing to what you know," I replied instantly. "But my brother is wrong. And I just don't want you going along with him just because he helped you."

Eve was silent for a time, still, calm. I could almost hear the gentle whisper of the surf, as though she was remembering home. Then she rose to her feet with the swift agility of someone my age and crossed the room. She had no belongings, but there hung on the wall a scrap of shattered mirror. I knew my brother had placed it there, trying in some way to make this feel like a home for Eve. She gazed into it, but from my angle on the floor I could not see her face.

"Why are you here?" she asked finally.

The question was unexpected. "Because I don't think war is the answer, even if we could win."

Eve kept her back to me. I had trouble sensing her mind, leaving her an expressionless opponent in a dance to which I was rapidly forgetting the steps. "What is the answer, then?"

I let my breath out in a low sigh. "I don't know," I admitted. "But there must be one. I think the answer lies in the Institute's records, if only they'd let me look for it. The people beyond the Wall say that it was a single event that caused the world to be as it is, not the slow deterioration that we were always taught."

Too late, I remembered that Eve was one of those people from beyond the Wall. According to our shared memory, she'd been sent by the Iron Wood. She turned her head just enough so that I could see her smile in profile. This time, it didn't have a calming effect. "It was a single event," she confirmed. "For a time, before they placed me in the chamber where you found me, they ran a series of tests. What they didn't know was that I was learning almost as much about them as they were learning about me."

I straightened, heart jumping. "Then you know what happened?"

Watching me out of the corner of her eye, Eve nodded.

"Tell me!" I cried, rising up onto my knees, unable to restrain my excitement. If I knew what had happened, I could fix it. I could bring a real solution to Caesar, instead of my spineless pleas for peace.

"They did it." Eve was as still as stone.

"They?" I echoed blankly. "I don't under—"

A torrent of images flooded my mind, robbing me of my words. I saw myself surrounded by architects, red coats swarming like ants, needles being inserted into my flesh and magical leads attached to my fingertips. I saw their lips moving as they spoke to each other over my prone body. They thought I couldn't hear.

"Well, can you see any reason why they're never born here?" one was saying. A man, I thought. His face blurred in and out, only his mouth clear as it spoke.

"It has something to do with the accident," said another. This voice I knew. Gloriette. But I couldn't see her face either, and I knew it was because these were not my memories. They were Eve's.

"How could it be? It's been a hundred years. No one's even alive who was a part of the project."

"The fallout is still here. A hundred years, a thousand. It doesn't matter. The Resource doesn't forget. We're never going to see another Renewable born here." Gloriette's lips blurred and her hand came into focus instead, reaching for me. "That's why we need her." She touched a button by my face, and my body flooded with agony.

Struggling, I thought hard, *Lark. I'm Lark, not Eve. I'm watching* her *memories.* But the deeper she took me, the harder it was to hold on. Bits of myself floated away like fragments of a dream.

Time had passed. I was in the chamber now. The glass filaments connecting me to their machines bristled in my skin every time I twitched, like spines radiating out from my heart. Gloriette was standing below me on the catwalk, her face upturned and lit by my glow. For an instant the blur sharpened, and I could see streaks glistening on her face.

She was crying.

"All they wanted was to get rid of the Renewables," she was saying, anger and grief roughening her voice. "Without them there'd be no wars. That endless fight for power was destroying lives—the Institute's mission was just to end that.

To get rid of the problem.

"They had no idea that it would backfire. That it'd destroy the fabric of the Resource, leaving us unable to survive *without* the thing they were trying to eradicate. We need you, Eve. You have to tell us where your people are. We won't hurt them, we only want to ask for their help. To fix this."

I moaned, unable to form words. I tore my weeping eyes away from her face and gazed upward, watching the play of light from my own body shifting against the chamber ceiling.

I heard Gloriette drag in a breath, ragged and raw. "Fine. *Fine.* Live forever in this hell, if that's what you want. We'll pull it out of you fragment by fragment. And when we find them, we won't give them the choice we gave you. We won't fade quietly into this darkness."

Eve screamed, and abruptly I realized it wasn't a part of the memory. She'd sagged sideways against the wall, knocking the mirror down. It shattered on the floor just as she dropped to her knees, gasping with the impact of the memory.

I was kneeling too, frozen where I'd been before she touched my mind. I wanted to vomit, my insides roiling and limbs quivering. I braced my hands against the floor, ignoring the fragments of glass digging their way into my palm. Compared to the agony of the glass siphons, the pain was nothing.

Eve was bleeding too, I saw; but the smear she left behind as she straightened wasn't red but a gray, faded tar. Even her blood had been altered. Her eyes met mine as her chest heaved, searching for breath.

I couldn't process what she'd shown me, and I gasped, "It's not true. It can't be. We did this—we did this to the world?"

Eve's eyes were burning, no longer the calm shore but a raging storm lashing the cliffs. "Your ancestors," she replied. "And your Institute knows. They've always known, and they kept it from you."

I lifted a shaking hand and scrubbed it across my eyes, trying to clear my blurring vision. "They destroyed the world in an attempt to destroy the Renewables." The ravaged landscape, filled with shadows and pockets of irregular magic, the harsh, brutal reality of life outside, it was all my own city's fault. Horror swept through me, more visceral and real than any nausea or hunger or pain.

"You see now why talking to them will never work."

I raised my eyes to meet hers. "You . . . you wanted this. For revenge."

Eve's gaze hardened. "I am not a vengeful person. In the first year, two years, even five, I would have blown them from the face of the earth if I could have. But I'm not the same creature I was then. Revenge means nothing to me."

"Then why?"

"Because they're right."

I stared at her, lips frozen, unable to speak.

Eve's eyes dragged me in, the rage and the pain so exquisite that I couldn't look away. "There are two kinds of people: the Renewables, and everyone else. This world cannot exist with both. Your city, your architects, they had the right idea in trying to eradicate one. They just chose the wrong side."

"Caesar wasn't manipulating you into being a weapon," I whispered. "You're manipulating *him.*"

"Your brother saved me from a life of torture, and for that I'm grateful. His rebellion gives me a place to heal, to regenerate, and I'm grateful for that too. But he shares your city's sins, he's as much to blame, living here in stolen safety, as anyone."

My skin crawled. "You're the one who wanted to attack, not Caesar. You're—you're *trying* to get everyone killed."

Eve crawled forward a pace, ignoring the glass crunching under her hands. Her gaze, burning and turbulent, held mine. "Listen to what I'm saying," she hissed. "Really think about it. A world with no normals. If only Renewables lived in this world, there would *be* no struggle for magic. No war, no walls, no fear of what they don't understand. The world outside wouldn't matter, we'd carry everything with us always." She leaned forward. "Isn't that the kind of world you wish you lived in?"

"But murdering all these people—"

"Don't think," Eve interrupted me. "Just answer. Isn't that the world you wish was yours?"

In my mind was the sea I'd never seen, with every color of blue and green and gray, dancing against the shoreline. Every detail was crystallized in this stolen memory. It was something I'd probably never see in this lifetime.

"Yes," I whispered, hating myself.

Eve rested back on her knees, watching me with such sympathy that my heart wanted to reach out. "We're two sides of the same coin, Lark. I know this fight inside you; I had years to fight it inside my own heart. You have had only days, only moments. We're the same."

I gritted my teeth, though I could not look away. The rage in her eyes was hypnotic, engrossing. Like a fire rushing through the forest toward where I stood. A fire—or a storm at sea. "We'll never be the same."

"The same coin," she echoed. "One of us fell one way, and the other fell another. You escaped; I didn't. You've seen the world out there; I've seen this one. You believe that people can change, can learn; I don't." She lifted a hand, stained with her dark, unnatural blood, toward me. "You believe these people can be saved."

"And you don't," I whispered. Something in her gaze compelled me, made me long to reach out and let her take my hand in hers. I wanted to throw all of Kris's caution to

181

the wind. It would be so easy. Let her cure me as she'd cured Oren—even if it destroyed us both.

Instead I backed away, dragging myself as though I was chained to the ground. I didn't have to speak for Eve to know my answer. She could read it in my face, sense it through our connection. The rage flared in her eyes, and in that instant I recognized it for what it was.

Madness.

"You know my solution, Lark." She released me from that compulsion, closing her eyes. My skin felt raw, as if I'd been scorched to the edge of burning and then let go. "What's yours?"

CHAPTER 20

Nix found me as I stumbled away from Eve's room, shattered and shaken. "I think I'm going to be sick," I whispered to it as it buzzed past my face.

"I have said from the beginning that she is dangerous." It landed on a loose brick that stuck out a little from the wall.

"You and Kris both," I managed, leaning with one hand against the wall. Part of it was just being around Eve—Kris had explained that we were opposites, that being together was unhealthy and dangerous. But after listening to Eve speak I wanted to erase my memory of it, to scrub out the inside of my mind and never think of it again.

Nix gave an abrupt whine of its mechanisms and swarmed over my hand. *"You are damaged,"* it exclaimed, indignation infusing every word.

I looked down at my hand, embedded all over with tiny shards of glass and throbbing with my pulse. "It looks worse than it is," I assured the machine. "I almost didn't notice; Eve is distracting."

Nix began crawling all over my palm, using its spindly legs to pry the shards out of my hand, one by one. *"She is powerful, though."*

"But a last resort," I said firmly, wincing as Nix dislodged a particularly deep bit of glass. Most of the shards were barely more than splinters, but a few had struck nerves. "What happened today was a fluke. Next time she goes off like that, she could destroy the entire city."

"Then we should leave," Nix said firmly, *tsk*ing to itself as it inspected my hand.

"I've done that once." I shoved away from the wall, sending Nix buzzing into the air. Even Nix had to see me strong, not on the verge of falling apart. "Not this time. We need help. We need power, if we're going to finish this before Eve grows strong enough to do what she's planning to do."

"What do you propose?"

I closed my eyes, weary now after struggling against Eve's power, and her ideas. My thoughts still went to Basil whenever I felt I was backed into a corner. In the tunnels, he'd tell me to retrace my steps until I was certain again. But now . . . He wasn't the same man I remembered. But then, I wasn't the same girl, either. I lifted my head, eyeing the pixie hovering in front of my face.

"Nix, how long can you last beyond the Wall?"

"As long as you can," it replied promptly as it settled again onto a loose brick.

"No—I mean alone. Without me."

Nix was silent, its multifaceted blue eyes fixed on my face. It had no facial expressions, but somehow I could read its distress there in its stare. *"Without you?"* echoed Nix.

"I need to send a message to my brother. To Basil."

Nix finally moved a little, lifting one leg to scrub it over one eye, gears whirring a little more quickly as it thought. *"You want the Renewables in Lethe to come help you fight."*

"I don't know what else to do. We don't have the ability to fight them, not like this."

"Why would they come help you? They're safe where they are."

"Maybe." I tried not to think of Basil, tried not to wonder if he'd come simply because I was his sister and I'd asked him to. "But if the Institute wins, the architects will find Lethe eventually. Either they'll torture the information out of me, or they'll find some new way of tracking them, or they'll con some new girl into running away to find Lethe and this will all start over again. They're not safe. They'll never *be* safe, not until the Institute is destroyed."

"And you want me to go."

"You're fast, you know the way, and Basil knows you." I swallowed, my voice betraying how dry my throat was. I didn't want to be without Nix, the only real ally I had left, the only thing in this entire city I was certain of. "And I trust you."

Nix gave a dismissive clicking of mechanisms, but I could see its wings flutter and sensory antennae flick with energy and pleasure. A machine, susceptible to flattery. I fought the insane urge to smile. *"I would go. But I won't last long enough without you to recharge me."*

My heart sank. "There has to be a way. When Kris went to find the Iron Wood, both times, he brought stored magic with him—"

"I cannot carry enough weight for that. I would not be able to move, weighed down by a crystal large enough to see me that far. I wasn't designed for it."

My mind whirled, trying to find a solution. I could go myself, except that there'd be no one here with even a hope of dealing with Eve if she lost control again. I didn't trust her to keep my city safe—all she wanted was vengeance and destruction.

Can you blame her?

I shoved that thought aside as ruthlessly as I could. "Kris has been outside before, but he'll be too weak to travel for days at least, and we'll need any intelligence he has on the Institute anyway."

"What about that other one?"

Despite its vague words, I recognized Nix's tone. It always had the faint aura of smug distrust when it spoke of Oren, though it never referred to him by name. It wasn't a stupid idea. If we could rig up some kind of magical storage unit for him like Kris had used, he'd stand the best chance of surviving out there. Nevertheless, some danger nagged at the back of my mind, something I couldn't name. But I'd grown to trust my instincts.

"It's too soon after what Eve did to him," I said slowly, trying not to think too hard about my motivations for keeping Oren close to me. "And he's still struggling with it."

"You could send your brother to find your brother."

That made me laugh, albeit a little wearily. "I trust Caesar about as far as I could throw him. I'm certainly not giving him the location of Basil's new home."

"You think he's still working for the Institute?"

"No," I admitted. Because that much was true. If nothing else, Caesar had proven his hatred of the architects. "But I don't think he really thinks we can win this war. And I don't think he'd relish the idea of outsiders coming to rescue us."

"Neither do you."

I cast a sharp glance at the pixie. I'd been carefully regulating my tone, trying not to show my own distaste for this plan. The machine was far more perceptive than it had any right to be. It went beyond programming, beyond magic. "No, I don't. But we don't have any choice."

"I believe you know who to send."

I didn't want to admit it to myself. But, as it almost always was, the pixie was right. Without needing a cue from me, Nix launched itself from the wall to my shoulder with a smug little flutter of its wings, and we went off to comb the Hub for our messenger.

. . .

"But it's death beyond the Wall." Tamren's face was white under the general grime marring his features.

"It's not," I protested. "It's dangerous, certainly. But no more dangerous than it is here. Less now, even. At least the monsters out there, you can see them coming. Not like the pixies here."

Tamren's face was still healing from the pixie attacks, long red gashes in his skin like lines on a map. "Why me?"

"You've spent the last few years cycling around this city. You're fit, you're clever, and you're determined. And I trust you." I felt Nix stir against my neck, hearing me use the same words to win Tamren to my cause as I'd tried to use on Nix. I swallowed the lurking discomfort at the back of my mind. Tamren was even younger than I was—and he could die out there.

He could die in here.

Tamren's gaze was still frightened, but no longer full of the raw panic that had flared when I'd first proposed my plan to him. "Everyone says there's no Resource out there, that we'll all die if the Wall ever goes away."

I hesitated, not wanting to explain Kris's revelation that everyone in the city was a breath away from becoming a shadow. Instead, I said, "Kris has been out there twice on his own, and he's fine. He can help us find you some portable magic you can bring with you. Like a bubble of air around you, only magic."

Tamren gazed askance at the bustling core of activity that was the Hub. I'd pulled him aside without much explanation, waiting until we were out of earshot to explain my plan.

I wanted no one else to know of it. No use getting everyone's hopes up if it no one came. Or if Tamren never even reached them in the first place.

I found it hard to meet his gaze when he looked back at me again. I wanted to hold my breath, but I couldn't let him see how desperately I needed him to say yes. He had to decide this by himself, not because I made it impossible for him to say no.

"You know I'll do anything you ask, Miss Lark," he said slowly. "If you tell me we need this, then I'll do it."

My eyes burned. This is why Kris was wrong, why I could never be a real leader. Caesar made decisions like this every day, potentially sending friends and loyal allies to their deaths, as though he was simply deciding on what to eat for breakfast. I felt as though I was tearing off a limb. "Thank you," I whispered. "I'm going to figure out how to get you the magic you'll need to take with you. In the meantime, keep this quiet. Don't tell anyone."

Tamren nodded. "I understand."

My feet yearned to flee, to escape the weight of his expectant gaze. Abruptly I was glad I could count the number of people this devoted to me on one hand. How could I ever hope to earn that kind of trust? "Thank you," I said again and hurried away, leaving him standing there in the Hub to think about what lay before him.

• • •

Kris was in the infirmary, which was no more than a corner of the Hub with a few cots and a poorly trained medic. The city's doctors were all architects, so we had to make do with a medical research assistant with a shaky grasp of practical application. Kris looked up when I inched around the grubby curtain dividing the infirmary from the rest of the busy Hub.

"How are you?" I asked softly. There was only one other

patient in the infirmary, an elderly woman suffering from malnutrition, and I didn't want to disturb her.

"I feel as though someone dropped a building on me, but I'll be okay." Though he didn't smile at me, the tiny flicker of humor in his words washed over me like a cool breeze.

"I need your storage crystal," I blurted, too tired of justifying my plan to launch into it a third time.

Kris's brows went up, and he was silent a long time. I didn't understand the source of his hesitation until he spoke, his voice barely above a whisper. "Don't leave us again. Please."

"What?" My mouth fell open, but I realized my mistake almost immediately. "No—Kris. I'm sending someone with a message for Basil and the Renewables for the Iron Wood. I'm sending for help."

Kris's eyelids fluttered closed for an instant. "I'm sorry, I never should have assumed."

"It wasn't that much of a leap," I said wryly. "I ran away once; what's to say I wouldn't again?"

"You're different now, and I know that."

I couldn't take my eyes from his face, the weary haggard lines that weren't there a day ago. He needed a shower and a change of clothes, and he needed sleep. He needed to believe in things again, but everything he'd ever put his faith in had betrayed him. I longed to put him to bed and take my troubles to someone else, but I had no one else. Only Kris had been outside, using the architects' technology.

Did you know that it's the architects' fault that the world is what it is? The words bubbled up in my throat, but I bit them back. If he knew, there was no point in dwelling on that fact now. And if he didn't, the last thing he needed right now was more reason to feel betrayed by those who had once been his family.

"I'm sending Tamren. He's been harvested, and if I send

him out there with no magic he won't last a day. I need your storage."

Kris reached inside the collar of his tunic and pulled out the crystal he wore around his neck. "You're welcome to it, but it won't do him any good."

"Why not?"

"It's empty, remember? I wasn't sure I'd even have enough to make it home when you found me out there. There's certainly not enough to get Tamren to the Iron Wood. Or to wherever you've hidden the Renewables."

I let out my breath slowly, summoning calm. "Okay. Fine. Then we recharge it. How do the architects do it?"

"How do they do anything? With machines. It's an extremely tricky and delicate procedure, involving machines that our ancestors designed. I can't do it here."

I wanted to shake him, to point out that he could do *anything*, he was their most brilliant engineer. But he was right, and short of breaking into the Institute, we weren't going to find the magic that way. "All right," I conceded. "What about me, then? I give Oren and Nix power. I can give this power too, can't I?"

Kris hesitated, thoughtful. "Maybe. But Oren's a negative drain—he draws power from you, it's not a passive process. Nix, too, I designed it that way. The crystal is just inert. You'd need a large surplus of power to get it to fill, more than you have."

He looked up and met my gaze, and at the same time it hit us both.

Eve.

CHAPTER 21

I stood outside Eve's door, skin crawling. I didn't have to knock to know she was in there. Her presence burned through the stone, even now, so soon after she blasted a hole in the side of the Institute compound.

While I wasn't sure Caesar would want me to bring in outside help, I was certain Eve wouldn't. She wanted mutual destruction of all those without magic, not one side's victory. I wasn't sure even the entire Renewable population of Lethe would be able to stand in Eve's way, but it was better than nothing.

I couldn't simply ask her for her help. I had to just keep her talking long enough to find out if proximity would be enough to charge the storage crystal for Tamren. I took a deep breath, knocked, and then slipped inside.

Eve was sitting cross-legged on the bed, eyes closed. She didn't open them immediately, leaving me to shut the door behind me and stand there, waiting. She wasn't asleep, but I wasn't convinced she was entirely inhabiting her body either—she seemed so at peace, her outward calm so perfect and encompassing. If I hadn't seen that rage burning behind her eyes, I would think she was the most rational of us all.

I studied her face, looking for some sign of her true age. Her face was unlined, lips full, eyes unshadowed. Her hair was white, but unnaturally so, the way all of her had been drained into nothingness by the years of torture at the hands of the Institute. In Eve's memory that we'd shared, Gloriette had been a much younger woman. But Eve hadn't aged a day.

Without warning Eve's eyes opened, pupils dilating in the sudden light and then fixing on mine. "Hello, Lark. I'm surprised to see you here so soon. I expected it would take longer for you to see how things were."

After I all but fled from you this afternoon? But I didn't say it. Instead, I summoned up my most humble tone and replied, "I can't stop thinking about what you said when you cured Oren. That you could cure me too."

Eve's eyebrows lifted, a rare moment in which she was startled. I could never surprise her, given that she and I seemed to hover at the edge of each other's thoughts. And no wonder this came as a surprise—in reality the last thing I wanted was for Eve to come anywhere near me.

"It won't be the same as Oren," she cautioned me. "Though the darkness is in both of you, it's different."

"I know." *I don't tear people apart*, I thought. *I just stop their hearts.* "But you think you can make it go away? Can you tell me how it works?"

Eve watched me, and for a long moment I thought she knew why I was there. I could feel Kris's amulet around my neck, warming to the temperature of my skin, but it was too early for me to tell if it was refilling with Eve's wild magic. Then Eve nodded, and I fought the urge to sigh with relief.

"You're so fond of comparing this affliction to shadows. If you think that way, shadows cannot hide from light," Eve said, her lips curving to a smile. "I simply fill the sufferer with my light, my magic. In the torrent the shadow simply cannot survive. I burn it away."

I wanted to shiver, fascinated and horrified at the same time. Instead I concentrated on the crystal around my neck. There—was it my imagination, or did it feel a little warmer than my body temperature now?

Keep her talking. "Does it hurt?"

Eve laughed, her eyes looking through me for a long moment. "Nothing like what you have already endured, sister."

"I meant you," I whispered. "Does it hurt for you?"

Eve hesitated, looking briefly, truly taken by surprise. "No more than breathing does," she said finally.

I swallowed, scanning her features. Sometimes they were hard to read, blurred by the glow that sometimes emanated from her skin. But just now I realized that there *were* lines there. Lines of pain. Before I could stop myself, the edge of my thoughts sought hers, brushing against them like a fitful breeze. A creeping horror slipped up my spine, accompanied by a realization. Eve's torment hadn't ended the day Caesar liberated her from the Institute. She carried it with her everywhere. Whatever they'd done to her, it was permanent, and this uncontrollable magic burned in her veins every day.

I jerked back before my sympathy could rise, lifting my eyes to hers and searching their depths for that burning madness I'd seen there. Her gaze stiffened a little, and she turned away. "You can continue to think about whether you'd like me to help you," said Eve. "But perhaps it won't matter."

Not if all of us are burned away by your rage.

The amulet had begun to burn where it rested against my chest, as though I wore a live coal around my neck. I took a step backward. Any more magic absorbed and I'd risk the thing exploding. "I'll let you know," I mumbled, turning for the door.

"Lark." Eve's voice was soft, but it brought me up short. "If you wanted some of my magic, all you needed to do was ask me."

My heart stuttered, my tenuous calm shattering. "I—I wasn't—"

"The ocean wouldn't miss a bucket of seawater," said Eve. Now that I knew it was there, I couldn't hear her speak without sensing the thinly veiled anger behind it. The worst part was that none of it was directed at me—I was merely nearby, her fury spilling out in every direction.

I wanted to scream at her, to dig beneath that calm exterior the way I had this afternoon. I wanted to force her to show what she really was. "Fine," I said shortly. "You're right, I was after your magic."

"I wish you could see that we're the same," Eve whispered, her gaze infinitely sad. "We're sisters, you and I. Connected. If you let me, I could cure you. I'd keep you safe when the others are no longer necessary. I could make you whole."

"I *am* whole!" I burst out. "I don't need curing. The Institute did this to me, but it's part of what I am now." The words startled me even as they flew from my lips. It was one thing not to want Eve to cure me. It was another not to want to be cured. "I'm not looking for help."

Eve's expression hardened as I spoke, like water crystallizing slowly across a lake's surface. "And when you realize you're drowning? What will you do then?"

"I'm not drowning. I never *was*. I need my darkness." I gasped for breath, listening to my own voice speak truths I hadn't stopped to admit myself. "My darkness, my light—I need them both. They're what give me strength."

"False strength," Eve countered. "Hollow faith and hope. You'll see."

I shook my head. "No. You're wrong. And if you try to harm this city, I'll stop you."

Eve never took her eyes from my face. I could feel her gaze, slow-burning and heavy, as though she was memorizing my features. "You have only the power you can scrape from those around you, nothing of your own. How would you do anything to me?"

"If I have to, I'll kill you," I said quietly.

While I watched, her lips curved into a slow, secret smile. "Won't that be an interesting day."

I could feel her thoughts, amusement and grief warring with the anger and the pain that was already there. She didn't know whether to laugh at my threat or mourn our tattered connection. I felt the blow as deeply; we *were* tied, bonded together by our shared experiences, by the magic that had made us what we were. I felt her rage and her agony as tangibly as my own, mingling with my own grief. She was lost, beyond my help. And as clearly as I knew that we *would* face each other one day, I also knew that day wasn't today. Not yet. Right now we were still on the same side.

But for how long?

· · ·

I found Kris with Tamren when I returned to the Hub. As I drew closer I heard the architect-turned-rebel describing what he had encountered on his way to the Iron Wood and how to deal with the hazards beyond the Wall. I kept silent, listening. The way I'd handle the hazards was completely different—and useless for Tamren, who didn't have my abilities. Of all the people equipped to advise Tamren, Kris was perhaps the best choice.

Kris noticed me after a few moments, catching my eye. I nodded, placing a hand over the crystal that hung from my neck, still burning a hole against my skin. It felt tainted, uncontrollable, as wild and dangerous as Eve herself. But someone as untrained as Tamren—I doubted he'd even be able to feel its warmth, much less detect anything off about it. And magic was magic. It would do.

I let Kris finish his lecture, and then the three of us headed out to the entrance Tamren used to guard. It was still blocked by the cave-in I'd caused, but Tamren claimed he knew a way around it, learned during his long nights spent guarding the entrance. I gave him the crystal, which he eyed dubiously. I knew he couldn't sense the magic inside, so to him it seemed little more than a piece of ugly jewelry.

I promised him it would keep him safe, then crouched down with a bit of recycled paper liberated from the Hub. While Kris held the lantern overhead, I sketched out a map.

"The first time I went to Lethe," I explained, "I went there via the Iron Wood, which is to the west of us." I pointed to a blank space off to one side. "But Lethe is north, making the third point in a sort of triangle. There's no need for you to go to the Wood, so you'll go straight north."

"Is there really a sun out there like ours?" Tamren asked, eyes flicking from Kris's face to mine. "To tell me what direction I'm going?"

I nodded. "But it's much brighter. You'll get sunburned like I did, so try to stay under the trees as much as you can."

"Burned?" Tamren stared at me.

"Not like with a fire. It itches more than hurts. You'll be fine, I promise." I had to fight irritation and impatience. "Kris told you about the shadows?"

Tamren nodded, face draining a little more of its color. "Yes."

"Stay by water as much as you can. Crossing it will confuse your scent. Avoid making fires, but if you must, dig a pit down into the earth so its light doesn't go far. And cover it back up in the morning."

Tamren hefted his pack, which was laden with tools: a knife, some cord for building shelters, extra socks, a makeshift hat for the sun, a flask of water. He was infinitely better prepared than I had been, stumbling through the wall with only the clothes on my back and not even a pair of shoes. And yet my heart lurched as I looked at him. No amount of preparation would really, truly *prepare* him.

But this was war. I hardened my heart and gave his shoulder a squeeze. "You'll be fine. Just follow the map and stay away from the shadows. I know you can do this."

Tamren swallowed. "I'll do my best," he said, in what he no doubt thought was a strong, firm voice. But he only sounded younger, voice cracking on the final syllable.

He turned and knelt down by what seemed to be a bit of crumbling brickwork, but turned out to be a hole barely big enough for him to crawl into. He gave me one last look, then wriggled through, vanishing into the darkness beyond.

I couldn't stop staring at the tiny hole until Kris came up behind me and took my hand, gently turning me and leading me away.

"He'll be fine," Kris said in my ear. "You sent the right person."

"I know," I said grimly. "But that doesn't make me feel any better. Even if he succeeds and brings the entirety of Lethe's Renewable population here—" I tried to imagine the carnage that would occur once both sides had fearsome weapons, and my mind refused to picture it.

"We should get back to the Hub before Caesar begins to wonder where we are."

"Or what we're up to." But it was not my brother's fury I feared, not anymore. When I closed my eyes, it was a different

rage altogether that I felt, slowly burning away my reserva-
tions, crowding in at the edges of my mind. I felt only the sea,
and the spray, and the coming storm.

CHAPTER 22

Oren joined us for dinner, and but for the thick tension stiffening his spine, it was the closest thing to normal that I'd felt in a long time. Myrah sat with us after serving us our evening rations of mush, taking a break to eat her own dinner. My mind was still reeling from all that had happened during the day, so I was content to listen to her telling stories about the ways people tried to get around food restrictions. Even Oren seemed to be listening to her, and Kris laughed from time to time, and I felt almost normal with Nix humming lightly against my neck.

That is, until my ear caught something unusual. "Wait— what was that, Myrah?"

Everyone turned to look at me, as though they'd forgotten I was there. Myrah recovered first. "One of the missing people was found."

In the midst of everything, I'd nearly forgotten the reason Caesar gave for moving up our plans, that missing people meant potential captures and information leaks. I'd half dismissed it as a lie meant to excuse sending me off on my fool's errand.

"Found where? Who was it?"

"Sorsha, one of the guards. They pulled her out of the reservoir."

"She was dead?" The bottom fell out of my stomach. Nix's humming by my ear had stilled, and I knew it was listening too. If pixies had gotten inside again, undetected, there was no telling what damage they could do.

Myrah nodded, utterly sober now that conversation had shifted. "They're saying she drowned herself. If only she had lasted one more day, she could have seen today's victory, and maybe that would have given her hope."

She went missing after Oren's encounter with Eve, so there was no chance that she was there when we were, and we'd missed it. Still, I found myself looking across the table at Oren, who was staring hard at his food, his scowl returned.

Kris had stopped eating and was gazing at Myrah. "That doesn't make sense," he said slowly. "Sorsha was fine a few days ago. No sign she was even unhappy, much less so depressed she'd want to kill herself."

Myrah just shrugged sadly. "You never can tell. I see it sometimes with the older people down here. Eventually they just stop eating, decide they're done. They're often peaceful, almost happy with their decision. You don't know what's going on in a person's heart."

I glanced at Kris, who was still frowning. He wasn't convinced, and neither was I. Even Nix made a disparaging sound of disbelief for my ears only. The rebels were hardly well-organized. It'd be exceedingly easy for the Institute to slip a spy into their ranks. If Sorsha had figured something out, it'd be the work of a moment to lure her away from the others and stop her from exposing the mole. Or—if that dark little tendril of thought was right—it would have been easy for my brother to kill her, turn her into a martyr for his cause.

I wanted to find out where Sorsha's body was now and

examine it for signs that my suspicions were correct. But before I could ask, a commotion at the other end of the Hub interrupted me. A clatter of dishes shattered the general convivial atmosphere, and a ripple of gasps and confusion spread outward, consuming the cavern. Voices rose, then erupted into a chorus of coughs and, increasingly, screams. I lurched to my feet, tangled in the bench bolted to the stone, and saw that the air at the other end of the cavern seemed thicker, hazier. People were running our way, covering their faces with their shirts and their napkins.

"Gas," I choked, stumbling backward. Something acrid tingled in my nose, and I tried to hold my breath. Nix launched itself from my shoulder, screeching an alarm.

Oren just stared, confused—he'd never seen such a thing before, not in the wild. But Kris reacted instantly, hauling off his torn shirt and ripping it into hand-width strips. He wound one around his face, covering his nose and mouth, then thrust the other strips at us.

Myrah sprinted away from us and toward the food lines instead, to be lost in the panicking crowd as she worked to get her coworkers and friends to safety. Oren, catching on, fixed his own mask and then headed for the exits with me and Kris.

My mind, trying to understand, immediately went to Eve. But if she'd finally snapped and decided to kill us all, she wouldn't do it with something so impersonal as gas. She'd walk into the center of the room and detonate, taking us all with her. *Besides,* I realized as we ran past a canister that opened as we passed, *this is technology. Motion-sensing mechanisms. This is the Institute.*

Tamren's entrance was blocked and the hole too small for us to pass through, so we made for the next nearest exit along with half the occupants of the sewer system. We burst into the fresh air and kept running, trying to help those who were staggering to a halt just outside to move further away. In this kind of panic, people would get trampled. I searched in the chaos for familiar faces, for Eve, for my brother, for Myrah. I saw only flashes of panicked faces, some streaming tears from reddened eyes, some retching into the sewer drains. Even Nix was nowhere to be found, lost in the confusion.

My lungs burned, but Kris's quick reactions had saved me from breathing in too much of the acrid gas. I tore the grimy rag from my face, gasping for breath. "How did you know?" I wheezed. The streets and buildings around us looked oddly familiar, though I couldn't place where we were.

Kris had his head between his knees, taking deep breaths. He lifted his head to look at me, his eyes shadowed. "Failsafe," he managed in reply. "Something the Institute always kept in case of a breach in the Wall. It was meant for shadows."

My gaze swept across the ever-increasing horde of rebels outside the entrance to the sewers, the family clusters and groups of friends supporting each other as they limped away, others nursing more serious injuries incurred in the riotous panic. We'd been flushed out of hiding, like vermin.

Maybe a hundred rebels had made it out of our entrance, including Oren, Kris, and me. There was no sign of Caesar or Eve, and no telling how many other groups had escaped through other exits. Scattered, bruised and alone, and without more than a few eating utensils and my knife for a weapon, our group was a prime target. We had to find cover.

Before I could figure out how to rally these half-broken survivors, an earsplitting crack resounded through the darkened city streets. Half the group dropped to the ground, expecting some new horror to drop from the sky onto their heads. The crack came again, this time accompanied by the sound of distant screams. I whirled to find Kris standing white-faced behind me, which told me all I needed to know.

The architects had found at least one other group of rebels fled from the tunnels at a different exit, and they were mowing them down. The others were slower to catch on, but as soon as one person gave a little shriek of dawning horror, the rest figured it out. In a few seconds I was going to have a full-blown panic on my hands. And there was no Eve to calm them down, no Caesar to cow them into obedience.

"Okay!" I shouted, my voice splitting with the effort to speak despite my battered lungs. "We've got to find cover, *now*. Either they don't know about this exit or they just haven't gotten here yet—either way, we can't stay here."

A ripple of quiet spread out from me as the gathered survivors of the attack heard me. Eager to listen to someone, *anyone*, who sounded like they knew what they were doing. I lifted my eyes for a moment to scan my surroundings, then abruptly realized where I was.

I was only a few blocks from the street I grew up on. It was inside the rebel barricades now, which meant the buildings stood empty. Empty but whole—and defensible. And visible beyond the square in front of us was the apartment building I used to call home.

"Come on," I shouted to Kris, who was still staring in the direction from which we'd heard the crack; some machine tearing through a building, no doubt. "Get these people moving. We're going to that brick building in the next block. Move!"

I started hauling people to their feet and shoving them in the direction of the building. It took Kris a few tries, but eventually he began leading them that way. He seemed to know where he was going, and I realized he probably knew exactly where I lived. He'd known everything about me before I ever set foot inside the Institute.

I turned, expecting to find Oren ushering people along as well. Instead he was huddled against the wall, face in his hands. My heart stuttered, sudden terror seizing my limbs. *He's hurt*, was the only thought running through my head.

I threw myself down at his side, reaching for his shoulder, but he jerked it away. "Stop it!" I cried as the crowd surged past us like a stream sliding around a boulder. "Oren, this isn't the time for your standoffish, arrogant—"

"Just go!" snarled Oren, shoving me roughly back.

I fell hard against the curb, bruising my tailbone badly enough to bring tears to my eyes. Fury swept over me. "Of all the times to throw a tantrum!" I shouted at him. "Grow up! There are more important things going on than you and me and whatever Eve did to you. Get up! *I need you.*"

I reached for him one more time, grabbing a handful of his sleeve and pulling him around to face me. This time he spun, with another snarl; and I saw his eyes. They were shifting as I watched, visible even in the low light. The pale blue that I'd come to know so well was fading, flickering as though it were a drowning flame. Drowning in white.

The sudden movement had loosened the strip of shirt hiding the lower half of his face, and as he panted for breath, the force of his breathing made it fall. As I watched, the faintest tracery of gray flushed his face. The darkness flickered through his skin like a drop of ink in water. "Go," Oren repeated, gasping through gritted teeth. "Need. Time."

What I was seeing was impossible. He'd never been *half* changed before. It was always either Oren *or* the shadow. The two were irrevocably split, and the change was like the flick of a magical switch. But the barrier between his two halves was gone—and the shadow was winning.

I reached out to touch his face, willing all the magic in my reserves to flow out into him. But nothing happened. No tingle of transfer, no steadying of his shaking body. My magic did nothing. I could no longer keep him human.

I felt a hand wrap around my arm, but I couldn't look away from Oren's face, watching him struggle against the shadow consuming him. No wonder he'd been hiding from me. Something *was* wrong. So wrong he didn't think he could come to me. He backed away, trying to put more distance between us.

I tried to follow, but the hands dragged me away, a voice screaming in my ear that we had to move, now. Kris's voice. Kris's hands. I struggled, clawed at his skin, kicked out with my feet in an attempt to make him let me go. I forgot the war, forgot Eve, forgot the dozens of rebels fleeing for my old home. I had to reach Oren before he ran from me again.

Kris lifted me off my feet, dragging me away, still shouting in my ear.

My voice, hoarse from screaming at him, gave out. For a moment everything stilled, my eyes meeting Oren's. "Fight it," I whispered. And then he was gone.

CHAPTER 23

Kris stopped just inside the door of my apartment building, long enough to press me back against the wall. "Snap out of it, Lark." His face was close to mine, and I saw that somewhere in the panic he'd cut his face, and a line of blood traced his cheekbone. "We need you."

"Did you see Oren?" I gasped, staring at that line of crimson, my vision blurring. "Something's wrong. I have to find out—"

"No, you have to calm these people down. Stay with me. This is why I brought you here."

I swallowed, blinking and trying to focus on Kris's face. "I know. I know—I'm sorry." I lifted a hand, shoving my hair back from my forehead and straightening. As soon as he saw I was standing on my own power, Kris leaned back, letting go of me.

Injured first. I bullied the people nearest me into helping to set up a makeshift infirmary in the first-floor apartments, then directed a handful of others to spread out and start searching the other rooms for supplies that the rebel raiders might have overlooked at first glance. Slowly, with each new set of orders, the group of refugees began transforming into something a little more organized. And I calmed too, working to put Oren's face, and the disfiguring flashes of shadow, out of my head.

It was late into the night before anyone was able to sleep. But gradually the need for action slowed, and more and more people began to drift off into uneasy sleep. I sat with Kris until he, too, fell asleep. We'd barricaded the entrances as best we could, posted sentries at every window on the third floor, laid out every weapon and tool we could find within easy reach in case of an attack in the night. There was nothing left to do, and yet I couldn't sleep. Oren was gone, and so was Nix, and the world felt too empty without them.

Something made me get to my feet, careful not to wake Kris at my side, and head for the staircase. My family's apartment was on the eighth floor, only a few stories below the roof. I hesitated just outside the door, not certain if I wanted to go inside. The last time I'd been here, my brother betrayed me to the people who wanted to enslave me.

Taking a deep breath, I pushed the door open. The lock had been broken by rebels raiding the place for supplies. Inside it was dark, the only light coming from the faint violet glow of the Wall outside the windows. The place had been ransacked; that much I had expected. The couch was torn to shreds, salvaged for its upholstery and padding. The kitchen cupboards were bare, the sink dismantled for its piping. The floor was littered with scraps of fabric and metal, whatever was too small to be useful in the nest the rebels were building under the city. Somewhere down there was the faded floral fabric that used to cover the couch where I used to sleep. Useless now, gone forever in the gas-filled maze that was, no doubt, being crawled over by hundreds of pixies, searching for and counting the bodies.

I tried to imagine my mother here, her horror at the state

of our home; I tried to imagine my father coming home after a ten-hour shift at the plant, dropping heavily into the now-broken chair in the kitchen. But their faces were blurry in my memory, slipping away from me like the remnants of a dream. *It's better they go on thinking you're dead.* Caesar's words, however, were as clear as fire, burning the backs of my eyes.

I knelt next to the couch, by the chest that had once held my meager possessions. The latch was broken, and it was empty, but the rest of it was intact. I lifted the lid, adjusting it in the dim glow from the windows until I could see the inscription carved there.

Don't panic. The words had been left there by my brother Basil, long before he left in search of the Iron Wood. When I was young I'd had the tendency to shut down in the tight spaces we explored underneath the city, feeling like the world was crushing in on me. He would keep telling me that it was panic itself that made me clumsy and weak; that if I just ignored the fear, I'd be strong like him.

Now, I traced my fingers over the etching, vision blurring until I could no longer read the words. I couldn't even wish my brother were here the way I used to. Not now that I knew he was only human, only fallible like the rest of us.

I drew in a shaky breath, tracing over the words—*Don't panic*—and closed my burning eyes. Oren was gone. *Gone.* I had no way to find him now, no connection with the shadow inside him. The thing I'd once hated, the feel of that black void inside him, was gone. And I felt its loss, *his* loss, like a missing limb. I should feel him at my side, always, and now there was nothing there but the ache.

I grabbed at the edge of the trunk, slumping until I could rest my forehead against the wood, a sob tearing its way free of my body. There was no one here to see me cry, only the memories of my family, the remnants of our home. For just a moment, I could let myself drown.

And then I felt it.

A surge of magic fluttered fitfully against my mind, familiar in its burning intensity. I refocused my attention—it was coming from above me. The surge came again, and this time I reached up with my own awareness, trying to touch that surge. It responded to my touch—then latched on with the strength of a drowning woman.

Eve cried, *Help me.*

I lurched to my feet, sprinting from my apartment and making for the staircase leading upward to the ninth floor; then the tenth; and then the roof. I burst out, expecting to see Eve being held by the architects' machines, convinced they'd found us and her. But instead I ran headlong into Caesar, colliding with his broad back and falling back with a gasp.

Caesar staggered back with a grunt, but I had no time for him. My eyes were on Eve, who was crouched in the center of the roof. In the darkness she shone, and she lifted her glowing head to fix her eyes on me.

"You did this!" I screamed at her, voice breaking. The sounds of machines marching through the city streets drifted across the night. They were no longer punctuated by screams; the pocket of escaping rebels they'd found had been neutralized. Captured, dead, or lying wounded in the street. "They're attacking us openly now because of what you did. You and your plan, you're the one who's—"

Eve gave a stuttering laugh, and my vision clouded with white-hot rage. I started toward her but felt a strong hand grab my arm and jerk me back. "Lark, stop—something's wrong."

Panting for breath through my fury, I pulled blindly, trying to free my grip. But Caesar held fast, and just as I considered blasting him back with magic, I realized that something *was* wrong. The magic I felt all around leaped and sparked like a wildfire, unstable and hot and fueling my rage. I blinked back tears and tried to focus on Eve, who was glowing like a tiny sun.

Flares of visible magic arced around her, flashing like lightning strikes. The violet Wall overhead roiled and surged like a storm cloud, responding to her power. My fury vanished, dread taking its place instantly.

"What's going on?" I whispered.

Caesar let go of my arm, sensing the shift in my mood. "I don't know. She was fine, and then the gas happened—it's like she went crazy. Lost control. It's like when she blew the supply depot at the Institute, only—"

"Only you didn't plan it this time," I finished for him.

He lifted his chin, his one good eye meeting mine. His lips pressed together, refusing to speak, but I saw it in his face. Regret. Apology. Anger. "I took her home because I thought it'd be safe," he said. "But then I heard people coming in from the street. I brought her up here, I thought it'd be safer if—" He swallowed hard.

"If she exploded."

"Stop her," he gasped, weariness evident in the way his shoulders drooped. He must have had to bodily drag her up here. "I know you can, why do you think we sent you away before the explosion? But this—this isn't what I wanted."

I wanted to scream at him that this is what happened when you tried to use these forces, to bend them to your liking. But Eve moaned in my mind, and my attention snapped back to her. Her head was thrown back now, eyes skyward, lips parted in that same silent scream I'd seen in the underground chamber at the Institute. Though no glass wires connected her to anything now, I saw the power flaring up around her, seeking the machinery that had once kept her captive.

"Eve!" I shouted, trying to move toward her. The power

pushed back, and my shoes slipped against the pavement. "You're just panicking." My voice was barely audible over the crackle and hum of magic.

She couldn't hear me. An arc of power snapped upward, connecting with the roiling storm of the Wall overhead with a deafening crack.

EVE. I shouted it with my mind, putting all my power behind it.

She didn't reply, but I saw her body twitch in response. She'd heard me that time.

You have to stop! I shouted. *You're remembering what they did to you. You're safe now. Caesar's here. I'm here. You have to calm down.*

Fractured images slid down the bond connecting us. Needles. Wires. The color red. A saccharine smile. Screaming. I nearly dropped to my knees and fought to stay upright, knowing that if I fell, I wouldn't be able to get back up.

"Lark!" A voice behind me penetrated the haze of magic. Kris.

I couldn't turn to look, but threw up a hand to keep him back. I couldn't have him near me. And he would only make it harder for Eve to get control of herself.

Eve's back arched, her hair lifting from her shoulders as though tossed by an impossible wind, wind that couldn't exist inside the Wall. I felt the hairs lifting on my arms and took another step, fighting against the push of her power. I couldn't touch her, Kris's presence was enough of a reminder of that. But if I could get near, perhaps I could shield her and soften the blow.

Fight it, I thought at her. *Don't become what they made you. Power doesn't make you a weapon. It gives you a choice.*

Eve's eyes snapped open and met mine. For an instant I could sense more than feelings and images; I was a part of her, thinking what she thought and feeling what she felt. The panic ebbed, easing back and parting to show what lay inside. Rage and hatred and the utter, utter certainty that she was right. That *this* was right.

Panic wasn't leading her to do this. She was choosing it.

No—Eve, wait—

Eve threw her head back. I had a single instant to act, and I flung the shield around her that I'd used to hide from the pixies.

Her power bashed against mine once, twice—and then the world exploded.

I was thrown against the door to the staircase, colliding so hard I blacked out for a second. When I came to, the world had gone dark again. I blinked, struggling to regain my balance, drag myself upright. The building was still here. Kris and Caesar were alive—I could hear them groaning and stirring. Eve was slumped where she'd been crouched, still—but breathing.

Afterimages blinded me as I battled confusion, trying to figure out why it was so dark. Eve was no longer glowing, but it was more than that. Always at night there was still some light, a soft, gentle glow from the violet cocoon enclosing us.

The Wall. My head tipped back, and my heart froze.

The shimmering violet of the Wall was gone, replaced by inky blackness. No comforting shimmer, no background hum of magic. But neither were there stars overhead, or clouds or the moon. Just darkness, stretching on forever.

My ears rang with the sudden silence, broken only by the pounding of my pulse. Panic gripped my throat and squeezed, dropping me back down onto my knees; my eyes searched for something, anything, to interrupt that black expanse. Once, I had thought the stars were the most terrifying thing I could imagine. Now I would have cried to see just one twinkling above me. The darkness closed in around me, smothering and thick.

I heard a shout in the distance, Enforcer or rebel, I could not tell; it was a wail of confusion, despair. The Wall was supposed to be eternal. No matter what, it was our protection against everything in the outside world. It was what made this home.

My eyes had begun to adjust and see that it wasn't just darkness enclosing the city. There was a weight to it, definition. I strained, staring hard through the gloom.

It was iron. Like the Wall had looked on the outside, only now it was encasing us. Cold, dead metal spread across the city, impenetrable and finite. The Wall had petrified; we were trapped.

My eyes fell on Kris, who looked across the intervening space at me. He'd gone white, and I knew why. I hadn't forgotten what he'd told me, that everyone in this city was a shadow waiting to happen the moment the magic ran out. Without the Wall and its gentle magic glow, there'd be nothing to sustain this city's humanity. It was impossible to know how long it would take; we could no longer afford to wait for reinforcements. Because once the residual magic drained away, everyone I was fighting to save would become a monster.

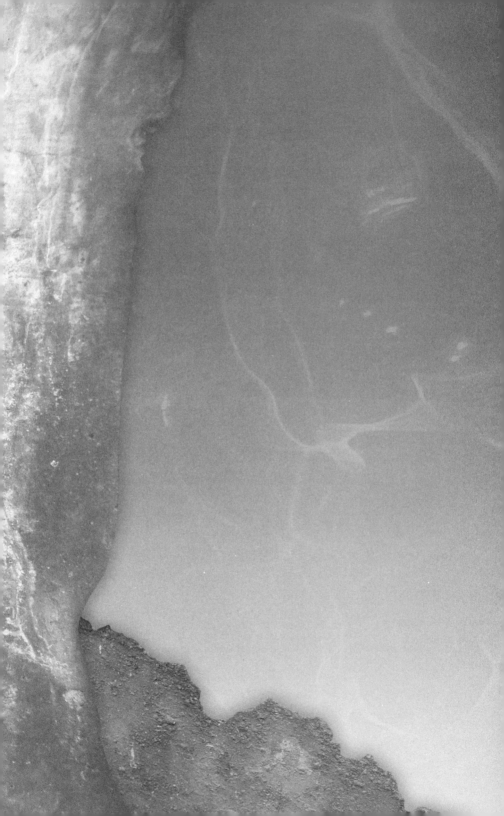

PART III

CHAPTER 24

"We have to press the attack." Asher, who had been among the rebels who escaped along with me, paced from one end of the couch to the other, nervous energy spilling out at his every movement. "Use their disorganization."

"What makes you think they're any less organized than we are?" I argued, frustration beginning to show in the shortness of my words, the bitter edge to my voice.

"We're smaller. We can mobilize faster."

We were gathered in what had once been my parents' living room, after having dragged Eve into the basement to lock her there until we could figure out what to do with her. I glanced at Caesar, who was uncharacteristically silent. I'd expected him to join in Asher's war cry, but instead he sat there, kneading the fingers of one hand into the palm of the other. His knuckles were red and irritated, but he didn't seem to notice.

I sighed and spoke slowly. "I know you want to find Alice. We all have people missing." My mind seized on the image of Oren's face, the fear and shadow consuming him as Kris dragged me away. "But assuming we'll win because we're the smaller force is mad."

Asher kicked the ruined couch, grimacing in pain before dropping down onto a creaky chair. "Well, what do you propose then?"

I felt his eyes, Caesar's, even Kris's, from where he sat in the corner, all come to rest on me. Eve had asked me the same question. I had no answer. "We have to keep Eve under control. We have to stay hidden. The Institute will be occupied for a time, trying to figure out a way to slow the drain of magic."

Kris lifted his head. "This will only make them more desperate," he pointed out. "They'll be taking prisoners to be harvested."

Asher's face flashed agony, his missing sister at the top of his thoughts.

I shook my head, narrowing my eyes at Kris. "We can't let that get out," I warned him. "If the others knew what would happen to them once the magic ran out, we'd have complete panic."

Kris raised his eyebrows at me. "More than there already is?"

He had a point. The fraction of the rebel army that had ended up with us was huddled below in the lobby and first- and second-floor apartments. I'd only spent a few minutes there before the stench of fear and despair overwhelmed me, and I'd called this meeting of the leadership. Such as it was.

Now, though, all I wanted to do was yell at them to leave me alone, to let me absorb the implications of what had happened. I needed time to make decisions. I needed Caesar to wake up, to start taking charge again. Even a bloodthirsty leader was better than no leader at all.

But they were all looking at me, so I lifted my head. "Keeping the people we have safe is our top priority. We're not going to waste these lives on an all-out attack. The streets are crawling with machines; we'd never even make it to the Institute gates."

"But if we keep retreating, they'll just keep finding ways to pick us off bit by bit," protested Asher.

"We aren't going to keep retreating. We'll hide here for now." I leaned forward. "Kris, you know them better than anyone. Do you have any idea why they're still using machines, when magic is at such a premium?"

"It's hard to extract the magic once it's been transferred to a machine," Kris explained. "You can retrieve some of it, but it's an imperfect process and they'd lose a lot of the power. They're not going to drain the machines already running."

"So we just have to last until this round of machines runs out of fuel?" I asked.

Kris nodded uneasily. "I think so. If I were them, I wouldn't waste any more of the Resource on their machines. They'll assume they've caught most of the rebels by then anyway."

Unspoken was the very real possibility that we'd be caught by then too. But no one voiced that fear.

"What about Alice?" Asher murmured. "What about the rest of our people?"

"We'll look for them." I spoke instantly. It seemed to me that leadership, even pretended leadership, was simply about sounding more sure than I felt. "The Institute's patrols are looking for people on the ground. In the Iron Wood, they had the advantage over the shadows because their scouts kept to the trees. We'll stick to the rooftops and send out a few people at a time to scout for survivors."

"Why not send all of us out?" Asher pressed. "With that many eyes, we'd be sure to—"

"Sure to get noticed," Kris interrupted. His wit had not vanished with his ordeal, only his humor. I missed the old Kris.

Asher glared at Kris with thinly disguised dislike, his lip

curling. I couldn't blame him. Kris was still wearing the red coat he'd worn when they tossed him out on the steps and left him for dead. It was hard not to see him as a symbol of those who'd done this to us. "Isn't Lark's magic limited now too? Like the machines we're trying to outlast? We should strike while she still has power left."

I swallowed. "Yes, it's limited. All the more reason to conserve what I have until we've got a plan. And I can still siphon off of Eve, in an emergency." I glanced at Kris, who said nothing. He knew what I'd just said was a lie.

"Like the architects did." Caesar's voice was hoarse. He didn't look up, his shoulders bowed and his hands dangling between his knees.

My jaw tightened. "Yes," I agreed. "But we don't have a choice. And what I'm taking is tiny compared to what they took from her. She can't even feel it when I do it."

"What *are* we going to do with Eve?" Kris asked quietly. "I know no one wants to discuss it, but we can't keep her here. Those chains won't hold her when her power regenerates."

I closed my eyes. I could feel her, as I always could. She was in the basement, but I could sense her there, through the layers of concrete and iron and the crowds of people in the lobby. I could see her as though she was standing next to me. I could feel the iron chains weighting her wrists and ankles as though they were shackled around my own.

"I don't know," I admitted. I had no answer where Eve was concerned. "We don't have the capability to contain her. The only place with the right facilities to deal with her is the Institute." I felt Caesar's gaze on me like a red-hot knife's edge. I didn't look at him.

"We should just give her back to them," Asher spat. "Better she explodes in there than out here."

I expected Caesar to snarl a response, but he just sat there, staring at Asher with red-rimmed eyes, his gaze haunted. Part of me had to agree with Asher's logic—giving Eve back to the Institute as a gesture of goodwill would potentially solve both problems, containing her and opening a dialogue with our enemies.

Asher drew breath for another jab, but I lifted a hand and interrupted. "We're not giving her back to them. No one deserves the kind of life she was living in there."

"She's still recovering," said Kris. "But this will all happen again when her power builds too much for her to contain."

"Then we have time to figure out what to do with her," I replied firmly. Delivering her back to that hell was not a part of my plan.

Caesar lurched to his feet, and without another word, left. The door banged shut behind him. Asher half stood, ready to go after him, but I convinced him to stay. I knew why Caesar was so ragged. I'd seen it in his face when he begged me to stop Eve on the roof. What that betrayal had cost him. He loved her.

I listened with half an ear as Kris and Asher debated ways to gain the upper hand over the architects. My attention was on the basement. I felt Eve's power flicker and surge and then die again as Caesar appeared there in her basement cell. When I closed my eyes I could almost see them, the knot of white-hot power that was Eve and the shape encircled by it, outlined by little sparks and crackles of magic. He didn't touch her, but sat only a few inches away. I had no way to know if he spoke to her, but he didn't move.

I wrenched my attention away. "I'll go tonight," I said, interrupting the stream of increasingly impractical suggestions from both Asher and Kris. "To scout the Institute and make sure they're not planning another attack."

"You'll go tomorrow," Kris retorted, lips firming with

resolve. "Even you can't run without sleep."

I started to protest, but Asher shook his head, interrupting me. "He's right," he said grudgingly. "With Eve so unreliable, you're all we've got against them. If you don't sleep first, you'll make stupid decisions."

I decided to ignore the not-so-hidden barb, the implication that I was already making stupid decisions. "Fine. Tomorrow, then."

Asher got to his feet and made for the door. Though the couch was ruined, there were a few blankets and towels that the raiders had overlooked. I'd be able to make a bed here, and even though it felt twisted and unreal, there was a strange comfort in sleeping in my own house. My former home.

Kris exhaled as the door closed behind Asher, getting to his feet as well. "It's a plan," he said quietly. "It'll work for now."

"I don't know what I can do even if I do find the Institute gearing up for another attack," I said slowly. "I don't have much power left."

"You did the right thing," he said, voice low. "Letting Asher and the others know that you can't siphon from Eve anymore would destroy any remnant of hope they have."

"She's white-hot," I said, closing my eyes with a shudder. "It's like trying to breathe fire."

"Maybe she'll cool down eventually," Kris said. I knew he was trying to be comforting, but I could tell that behind the attempt was the certainty that Eve wasn't going to cool down. It was only going to get worse.

"Maybe," I said with what I thought was a smile. He grimaced back, and for a moment it was a little easier to pretend we both believed there'd be an "eventually" to look forward to.

I stood and went to the window. I didn't want to twitch aside the curtain for fear someone in the street might be able to see the movement. Instead I just leaned my head against the wall and peered through the crack at the sliver of darkened street below. The street was empty, but I found myself staring at the shadowed alleyways, trying to detect movement, until my eyes watered with effort.

Kris watched me from his spot across the room. "He'll be okay," he murmured. "He had a lifetime of being a shadow before he met you. He can take care of himself."

I swallowed hard, disengaging from the feel of my burning eyes. I couldn't afford to fall apart right now. "I know."

He cleared his throat. "Get some sleep, Lark." He turned for the door.

"Wait." My voice broke on that single syllable. I turned so I could press my shoulders against the wall. "Stay here tonight."

That was enough to penetrate Kris's thick misery. He blinked at me, hesitating with one hand on the door handle. "Stay here?" he echoed.

"I'm tired of feeling like I'm on my own." I nodded at the pile of linens scavenged from the back closet. "And there's room for two."

Though I didn't have the courage to look at him directly, I saw his hand clench around the handle, white-knuckled. He drew in a deep breath. "I'm not the one you want. Don't ask this of me, not when I'm a substitute for—for someone who isn't here."

I wanted to hate him for turning me down. I wanted to yell at him that I wasn't asking him to marry me, just stay with me while I slept so that I wouldn't be alone. But somewhere, deep down, I knew it was more than that, what I was asking. I tried to find anger somewhere, even humiliation I could express as anger. But I was too tired. I couldn't find any of it. So I just shrugged. "Goodnight, then."

Kris stood there so long that I began to think I'd have to tell him to go. But finally I heard the door open with a creak and close behind him again. I shut my eyes, pressing my forehead against the cool wall. My heart was with Oren, wherever he was, and I couldn't sleep without it.

CHAPTER 25

Waves lapped at my toes, tugging at the sand around my feet. The wind tugged at my hair, sending it whipping around my face. Brown strands like seaweed floated before my eyes, and I closed them. My nose stung with salt and sea spray, but I didn't move.

The sand shifted beneath the soles of my feet, pulling away as the waves receded. There was no other feeling in the world like this one—that even the ground beneath me was fluid, changing, always adapting.

This was home. I slept in the decrepit house up on the cliff, making my bed on the creaky boards in the living room, but this shore, with the cliffs to the north and the aspen grove to the south, was my home. Where I belonged. The house on the hill was too full of ghosts.

I knew that the sea ought to feel haunted. It's where my mother died, where she chose to bury her own body after my father became one of the monsters we so feared. For months he crept around the house, trying to find a way in, as we huddled on the floor, listening to the scratching and the howling screams.

One day the howling simply stopped. And on that day my

mother walked into the sea.

Somehow, though, it didn't matter that this ocean was a grave. I felt happy here. Comforted. Safe. I could walk into the sea too, if I ever wanted to go away forever. If I ever got tired of being the only one left. Sometimes I did. But standing here, with the sand between my toes, was always close enough for now.

I turned, shielding my eyes against the diffuse, overcast sunlight. In the distance, the colony of aspen trees shivered in the wind, whispering to me in its shared language. The house on the dunes waited for me, and my stomach rumbled. I had a few more weeks of food there. I'd eat it, and then I'd move on. Onward down the shore, or else into the sea. It didn't matter much what I chose.

I freed one foot from its sandy trap, but then froze. The curtains in the house just moved. Before I had time to consider what it meant, a face appeared there. It stayed just long enough that I was sure it had seen me before it vanished.

I turned to run, gathering up my shoes from the high tide line and making my way to where the sand was firm enough to run on. I'd barely gotten a few steps before a voice called out, "Wait!"

That, more than the moving curtain, more than the face at the window, froze my heart. Shadows didn't speak.

It was a boy about my age, no more than eleven or twelve. He was shorter than me, with big feet and stringy hair that needed washing. His face was badly windburned, and I thought of the storm two nights ago that had broken the roof upstairs.

"Keep back!" I shouted, whirling and pulling out the little knife that my father had given me. "Who are you?"

The boy skidded to a halt with a shower of sand. He lifted his hands, showing he was unarmed, and in silent plea. "Don't hurt me," he gasped, panting with the effort of sprinting down here. "I'm sorry if I scared you. Is that your house? I was just looking for something to eat."

His cheeks were hollow, eyes bright with hunger. I glanced up at the house on the hill. "It used to be," I said. "How are you—why aren't you shadows like everyone else?"

He shook his head. "I don't know. My dad was like me, though."

"Where is he now?"

The boy didn't answer, his face reddening still more under the windburn.

"Never mind," I said. "If you're hungry, you can eat something from the house, but you can't stay. I don't have enough food for two."

"What will you do when you run out?"

I glanced at the sea. My mind's eye summoned an image, dark brown hair spreading out over the waves as my mother's head vanished there. "I don't know."

"Why not come with me?" said the boy. "It'll be safer with two of us."

"Where are you going?" I asked. "There's nowhere to go."

"In the last town we lived in, before the shadows got it, my dad heard a story about a place. With people like us. Renewables."

My mom had used that word sometimes when I was growing up. She'd go get supplies from a nearby town where a few Renewables, people like her, had holed up against the shadows. I wondered if that was the town where this boy was from.

"I don't want to go chasing after stories. I want to stay here. I'd like to die at home." I thought of my aspen grove.

The boy nodded. "I guess that's your choice. But if I'm going to die, I'd rather die fighting."

I tore my gaze away from the sea, frowning at him. He

was such a skinny, weird-looking boy, with his big hands and feet and ears, like they were trying to grow to grown-up size before the rest of him could catch up. The idea of him fighting anything was ludicrous. He caught me staring, saw my scowl—and smiled.

It was strange talking to another person after months of isolation. I felt as though my heart were one of the dried husks of seaweed at high tide, slowly coming back to life as the water returned. "How far is this place?"

"I don't know," he admitted. "But it's west of here. You'd have to leave the sea."

"Does this place even have a name?"

"My dad said it's called the Iron Wood."

I shoved my hands into the pockets of my dress. "What does that even mean?"

"Dunno." The boy shrugged. "My name's Dorian, by the way."

I hesitated. "Eve. I'm Eve."

. . .

I woke expecting to hear the roar of the waves. I brushed at my face, trying to dislodge the sand I knew was stuck there, only to find nothing but the imprint of the floorboards on my cheek. I stared around the dark apartment groggily, trying to reorient myself. Only then did I feel the little thread of power coming up from below, the connection Eve and I always shared. Dream, memory—it didn't seem to matter. I rubbed at my eyes, trying to shake it away. I didn't want to feel closer to the woman I'd chained to the floor in the basement. I couldn't afford to.

There was no way to tell how much time had passed. It was as dark outside as it had been when I fell asleep, and it would be dark forever. Unless the Wall was powered again, the sun disc would never light our city. And no sun from outside could penetrate our leaden sky. I could only tell by how stiff my arms and legs were that I'd been lying on the floor for hours, at least. So I stood, stretching as best I could, and made for the door.

I nearly tripped over someone lying on the floor outside. I stumbled, catching myself before I could crash noisily to the floor. Bending low, I made out Kris's features in the dark. My breath caught painfully in my chest. He stirred but didn't wake. He wasn't Oren, someone who'd jump to his feet out of a dead slumber at the slightest noise. But he also hadn't left me alone.

I retrieved one of the ratty blankets from the apartment and draped it over him before I stepped silently down the hall to the staircase, retrieving a lantern and giving it a crank as I went. I hesitated when I reached the basement door, but only for a moment. I knew Eve was awake. She'd awoken the instant I had.

The door opened silently when I gave it a nudge. This place was too recently inhabited to have gathered much rust yet. I almost thought it'd be easier to see my home falling apart, as though it had been abandoned generations ago—rather than just the way I'd left it, only empty and still.

Eve sat cross-legged where we'd left her chained to the hot water generator. Of course, there was no power running through it now, and no heat—but it was bolted to the floor and impossible to budge. Eve didn't lift her head when I entered; her eyes were downcast, fixed on my brother, who lay with his head cradled in her lap.

I jerked to a halt at seeing this, struck by the image. My oldest brother seemed so small.

"We can speak," Eve said softly. "He's dreaming."

I swallowed, inching into the room but giving the pair of

them a wide berth. "How do you know?"

Eve just smiled, her fingers running slowly through the hair at my brother's temples. I hadn't noticed before, but there were threads of silver there among the brown. "I can taste it in the air. Your brother has the kindest dreams."

That I doubted. But maybe dreams were the way to reach her. "You knew Dorian," I whispered, letting the door close behind me. Eve was glowing again, but with a gentle, warm light—not the burning glare she'd given off on the roof. Just enough to light the room and illuminate her face.

"Dorian," she echoed, finally lifting her eyes to meet mine. Her brow furrowed, lips repeating the shape of the name again and again, as though it might taste different if she tried it one more time.

"The boy who brought you to the Iron Wood. The man who sent you here to find out about the Institute."

Eve shook her head abruptly, the force of her movement causing my brother to stir uneasily. "No. I've always been here."

I looked at her face again. She met my gaze, pupils barely more than pinpricks in her white irises. "You came here years ago," I said slowly. "You don't remember that anymore?"

"I'm like the sea. I've always been and will always be."

"How would you know anything about the sea if you've always been here?" I challenged.

Eve hesitated, lips curling. "What do you want?"

"I want to help you." I pinched the bridge of my nose with my fingers, trying to stave off the headache that inevitably assailed me when I was around Eve for too long. "I don't want to keep you here like this."

"You want me to say I love these people like my own. Like you do."

"You don't have to love them," I argued. I wasn't so sure

she was right about *me* loving them. "You just have to not want them all to die."

"You think death is the worst end for souls like these," Eve whispered. Her eyes burned with memory; I could still picture her memory of her mother's suicide. "If they knew what was coming for them they would choose it. Isn't choice the freedom you keep trying to push on me?"

"Maybe they would," I allowed, heart pounding. "But that isn't your choice to make."

"Isn't it? If I'm the one with the power to save them?"

"Your idea of saving them isn't the same as mine." I took a long, slow breath, trying to keep hold of my calm. Even now her pull was irresistible; even knowing what she did to Oren, what she wanted to do to my people. "Eve, tell me why the architects disconnected you from the power grid in the Institute."

She blinked at me, a languid dip of translucent white lashes. "Why do you think I know?"

"You delight in reminding me that we're connected," I pointed out. "I may not have your experience, but it goes both ways. I know there's more here than you've told anyone. What were they going to do to you?"

"Kill me," she replied evenly. Her fingers combed through my brother's hair, a disturbingly tender gesture. "They wanted to kill all of us."

"I can't believe that," I snap. "The people in there aren't evil, Eve. They're not murderers by choice, they wouldn't come this far only to decide to wipe out everyone in the city."

"Not them." Eve's voice sharpened, a spray of irritation mottling her tone. "Not the normals. They wanted to kill the Renewables—to finish what their ancestors started."

My pulse quickened; I had to fight the surge of excitement, keep it restrained where Eve couldn't sense it in my thoughts. "Finish it? How?"

Eve narrowed her eyes, inspecting my features for a long moment. "They have a device. The one your city's founders used. They believed I had grown strong enough to trigger the process again. They did not get a chance to test their theory."

Before Caesar broke her out.

Mind racing, I tried to piece together the truth from Eve's fragmented, paranoid memories. The architects wouldn't have tried to destroy all the Renewables now, not when their magic was the only thing that could power the Wall and all their machines. There had to be something else, some other factor that Eve was unable—or unwilling—to understand. If it was possible to complete the founding architects' plan, perhaps it was possible to reverse it—to reverse the damage to the world. There were answers somewhere behind those high granite walls, if only I could reach them.

I swallowed heavily, trying to rid my throat of the lump lodged there. "Eve, why not help me? Together we could get into the Institute and find a solution. One that doesn't involve genocide."

Eve's eyes had wandered, but when I spoke they snapped back, the pinprick pupils darting this way and that over my face. "Return to that place and to their device? I will not hand my enemy the power they need to destroy me."

"But what if we could use their device against them? Maybe we could change things."

Eve's fingers were still idly stroking my brother's hair; I couldn't tell if she was even aware of the movement. She was silent for a long time, and when she finally spoke, I wasn't even sure if she'd heard me. "Sometimes I think about your brother, and his death. I wonder if he would still love me in that moment."

It was pointless. She'd lost what little sanity she had left, up on that roof. I fought the urge to shout at my brother, to wake him and drag him bodily from the room if I had to. "It's not love," I retorted. "He's under your magic. No more."

"Of course he is." Eve dropped her hand, fingers stroking along Caesar's knuckles, where he'd fallen asleep with his fingers wound in the hem of Eve's dress. "How is your pet any different?"

"My—" I started to ask, but it took one look at Eve's face, the tiny smile there, to understand. "You don't get to talk about Oren," I breathed. "Ever."

Eve shrugged. "I gave him what he wanted," she whispered.

"He wanted a cure!" I had to dig my nails into my palms to keep from shouting.

"He wanted freedom from you."

My stomach seized as though I'd been punched in the gut, and I nearly staggered. She was wrong, I knew she was wrong. Oren cared for me—he'd always told me that he'd follow me whether he needed my magic or not.

And now he didn't—Eve had made it so his shifts to shadow and back weren't affected by magic. Now that he didn't need me . . . where was he?

Eve rested her hand on Caesar's cheek, watching me. "When you change your mind about these people, I'll be here. I'll let you help *me*." Something flickered in my mind, the slick tingle of deceit. I was growing more deft at reading her thoughts the way she read mine.

Sick, I turned my back on her and left, pausing on the other side of the door to rub at my eyes and my face, trying to scrub her presence away. There was no saving her anymore. The magic was poison—without the Institute leeching it away, it was destroying what little was left of her mind. Killing an entire city so that only Renewables would be left was a madness I couldn't even understand.

Except that part of you knows she makes sense.

I hurried away, taking the stairs two at a time in a futile attempt to leave the touch of her mind behind.

CHAPTER 26

The lobby of my apartment building was full of refugees from the sewers, no more than lumps of blanket and clothing scraps littered around the floor. A few of them stirred as I passed, the dim lantern light brushing their faces, but none woke.

I slipped outside, dropping the lantern and sinking into a crouch as I tried to force the remnants of Eve's mind from mine. Being around her was like walking through cobwebs, leaving traces of invisible, creeping thread all throughout my thoughts. It seemed colder than I was used to, but I knew I was imagining things. Even if the environmental controls went offline when the Wall did, it would take more than one night for the temperature to start dropping.

I rose to my feet and stumbled down the steps into the street. If the sun disc had been working, it'd be dawn. As it was, the street was shrouded in midnight. Not even the lamps were lit. As I left the stoop of my building, and my lantern, behind, the darkness swallowed me.

"Oren," I whispered, eyes searching the darkness. "Come back to me."

Instinct made me search for him with my second sight, reaching for the well of shadow that had always been beside me. But that was gone now, after what Eve did to him. There was no more division between his darkness and his light; there was only him, and I couldn't find him in this impenetrable midnight.

But then my straining eyes did pick something out; a shadow slipping from behind a corner into the shelter of a doorway. My heart skipped, and I moved toward it. "Oren?" I whispered, knowing it was foolish, and not caring. If it was one of the Institute's Enforcers, so be it. They'd find us anyway, if they were this close.

The shadow froze, and for a pounding moment there was only silence. Then came a voice. "Lark?"

My feet went numb, and I stood rooted to the ground. "Basil?"

The figure bolted from the doorway and came at me. I could barely see his face in the dark, but as soon as his arms went around me, I knew I'd been right in recognizing his voice. "You're here! You're alive!"

For a moment it didn't matter that my brother wasn't the hero I remembered; it didn't matter that he'd been just as corrupted by magic as everyone it touched. I buried my face against his shoulder and clung to him.

We stood there in the false midnight, mumbling reassurances to each other, like children afraid of the dark. Eventually I pulled away, reaching out to touch his face and remind myself that he was really there. I took his hand and pulled him back toward the stoop and my fading lantern. I let go of him long enough to give the lantern a few more cranks, then turned back.

"How did you get here so fast?" I gasped, still breathless with relief. "Where's Tamren?"

Basil's face, now that I could see it in the light, was worn and ragged. He'd been on the road, and it clearly hadn't been an easy journey. "Tamren?" he echoed, brows drawing inward. "Who's Tamren?"

My relief vanished, the bottom dropping out of my stomach. "You mean he didn't find you?"

Basil shook his head slowly. "I left on my own, with Dorian. He's a street or two back. We came to help you. I didn't know where you'd be, I thought I'd try home . . ." His eyes lifted to the battered façade of where we'd once lived together as a family.

"So Tamren could still be on his way to Lethe," I whispered, trying to ignore the sick pit in my chest. "Wait, Dorian's here?" I straightened, trying to cast out with my thoughts. Unlike the Renewables in Lethe, the Renewables from the Iron Wood weren't good at shielding themselves. After a moment I found him, a few blocks away, feeling his way through the darkness like Basil had.

"I couldn't go alone, without someone to give me magic. Dorian volunteered. He said he had unfinished business here, though he refused to explain what."

I swallowed hard. "Eve."

"Who's Eve?"

"That's the name of the Renewable the Institute's been using for the past decade or two. She was originally from the Iron Wood. Dorian is the one who sent her here."

"You mean—the Renewables in the Wood are the ones who started all of this?"

I nodded. Even the peaceful residents of the Iron Wood, content to live in rustic simplicity in the middle of a frozen orchard, abused this magic. "I thought you couldn't absorb magic except through machines," I pointed out. "That you and I were different."

Basil grinned and lifted his hand, revealing a simpler, smaller version of the glove he'd used as Prometheus. Wires and circuits wrapped around his fingers, crystal pads on each fingertip, conductors for the transfer of power. "Piece of cake for me, little bird."

I tried not to react, tried to remember that he recreated this machine so he could come help me. But all I could see was the way Adjutant had used it to rip the magic from Tansy, killing her brutally in front of me.

"How did you get inside?" I asked instead. "Even I struggled to get through the iron."

Basil blinked at me, then looked more closely at my face. "You mean you don't know?"

"Know what?"

Some kind of realization was dawning on his face. "You think . . . you think the Wall is shut down. Dead."

"It is," I said, gesturing at the sky. "Just look up."

He shook his head. "It's not. It's inside out. We were waiting outside, trying to figure out a way in, when suddenly the iron turned to magic. We thought it was you."

I shook my head, my throat tight. "And when you came through . . ."

"Then we realized we were trapped. The Wall we know is on the other side now."

The hairs on the back of my neck lifted. "You mean anyone—any*thing*—from outside can just walk into the city?"

Basil nodded, his expression grim. "I thought you knew. But there's magic in here yet, I can feel it. Any shadows who come in will revert to their human selves."

"For now," I murmured.

Before Basil could ask what I meant, Dorian caught up with us. Basil told him what I'd said, but Dorian was watching me, his gaze difficult to read, but haunted nonetheless, his eyes shadowed.

When Basil had finished, Dorian swallowed. "It's good to

see you again, Lark."

"You too," I replied. I knew what he wanted to ask, but I wasn't going to make it easy for him. From one perspective, he was the one who had set all of this in motion, by sending a spy to infiltrate our city all those years ago.

"The Renewable," he began. "The one you said helped you find the Iron Wood. Is she—"

"She's not really Eve anymore," I said gently. "You had to know that."

He flinched, but didn't retreat. "But she's alive? She's here?"

"I'll bring you to her."

I turned to lead the way back into the building, my thoughts surging. Until now, Eve had been the only Renewable we had access to. I hated myself for thinking of Dorian as a weapon in our arsenal, but given how wildly out of control Eve was, his arrival changed everything. He'd be able to help us infiltrate the Institute; he'd give us a fighting chance.

And maybe all hope wasn't lost for Eve. In the earliest memories I'd shared with her, before she became the Institute's captive, she'd thought of Dorian often. I'd felt the wistfulness of those thoughts, how deeply she cared for him. At one time, Eve had loved this man, when they were young together in the Iron Wood. That young girl had left her home and volunteered for his mission because she cared for him so.

I had to hope there was some part of that girl still somewhere inside the glowing, mad creature chained in our basement. I had to hope Dorian could reach her.

I let the lantern die a little as we picked our way across the lobby. It was definitely closer to morning; the light made the sleeping bodies stir, and a few sat up behind us as we went. I hurried on, not wanting to have to pause to explain these two new faces.

Dorian's magic, natural and untwisted, was like a gentle balm after the raw, raging storm inside Eve. I wanted to stop and bask in it, but I settled for letting my shadow taste its edges as I made my way down the stairs. I should have been paying attention to what I wasn't sensing. We reached the basement floor, and I lifted my lantern high, expecting to see Caesar still sprawled out in Eve's lap. But instead all my light illuminated was a set of rusty chains wrapped around the boiler, empty.

She was gone.

CHAPTER 27

I could hear footsteps and confused shouts as I pounded back up the stairs and through the lobby, but I didn't dare stop to explain. I could still feel Eve's magic, and though I couldn't pinpoint exactly where she was, my senses drew me toward her. I burst out of the doors into the thick darkness and flew down the stoop into the street. There was nowhere in this city that she could hide, not from my senses, but if she found a way to break through the shell of the Wall, she'd be lost forever, and her power with her. I had to get to her before that happened.

And insane or not, we needed her.

I closed my eyes, which were useless in this darkness anyway. I let my senses take over, using what Eve had taught me through her memories. Casting magic around me I could feel the reverberations off buildings, curbs, parked carriages. I vaulted over a barricade, lungs burning and soles skidding as I turned down an alley. I was getting closer. Maybe Caesar was slowing her down—for he had to have helped her escape. I wondered why she didn't just leave him and flee.

A few blocks more—

A blinding light swooped in front of my face, dazzling my

second sight and sending me reeling back. I fell, landing with a jarring pain on my tailbone. The thing swooped again, and I opened my eyes, crying out. A pixie. It was dark—I'd forgotten that night was the time the pixie patrols ruled the streets. I threw up my arms, trying in vain to gather my scattered senses.

"What are you doing? You'll run straight into the Institute's patrols."

I gasped for air, dazzled eyes searching until I made out two tiny pinpricks of blue. "Nix!" I breathed.

"If it wasn't me, you probably wouldn't have a face anymore."

My breath sounded like a sob, not the laugh of relief that bubbled out of me. "I'm glad to see you, but I have to—"

Nix waited patiently for me to finish, but there was nothing to say. The hints of Eve's magic were *gone*. I looked up, but there was no shift in the iron shell around our city, nothing to indicate that she'd blasted her way through it. She was still here, somewhere. But somehow, against all I'd come to understand, she was hidden from me.

It ought to be impossible. I could feel her even when I was out in the wilderness beyond the Wall. And yet it was as though that connection had never existed.

I closed my eyes, trying to make my pounding heart calm. I'd grown so used to feeling Eve in my mind that her absence was unsettling. "Nix, where have you been?"

"Investigating." Nix landed on my shoulder, tunneling in under my hair. *"The dead woman these people found right before the attack scattered us."*

My eyes flew open as I started, remembering the rebel woman's so-called suicide with a guilty pang. I'd nearly forgotten about her. "Did you find anything?"

"No evidence of a spy," Nix replied. *"I thought it wise to check, to prevent it happening to someone more important."*

"Everyone's important, Nix," I interrupted, my tone sharp. Nix sounded like Eve. "But it's good we don't have a mole amongst us."

But the pixie merely hummed indifference, its legs busy plucking sweaty strands of hair away from my neck with distaste. *"I do not believe she drowned, however."*

I pulled myself upright onto my knees, still trying to catch my breath. "What do you mean?"

"Her body was torn to shreds. And not by the currents and the stones, as they assumed."

My heart shriveled, stomach turning over with dread. "Torn apart like—like by a shadow?"

Nix was quiet, body tucked close against my throat, cold metal warming to my own temperature. *"How long was that other one missing after you spent the night at the reservoir?"*

I shook my head, swallowing hard. "It wasn't Oren," I hissed. "It couldn't have been. He was fighting it—I saw him fighting it."

Before Nix could answer, someone came skidding around the corner, carrying a lantern. It was Basil, and his face fell as he saw me on the ground. "Lark! Are you—"

"Fine," I interrupted, getting wearily to my feet and trying to ignore the ache in my bruised tailbone. "I was trying to follow Eve, but she's gone."

"Gone? She left the city?"

"I don't think so," I answered slowly, head tipping back even though there was nothing to see overhead but empty darkness. "I think I would've felt it if she used enough magic to punch through iron. But I've always been able to sense her before."

"Let's get back," Basil said. "You scared everyone to death, sprinting out of there like that. Better show them you haven't lost your mind. From what you've said, I don't think they could deal with losing both Eve *and* you in the same night."

. . .

Kris was awake by the time Basil and I made it back to the lobby of our building. When I walked in, he was asking agitated questions of Dorian, voice raised.

"And what, it's a coincidence that she took off when *you* showed up?" Kris stabbed a finger angrily into Dorian's chest, and I remembered abruptly that they'd met—that Kris had lived in the Iron Wood for some time before he was uncovered as a spy for the Institute.

"Stop!" I interrupted as Dorian opened his mouth to respond. "She didn't know Dorian was here. He had nothing to do with it."

Kris whirled, mouth falling open for a split second before he recovered. "I wasn't talking about Eve," he muttered, moving toward me. "Are you okay?"

"I'm fine. I was trying to follow Eve." My gaze swept the lobby; all the survivors we'd led out of the tunnels were awake now, clustered around the edges of the room. Their numbers greatly reduced after scattering in the wake of the Institute's attack, they didn't seem so much fighters as refugees. There was something hauntingly familiar about the droop in their shoulders, the emptiness of their eyes.

I shivered and turned back to Kris. "We shouldn't talk here. You, you, and you—come with me." I tilted my head at Dorian and Basil, summoning them and Kris to follow me back upstairs to the apartment I'd once called home.

I waited for them to precede me, focusing on the comforting weight of Nix on my shoulder once more. I let my eyes drift back to the refugees, watching us go, and an image flashed into my mind.

I realized where I'd seen that look before. What felt like years ago, standing by the shore of the summer lake, a shadow woman searching for her lost child had looked at me like that. Empty and hopeless, one step away from darkness.

I shut the door on the lobby and followed the others upstairs.

. . .

"We should make a list of the places she could hide." Dorian was intent, hunched over the makeshift map of the city Kris and Basil had sketched out in chalk on the floor of the apartment.

"That's the problem," Kris said, impatient. "She shouldn't be able to hide from Lark. They're linked. Lark can feel her anywhere."

I glanced at Basil, who was standing by the window. He'd been quiet since we entered the apartment, which he was seeing for the first time since he'd left the city so many years ago. Looted and trashed by rebels searching for supplies, it bore little resemblance to the place where we grew up. I didn't have to warn him not to look outside; any twitch in the curtains might alert pixies or Enforcers to our position. I'd already put us all at risk during my headlong flight in pursuit of Eve; if I'd run into an enemy patrol, we could all have been on our way to the Institute's machines.

"Forget about Eve," I said, breaking into the debate between Kris and Dorian. "Even if we got her back, what could we do? I couldn't stop her from exploding before. It'll only be a matter of time before it happens again, and next time there won't be a Wall to absorb the blow."

Kris leaned forward, his gaze intent on my face. "Then you're just giving up?"

I wished I could. I wished I'd just stayed in Lethe, or even the Iron Wood. I wished— But I shook my head slowly, taking in a steadying breath. "No. But since we can't stop Eve, our only hope is to stop the Institute before she explodes again. We have to fix this city—we have to fix everything, or all of this will continue until we're dead."

Basil left the window, returning to the tiny circle of lantern light that was all we could risk. "How? Even you don't have that kind of power, Lark."

"No," I agreed. "But I think the answer lies inside the Institute."

I turned my gaze on Kris, who lifted his head to meet my eyes. His jaw clenched, a muscle in his cheek twitching as Basil and Dorian followed my gaze. "You know?"

I thought of Eve's memory, the one where Gloriette had let slip that it was the Institute who shattered this world all those years ago. I nodded, trying not to let Kris's confirmation hit me like the blow it was. Until now, I could believe Eve's memory was somehow faulty.

"Know what?" demanded Basil, glancing from me and Kris.

"Eve showed me in a memory that the architects have been hiding the truth from us," I said, looking up from Kris's stricken face. "They're the ones who caused this."

"This war?"

"No—they're the ones that caused the world to be what it is now. A century ago they decided to end the Renewable Wars by destroying the Renewables themselves. Only, their plan backfired, and it unleashed this hell. They're the ones who destroyed the world."

Basil sat back on his heels, staring silently at me. I couldn't be sure in the low light, but I thought his face had paled; I knew he was feeling as sick as I was. Despite everything the Institute had done to us, we'd both been raised to believe they were the saviors of this city—not its executioners.

Dorian, on the other hand, leaned forward, eyes glowing in the lantern light. "I knew it," he hissed. "I was right to send Eve here."

I stared at him. "You were *right?*" I could barely control my voice, the tremor in it vibrating through my skull. "Right to send a girl to be captured and tortured for years, turned into an insane monster, robbed of her freedom and her soul?"

Dorian swallowed and didn't answer me.

"Kris," I said, unable to look at Dorian any longer. "Eve told me that the founding architects used a device to shatter the world; that the architects today still have it. Why haven't they just reversed the damage already?"

"We've tried," Kris replied helplessly. "You have to understand, the architects who did this all died a hundred years ago. We don't have that technology anymore. But even if we did, we don't have access to the kind of power they had back then. All we had was Eve."

"And that's why they removed her from the power grid," I finished, glancing at Dorian. "To let her recharge, hoping she'd grown powerful enough to use with this device."

Kris shook his head. "I told them it would never work. When the original attempt to destroy the Renewables failed, it tore the fabric of the Resource apart. We're not dealing with the same laws of nature anymore; it's impossible."

Nix thrummed against my neck; it was being quiet during this meeting, but its presence was a comfort. Without Oren, it was the only thing keeping me from feeling utterly alone. I jerked my thoughts away from him with an effort. If I let myself think about him, about where he was, the pain he was in, his struggle to stay human—I'd fall apart.

"Don't talk to me about impossible," I said, remembering what the pixie had told me once. "The Institute did this. The answers are in there somewhere, and we've got two of the best minds the world has to offer." I glanced from Kris to Basil and back again.

Kris shifted uncomfortably. "And you want to—what? Walk up and knock on the Institute's gates and say 'Hey, we'd like to come in and root around in your ancient machinery'? They'd kill us."

"Maybe," I replied. "Maybe they're searching as hard as we are for answers. Regardless, I think we have to get inside. We find their records, figure out how they did this—and maybe we can find a way to put an end to it."

Basil was nodding slowly, his gaze distant and thoughtful. "There are sewer tunnels threading the ground beneath this entire city, including the Institute. Maybe we could get inside unnoticed that way."

I nodded, finding a bit of a smile for that—Basil was the one who showed me those tunnels. And even if we didn't exactly break into the Institute through them, it was doable. "That's how Eve got in, all those years ago when Dorian sent her."

"Those tunnels were sealed," protested Kris." The entrances were blocked off."

"With what—iron?" Dorian raised his eyebrows, a smile playing at the corners of his mouth. "Because that's no problem for Lark."

Kris paused, his gaze thoughtful. "True."

"They might be prepared for resistance fighters to try a break-in," I said, trying to think through my exhaustion. "They might even be prepared for me. But they're not prepared for Dorian. He's the first Renewable they've seen since Eve."

"I can serve as a distraction," said Dorian, reaching out to stab his finger at the Institute's front gates. "Let them throw their machines and their attention at me."

"And I still know those tunnels better than anyone in this city," said Basil. "I can get us in undetected."

"And Kris can lead us to the archives," I said, lifting my eyes from our map. "There has to be something in there from before the cataclysm. Something that can tell us how to fix this world."

I looked around the circle, at the faces upturned and lit by the lantern. There was something new there, animation on faces that had been nearly as weary and worn as my own. I felt something flicker in my own chest, a tiny flame. Hope.

CHAPTER 28

The tunnels had always been dark, which made it easier to forget that the world outside had changed irrevocably. This place had become a second home to me when I was younger. To be navigating the tunnels at my brother's side almost made me feel like I was a child again, before any of this had happened.

Almost.

We were stopped at a T intersection, the four of us huddled down against the wall, waiting for Nix to return from scouting. Between Dorian and me, we could handle any pixie attacks if necessary, but there was no telling what we'd find in the Institute. We might need our magic to reverse what the Institute had done. And though I could siphon some power from Dorian, it was all too easy to see Nina's comatose face, with me always.

A distant buzz echoed back to me, and I cast out carefully; just because we were expecting Nix didn't mean a lone pixie sentry couldn't find us instead. But I recognized the particular thrum of power in its center and nodded to the others. A few seconds later, Nix appeared from a corridor up ahead and swooped in to light upon my palm.

"*Nothing,*" it reported, its mechanical voice whisper-soft.

"A few sentries several tunnels over, but they don't appear to be coming this way."

I transferred Nix to my shoulder and led the way forward—keeping my own senses as sharp as I could. My stomach started to growl, and only a few minutes later Kris broke out the few rations we'd brought. I chewed on my stale cracker as we slunk forward.

Nix gave a light hum against my neck, reassurance that it was still not detecting anything ahead of us. I let my mind wander just a little, my thoughts returning—as always—to Eve. I should have known her immediate goal wasn't to flee the city. She claimed that vengeance played no part in her desire to put an end to everyone who wasn't a Renewable, but I'd felt her mind. I'd shared her torment, if only for a fraction of the time she'd lived it. There was a part of me, buried but no less potent, that wanted every last one of them to die. Whether it was coming from me or from the corner of my mind Eve occupied, it didn't matter.

Kris was right. We were linked. And I knew Eve wasn't going anywhere until she'd done what she'd set out to do. I thought of Caesar and the tender way she'd brushed his hair back from his face. He was a "normal," as Eve had called it—if she succeeded, he'd die too. I hoped she had enough humanity left to spare him until the end.

I paused at the next junction, searching the space around us with my thoughts, then turned right, following Basil's instructions. I'd taken no more than two steps when something black and huge leaped at me, knocking me backward, body rolling over on the concrete floor. The impact drove the breath out of me so completely that I couldn't even scream. My vision dazed, the light from Kris's lantern dancing wildly, I could hear snarls and the crack of someone else hitting the ground; I heard Nix take off from my shoulder with a scream of outrage, ready to defend me.

My eyes struggled to focus on the thing the others were fighting; a dark shadow, quick and nimble, everywhere at once. Recognition flared deep in my mind even as somewhere behind me, I felt Dorian gather his magic in for a blow.

With an eye-watering effort I forced my lungs to suck in air and croaked, "Stop! *Stop!* It's Oren."

The shadow thing danced back as Kris swung at it, momentum carrying the movement through despite my shout.

Dorian hesitated, and it was enough for me to drag myself onto my hands and knees and crawl forward.

The thing hovered just at the edge of the lantern light, breathing labored. I heard pacing footsteps, a groan that tore at my heart.

"Oren," I whispered, hoping the fight hadn't attracted the attention of the sentries Nix had sensed. "It is you, isn't it?" I couldn't sense him, couldn't identify the shadowy pit that I'd grown used to.

The pacing stopped, and I gestured to Kris to step forward. The light revealed Oren, the shadow swirling beneath his skin like inky water. He lifted his head, eyes dilating in the glow of the lantern while his irises deepened, shading slowly from white to blue.

"I'm sorry," he gasped. "I'm so sorry."

I dropped my pack and stumbled forward, arms going around him as he dropped. "It's okay. You didn't hurt me." I lifted my gaze to find the others staring. Kris still had one hand balled into a fist, and Basil and Dorian were poised to run at us. I shook my head, trying to warn them off, pulling Oren close.

"I thought if I lost myself down here in the tunnels, I wouldn't hurt anyone."

"You didn't," I whispered, thinking of the woman in the

reservoir. Had she been torn apart before her death or after? Did Oren kill her? Either way, there was no point in telling him. I tightened my arms. "Don't run away from me again. Please."

He lifted his head, and as I watched, the last traces of shadow vanished from his skin, sinking back down into the depths. "What am I?"

I swallowed. "I don't know."

He shuddered. "I can control it, mostly. You just startled me. But it's gone—it's gone now."

I reached up, one shaking hand brushing the hair back from his brow, letting me see his face more clearly. He looked like he hadn't slept in days, or eaten, for that matter. But as he gazed back at me I saw a little of that calm return, the calm that Olivia had taught him in Lethe. With that calm came control.

"Lark, what's going on?" Basil asked as Kris lifted the lantern higher, his face grim.

I hesitated, glancing at Oren. It wasn't my secret to tell. But he nodded at me, so I turned back to the others. "Oren is—was—a shadow person."

The reaction was electric; Dorian, recognizing him now as the boy he'd caged in the Iron Wood, flung his magic back up in a defensive pattern; Basil's face drained of its color. I kept speaking, hoping to forestall their hostility toward him. "In the past my magic always kept him human. But Eve did something to him. She said she burned the shadow away with her magic, but . . ."

"But it's still here." Oren's voice sounded a little stronger. I felt his arm tighten around me just a fraction. "And now I can only control it with focus. With concentration. Lark can't help me anymore."

Kris moved forward cautiously until he could crouch

down in front of Oren, lifting the lantern higher. "So it wasn't a cure."

I glanced at Oren, whose exhausted face bore the tale of the last few days, the internal and external struggle. But it also showed no sign of the shadow he'd banished—by himself. With no help from anyone else.

"I don't know what she did to him," I admitted. "But something's changed. I can't feel him anymore—I can't feel his shadow, and I can't feel his humanity. If I wasn't looking at him right now, I'd swear there was nothing here."

"Fascinating." Kris had left his caution behind and was peering more closely, inspecting Oren's face as if it were a circuit board he could coax to reveal its secrets. "I wonder . . ."

I waited, but he just crouched there, scanning Oren's features. "Kris. We don't have hours. What are you thinking?"

"I'm wondering if she somehow removed his magic altogether—not just drained him, but completely made him impervious. It'd explain why Lark can't sense him, why her magic doesn't affect him anymore. He exists outside of magic."

"Outside of magic?" Dorian sounded as confused as I was. "What does that mean?"

Kris shrugged. "It's not possible, theoretically. Everything is governed by the laws of magic. Physics, chemistry, life and death—it's all tied to magic. But Oren isn't anymore, according to Lark."

I felt Oren shift uneasily.

"Well, we don't have time to theorize any longer," I said, reaching for Oren's hand and helping him to his feet. "Let's go.

"And bring—that?" Dorian jerked his chin at Oren, fear and mistrust on his face.

"I know you think the shadows are monsters," I said wearily. "But the shadows are victims as much as we are. More, even. They're just people. And Oren's got it under control." I glanced at him, and he nodded, hand tightening around mine.

Dorian just stared at us, unbending. Even Basil looked uncertain, eyes flicking from my face to Oren's.

It was Kris who spoke up, surprising me. "Lark's right," he said softly, watching Oren. "At the very least, we could use him. None of us are all that useful in physical combat. And if magic doesn't affect him, then we might need him in there."

Dorian snorted. "Fine. But he walks in front of me."

Oren lifted an eyebrow but said nothing; still, he spoke a world in that one tiny gesture. I couldn't help but exhale a breath I hadn't known I was holding inside. He was still Oren. I squeezed his hand.

"Let's go."

CHAPTER 29

It took a little over two hours for us to reach the Institute via the tunnels; our route had to be circuitous to bypass collapsed tunnels and avoid sentries. But aside from the encounter with Oren, we got through without incident. Basil stopped beneath a round hatch in the ceiling, face upturned.

"This is it," he said, voice lowered.

Kris lifted the lantern, illuminating the hatch. There was something achingly familiar about it, but I'd never broken into the Institute before; there was no way I could have encountered this particular entrance before.

There was a ladder leading up to the hatch, and I climbed up to test the wheel-shaped locking mechanism. It didn't budge, and I peered closer. It was soldered closed, but when I reached out to test it, I realized it was lead—not iron.

"Can you break in?" whispered Dorian.

"Easily," I replied. But despite the lack of iron in sight, my senses stopped at the threshold of the Institute. "But I can't tell what's beyond it. It's shielded somehow. There could be architects right on the other side."

"The shield's a standard defense," Kris called in a hoarse whisper. "I thought maybe they'd run out of magic enough to power the shield, but clearly they haven't."

"This hatch should lead directly into the rotunda," Basil said.

"Then we're probably fine," Kris replied. "When I was being held, the architects had pulled back to only a small portion of the Institute in order to preserve power. There shouldn't be anyone in the rotunda."

There were enough "maybes" and "should bes" in there to make anyone balk, but we didn't have much choice. Something tugged at the back of my mind, even as I tried to push through the shields with my senses.

"Eve," I whispered, my voice echoing in the cavern.

"What about her?" Dorian's voice was hoarse.

"She came this way." My vision blurred, taken over by a distant memory, one I'd dreamed before I'd even come into the city. A memory of how Eve arrived in the city; how she infiltrated the Institute; how Gloriette had captured her.

"Then we know we can get inside this way. Maybe we can . . ."

Their voices faded into the background, a buzzing rising in my ears. Only Nix seemed to sense anything was wrong; it reached up and tugged on my earlobe.

"What is it?"

"She's here. Eve's in the Institute. That's where she's hiding." I blinked, looking down to find everyone staring at me.

"Are you sure?" asked Kris.

"Where else could she hide from me? She's using the Institute's own shields against them, and me."

"But why deliver herself into the hands of the people who held her captive?" demanded Dorian.

"She didn't." I closed my eyes, dread closing over me like frigid water. I'd said it myself: *What if we could use their device against them?* "She's right where she wants to be."

When I looked down again, the faces gathered around the ladder were sober, frightened. I should have kept what I knew to myself; my allies were few, now, and I couldn't afford for even one of them to lose hope. "This doesn't change anything," I said firmly. "We just need to find out how to use this device first. If we run into her, we just have to hope she's too focused on mass murder to pay attention to individuals."

"It seems illogical, under the circumstances, to hope that anyone's thoughts are preoccupied with mass murder." Nix's voice was dry; I could detect undercurrents of concern there nonetheless.

"Hush. Let me concentrate."

It was only the work of a few moments to slide an edge of magic through the lead sealing the entrance hatch. It was nothing like magicking iron, for which I was grateful. I couldn't afford to walk into the enemy's den already handicapped by exhaustion.

I gave the lock an experimental turn, and it budged half an inch. Oren climbed up on the ladder beside me, balancing on one foot while leaning into the wheel, adding his strength to mine. Bit by bit the lock turned with a screech of long-undisturbed metal.

If there were architects up there, they wouldn't miss that sound. Stealth was out the window, so Oren climbed up a few more rungs and leaned his shoulder into the door, banging against it until the whole thing popped free with a clang.

Oren climbed through and then reached down to offer me a hand, pulling me up after him. The tunnel opened up under the rotunda, exactly as Kris suggested, and as I remembered from Eve's dream. The hatch itself, when closed, formed the center of an ornate compass rose inlaid in tile and stone on the floor.

Overhead was the dome I remembered, stars forming complex constellations above us, moon and sun in separate tracks meant to move with the time of day. But unlike that first time, the dome was dark and still. The tracks didn't move, the stars were nearly invisible with no light to reflect. As Kris climbed up after us, the lantern light picked out a few of them, but it was a poor comparison to the splendor I'd seen when I was first brought here for harvesting.

Basil and Dorian followed, letting the hatch close quietly behind them. Kris's intel had proved correct; there were no architects around, but we had to keep our voices to a whisper. The rotunda may have been dark and empty, but it still echoed and amplified even the tiniest of sounds.

"The archives are this way," breathed Kris, nodding his head toward one of the many corridors leading off from the rotunda. "Maybe we won't need you for distraction after all, Dorian."

"Let's hurry," was Dorian's only reply. He'd been on edge, even more than the rest of us were, ever since we'd entered the tunnels. The problem with being our backup plan was that if we failed, there'd be no one to rescue him from the architects after he'd distracted them. He'd be stuck here and likely suffer the same fate as Eve, experimented upon and tortured.

We headed down the corridor marked *Museum and Archives*, making cautious progress. Nix, picking up on the tension in my body, kept making nervous little forays away from my shoulder and back, landing on the wall, the darkened light fixtures, even Kris's shoulder a couple of times.

The fear thickening the air only deepened when we reached the museum corridor that led toward the records room. The hall was lined on either side with mechanimals, along with stuffed creatures from beyond the Wall, many of which had gone extinct in the century since the cataclysm. Kris's lantern glinted off the bared teeth of the *Ursus arctos horribilis*—the huge bear I remembered, rearing up on its hind legs.

This place had been thrilling and a little frightening when I walked through it the first time, under full illumination and without realizing yet what lay at the heart of the Institute. Now it was nightmarish. The shadows gathered thickly behind each creature, the inconstancy of the lantern making my eyes pick up imagined movement everywhere. Some of the pedestals were empty, as though their occupants had come to life and slunk away, into the darkness, to wait for us.

More likely, the Institute had reactivated them to aid in the war against the rebels. Against me. I hurried past the empty spots, not willing to read their labels and find out what they were. I didn't want to know.

No one spoke until we passed the last case, containing a deactivated pixie settled upon a dark blue velvet background. Nix darted from my shoulder to land on the case, its tiny feet clinking against the glass as it turned this way and that, inspecting its ancient cousin.

I paused as soon as we were out of the museum, letting my breath out in a rush.

"That was horrific," murmured Dorian—I realized he had never seen it before.

Neither had Oren, and when I turned to look at him his face was as hard and as cold as granite. He'd no doubt hunted animals for food in his life spent surviving in the wilderness, but he never would have seen their pelts stuffed and put on display before. I reached out to touch his arm, which was rigid under my hand.

"Shh—do you hear something?" Kris tilted his head, brow furrowing and eyes sharp.

Oren lifted his head, setting aside his horror. "A whispering—crackling?"

I took a slow step forward, ears straining until I picked up the sound. It was like a sputtering flame, barely more than a whisper, but in the silence it rang like a shout. I kept moving, slowly, changing course whenever the sound grew fainter. I ended up alongside a wall, though when I pressed my ear to it the sound grew dimmer. It wasn't until I looked up that I realized what it was.

One of the Institute's speakers in their announcement system—the same one that had alerted them to my presence when I snuck in here the first time—had come to life.

"It's here," I whispered."

Kris came to my side, lips pressed together as he tipped his head back. "They're only maintaining the speakers in the part of the building where they are. The circuitry on these is degraded, it's interfering with the sound."

"Give me a boost," I told him, and then stepped up when he cupped his hands. With my ear close to the speaker I could make out individual words.

"... detected in ... Security ... alpha report to ... Museum."

I gasped, pushing back away from the wall abruptly enough that Kris staggered, half dropping me ungracefully back to the ground.

"They know we're here," I hissed. "That was a security announcement. I think they're sending guards here, now."

"Then I'm up." Dorian stood a few paces behind us, hands clasped behind his back. For a moment I remembered how he used to seem to me—thoughtful, wise, a leader well respected by his people. If he was afraid, he didn't show it.

"You don't have to do this," I blurted. "I'll go. I can handle them."

"Lark, we need you here." Kris stepped up behind me. "We may need your power to undo what the architects did."

"I'll be fine," Dorian assured me. "Eve survived them for

years. If they capture me, then so be it. Perhaps I need to understand what she went through."

I felt his magic flare like a beacon. "Make this worth it," he added before he took off at a jog back down the museum corridor. After a few seconds I could no longer feel his magic, the sensation absorbed by the dampening shield enclosing the Institute.

"Good luck," I whispered as he vanished into the darkness. Oren's arm brushed mine, his hand pushing aside a bit of my hair. His touch, strange though it felt without the shadow inside, was all the reassurance I needed, and the four of us that were left hurried for the archives.

CHAPTER 30

The records hall was as dark as the rest of the Institute, and the air was even thicker, dust assaulting my nose as soon as we stepped inside. Kris and Oren manhandled the heavy doors closed while Basil veered off, heading for an iron cabinet inset in the wall. I saw him pry it open, revealing a series of glass spirals, all set in rows. There were labels written beside each in an ancient, curling handwriting that I couldn't make out. A few of the spirals were fractured, the cracks turning them all opaque.

"Pixie," Basil called, prompting Nix to stick its head out through my hair. "Can you come help me? Some of these circuits are fried, but I think I can get around them."

Nix hesitated just long enough to make Basil turn around, exasperated, then launched itself from my shoulder to land upon one of the spirals.

Together they began moving the coils around, Nix's tiny, needlelike legs prying the broken ones loose while Basil replaced others. His tongue stuck out of the corner of his mouth as he concentrated, for an instant so painfully familiar, so like the brother I'd known as a child, that my throat closed. The cabinet was next to a row of lever switches and another box with a speaker on it like those that crackled at us in the museum.

Basil snapped the last circuit into place, then glanced at Kris, still by the door. "Try it now."

Kris reached for a lever the length of his hand inset beside the door and, leaning his shoulder into it, pushed it upward.

I felt the hum first; then, with a seeming effort, a few of the panels overhead flickered to life. Nix darted back toward my shoulder, performing a quick, almost perfunctory loop before landing, satisfied with itself.

The records hall was a cavernous space broken up by tables and shelves. At the end was the Archivist's desk, but unlike the first time I was here, it was empty. It had previously been occupied by an ancient, wispy-haired man. I wondered if he was holed up with the other architects—or if he was still alive at all.

The lights overhead continued to flicker, but it was enough illumination to navigate the area and scan the documents.

"Good work," I said, flashing Kris a smile. The expression felt strange, and I realized I hadn't really smiled much at all in days. "Any idea where the records we want might be?"

"I was always more interested in where our technology could go than where it had been," Kris replied apologetically, turning off his lantern and setting it aside. "Maybe we should split up. Dorian can't hold them off forever."

I nodded, and we fanned out through the stacks. Oren kept close to me as I headed for the section where I'd once found boxes of records pertaining to my brother, Basil, when I'd thought he'd disappeared forever. There had been one box with my name—now, as I scanned the top of the shelf, there were nine. Kris was right; what I'd done in the Iron Wood had rattled the architects. I wondered what wild theories and explanations the boxes contained, but there wasn't time to find out, not with Dorian at risk every moment.

My eyes raked the shelf. Many of the volumes on this shelf were crumbling with age, coated with dust. Old was good— old meant it might be from the time we were looking for. But as I scanned, my eyes fell on something that stood out, and I stared at it for a few moments before I realized what it was. There were tracks in the dust on a shelf at eye level; the record there was brighter than the others, though no newer. It had been read recently.

I reached out to pull down the thick portfolio, its spine so worn with age that its title was unreadable. I stepped back to move under one of the lights and backed into Oren, who jumped.

I shot him a wry smile. "You don't need to be my body-guard in here," I said. "Just start looking for something about the cataclysm, the ancient machinery, anything that might give us answers."

Oren shifted his weight from one foot to the other, always poised; that was the wilderness in him, making him prepared for anything. "I won't be of much help in here," he said quietly. "I'd rather stay close to you."

"We need as many—" But I stopped, my mind catching up with my mouth. The wilderness. Oren had grown up in the wild and spent most of his life alone, trying to survive. "You don't know how to read," I whispered.

Oren shrugged. If he was embarrassed, he didn't show it. "I remember my parents starting to teach me when I was very little. But then we were on the run, and we didn't have any time for reading. And then it was just me."

I shivered. My parents might be happy thinking I'm dead, but at least I knew they were safe. Oren talked about the death of his family as if it had happened to someone else.

When we get through this, I'll teach you. The words hovered, faint and warm, at the tip of my tongue. But there they stopped, fading away until all that was left was a sour taste. Because there probably wasn't going to be a *when we get through this.*

Oren gazed back at me, one corner of his mouth lifting a little bit in a smile. He reached out and brushed a finger against my cheek, dislodging some dust that had clung there during my search of the stacks. If he knew what I was thinking, he didn't speak about it either.

I cleared my throat, ducking my head to the volume. The cover of the portfolio crackled as I opened it, and Nix crawled curiously down my arm to peer at the pages. The title page was in Latin, the language of the architects; it was unsurprising, but disappointing. I knew only the tiniest bit of Latin, but I made out the word *magia*—magic, which I knew from the Institute's motto. I also saw the word *machina*, which I assumed was the Latin for "machine."

My pulse rising, I whispered, "I think this might be something. The title is talking about magic and machines, and it's old enough, certainly."

"*I should have been programmed with multilingual capabilities,*" complained Nix.

"In Kris's defense, it's not like I was going to stumble across much Latin as I fled across the wilderness, running from you."

Nix buzzed indignation but didn't argue with me.

I started turning pages, my eyes ready to pick out as many of the Latin words I could recognize, but I stopped, squinting. This wasn't a history—it was a collection of blueprints. Technical diagrams crawled over every page, spiderwebs of circuits and depictions of power flow that made my head spin. With this, I was as useless as Oren was—I might as well be illiterate.

But we had someone who could speak this language.

"Basil!" I hissed. He was only a few stacks over, and he

appeared around the end of the shelf with dust in his hair and a sour look on his face.

"This place is a mess," he complained, hurrying to my side. "What'd you find?"

"Can you make any sense of these? The writing's in Latin, but the diagrams . . ."

Basil took the portfolio from me, eyes sweeping across the page. "Design schematics," he murmured, turning the page and scanning the lines on the next.

"There must be a thousand different machines in there." Frustration coursed through my voice. It'd take hours to catalogue them all, and Dorian wouldn't last that long on his own. And we had no way of knowing if any of these machines were going to help us.

Basil didn't answer immediately, shifting the portfolio so that the flickering lights overhead illuminated the paper more fully. "I don't think so," he said slowly. "I think this is all a schematic for one machine. One very large, very complex machine."

The portfolio was easily four inches thick, and the pages were hair-thin; there were thousands of them. I stared at Basil. "How is that possible?"

"I don't know, but look." He indicated the edge of one page with his thumbnail. "That symbol there, it's repeated here. He flipped back several pages until he pointed out the symbol again, on the opposite side of the page. I think that means the pages are meant to join together there."

If it was a schematic for the device Eve mentioned, then it wouldn't be easy to hide. We had to know what we were looking for.

"Come on," said Basil, snapping the portfolio shut. "We need more space."

We headed for an area full of tables, no doubt meant for

research, though they stood dusty and empty now. We shoved the tables and chairs back against the stacks, clearing a space on the floor, and got to work. Kris abandoned his own search to help, and though Oren couldn't read, there was nothing wrong with his eyesight. Of all of us he was the quickest to match the patterns, lining up the pages like a giant puzzle. Even Nix helped, its unblinking crystal eyes scanning every page and committing them to memory.

I pulled another handful of pages from the portfolio and started handing them out, scanning for anything familiar. Basil was scanning the portion we'd assembled, barely more than a fraction of the whole thing, with a frown on his face.

"This thing would be massive, if I'm understanding it all correctly." He stabbed downward at a line with tick marks crisscrossing it. "If this scale is right, it'd be nearly as big as this entire building. Bigger, even; the Institute's not that tall."

"Does any of this look familiar to you, Kris?" I glanced at Kris, still wearing the grubby remains of his red architect's coat.

But Kris was shaking his head. "I've never seen this design before. But I was always in theory, research and development. Like I said, I wasn't studying historical machinery."

Basil squinted, leaning close to the page. "This goes way beyond me," he said slowly. "Lark, I'm good with machines, but I'm no architect. It'd take me days just to figure out one of these pages."

"Maybe this is a waste of time," said Kris, sighing. "They'd never be able to hide something this massive. Perhaps Eve was lying about it from the beginning; should we get out of here? Lark?"

But I was staring the sheet of paper in my hand, my voice lost. The nuances of the technical schematics were lost on me—I'd never been interested in circuitry and use of the

Resource like Basil. But I recognized what was sketched on the page before me. It showed a series of long glass filaments, straight as arrows. Next to them was a symbol and an explanation in Latin—again I saw the word *magia*—and then the filaments again, but this time they were curved, sinuous, curling as though beckoning me into the page.

I'd seen those undulating glass tendrils before. I saw them still in my dreams, my nightmares. It didn't even matter whether they were my dreams or Eve's—they drew the same nameless horror from us both.

"I think they did hide it," I whispered.

"What?"

"This is the design for the Machine."

"What machine?" asked Basil.

"*The* Machine," I said, lifting my gaze, trying to banish the memory of those glass shards and how they sought out my magic and Eve's. "The one they used to change me, the one they used to harvest the kids. The one they used to hold Eve all these years. It's all the same Machine."

"But Lark, it would have to be the size of a small city—"

"The Institute!" I blurted, willing them to see it. "The Institute *is* the Machine. It's hidden here, beneath our feet—it's been here all along. The machinery is threaded through the whole place, like underground rivers. Like veins."

For a long moment, all I could hear was the pounding of my heart as the others stared at me. If the Machine was the ancient device Eve was talking about, then we'd have to retrace my route down into the bowels of the Institute. We'd have to pass through the sections still occupied by architects, and we'd have to do it without Dorian's help. Eve had been here hours already; we couldn't afford to waste time sneaking.

I rose to my feet, my sudden movement stirring the pages and sending half of them skittering back into the stacks.

"Hey!" cried Basil, trying in vain to grab at the delicate sheets.

"Leave them," I snapped. "We don't need them anymore. Kris, can you make this intercom work?" I jabbed my finger at the speaker-box next to the light switches.

Kris rose slowly to his feet, glancing from me to the others. "What? I think so, but—"

"Do it. Hurry."

Kris pried the casing loose, exposing a number of wires and glass filaments turned flexible with magic. It took him only a few moments to shove the panel back into place. "It should work now, but you'll only hear anything if—"

"I don't need to hear anything." I moved past Kris, headed for the intercom, and pressed the switch to talk. Kris and Basil both leaped for me; even Nix screeched alarm.

"Gloriette!" I shouted into the intercom, holding up my hand to forestall my friends. "I know you're here. And I know you're looking for me."

"What are you doing?" hissed Basil, eyes wide with alarm. Only Oren, strangely enough, seemed unperturbed; when I met his eye he gave me a small, grim smile. *I trust you.*

There was no reply from the intercom, so I pressed the switch again. "Well, I'm here. I'm in the archives. And I know about your Machine." I could hear my own voice echoing from far away, down the empty corridors, through the abandoned rotunda and the dark, dusty museum.

"This is not a good plan," Nix whispered in my ear, its voice jangling with perturbation. *"We must run, now."*

I swallowed hard and leaned in toward the speaker. "Come find me."

CHAPTER 31

"Have you lost your mind?" Kris exclaimed, trying without much success to keep his voice down. "We have to go *now*." He reached for my arm, clearly intending to drag me bodily from the room if need be.

Oren stepped in, putting himself between Kris and me. "All this way, you claim to trust her, and now you think she's failed you?"

"We have to stop hiding," I said quietly, my voice carrying with it the eerie sense of calm I felt, waiting for the Institute's forces to organize and find us. "It could take us weeks to figure out the Machine from those schematics, and we don't have that kind of time. Eve is here, somewhere, and she's stronger than I am. Gloriette will come, and we'll make her bring us to the Machine."

"If she doesn't just take us to the nearest cell," Kris hissed. "And that's if we're lucky. Or maybe you forgot, these people already tried to kill me once."

I looked up, meeting his eyes; the fear there was bright and hot, pleading. "You can run," I said softly. "I won't think less of you, Kris. They're after me—they won't stop you if you try to leave. I choose to believe that you were right all along;

that the Institute is only trying to find a way to save this city, just as we are. I have to believe it."

Kris swore, turning away to pace, though he made no movement toward the exit. Basil was quieter but didn't look any more pleased than Kris, his expression grim. Oren stood just beside me, and when I glanced at him, he was as collected as ever; but then, he'd learned to control that wildness in his nature. It didn't mean he was any less prepared to fight.

I lifted my hand to my shoulder, and Nix crawled out from under my hair in order to bump its metallic head against my knuckle. "What about you?" I whispered. "Not too late for you to fly away."

Nix gave a tiny sniff. *"I dislike extended effort,"* it said. *"I'll remain here for now."*

I grinned, but before I could reply, the door leading from the archives shifted, clanged, and then swung open.

I turned, the noise jolting me from my calm; I expected to see a dozen armed Enforcers and a dozen more architects standing there, waiting to arrest me. But instead my eyes found just one architect. Gloriette.

"Well, gosling," she said slowly, her eyes sweeping from me to my friends, lingering on Basil with some surprise. "That was unexpected."

I'd forgotten the effect her voice had on me. Unprepared, the sweep of hatred through my body left me unbalanced. "Hello, Administrator," I said through gritted teeth. There was only one of her, and yet she stood there like she had an army at her back. There had to be some trick, some reason she felt sure we couldn't overpower her. "No army this time?"

"It seemed wise not to bring machines you could harvest." She'd lost weight since we faced each other in the Iron Wood—I'd been too distraught to notice when she'd been standing over Kris's body. The rebels weren't the only ones going hungry. "Besides, how could I respond with violence to such a polite invitation?"

"We expected Enforcers," Kris broke in. "Not smart, coming alone."

"You can't touch me," she replied, her black eyes glittering. I couldn't read her expression, but I thought I saw a flinch, a tiny chink in the drawling façade. There was fear there, deeply hidden; but very much alive. "Didn't I kill you?

"You're unarmed," Kris replied, ignoring her barb, though I could see it cost him. "There's no one else here, and there are four of us."

"*Five,*" spat Nix, its mechanisms trembling.

"And your friend down below?" asked Gloriette, raising an eyebrow. "What happens to him if something happens to me?"

"You caught Dorian." Oren's voice was low, but tense.

"Did you really think one Renewable would get the better of all my architects?"

"We've got Lark," replied Kris, tension singing through his voice. "You want to try your luck against her?"

"Stop it," I broke in sharply. "She came alone. It's a show of good faith."

Gloriette's eyes slid back toward me, hesitating for an instant before her mouth widened into that saccharine smile. Everything in me wanted to leap at her, to tear at her face and eyes, to throttle her with the chain she wore around her neck. She'd ruined my life, turned me into a monster, destroyed my family beyond repair. I wanted to rip away the magic beating in her heart, and see it in her eyes the moment she realized what had happened.

There was no good faith there. But even a lie could get me where I needed to go.

"Indeed," Gloriette replied. "I didn't come here to kill you or arrest you. Your Renewable friend attacked *us*." Though her words were directed at the others, her eyes were on me. "I came to ask for your help."

Her words were met with a thick silence, until Basil lurched to his feet, striding forward until he stood at my side. "Why the hell would we help *you?*" he spat. "You betrayed Lark—you betrayed me. You hid the truth from all of us, you made us think the Renewables destroyed the world, when it was *you.*"

"It was our ancestors," snapped Gloriette. "My parents weren't even born when the cataclysm occurred."

"But you *lied* to us." Basil's hands curled into fists. "Everyone in this city thinks that the world was shattered during the Renewable wars. But you've been the enemy all along."

Gloriette's face was hard, her eyes narrowed under her sharp brows. "If this city falls, we fall too, Mr. Ainsley. What good would it do if every citizen knew the truth? How would that change our circumstances?"

"She's right," I said quietly, cutting through the rising swell of angry voices. I didn't bother to hide the dislike in my voice; there were no illusions here, no pretense at friendship.

When Gloriette turned back to me, I could see the hatred there in her gaze, reflected at me as in a mirror. Her eyebrows lifted in a show of surprise. "And here I thought I'd have to fend you off with a stick. You used to be such a little savage."

"I used to be a lot of things," I replied softly. "Before you happened."

Gloriette made a derisive sound in her throat, but her gaze slid away from mine as though she no longer wished to look at me. She looked instead at the partially assembled diagram at our feet. "I see you already know about the Machine."

"And so does Eve."

That shattered Gloriette's façade, her eyes widening. "Eve— Eve's here?"

"And she's not pleased," said Kris, a little of that dry humor underpinning the tension in his voice.

Gloriette's fear shifted, her gaze falling on me. "If you'd just done what you were programmed to do, we'd have brought more Renewables in, and none of this would be happening."

"Torturing people in order to power a city is not a sustainable situation," I replied through gritted teeth.

"And if we'd brought the entire population of the Iron Wood into our city? With that much magic, it wouldn't be torture. It'd be an hour or two of discomfort every few weeks. And there's no argument you can make against that."

I glanced at Basil; I couldn't help it. Because that's exactly what we'd done to save Lethe, bringing the Renewables there to volunteer to have their magic siphoned off to run the city.

Gloriette turned away, pacing back toward the shelves, her eyes on the sputtering lights overhead. "It's not worth fighting about now; the Renewables are gone, except for that one we've got in the chamber down below. That option is gone."

"Eve told me that the original architects used the Machine, and that's what tore the Resource apart." I tried to keep my tone even. "Let us try to reverse it."

"Reversing it is impossible," Gloriette snapped. "Don't you think we tried that?"

"Then why come to me asking for help?" It was becoming harder and harder not to let the fury win. Talking in circles was making my jaw ache with tension.

"We can't reverse the process—but with Eve's power, or with yours, we can try to finish what they started."

"Finish—" My voice broke and I stopped, staring at her in confusion. "I don't understand. The founders were trying to destroy all Renewables. Why would I ever help you do that?"

Gloriette's head dropped for an instant before she turned back, hands clasped in front of her. "They weren't trying to destroy the Renewables, you stupid girl. You think everything's so easy, that morals are black and white, that some actions are good and the rest are bad. You think we're monsters."

"You are," I whispered, feeling the shadow inside me stir in response to my anger. "Desperation has made us all into monsters."

"We're the reason you're alive today," Gloriette replied, her voice shaking with effort—effort to speak calmly, I assumed. This time, when I met her gaze, I saw the loathing there. She hated me as much as I hated her. "We're the reason you were even born——the reason everyone in this city has a home."

"Pardon me if I don't fall on my knees to thank you." I felt Nix buzzing against my neck, the comforting weight of its body lending me a little strength.

Gloriette shook her head. "It's easy to preach moral superiority when you aren't the one who has to come up with an alternate plan." She gazed at me with her sunken eyes, glittering black in the sagging flesh on her face. "It's easy to be good."

"Poor you," I said, coldly, holding onto that anger. It was all too easy to let those words stab into me, echoing the same thoughts that had been following me ever since I fled the Iron Wood. Because it was easier. When there was nothing riding on it but my own beliefs, it was easy to call the architects monsters. But had I ever come up with another way to save my people? I cleared my throat. "You still haven't told me why I'm going to help you commit genocide against the Renewables."

"It was never going to kill the Renewables," said Gloriette briskly, shrugging off that loathing for the time being. "Well, it might have killed a few, the very old and the very young, those without defenses. But it wasn't designed to kill them, it was designed to——"

"Harvest them," I interrupted, staring. "The Machine. The part that you use to harvest children, it's the same principle."

Gloriette nodded. "Originally the Machine was designed to operate on a global scale. It's tied into the fabric of the Resource itself. The Machine was supposed to remove the power from those too selfish not to abuse it and place it in the hands of those who'd act responsibly and judiciously."

"The founding architects."

"Indeed. But it failed partway through the procedure. Instead of gathering the fabric of the Resource, the Machine fractured it, stripping the land and leaving it as it is now."

"And you think completing the process will heal the land and place the power back in your hands, where you think it should be."

Gloriette hesitated. "We don't know what it'll do, but that's our hope, yes."

"So why not just do it? Why do you need me?"

"We don't know how it works."

I stopped short, blinking. "What do you mean, you don't know?"

"The technology is over a hundred years old. The people who built it and operated it are long dead. We've held onto a few things—the ability to harvest individuals, for one. And we've been able to keep the Wall running, until now. And we figured out how install Eve."

Install, like she was no more than a component in a machine. Which, from their perspective, she was.

"Miss Ainsley," said Gloriette, her voice sharpening a little. "We didn't run all those tests on you all those months ago for fun. We wanted to know why only you, and your brother, survived the process. Being stripped, then refilled, and stripped again. Because you're the key. You and Basil, and

Caesar too. Some twist of genetics, some mutation just now coming to light generations after the cataclysm. The world has been stripped of magic, and we're trying to put it back."

"Just like you did to us." My head spun as I glanced at Basil beside me, who was staring grim-faced at the red-coated architect in front of us.

"Come with me," Gloriette said quietly. "You want to get to the Machine? I'll take you there myself."

My mouth tasted like ashes. I'd expected to confront Gloriette and force her to take us to the Machine; I'd expected her to fight me every step of the way. The mere thought of working *with* Gloriette, the figure who dominated my nightmares, who had planted this darkness inside me—it made my eyes burn, my thoughts scream protest. But isn't this what I'd wanted? To talk to the Institute, not to fight them?

"Give me a moment," I said, my voice emerging with no more human inflection than Nix's. Empty, wrung dry. "Let me talk to my friends."

Gloriette hesitated, her eyes flickering from me to Kris and Oren. Then she nodded and turned away. I watched her as she walked back toward the door and then stopped there, waiting. Her eyes were on the metal panel containing the glass fuses, which Basil hadn't bothered to close.

"You can't possibly be thinking of doing this," Oren broke in first, agitation drawing a few inky filaments of shadow to his cheeks, like a colorless flush. "After everything they've done to you, how can you trust them?"

"I'm inclined to agree," Kris said slowly, eyes downcast. His mouth drooped, making him look older; almost as tired as I felt. "Gloriette is a manipulator, you know that. There's a reason she came alone, even though you have every reason to want her dead."

I glanced at Basil, who was still silent. For just a moment,

I wanted my big brother back. I wanted him to make the decision and tell me what to do. I wanted him to hug me and whisper, *Don't panic.* Instead he met my eyes for a long moment without speaking. Then he just lifted one shoulder in a half shrug. "I trust you," he said simply. "You haven't led us wrong yet. This is your call."

I let my breath out, the air heavy in my lungs. Two votes against, one abstention. I glanced down at my shoulder, craning my neck. "What about you?"

"I believe she is offering to take us to the heart of the Machine that caused all of this," said Nix, its voice so quiet I wasn't sure the others could hear it. *"Whether we do as she asks or not, we will be where we wish to go."*

I glanced at Kris, who was watching Nix on my shoulder with a frown. When he saw me looking, he sighed. "Sometimes I wish I hadn't programmed it to think for itself."

I grinned, taking that moment to breathe again fully for the first time since the Administrator had walked into the archives. Straightening, I raised my voice. "All right, Gloriette. Take us down."

CHAPTER 32

The path Gloriette took mirrored the one I'd used when I was wandering the Institute, half lost, before my harvest. If she was doing it on purpose to set my mind at ease, it wasn't working. The memories of that day were screaming through my mind, calling alarm and danger, warning me away. It was discovering Eve at the Machine's heart that sent me fleeing for the Iron Wood. Maybe if I'd never come here, I'd be home now, with my parents, living a blissfully dull life.

At first the corridors were dark, still part of the abandoned section of the Institute. We had only Kris's lantern for light, making me wonder if Gloriette had come to find us in the dark. The corridor was narrow enough that we walked single file, which felt eerily as though we were marching to our own executions. Nix stirred now and then, whispering remarks in my ear to remind me I wasn't alone, even though I couldn't see my friends behind me.

Then Gloriette opened a door at the end of the corridor, and light flooded in. These lights were more stable than the ones we'd hijacked for the records hall, though even they had a telltale jolt every now and then. Gloriette paused, eyeing Kris.

"You can leave that here," she informed him.

Kris didn't reply; though he turned the lantern off, he didn't set it down, clutching it stubbornly. I didn't blame him. If Gloriette was trying to play us, at least we wouldn't be left in darkness.

When we started moving again, I recognized the corridor. It was a long, slow spiral, the barely perceptible curve playing tricks on my eyes. Though I hadn't known it at the time, Eve had led me down this very hall, using the lights to goad me farther and farther. This time there was nothing to guide me but Gloriette's form ahead of me.

We'd gotten about halfway down when something tickled at my mind, barely more than a whisper against my thoughts. I paused, causing Oren to stumble straight into me, though he caught himself an instant later. Gloriette hadn't stopped, and no one else seemed to notice what I was feeling, not even Basil. It couldn't be magic, not with the dampening field that shielded the Institute from my senses. I started moving again, but I couldn't shake the feeling—like there were cobwebs inside my mind.

The feeling grew stronger as we descended, until my heart was pounding with it. Flares of sensation in my mind, flashes of light across my vision and whispers in my ears. Nix sensed my tension, if not what was causing it, and pressed close against my neck, mechanisms whirring and ready for quick action.

We were a few yards from the door at the end of the spiral when I stopped, mind spinning. The dampening field made it hard to concentrate, but—

"It's Eve," I gasped, staggering sideways until I hit the wall for support.

"What?" Kris skidded to a halt next to me.

"She's in there. She's—" But I couldn't describe what she

was doing. Flares of magic lanced at my bones. Eve was losing control.

Gloriette was staring at me. "She's inside the Machine?" As I watched, her face drained of color.

I dragged myself upright again and headed for the end of the corridor at a run. The door flew open when I collided with it, and I spilled out onto a catwalk.

Though I'd seen this place a thousand times in my nightmares, nothing prepared me for coming face-to-face with the reality again. The doorway opened into a cavern vast enough that it could have held several reservoirs, machinery and circuits and gears lining every inch of the curving walls. Catwalks crisscrossed the space in every direction. The glass wires dripping from the ceiling no longer held the glowing Renewable, but instead writhed as if in response to a sentient mind; sinuous, intent.

Eve was at the Machine's heart, shining like a miniature sun. Dozens of architects ran this way and that, some heading toward her and others running away. As I watched, a cluster of glass wires lashed out and knocked one of the fleeing architects over the edge of the catwalk. For an instant, Eve's glow lit his face so clearly I could see it from across the cavern as he reached futilely for the railing above him. His screams echoed in the spherical Machine long after he'd hit the bottom three hundred feet below.

"We're paying for our sins." I don't know how I heard Gloriette's whisper over the echoing shouts and screams in the heart of the Machine, but when I turned to look at her she was clutching at the railing as though it was all that kept her from falling to her death.

"Stay here!" I screamed, glancing from her to the others. I knew they wouldn't listen, but maybe they'd hesitate and buy me a little time.

"*She'll kill you!*" screamed Nix, clutching at my collar, refusing to stay. The pixie always knew what I was going to do a second before I did it.

"Probably," I panted. "But maybe I can stop her first."

I scrambled away, breaking into a sprint. My feet pounding against the metal sent aching shockwaves up my legs, the clanging of my footsteps rising over the screams.

"Eve!" I shouted when I was close enough for my voice to carry. "Eve, you told me you didn't want revenge!"

She was glowing so brightly that she was encased in a ball of light, too blinding for me to make out her features. But the magic didn't so much as flicker at the sound of my voice, as though she couldn't even hear me.

"Don't let them make you into this!" I drew breath to speak again, but a glass tendril swung my way and I had to throw myself to the catwalk to avoid being brushed into the chasm like a pesky insect.

I craned my neck, eyes watering as I tried to look through the glare of her light. Beyond her, on a catwalk slightly below mine, was a cluster of architects and a man on his knees. He had a hood over his face, but I knew by the bands of iron locked around his arms and feet who it must be: Dorian.

I'd have to run past Eve's position to get to him, but I knew her magic would destroy me before I ever reached her. I ran to the edge of the catwalk, grasping the railing and leaning out as far as I could. I tried to gauge the distance to the next bridge below me, shifting back a few paces until I was lined up.

"*Lark, no.*" Nix launched itself from my shoulder to hover in front of my face. "*Self-preservation must come first.*"

"Not this time," I gasped. "Programming only takes you so far, Nix. There are things more important than survival."

I lifted my eyes again and then climbed over the edge of

the railing. I tried to ignore the way the metal shook and shuddered under the stress of Eve's magic lashing out at the architects trying in vain to subdue her. Hands shaking, I lowered myself, glancing down again to judge the amount of swing I'd need; then immediately wished I hadn't looked.

I heard a shout that rang out above the others, and when I looked up I saw Oren sprinting my way. I couldn't let him reach me, or he'd stop me, and there was no way I could explain in words why I was so certain that Dorian's presence would reach Eve in a way mine never could. My gaze met Oren's for a brief second, a moment in which his eyes widened, the shadow crowding in around his features in response to his desperation to reach me.

Hold on, I willed at him. And then let go.

I swung my body in the direction of the next catwalk down, expecting to feel a moment of calm, of weightlessness. Instead everything happened at once, in a rush of panic and sour-tasting adrenaline. A passing tendril caught my shoulder, knocking me back; Nix's voice screamed alarm as it whizzed past me, too small to help redirect my fall; Oren's face appeared over the edge of the walkway, too late to stop me, helpless eyes meeting mine.

I wasn't going to make it. The tendril had knocked me too far away. The realization hit me in the same moment that I saw Oren's face, sudden and final.

Then a second tendril came at me, colliding with my back so hard my head snapped back; then another, whipping past and redirecting my course. The catwalk came up on me so fast I barely had time to reach out; the railing caught me under the arms, and for a moment triumph flooded through me. Then pain seared through my arms and up into my chest, and my nerveless arms let go.

This time a scream half erupted from my throat; then a

strong hand wrapped around my forearm. For a second I was dangling from this savior's grasp, until he swung me back toward the catwalk and I could hook a foot over the edge and crawl through the railing to collapse, shaking, on the metal grid.

I wanted to curl into a ball and sob there, but I didn't have time. I lifted my head, my gaze spinning with the pain of my bruised ribs and arms.

"You're mad." Caesar's rough face, even more haggard than I remembered, swam into focus a few inches from mine.

"Thank you," I choked, my voice hoarse from the scream that tore free. Nix caught up to me and flew at my chest so hard I gasped from the impact. The pixie crawled up the front of my shirt, vibrating with wordless fury—and relief, I hoped.

Caesar was still holding onto my wrist, and after a moment his other hand came to enclose mine in both of his. "Little sister," he whispered, broken. "I'm sorry. They were talking about turning her in. I had to protect her. She asked me to bring her here—I had to take her away."

I wanted to scream at him. But I scanned his features, the way his gaze met mine, defiant still behind the shattered façade.

"I know," I replied, raising the hands clasped around mine to press my cheek against them. "Will you help me stop her?"

Caesar nodded and helped me get to my feet. His limp had grown worse, but he supported his weight on one hand on the railings. We headed for the cluster of architects around Dorian.

"The Renewable they've captured," I explained. "She knew him, before she came here. I think—" I hesitated, glancing sideways at my oldest brother. "I think they were in love."

Caesar's face barely changed, registering only a flicker. Only his eyes betrayed him, closing for a long moment before

284

he stumbled, catching himself on the railing. "I couldn't reach her," he said quietly. "This man is worth a try."

One of the architects saw us and raised the alarm; though I only recognized one of them from my time there, a younger woman with dark hair like mine, they all knew me.

"I'm trying to help," I snapped, raising my voice in an effort to be heard over the battle raging above and around us. "Your prisoner. We need him." I saw the hooded man lift his head, turning blindly toward the sound of my voice.

"Absolutely not," shrieked one of Dorian's keepers, the shrill note of hysteria making my head ache. "He's our only hope of stopping her."

"That may be true," I agreed, gritting my teeth. "But you don't know Eve like I do. Give him to me, and I'll stop her."

The man hesitated, glancing at the young woman I recognized. I couldn't place her name, but I knew where I'd seen her before—she was the guide I'd escaped from the first time I stepped through the Institute's doors. But she had no answers for him either.

"Give him to me," I said, lowering my voice a little, willing them to believe me, "and he's not your responsibility anymore. You don't have to be a part of this."

The man holding Dorian's arm gazed upward, in time to see a blinding flash of magic ignite the air, prompting a chorus of screams from the architects trying to fight—or escape—Eve. His eyes snapped back down to meet mine, and after only a split second longer, he shoved his prisoner at me. He said nothing, only grabbed the girl's arm and tugged her back down the catwalk until they could break into a run for the exit.

CHAPTER 33

Caesar helped steady Dorian as he stumbled forward, and I stood on my toes to pull the hood off. I braced myself for blood and bruises, the signs of a fight, but his condition was far better than I expected. His eyes were clouded, though, and he stared around wildly, unseeing. When I laid my hand against his cheek to summon his gaze back to us, I could feel the currents of magic inside him, wavering and sluggish. He'd spent himself fighting them, to buy us more time.

"Dorian," I hissed, trying to get him to focus on my face. "We need you."

"Lark," he groaned, squeezing his eyes shut. "What's happening? I can't feel anything."

"They've got you in iron bonds," I replied, dropping to my knees to inspect the manacles around his wrists. They were fused solid, and with Eve's magic flying in every direction, I couldn't hope to gather enough focus to break through it with my own power. "I don't think I can free you."

"Then I'm useless to you," he protested, leaning heavily against the rail. "Just leave me here."

"Like hell," I snapped. "Dorian, Eve has lost her mind. She won't listen to Caesar, and she won't listen to me."

Dorian's eyes rolled over to Caesar's face and widened a little. "You're the other brother," he breathed. "The one who took Eve."

Caesar's one good eye narrowed. "Yes."

Dorian pulled himself a little more upright. "If that," and he jerked his chin upward to indicate the blinding energy encasing Eve above us, "isn't Eve anymore, what do you think I could possibly do?"

"I think she saved my life," I said, trying to catch my breath. "When I jumped for this catwalk I wasn't going to make it. The glass saved me, and she's controlling the glass."

Dorian and Caesar both stared at me with expressions so similar it would've been funny, if they hadn't both been so grief-stricken. "I don't understand," said Caesar, brows furrowed.

"Some piece of Eve is still in there. And if there's a part of her that doesn't want me to die, there has to be a part of her that doesn't want anyone to die." I nodded at Dorian "She loved you, before all of this. I've had her memories in my head; I've felt it."

"I thought she died long ago. I made my peace with that, with the guilt." Dorian swallowed hard, the lines around his eyes deepening as he tried to pull himself together. "The Eve I knew would never do this."

"That's why I think you can stop her. She claims not to remember you, but I've seen her memories. I know you're still inside her. I can protect you long enough to get close to her."

"And if I can't stop her?"

"All I need is a second. If you can distract her, I might be able to interrupt her trance."

Dorian hesitated, watching me. I could see Eve's light reflected in his eyes, flashing and exploding like stars. Then he nodded.

I turned back toward Eve. She was one level above us, on the central platform that housed the very heart of the Machine. Ladders led up to it in several places, forcing Dorian to climb precariously with his hands bound in front of him. More than once Caesar, climbing behind him, had to stabilize him on the ladder. My brother's face was like iron, lips pressed into a line. I knew how much it killed him that he couldn't reach Eve.

I reached the top of the ladder and dragged myself over the edge, staggering in the sudden onslaught of light. Nix, its legs twined in my hair to hold on, gave a tiny metallic shriek of protest as a shockwave from a tiny explosion of magic knocked me backward.

I gathered my wits and my strength, throwing up as sturdy a shield as I could with my own magic. My best efforts were no match even for Eve's offhand blasts; if the architects thought I was powerful in the Iron Wood, Eve made me look like a child. Still, I only had to hold out long enough to get Dorian inside Eve's cocoon of magic.

Dorian stumbled, hobbled and blinded by the iron bindings, forcing Caesar to keep him upright. I couldn't afford to glance over at them, but out of my peripheral vision I saw another man catch up to them and sling an arm under Dorian's other shoulder.

Basil. He and Oren had caught up to me, probably via a less insane route than the one I'd taken. Basil was wearing his modified Prometheus glove, and as a glass tendril came whistling out of the chasm at us, he planted his hand firmly against Dorian's chest. I felt him wrench a torrent of magic free, enough to lash out at the tendril and shatter it. Glittering shards fell in a cascade down, down into the darkness.

Dorian might not be able to use his own power, too crippled by the iron manacles, but there was nothing stopping Basil from using it.

Caesar faltered, his eyes falling on his little brother for the first time since he'd crossed the Wall, all those years ago. Basil looked back, his expression grim—there was no time for reunions, no time to compare betrayals or levy grief. Basil nodded at him, and Caesar nodded back.

We pressed on, sweat beginning to bead on my forehead and roll down my temples and the back of my neck. Eve's magic was like a physical force pressing back at us, so that we had to brace ourselves and walk as if into gale-force headwinds. Though most of it parted around my shield and flew past us in streamers of white-gold light, occasionally a thread sliced through it. I only noticed my face was gashed when Nix stretched up to press its feet against the wound, holding it closed and trying to stop the bleeding.

I tried to take another step and found myself sliding backward. I felt Oren's arm wrap around my waist, lending his strength to mine. We made it a few more paces before even his strength gave out, and we lurched to the side to grab onto the railing.

"This is as far as I can get us," I screamed over my shoulder, as Basil braced one leg against the railing and Caesar set his shoulder against Dorian's to prop the faltering Renewable up.

On the far approach to the platform my streaming eyes made out a familiar form wearing a coat much more faded and torn than the ones the other red-clad architects wore. Kris was trying to warn the Institute's forces away. I couldn't be sure if they were listening to him, but if his attempt stopped even a few of them from renewing the attack on Eve, it might help us reach her.

"Dorian," I shouted, my voice breaking with exhaustion and desperation. "Talk to her."

For a long moment the Renewable said nothing, his face

illuminated in flashes and sweeps of light, his eyes wide and staring. "Eve," he said, his weary voice barely carrying as far as my own ears. Caesar gave him a rough shake and bent close to whisper something harshly in his ear. I couldn't hear the words, but Dorian lifted his head and nodded.

"Eve!" he called, more loudly this time. "Can you hear me? It's me. It's Dorian. Do you remember me?"

There was no change, no sign that Eve could hear any of us inside the sphere of magic encasing her.

Dorian leaned to the side, grabbing onto the railing with his bound hands. "I never meant for you to do this. Any of this. I had so many plans for us when you got back from this mission." His head dropped, voice roughening. "I never should have sent you. I was arrogant and young and too obsessed with knowing the truth about the cataclysm."

Pain seared along my eyes and my spine, the effort calling my shadow up until it screamed at me to give up my foolish attempt to spare Eve and just let her magic take me. It'd be so easy to let it use her power against her, to let it take over; but I couldn't. Eve's magic and her madness were one and the same, too hot and too raw to control. If I let Eve's magic in, it would sear my soul.

My shield faltered, and a lash of magic slid through and slammed into Oren's shoulder. He grunted but didn't let go of the railing; his arm tightened around my waist as I groaned, trying to shore up my defense. I had only a split second to spare to glance at Oren to see that he was all right. The shadow had returned in him, as well; his eyes were white, reflecting Eve's glow like mirrors, and the darkness flickered through the veins of his face. His grip tightened on the railing. He was using the shadow for strength; for the first time, it wasn't using him.

"After you left," Dorian went on, his head still down, as

though looking at the singularity of magic was too painful, "I made our home safe. We had a life there; we were all safe. I wanted to come for you, to see if you were still alive. But if I left, who would watch over the Iron Wood? I thought you were gone. I thought I'd never see you again. Never hear your voice again."

Was that a flicker in Eve's cocoon? I wiped my eyes against my sleeve and squinted. There it came again, and the tendrils whipping around us slowed. Dorian didn't seem to notice, his every effort fixed on clinging to the railing.

"I'm so sorry, Eve. Please forgive me. Please. Remember me, and come home."

The air went out of the room in an instant, the void bringing with it a silence that made my skull ache. The glass wires fell limp, and for an instant the magic wrapped around Eve froze, a delicate tracery of shimmering light in branching, fractal patterns, no two alike.

Then the shell exploded.

Magic flew outward, a shockwave that vaporized the glass wires and sent us flying. I hit the railing and rolled down the walkway, stunned and aching. I tried to lift myself up on my arms, only to find that they were numb and I could barely raise my head. Oren had been half knocked from the platform, but he had a grip on the railing. Caesar was dragging Basil back over the rail, where he'd nearly flown off; Dorian was on his hands and knees, head down. I couldn't see Kris or the other architects.

Instead all I saw was a light moving toward us; slow, light steps that nevertheless made the metal beneath us quiver and shift like waves on the sea.

"I know you," she whispered, her gaze passing through him.

Dorian nodded, lifting his head. Tearstains cut long

swaths down the ragged expanse of his face. His lips twisted as he tried to speak and failed.

Eve stopped a few paces away from him. "You beg for my forgiveness. You ask for yourself, to feed your guilt. Your demands are selfish."

"Eve," gasped Dorian, sinking back onto his heels as he looked up at her. "Let me take you home."

"That place is not my home." Her white eyes burned, making my own water. "My home is an aspen grove by the sea."

"Then we can go there," Dorian said, his voice rising in desperation. "Just you and I."

"I'm not yours anymore," Eve said quietly. Her eyes went from Dorian to Caesar, who was leaning against the railing, his bad leg bent with pain. He lifted his head but said nothing, just watching the woman standing before them.

"Eve." I pulled myself upright with an effort, ignoring the way my arms quivered. "We have a chance to finish this."

Her gaze flicked toward me, and I resisted the urge to flinch away. Gone was the gentle, subtle creeping attraction that she'd used so well among the resistance; in its place was fire. "If you want this finished, then allow me to continue. These are your enemies too."

She gestured at the far edge of the platform, where I could see a few of the architects there starting to pick themselves up. My heart leaped when I saw Kris among them, his gaze meeting mine.

"This is the Machine," I said, ignoring her offer to destroy my enemies. There was no point in arguing that they weren't; not even I believed that anymore. "The device, the one they used to shatter the world."

"To try to kill us," she hissed, moving back toward the central mechanisms and the architects beyond.

"No. It was designed to drain the Renewables of their

magic, not kill them. Eve, we can use it to finish what they started."

She paused, glancing back at me, her eyes shadowed.

I pressed on. "Between your power and mine, we can do it." I took a deep breath, taking a few cautious steps after her. "I think if it works, you'll be cured. And so will I."

Eve turned back to the center of the platform, turning to circle it, gazing down at the mechanisms. It was the first time I'd seen this, the heart of the Machine, the heart of the Institute. I'd expected piles of circuitry and intricate gears; instead it was simply a glass dome, inset into an iron pedestal, like a tiny replica of the Wall. Now that Eve's magic had subsided, I could trace the currents down through the dome, through the glass wires that traveled down and away, into every part of the Institute, and beyond.

"This Machine's veins go deep," whispered Eve, her thoughts flowing alongside mine. "Down into the earth, into the core of this world."

"Like roots," I replied, traveling the pathways with her. This was how the founding architects had sought to change the very nature of magic; they'd tapped into the life force of the planet itself.

Eve's thoughts pulled out abruptly. "Like a parasite."

"Listen to me." I turned toward her, bracing myself for the madness in her eyes, the fear and hatred and despair that threatened to pull me through the thin veil between our minds and down into the dark with her. "You asked me once what my alternative was. That until I had a solution, yours was the best one. This *is* that solution, Eve. No one has to die."

"And the magic, where does it go? Here? With them?" Eve glanced at the half dome in the floor, lips curling.

"With all of us," I replied firmly. "We'll use it to care for this city, and for Lethe, where the other Renewables are."

"This Machine," she whispered, her eyes still on the dome. "I wonder what would happen if we were to use it against them?"

My pulse quickened. "No, Eve," I said sharply. "It'd kill these people, if you tried to harvest them instead of the Renewables. It's impossible, anyway."

Eve glanced up, her eyes meeting mine. "They are children, playing with things they'll never understand. Not the way we do, you and I. They say to magic iron is impossible."

I tried to gather my thoughts to respond, to find some other way of reaching her. Before I could find it, movement behind her caught my eye. I had only an instant to register the red-clad form of Gloriette lunging for Eve's back, her hand upraised and clutching a bloodied shard of glass from the shattered tendrils.

"No!" I shrieked.

Eve lifted a hand, and Gloriette hung suspended, frozen as though the air had grown thick around her. Eve's gaze still held mine, as an instant later Gloriette shot backwards to slam into the railing on the far side of the platform, something cracking with sick heaviness on impact. I could see her gasping, still frozen, as though whatever Eve had done to the air had made it impossible for her to breathe.

From all around us the shards of glass lifted, coalescing back into the shapes they'd once held. Ghosts of the wires that had held Eve for all those years, a memory of the torment that turned her into this.

"Don't," I whispered. "Eve, don't—Eve, listen to me, look at me—!"

Eve smiled; and then all at once the shards shot down and in, driving into Gloriette's body. She twitched, the wires shivering as her flesh quivered; her eyes bulged, staring into the darkness. Then she was still.

I tore my eyes from Gloriette's corpse and stared at Eve, gasping for air. She met my eyes, and for an instant everything was still. The muffled screams of the architects, Dorian's shout of disbelief, Oren's snarl of fear as he started to head for me, even the frantic whirring of Nix's gears; it all faded away.

It was always already over, sister. I won the moment I told you to run, an eternity ago. I won when I told you to follow the birds, and you listened, and you turned your back on this place to flee. Let me do this for you, let me bear the burden. My sister, my child. You were always a frightened little girl. And you always will be.

"Not anymore," I whispered aloud.

At the same instant both Eve and I lunged for the crystal dome at the center of the platform. It came alive as we touched it, reacting to the power as though it hadn't lain dormant for over a century. Eve's magic was an onslaught of heat and light, rushing over me, overwhelming me; she was pushing toward annihilation, to destroy anyone without the power reserves of the Renewables.

I clapped my other hand to the dome, my voice tearing from my throat as the power burned through me. My shadow howled within me, snarling, pacing, ravenous. It thrashed against the restraints that held it at bay, screaming to be set free. All this time I'd spent building walls, pulling away from it, burying it deep unless I had no choice—the barriers faltered, like rusted bars caging an enraged beast. It wanted out.

And I let it come.

It erupted with a scream I felt in my bones, a scream I must have uttered, for I heard the others' answering calls of alarm and helplessness. At last I let every instinct but the shadow fall away, heart singing at this single moment, this instant in which I was finally, *finally* whole. The darkness in me lashed at Eve's magic, absorbing it and turning it back upon her, reveling in the gluttony of unlimited power.

Though my eyes fixed on the dome, burning in the light, I could see, sense, taste everything around us. I felt the heat of Eve's body as it burned, I felt the metal grid below us groaning as it buckled and shook.

I saw, with painful clarity, Oren leap forward, only to have Kris grab at his arm and haul him back roughly; Oren twisted and slammed him back into the railing, snarling.

"Interrupt them and you could kill Lark!" I heard Kris scream.

"I have to help her," Oren snarled, lips curled.

"She doesn't need your help!" Kris's breath came in sharp gasps, panting.

"Lark's sided with the architects," gasped Dorian, his voice hoarse. "We have to stop her."

"Are you insane?" Basil broke in, fury erupting in a roar.

"The Renewables have been the keepers of this power for generations," replied Dorian, striding past Basil and heading for the central dome. "Who are you to say you're—"

"It belongs in the hands of the people!" Kris strode up and shoved Dorian back against the railing. "Not people like you. We'll rebuild this city, make it what it should've been, a sanctuary for—"

"For monsters like them?" Dorian, still half supported on Caesar's shoulder, spat in the direction of the few surviving architects, still huddled on the far end of the platform.

I let out a tiny moan, the black fire running through my veins turning their voices into a dim roar in the background. I could smell burning flesh; even though I couldn't feel it, my palms were charring against the heat of the glass beneath them. I looked down and saw tendrils of black shadow snaking down my arms from beneath my sleeves, running through my veins like ink.

I could no longer tell one man from the other; I felt one

strike another, knocking him to the ground; I felt one make a run at the platform only to be dragged back by a grasping hand. I felt their fear and their helplessness and their rage and their greed.

"I have to destroy it," I whispered.

"Destroy what?"

Nix. Nix was still with me, tucked away between my collar and the hollow of my throat, clinging to me, whispering to me, encouraging me. It didn't care which side won. It wanted only to be with me. I felt its warmth, the purr of its mechanisms, the tiny hum of power at its heart. I felt a tiny thread of strength wind its way through me, renewing me, pushing back against Eve.

"Listen to them," I gasped. "Even if I beat her, even if I can take the power from the Renewables and return it to the world, it won't matter. This power, it will always corrupt, it will always destroy... this magic will always shatter the world."

"Destroy magic, and they will all be like Oren."

"Able to control their own destinies. No dependence upon magic. No dependence on machines. Light and dark together."

Nix was silent for a long moment, then crawled out of my collar and onto my shoulder, braced against the winds rising from the dome beneath my hands, beneath Eve's hands.

"We're opposites," I panted between gasps for breath. "Eve and I. Kris said to touch each other would be catastrophic—I can feel it. Dark and light meeting, that'll be the end. I just need to—"

I tried to push harder, to throw Eve off-balance long enough to reach out for her, but her strength was exactly equal to my own. My shadow could only use as much power as she spent; and no matter how much magic she exuded, my shadow matched it. We'd be locked in a stalemate for eternity.

"*I will help you.*" The quiet dignity of Nix's artificial voice stabbed deep into my heart, and for an instant I didn't know why.

Then my heart froze.

"Nix—wait, no. No. Without magic, you'll die."

"I am a machine. I cannot die."

I gasped for air, faltering. Eve sensed it and unleashed an onslaught that drove me to my knees. The searing pain in my hands penetrated my numbness, burning down to the bone, an agony I could no longer ignore.

"Nix—NO. I can't lose you. I'll find another way. Just—stay with me."

Nix leaned close, bumping its head against the line of my jaw, the vibration of its mechanisms carrying through the bone to sing a soft, sweet note directly inside my mind. Then it flew up until I could see it, hovering in front of me and watching me with its lidless, unblinking blue eyes.

A ripple went through its outer shell, and then it began to fold and change in midair, shifting shapes the way it used to, taking joy in flight in every form. Its body lengthened, its winds elongated and reshaped; its head softened and antennae smoothed and dipped, merging. Before my eyes, Nix became a tiny bird.

A lark.

"Nix," I whispered.

"*I am a machine,*" it echoed, its new wings sweeping the air. "*And I am your friend. Always.*"

Then it turned and dove through the air, tucking its wings close to its body to gather speed and dart at Eve's face. It knocked her off-balance, and for one instant her hands left the dome. Her instincts were lightning-fast, her magic snapping up and beginning to shred Nix's body, tearing away the copperplate feathers, grinding through its mechanisms.

I sobbed, tearing my own ruined hands away from the dome. Forcing my failing muscles to move, I threw myself forward at Eve.

I wrapped my arms around her—and the world tore apart.

CHAPTER 34

"How is she?"

"Still alive."

"Can you—can you do anything?"

"Do what?"

"Something. Anything."

"If I could, I would."

"It's been days. I don't know how much longer we can hide her here. They're going to find her."

"You won't let that happen."

"Will she ever wake up?"

"Maybe it's better if she doesn't."

"How can you say that?"

"How do we know that what wakes up will even be Lark?"

• • •

A lantern shone in the darkness, blurring and wavering as I opened my eyes. I gazed at it, the light washing over me with gentle warmth, mesmerizing. Long moments passed before I understood what I was seeing. The lantern burned with a flame.

I was lying on a mattress stuffed with something lumpy,

in a sagging cot. My body felt hollow and empty, and wrong. The air smelled damp and musty, and like burning oil. I tried to move, but my muscles wouldn't respond, as though my body was no longer connected to my mind. I tried to scream; I whimpered.

A face appeared over me. I struggled to focus my eyes, but all I could see was the afterimage of the magic-less lantern, the flame flickering in the invisible air currents.

"Lark?"

I knew that voice. "Oren." I could do little more than breathe the name, but he heard me. Something was wrong with me; something was broken. I struggled for breath, trying to understand.

A hand touched my face; with his touch came clarity, the ability to blink away the haze in my vision. I saw his eyes first, sunken and intent on mine. They were blue again, his skin clear. The shadow he'd drawn on against Eve's magic had subsided.

"The magic," I gasped, realization striking hot and quick. The shadow inside me was gone; there was no energy, no flow to the world around me. I tried to look around with my second sight and saw only the world as it was, flat and ordinary. "I can't feel—"

"Shh," said Oren, fingers stroking my hair. "It's okay. You'll get used to it."

"Eve," I managed, trying to sit up. "Where—"

Oren grasped my shoulders, but rather than trying to hold me down in the bed, he helped me to lean against the wall at its head, slipping an arm around my waist to keep me from falling. "She's gone," he murmured.

"Gone?" I replied. The sudden movement had caused a ripple of pain to erupt from my hands and scream up my arms. Something was wrong with them. "Dead?"

Oren shook his head. "We don't know. Whatever you did nearly destroyed half the Institute; when we found you in the rubble, she was gone. No body, nothing."

"Rubble," I echoed, barely able to do more than speak single words. "Everyone else . . . ?"

"All fine," he said. "The platform dropped, but the walkways stayed where they were. Everyone's fine."

Not everyone.

"Nix," I whispered. And then, as though the name had thrown me back into my mind, stripping away the cocoon of numbness, I collapsed forward, weeping. Oren wrapped his arms around me, pulling me close. He whispered in my ear, phrases half-formed and wordless murmurs of reassurance. I tried to grab at his shirt, clutch anything I could touch, hold onto, but my hands were wrapped in bandages and to move them was an agony I couldn't bear. The sobs tore out of me, each a great wrench somewhere deep in my heart.

After a time, Oren's arms loosened enough so he could draw back and look at me. He reached up to touch my cheek again, this time touching the tears and smoothing the moisture away. "I think of my parents sometimes," he said in his low, thoughtful voice. "What they'd think of me now, whether they'd be proud. Whether they'd be frightened. Their bodies are gone, long turned to dust, but their thoughts, good and bad—those are always with me."

He reached over toward the lantern, which rested on a packing crate table. Next to it was something that glinted in the light. He lifted it and, with his other hand, sought my heavily bandaged palm to place the object there.

All that was left of Nix was the frame of its body, petrified in the moment of its death; a delicate iron tracery of circuits and feathers. It still wore the form of a bird, though its crystal eyes were iron now, colorless and still. The wings didn't move, the mechanisms didn't click. Only its heart had survived: a tiny glass crystal, empty of magic, shimmering gently in the lantern light.

Oren curled my fingers around the dead pixie. "Nix's body; it's just a thing. Its sacrifice and its friendship, nothing can destroy that."

I tucked the little metal bird close to my heart.

"Do you want to see the others?" asked Oren, tucking a strand of tangled, matted hair behind my ear. "Your brothers are here, and I can send for Kris."

I kept straining to hear the sound of purring gears, to feel some warmth in the cold metal against my skin. But I lifted my eyes and swallowed. "Help me stand?"

Oren half carried me out into the adjoining room; my legs were so wobbly I could barely walk. I must have been unconscious for days, though I was afraid to ask. What had happened to my city, my people, in that time?

Basil and Caesar were together, sitting on packing crates and conversing in low voices. I realized where we were—in the old home of the rebellion, the tunnels under the city that had been converted to living space. When Oren and I appeared in the doorway, both my brothers flew to their feet.

"You're awake!" Basil exclaimed, striding toward me and gazing hard at my face.

Caesar glanced at Oren. "Is she—"

"Feeling fine, I think" Oren interrupted him before he could finish.

I glanced from Oren to Caesar, a dim memory returning to me. "I heard you—I heard you talking, while I was sleeping. What did you think had happened to me? Who was I supposed to be?"

"You," Oren said fiercely. "You're you.

Caesar turned away, shoulders bowed. Basil watched him,

then came closer to me so he could take my shoulders and give them a squeeze. "When we found only you, and no sign of Eve, we thought—damn it, if Kris were here, he could explain it."

Oren eyed Basil sharply, but when I insisted, he caved enough to add, "Kris had a theory that since you were so connected, your minds, that there was a chance you'd be . . ."

"You thought I might be Eve on the inside." I glanced at Caesar's broad shoulders as he sank back down onto the packing crate, unable to look at me. "Sorry to disappoint you," I whispered.

Caesar's head snapped up, the grief in his gaze turning to anger. "You stupid girl," he snapped. "I'm not—I'm glad you survived, Lark. You're my sister. More than ever, you're a part of me. But that doesn't mean I'm not—" His voice broke, and he turned away again. "I'm allowed to grieve too."

I closed my eyes. "I'm sorry, Caesar." As I exhaled, the tiniest flicker stirred in the back of my mind. "But—I don't think Eve's dead."

"What?" Caesar's voice was rough.

"I'm not sure, but I can still feel her. We're still connected. Not in my mind, where the magic was, but—she's out there, somewhere."

A commotion at the door caused all three men to tense, leap to their feet, and step between me and the exit; when it opened to reveal Kris, Caesar grunted and dropped back onto his crate.

Kris's eyes fell on me, and for a moment it was like none of this had ever happened, and he smiled at me the way he had when teasing me about eating all the watermelon at the Harvest feast. "You're awake," he said softly, still standing with one foot outside and the other on the lip of the door.

"And I'm myself," I added wryly, noting the way his

shoulders dropped with relief as I spoke.

"That's the best thing I've heard all day," he replied.

I had one more question I needed to ask—even if I was pretty sure that the lantern by my bedside had given me my answer. "Did I—what about the magic?"

"Gone," said Kris, his smile vanishing. "No trace, no sign it ever existed at all."

I glanced at Oren, who nodded confirmation. "A city full of shadows like me," he said.

"Not exactly," corrected Kris. "A city full of people who no longer have magic to separate the light and dark. In time I think we'll learn to control it, as you have."

I sighed, grimacing when the air brought with it the stench of underground decay. "Why are we down here?" I asked. "Why not recover up in an apartment, with real beds?"

Basil and Oren both looked at Kris, who looked back for a long moment before looking at me. He opened his mouth to speak, but hesitated so long he had to let his breath out before trying again. "Lark," he said slowly. "The people . . . they don't understand what you did. They only know that you destroyed the magic."

"They don't know that you saved them all," Oren broke in, anger on my behalf making his skin flush dark.

"They want justice." Caesar's voice was heavy.

Numbness crept back in, sighing through my limbs until they hung like lead, the iron bird dangling from my fingertips. "You're hiding me—from all of them."

"Give them time," Basil said earnestly. "They'll understand. They will. Oren will teach them to control the darkness as he does, and they'll realize that they're free. They'll realize that you've given them back this world."

"They'll understand . . . the way my parents did?" I glanced at Caesar, whose good eye met mine for only a fraction of a second before sliding away. I closed my eyes, the truth welling up like tears. "I can't stay here, can I?"

My answer came in silence; Oren was the only one who would meet my eyes, the winter-sky blue muted by the lantern flame.

I swallowed. My voice sounded dull and empty. "I'm tired; I think I'd like to go back to bed."

• • •

It took weeks for me to be able to use my hands again, and even then it was hard to do much of anything without pain. My struggle with Eve over the dome had burned the flesh from my palms, the heat so intense that even the backs of my hands were wrinkled and scarred. I had to teach myself again how to do the simplest of tasks. Kris removed a set of stitches from my cheek, a gash I'd forgotten getting in that final battle against Eve and the architects. I knew there was a scar there, that there'd always be a scar there; I knew that, between it and my hands, I looked like a monster. But Kris never blinked, and if Oren even noticed, he never said a word.

Oren—Oren, who watched over me, Oren, whose faith never faltered. Oren, who never left my side unless he absolutely had to rest, letting my brothers take over the watch. Even Caesar, who struggled to be near me for long and never spoke, took his turn.

It was late one night—or possibly midday, I had no way of knowing—that Caesar finally broke the silence between us. "I'll always know what you did," he said quietly.

I looked up, bracing myself for censure.

"Even if these people never understand." He met my eyes, his gaze sober. Though the beard and the patch over his eye concealed his features, for a brief moment I could see past them. "I always will."

I didn't reply, my throat too tight for words. I dropped my gaze, and when I managed to look up again, he'd returned to the book he'd been reading.

Oren helped me learn to use my hands again, with a patience I never knew he possessed. And yet he was no less fierce, no less quick and wild—his fierceness was for me, for his belief that I could be whole again. He made me do stretches and exercises, curling my hands around his, squeezing until my eyes watered in pain. He kept at it, massaging the damaged tissue and nerve endings that would never fully heal, until slowly the scar tissue began to thin, and stretch, and give me hope that someday I'd be able to do again the things I'd taken for granted, like hold a pen, or turn a page, or slide my fingers in between Oren's and let them nestle there, the way they were made to interlock.

"But my face," I whispered one night, touching the scar on my cheek with fingertips too swollen to feel it. "My hands. How can you stand to—"

Oren leaned over to kiss me just beside my ear, where I could feel the change; the way his lips felt against the scar tissue was different from the flush of sensation in the healthy skin. "How could I stand not to?" He pulled back so I could see his face, and while I watched, he allowed a swirl of shadow to caress his features, flickering through his eyes and past his lips. "You've seen my face; do you love me any less?"

His dedication only made my heart ache all the more. Part of me would have been happy to stay here forever, hidden underground with Oren, and with Kris and my brothers. But that was no life for them, and no life for Oren. And sooner or later, the people I'd saved would find me. I had to go. And the boy who'd struggled so long on his own had a home now—how could I expect him to give it up for me?

Quietly, I began to make plans to leave the city. I knew

Kris and Basil would understand; though I hadn't been aboveground, I knew the city's hatred for me must be strong indeed, if they'd rather see me banished than stay. But Oren—Oren wouldn't understand. He *couldn't* understand. He'd tell me to stay, to fight for myself, that I was strong enough to face down anyone in the world. And so I couldn't tell *anyone*, for fear Oren would know, and stop me.

Basil was staying only long enough to see me safe and help Kris reestablish order in the city above. Lethe was his home now, and though there was no longer a crisis of magic to deal with, someone would have to teach his people how to live in this new world, how to deal with the new aspects of themselves. Dorian had left some days before I woke up, planning to return to the Iron Wood. It stood empty now, but without the need to protect its people from the Institute, he expected them to return.

Even Kris had his place; I saw less of him than the others, because he was helping to rebuild the government of the city. The Institute lay abandoned, in ruins, but most of the city was unharmed and, following the collapse of magic, in a panic. Kris's charisma and talent for handling people were proving vital.

I made mental lists of supply caches to raid on my way out, calculated my exit route, composed and discarded a thousand notes to leave for Oren. And I waited.

It was midmorning, according to the time up above, when Oren next left my side to get some rest. This time Kris took over for him; my brothers were both up marshaling the crowd, preparing for a rally in which Kris would begin assigning new work orders to the city's people. According to him they'd begun to adjust to having their darker sides manifest, now that the magic suppressing them was gone. There'd been incidents, but casualties were low. Kris was optimistic.

I feigned sleep until he began to doze, cheek resting on one hand propped up against his knee. I lingered for a moment after I slipped out of bed, scanning Kris's features. I thought he'd look older, wiser, more battered for our experiences; but he looked just the same as he always had, that brown hair tumbling down over his brow, the handsome features relaxed in sleep. I swallowed the urge to push his hair back and reached for my pack. The pack held my knife and the fire-starter I'd been carrying since Oren gave it to me all that time ago, when I was still a weakling, when I knew nothing of survival; when I was still just Lark.

I quietly slipped the straps over my shoulders and reached for the door; but then I heard a sigh and the rustle of movement. Kris was awake.

"Wait—Lark, where—" He blinked at me, frowning. "Where are you going?"

I bit my lip, hesitating. I could tell him I was going for a walk, let him think I'd be back in an hour or two.

But he read my answer in my hesitation, and confusion dimmed to understanding. "Are you sure you're ready?" There was no sign of his old smile on his features.

I flexed my fingers; they hurt only a little, and every day I could move them more. I could hold my knife; I could start a fire. I could survive on my own. But that wasn't what Kris meant. "I think so."

"He's going to try to follow you, you know."

I winced, glancing at the corner where Oren usually sat while I was asleep, watching over me. It was empty, but I could imagine him there anyway, quiet and unyielding. "I know. That's why I'm leaving now. Don't tell him, Kris—give me as much of a head start as I can get."

Kris's features hardened a little. He didn't approve, but he didn't argue, either. I'd noticed that none of them argued with me anymore. They let me win every conversation, always, like I'd earned some sort of free pass. It made my heart ache, made me long for the days when Caesar would call me stupid and Kris would protest my headstrong plans of action. It was like I was no more than a ghost already.

"Thank you," I said when he didn't answer; I took his silence as acquiescence.

"There's food in the room next door," he said, clearing his throat. "Now that people can gather food outside the Wall, they don't much care about the rations left down here. That's what we've been feeding you."

I swallowed hard. I'd been planning to detour to the old resistance caches and raid them for supplies—Kris had saved me valuable time. "You're not going to try to tell me to stay, or to say good-bye to everyone?"

The ghost of Kris's smile flickered across his lips. "I know better than to argue with you."

I found myself smiling back, in spite of myself. We watched each other, and our smiles faded slowly, like drawings in the sand, washing out on the tide.

"Lark," he whispered, moving toward me. "I don't . . . I don't know if I ever truly apologized for my part in what was done to you."

My throat closed. I shook my head, looking down at the floor so he wouldn't see my eyes growing wet, that even now the apology stung like fire. "You were doing what you thought was right."

"And I regret it every moment." His fingertips sought my chin, lifted it, forcing me to meet his eyes. "Promise me you'll come back to us, one day."

I stretched up onto my toes—I hadn't realized how much taller Kris was than Oren—and leaned in to press my lips to his cheek. "I promise."

I stopped long enough in the room next door to fill my pack the rest of the way with Kris's supplies, laying the fire-starter on top and tucking the knife into my boot. I'd regained my health in the days since I'd woken, but as I navigated the tunnels, I realized there was still a long way to go before I'd be fit again. Leaving the city this time would be only marginally easier than it had been the first time; I'd be just as weak. And this time I wouldn't just be leaving my home, I'd be leaving my heart.

It took all my strength to climb up the ladder and shoulder the hatch open. When light came pouring in, nearly blinding me, I realized I had no idea what the city above looked like anymore. As I dragged myself up to street level, I gazed around, blinking my streaming eyes. I lifted one hand to shield them from the light and gazed upward.

The iron Wall overhead had shattered, great sections of it crumbling to rust and raining down on the city below. Some of it remained, jagged shards like eggshells standing as a reminder of what the founding architects had built here; this great technology, lost and now useless without the Re-source —without magic.

The sunlight poured down, warm and bright, and as my eyes adjusted, the gloom of the tunnels below began to drift away. I took a deep breath, tilting my head back and letting the wind carry away the last of the smell of darkness and damp.

I headed through the empty city, keeping an eye out for anyone who might have skipped the rally. I saw no one, though, and after passing a few streets without incident, I began to breathe a tiny bit easier. Despite how easy it had been to sneak out, each step felt heavier than the last. I forced myself to ignore the ache in my bones and tried to keep myself from thinking about what I was doing. That I'd likely never see him again. That he'd never know why I left him here. That

I'd written a dozen letters and thrown them all away, because how could I tell him that I loved him in the same breath that I told him I was leaving, perhaps forever?

It was about half an hour's walk to the edge of the city, still marked by the groove where the Wall had once stood. I slowed to a halt, staring at the line, my thoughts grinding to a halt and trickling away. Spring was in full bloom beyond the remnants of the Wall, flowering weeds winding up through the cracked pavement and dangling from crumbling eaves. It was beautiful, and yet I hesitated, unable to take that first step beyond.

Then a wry voice split the quiet. "You're still as easy to track as a wounded deer."

I jumped, whirling to find Oren a few paces behind me, his expression unreadable. My heart leaped at the sight of his face; all it knew was that it had wanted him, and he was here. It didn't matter that it'd make saying good-bye a thousand times harder. I opened my mouth, but nothing came out when I tried to speak.

"Well?" said Oren, taking slow, deliberate steps toward me. "No explanations, no apologies, no attempts to make me understand?"

The morning sun caught his sandy hair, gilding it white-gold as it stirred in the breeze. In the light, his normally pale blue eyes looked brighter, more like the sky overhead, like windows through to the world beyond my city. I thought my ribs would crack from the pounding of my heart.

For a long moment, neither of us said anything. Then I stepped forward, reaching for his hand to pull him closer. I stretched up on my toes and kissed him, soaking in the way he responded, the shape of his mouth fitting to mine, the hand that wound around my waist. I held onto that instant, memorizing it, storing every tiniest detail in my mind.

Slowly, reluctantly, I dropped back down onto my heels again.

Oren swallowed, forced to clear his throat before speaking. "What was that for?"

"For you." I smiled, scanning his face. His face seemed so different now from the one I knew when I first met him; the wildness, the savagery, the way his gaze had scared me so. And yet I could still see that wild boy in there, the angry, lonely, desperate boy who had saved my life. Who had made me whole. "And for me," I added, smile turning a little wry. "So I don't forget."

"Forget?" Oren's expression darkened. "I knew you were going to do this," he muttered. "Were you really going to sneak out like some kind of criminal? Lark, I'm coming with you."

I ignored the faint relief that someone, at least, was arguing with me, and closed my eyes. I couldn't bring myself before to have this fight with him, but he had to know. He had to know it was all a dream, that I was right. Not speaking about it didn't make it go away. Leaving words unsaid didn't rob them of their truth.

"Oren—I have to leave. I can't change that. But you . . . you can stay here. You have a home, you have a place where you belong. You're just like everyone else now, no shadow to hide, no secrets. It's everything you've always wanted."

Oren didn't answer, and after a moment of silence I opened my eyes to find him watching me, his expression far more thoughtful—and less angry—than I was imagining. He reached up, tracing with one finger the line scored across my cheek. "Lark," he said slowly. "*You're* the one who's been searching for home all this time. Not me. You're the one who's been longing to fit in, to belong—to feel whole."

My eyes burned, and I shook my head. I couldn't speak, wordlessly trying to deny what he was saying.

He curled an arm around my waist and ducked his head, pressing his forehead against mine. "I already have a home."

A dark knot deep inside me, deeper than the shadow had been, tore its way free in response to his voice. The darkness rose up, carrying all my fears and lost dreams, everything I'd put aside so I could fight, so I could lead, so I could make the decisions that would save or shatter the world. And, like a shadow destroyed by the light, the darkness found Oren and fled. I dropped forward into his arms, letting him wrap me up and tuck my head below his chin. My shoulders shook, hands trembling, voice tangled in a sob.

"My home is you," Oren whispered, his arms tightening around me while I cried. "You think you're alone—you think that's your punishment for all of this, for being the one to save mankind from itself. You think I don't see that, but I know you, Lark Ainsley. I *know* you."

I let out a shuddering breath. Tilting my face upward, I let the sun shine down on it, warming my skin and drying my tears. The sun's rays warmed the pendant resting in the hollow of my throat, the tiny iron bird that I wore now always on a chain around my neck. "I am whole now," I whispered, not trusting my voice to speak aloud without breaking.

Oren grinned that quick, fierce smile, then ducked his head to kiss me hard. Though his words were confident, I could feel his fear and relief in the strength of his embrace, the quick heat of his mouth.

When he lifted his head, it was a long moment before I could speak again. I ran my scarred hands across his chest, loath to pull away, half afraid he was a figment of my broken heart. "How did you know to come find me?" I asked.

"Kris woke me."

My mouth fell open. "K-Kris? But I told him—he promised he wouldn't—"

Oren's mouth twitched, showing briefly an expression

dangerously close to a smile. "Maybe he's not quite as useless as I thought."

I didn't know if I was furious at Kris or so grateful I could cry; I couldn't help but wish better for him. Perhaps, in leading the city, he'd find purpose again. Maybe he'd find whatever he once thought I could give him.

Oren released me except for one hand, which he kept custody of so he could press his lips to the puffy skin there. "So, what now?"

I shook my head. "I . . . I don't know. I want to find Eve."

Oren's hint of a smile vanished. "Eve? She's dangerous, and she's mad. If she's alive—just leave her."

I raised my eyebrows at Oren. "She's no more dangerous than I am anymore. And . . . there's just something about the shape of her mind, when I can sense her. I can't feel that burning hatred. I feel . . . confusion, I feel fear. But I don't feel anger."

Oren still didn't look convinced. "Facing her nearly killed you."

"And it nearly killed her," I replied. "We're—we're connected. Still, somehow. I can't help Kris run the city, I can't help Basil with Lethe, I can't help my people adjust to their new lives. But before Gloriette, Eve was just a normal girl, like me. Maybe she is again, and if she is out there, there's no one to help her. I can do that. *We* can do that. Maybe . . . maybe she's the start of redemption."

Oren squeezed my hand, gently, so as to avoid pulling at the barely healed skin. "Then we should go. How do we find her?"

I took a deep breath, letting the spring air fill my lungs, fill every corner of my body. Turning so that I faced the outside, I stepped forward until the tips of my feet aligned with the groove where the Wall used to be. On this side the pavement was darker, less weathered. On that side, weeds grew up through the cracks, spindly flowers opening to the morning light. A fitful eddy of wind tossed a spray of gravel from under my feet, across the line.

"This used to be the end of the world," I whispered, closing my eyes. I could still feel the memory of the Wall, its vital crackle, the glow of magic against my skin. I hoped I would never forget the way magic felt. "Right here."

When I opened my eyes I could see only sky, a few distant clouds scudding across a blue so pure it could be the ocean where Eve grew up. I could still feel her, lingering in my mind halfway between a memory and a dream. She might have vanished, but she wasn't gone. She was out there somewhere; and, like the tendril of a breeze touching my cheek, I could sense her mind against mine.

A flock of birds, startled by something unseen, erupted from the ruins a block beyond the edge of the shattered Wall. Calling to each other, they swooped overhead, ducking down through the alley and then up again into the light. I remembered how Nix used to play with the birds in the Iron Wood's orchard, shifting shape in midair to confound and challenge them. There was such joy in their flight, as the unfolding spring and the promise of sweet sea air beckoned them north to the homes they used to have.

I smiled. "Maybe we'll follow the birds."

EPILOGUE

I'm standing by the sea, my feet swallowed by the sand. There is a storm coming, but not for a little while. For now the wind on my face is cold and lively, waking me. The salt from the spray burns my eyes, and I blink away the tears forming there. The water is cold, numbing my feet and promising a quick, painless end.

When I close my eyes, I'm standing at the edge of a cliff, daring myself to take that last step. The impulse starts in the base of my feet, deep in the sand, tingling like feeling returning after the cold. It burns up my legs and makes my thighs tremble, surging into my lungs and making the air feel like knives between my ribs. My heart sings, my hands clench and release. My chin lifts, and the wind grabs at my hair, whipping it like strands of ice around my face.

Not today, I realize as the impulse fades, returning me to the ground, connecting me once more with the sand beneath my feet. *And probably not tomorrow, either.*

It's the choice that leaves me breathless.

I turn away from the waves, heading for the twin quaking aspens at the edge of the rocks to the south. The ruined house up just beyond the dunes stands dark and empty, and full of ghosts. I slept there once and had such dreams . . . dreams of another life, of a wood of iron and a city of shadows, of a sister lost and love shattered. I choose not to sleep there. Instead I rest under the aspen trees, and listen to the leaves whisper things, and think that sometimes I can almost understand.

But then I stop. I am not alone.

There's someone there, standing under my trees, watching me. I move closer, leaving thin, cautious prints in the sand behind me. When I'm close enough to see her face, she smiles.

"I know you," I whisper.

"Hello, Eve." She tucks her hair behind her ear, and I see healed-over burns scarring the backs of her hands. "I'm glad I found you."

The aspens overhead stir in the wind of the oncoming storm, a ripple that starts over the girl's head and sweeps through the rest of its branches. "Come sit with me, sister." There's time yet, before the rain.

ACKNOWLEDGMENTS

I've tried and failed several times to write the acknowledgments for this book. Despite the solitary nature of writing, the creation of a book is anything but solitary, and there are at least a hundred people I need to thank for making these books, this trilogy, a reality.

My agents, Josh and Tracey, my editor, Andrew, the entire team at Carolrhoda Lab and Lerner Publishing Group. My family: Mom, Dad, Josie, Naomi and Jerry, Harry Wolf. The booksellers at One More Page and at Malaprop's Bookstore. The bloggers and librarians who've been with me from before the beginning. The friends who welcome me back for board games and dark 'n' stormies no matter how long I vanish into the book cave. My fellow authors, for their support and wisdom, especially the girls at the CL: Megan, Alexa, Beth, and particularly Stephanie, without whom I'm not sure I would've gotten through the shadows. And, of course, Amie, soul mate and general nuisance, always making sure I've done my words and that I haven't given up.

I was on my way back from a book festival the other day and I finally realized why these acknowledgments were such a struggle for me: I wasn't thanking who I really wanted to thank. Though *Skylark* certainly wasn't written in a vacuum, it was written privately; and to a certain extent, *Shadowlark* was as well. But by the time I got to the third book in this trilogy, I wasn't writing it just for me anymore, or even for me and my publisher. I was writing it for you.

You, who stays up late at night, reading by flashlight. You, who write to me after you finish each book. You, who I've never met, and perhaps never will meet, but for a few shared moments spent in this book. It's your enthusiasm for this story and these characters that has kept me going and pushed me to finish this trilogy. I couldn't have done it without you. And I mean that from the bottom of my heart.

So thank you.

ABOUT THE AUTHOR

Meagan Spooner grew up reading and writing every spare moment of the day. She graduated from Hamilton College in New York with a degree in playwriting and spent several years living in Australia. She's traveled with her family all over the world to places like Egypt, South Africa, the Arctic, Greece, Antarctica, and the Galapagos, and there's a bit of every journey in the stories she writes. She currently lives and writes in Northern Virginia, but the siren call of travel is hard to resist, and there's no telling how long she'll stay there.

In addition to writing the Skylark trilogy, Meagan is the coauthor of *These Broken Stars* with Amie Kaufman. You can visit Meagan online at www.meaganspooner.com.